THE
HOLLOW
HILLS

Mary Stewart

THE HOLLOW HILLS

Fawcett Columbine
New York

A Fawcett Columbine Book
Published by Ballantine Books

http://www.randomhouse.com

Library of Congress Catalog Card Number: 96-96703

ISBN: 0-449-91173-X

This edition published by arrangement with William Morrow and Company, Inc.

Manufactured in the United States of America

First Fawcett Crest Edition: July 1974
First Ballantine Books Mass Market Edition: April 1983
First Ballantine Books Trade Edition: August 1996

10 9 8 7

*To the memory of
my father*

CONTENTS

There was a boy born,
A winter king.
Before the black month
He was born,
And fled in the dark month
To find shelter
With the poor.

He shall come
With the spring
In the green month
And the golden month
And bright
Shall be the burning
Of his star.

M.S.

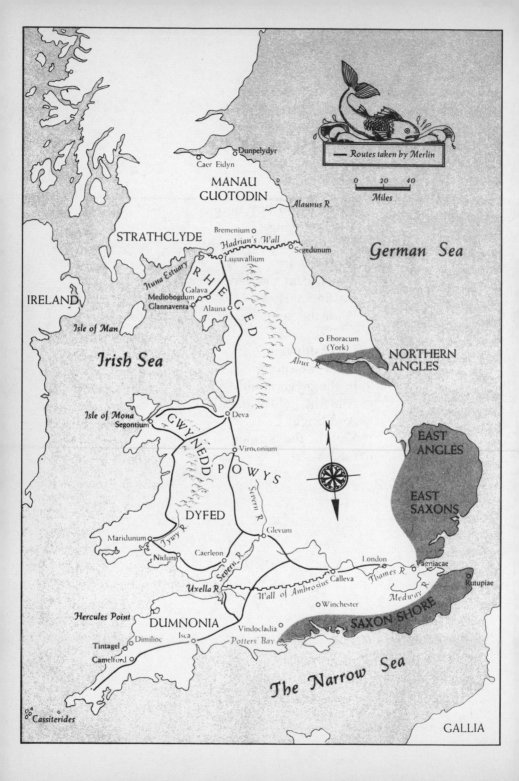

Dunpelydyr

Caer Eidyn

MANAU GUOTODIN

Alaunus R.

STRATHCLYDE

Bremenium

Hadrian's Wall

Luguvallium

Segedunum

German Sea

Routes taken by Merlin

0   20   40

Miles

Huna Estuary

R H E G E D

Galava

IRELAND

Mediobogdum

Glannaventa

Alauna

Isle of Man

Irish Sea

Eboracum
(York)

NORTHERN
ANGLES

Abus R.

Isle of Mona

Segontium

GWYNEDD

Deva

Viroconium

EAST
ANGLES

P O W Y S

EAST
SAXONS

DYFED

Severn R.

Maridunum

Tywy R.

Glevum

London

Vagniacae

Nidum

Caerleon

Severn R.

Thames R.

Rutupiae

Uxella R.

Wall of Ambrosius

Calleva

Medway

Winchester

SAXON SHORE

Hercules Point

DUMNONIA

Vindocladia

Tintagel

Dimilioc

Isca

Potters' Bay

Camelford

The Narrow Sea

Cassiterides

GALLIA

BOOK I

THE WAITING

1

There was a lark singing somewhere high above. Light fell dazzling against my closed eyelids, and with it the song, like a distant dance of water. I opened my eyes. Above me arched the sky, with its invisible singer lost somewhere in the light and floating blue of a spring day. Everywhere was a sweet, nutty smell which made me think of gold, and candle flames, and young lovers. Something, smelling not so sweet, stirred beside me, and a rough young voice said: "Sir?"

I turned my head. I was lying on turf, in a hollow among furze bushes. These were full of blossom, golden, sweet-smelling flames called out by the spring sun. Beside me a boy knelt. He was perhaps twelve years old, dirty, with a matted shag of hair, and clad in some coarse brown cloth; his cloak, made of skins roughly stitched together, showed rents in a dozen places. He had a stick in one hand. Even without the way he smelled I could have guessed his calling, for all around us his herd of goats grazed among the furze bushes, cropping the young green prickles.

At my movement he got quickly to his feet and backed off a little, peering, half wary and half hopeful, through the filthy tangle of hair. So he had not robbed me yet. I eyed the heavy stick in his hand, vaguely wondering through the mists of pain whether I could help myself even against this youngster. But it seemed that his hopes were only for a reward. He was pointing at something out of sight beyond the bushes. "I caught your horse for you. He's tied over there. I thought you were dead."

3

I raised myself to an elbow. Round me the day seemed to swing and dazzle. The furze blossom smoked like incense in the sun. Pain seeped back slowly, and with it, on the same tide, memory.

"Are you hurt bad?"

"Nothing to matter, except my hand. Give me time, I'll be all right. You caught my horse, you say? Did you see me fall?"

"Aye. I was over yonder." He pointed again. Beyond the mounds of yellow blossom the land rose, smooth and bare, to a rounded upland broken by grey rock seamed with winter thorn. Behind the shoulder of the land the sky had that look of limitless and empty distance which spoke of the sea. "I saw you come riding up the valley from the shore, going slow. I could see you was ill, or maybe sleeping on the horse. Then he put his foot wrong—a hole, likely—and you came off. You've not been lying long. I'd just got down to you."

He stopped, his mouth dropping open. I saw shock in his face. As he spoke I had been pushing myself up till I was able to sit, propped by my left arm, and carefully lift my injured right hand into my lap. It was a swollen, crusted mass of dried blood, through which fresh red was running. I had, I guessed, fallen on it when my horse had stumbled. The faint had been merciful enough. The pain was growing now, wave on wave grinding, with the steady beat and drag of the tide over shingle, but the faintness had gone, and my head, though still aching from the blow, was clear.

"Mother of mercy!" The boy was looking sick. "You never did that falling from your horse?"

"No. It was a fight."

"You've no sword."

"I lost it. No matter. I have my dagger, and a hand for it. No, don't be afraid. The fighting's done. No one will hurt

4

you. Now, if you'll help me onto my horse, I'll be on my way."

He gave me an arm as I got to my feet. We were standing at the edge of a high green upland studded with furze, with here and there stark, solitary trees thrust into strange shapes by the steady salt wind. Beyond the thicket where I had lain the ground fell away in a sharp slope scored by the tracks of sheep and goats. It made one side of a narrow, winding valley, at the foot of which a stream raced, tumbling, down its rocky bed. I could not see what lay at the foot of the valley, but about a mile away, beyond the horizon of winter grass, was the sea. From the height of the land where I stood one could guess at the great cliffs which fell away to the shore, and beyond the land's farthest edge, small in the distance, I could see the jut of towers.

The castle of Tintagel, stronghold of the Dukes of Cornwall. The impregnable fortress rock, which could only be taken by guile, or by treachery from within. Last night, I had used both.

I felt a shiver run over my flesh. Last night, in the wild dark of the storm, this had been a place of gods and destiny, of power driving towards some distant end of which I had been given, from time to time, a glimpse. And I, Merlin, son of Ambrosius, whom men feared as prophet and visionary, had been in that night's work no more than the god's instrument.

It was for this that I had been given the gift of Sight, and the power that men saw as magic. From this remote and sea-locked fortress would come the King who alone could clear Britain of her enemies, and give her time to find herself; who alone, in the wake of Ambrosius, the last of the Romans, would hold back the fresh tides of the Saxon Terror, and, for a breathing space at least, keep Britain whole. This I had seen in the stars, and heard in the wind: it was I,

5

my gods had told me, who would bring this to pass; this I had been born for. Now, if I could still trust my gods, the promised child was begotten; but because of him—because of me—four men had died. In that night lashed by storm and brooded over by the dragon-star, death had seemed commonplace, and gods waiting, visible, at every corner. But now, in the still morning after the storm, what was there to see? A young man with an injured hand, a King with his lust satisfied, and a woman with her penance beginning. And for all of us, time to remember the dead.

The boy brought my horse up to me. He was watching me curiously, the wariness back in his face.

"How long have you been here with your goats?" I asked him.

"A sunrise and a sunrise."

"Did you see or hear anything last night?"

Wariness became, suddenly, fear. His eyelids dropped and he stared at the ground. His face was closed, blank, stupid. "I have forgotten, lord."

I leaned against my horse's shoulder, regarding him. Times without number I had met this stupidity, this flat, expressionless mumble; it is the only armour available to the poor. I said gently: "Whatever happened last night, it is something I want you to remember, not to forget. No one will harm you. Tell me what you saw."

He looked at me for perhaps ten more seconds of silence. I could not guess what he was thinking. What he was seeing can hardly have been reassuring; a tall young man with a smashed and bloody hand, cloakless, his clothes stained and torn, his face (I have no doubt) grey with fatigue and pain and the bitter dregs of last night's triumph. All the same the boy nodded suddenly, and began to speak.

"Last night in the black dark I heard horses go by me.

Four, I think. But I saw no one. Then, in the early dawn, two more following them, spurring hard. I thought they were all making for the castle, but from where I was, up there by the rocks, I never saw torches at the guard-house on the cliff top, or on the bridge going across to the main gate. They must have gone down the valley there. After it was light I saw two horsemen coming back that way, from the shore below the castle rock." He hesitated. "And then you, my lord."

I said slowly, holding him with my eyes: "Listen now, and I will tell you who the horsemen were. Last night, in the dark, King Uther Pendragon rode this way, with myself and two others. He rode to Tintagel, but he did not go by the gate-house and the bridge. He rode down the valley, to the shore, and then climbed the secret path up the rock and entered the castle by the postern gate. Why do you shake your head? Don't you believe me?"

"Lord, everyone knows the King had quarrelled with the Duke. No one could get in, least of all the King. Even if he did find the postern door, there's none would dare open it to him."

"They opened last night. It was the Duchess Ygraine herself who received the King into Tintagel."

"But—"

"Wait," I said. "I will tell you how it happened. The King had been changed by magic arts into a likeness of the Duke, and his companions into likenesses of the Duke's friends. The people who let them into the castle thought they were admitting Duke Gorlois himself, with Brithael and Jordan."

Under its dirt the boy's face was pale. I knew that for him, as for most of the people of this wild and haunted country, my talk of magic and enchantment would come as easily as stories of the loves of kings and violence in high places. He said, stammering: "The King—the King was in the castle last night with the Duchess?"

"Yes. And the child that will be born will be the King's child."

A long pause. He licked his lips. "But—but—when the Duke finds out . . ."

"He won't find out," I said. "He's dead."

One filthy hand went to his mouth, the fist rammed against his teeth. Above it his eyes, showing white, went from my injured hand to the bloodstains on my clothing, then to my empty scabbard. He looked as if he would have liked to run away, but did not dare even do that. He said breathlessly: "You killed him? You killed our Duke?"

"Indeed no. Neither I nor the King wished him dead. He was killed in battle. Last night, not knowing that the King had already ridden secretly for Tintagel, your Duke sallied out from his fortress of Dimilioc to attack the King's army, and was killed."

He hardly seemed to be listening. He was stammering: "But the two I saw this morning . . . It was the Duke himself, riding up from Tintagel. I saw him. Do you think I don't know him? It was the Duke himself, with Jordan, his man."

"No. It was the King with his servant Ulfin. I told you the King took the Duke's likeness. The magic deceived you, too."

He began to back away from me. "How do you know these things? You—you said you were with them. This magic —who are you?"

"I am Merlin, the King's nephew. They call me Merlin the enchanter."

Still backing, he had come up against a wall of furze. As he looked this way and that, trying which way to run, I put out a hand.

"Don't be afraid. I'll not hurt you. Here, take this. Come, take it, no sensible man should fear gold. Call it a reward for catching my horse. Now, if you'll help me onto his back, I'll be on my way."

He made a half movement forward, ready to snatch and run, but then he checked, and his head went round, quick as a wild thing's. I saw the goats had already stopped grazing and were looking eastwards, ears pricked. Then I heard the sound of horses.

I gathered my own beast's reins in my good hand, then looked round for the boy to help me. But he was already running, whacking the bushes to chase the goats in front of him. I called to him and, as he glanced over his shoulder, flung the gold. He snatched it up and then was gone, racing up the slope with his goats scampering round him.

Pain struck at me again, grinding the bones of my hand together. The cracked ribs stabbed and burned my side. I felt the sweat start on my body, and round me the spring day wavered and broke again in mist. The noise of approaching hoofs seemed to hammer with the pain along my bones. I leaned against my horse's saddle, and waited.

It was the King riding again for Tintagel, this time for the main gate, and by daylight, with a company of his men. They came at a fast canter along the grassy track from Dimilioc, four abreast, riding at ease. Above Uther's head the Dragon standard showed red on gold in the sunlight. The King was himself again; the grey of his disguise had been washed from his hair and beard, and the royal circlet glinted on his helmet. His cloak of kingly scarlet was spread behind him over his bay's glossy flanks. His face looked still, calm and set; a bleak enough look, and weary, but with over all a kind of contentment. He was riding to Tintagel, and Tintagel was his at last, with all that lay within the walls. For him, it was an end.

9

I leaned against my horse's shoulder and watched them come level with me.

It was impossible for Uther not to see me, but he never glanced my way. I saw, from the troop behind him, the curious glances as I was recognized. No man was there but must have some inkling now of what had happened last night in Tintagel, and of the part I had played in bringing the King to his heart's desire. It was possible that the simpler souls among the King's companions might have expected the King to be grateful; to reward me; at the very least to recognize and acknowledge me. But I, who had dealt all my life with kings, knew that where there is blame as well as gratitude, blame must be allotted first, lest it should cling to the King himself. King Uther could only see that, by what he called the failure of my foreknowledge, the Duke of Cornwall had died even while he, the King, was lying with the Duchess. He did not see the Duke's death for what it was, the grim irony behind the smiling mask that gods show when they want men to do their will. Uther, who had small truck with gods, saw only that by waiting even one day he might have had his way with honour and in the sight of men. His anger with me was genuine enough, but even if it were not, I knew that he must find someone to blame: whatever he felt about the Duke's death—and he could hardly fail to see it as a miraculously open gate to his marriage with Ygraine—he must in public be seen to show remorse. And I was the public sacrifice to that remorse.

One of the officers—it was Caius Valerius, who rode at the King's shoulder—leaned forward and said something, but Uther might never have heard. I saw Valerius look doubtfully back at me, then with a half-shrug, and a half-salute to me, he rode on. Unsurprised, I watched them go.

The sound of hoofs dwindled sharply down the track towards the sea. Above my head, between one wing-beat and the next, the lark's song shut off, and he dropped from the bright silence to his rest in the grass.

Not far from me a boulder jutted from the turf. I led the horse that way and somehow, from the boulder's top, scrambled into the saddle. I turned the beast's head east by north for Dimilioc, where the King's army lay.

2

Gaps in memory can be merciful. I have no recollection of reaching the camp, but when, hours later, I swam up out of the mists of fatigue and pain I was within doors, and in bed.

I awoke to dusk, and some faint and swimming light that may have been firelight and candle flame; it was a light hazed with colour and drowned with shadows, threaded by the scent of wood-smoke and, it seemed distantly, the trickle and splash of water. But even this warm and gentle consciousness was too much for my struggling senses, and soon I shut my eyes and let myself drown again. I believe that for a while I thought I was back in the edges of the Otherworld, where vision stirs and voices speak out of the dark, and truth comes with the light and the fire. But then the aching of my bruised muscles and the fierce pain in my hand told me that the daylight world still held me, and the voices that murmured across me in the dusk were as human as I.

"Well, that's that, for the moment. The ribs are the worst of it, apart from the hand, and they'll mend soon enough; they're only cracked."

I had a vague feeling that I knew the voice. At any rate I knew what he was: the touch on the fresh bandages was deft and firm, the touch of a professional. I tried to open my eyes again, but the lids were leaden, gummed together and sticky with sweat and dried blood. Warmth came over me in drowsy waves, weighting my limbs. There was a sweet, heavy smell; they must have given me poppy, I thought, or stunned me with smoke before they dressed the hand. I gave up, and let myself drift back from the shore. Over the dark water the voices echoed, softly.

"Stop staring at him and bring the bowl nearer. He's safe enough in this state, never fear." It was the doctor again.

"Well, but one's heard such stories." They were speaking Latin, but the accents were different. The second voice was foreign; not Germanic, nor yet from anywhere on the Middle Sea. I have always been quick at languages, and even as a child spoke several dialects of Celtic, along with Saxon and a working knowledge of Greek. But this accent I could not place. Asia Minor, perhaps? Arabia?

Those deft fingers gently turned my head on the pillow, and parted my hair to sponge the bruises. "Have you never seen him before?"

"Never. I hadn't imagined him so young."

"Not so young. He must be two and twenty."

"But to have done so much. They say his father the High King Ambrosius never took a step, in the last year or two, without talking it over with him. They say he sees the future in a candle flame and can win a battle from a hilltop a mile away."

"They would say anything, of him." The doctor's voice was prosaic and calm. Brittany, I thought, I must have known him in Brittany. The smooth Latin had some overtone I remembered, without knowing how. "But certainly Ambrosius valued his advice."

"Is it true he rebuilt the Giants' Dance near Amesbury, that they call the Hanging Stones?"

"That's true enough. When he was a lad with his father's army in Brittany he studied to be an engineer. I remember him talking to Tremorinus—that was the army's chief engineer—about lifting the Hanging Stones. But that wasn't all he studied. Even as a youth he knew more about medicine than most men I've met who practise it for a livelihood. I can't think of any man I'd rather have by me in a field hospital. God knows why he chooses to shut himself away in that godforsaken corner of Wales now—at least, one can guess why. He and King Uther never got on. They say Uther was jealous of the attention his brother the King paid Merlin. At any rate, after Ambrosius' death, Merlin went nowhere and saw no one, till this business of Uther and Gorlois' Duchess. And it seems as if that's brought him trouble enough. . . . Bring the bowl nearer, while I clean his face. No, here. That's right."

"That's a sword cut, by the look of it."

"A glancing scratch from the point, I'd say. It looks worse than it is, with all the blood. He was lucky there. Another inch and it would have caught his eye. There. It's clean enough; it won't leave a scar."

"He looks like death, Gandar. Will he recover?"

"Of course. How not?" Even through the lulling of the nepenthe, I recognized the quick professional reassurance as genuine. "Apart from the ribs and the hand, it's only cuts and bruising, and I would guess a sharp reaction from whatever has been driving him the last few days. All he needs is sleep. Hand me that ointment there, please. In the green jar."

The salve was cool on my cut cheek. It smelled of valerian. Nard, in the green jar . . . I made it at home. Valerian, balm, oil of spikenard . . . The smell of it took me dreaming out among the mosses at the river's edge, where water ran sparkling, and I gathered the cool cress and the balsam and the golden moss . . .

No, it was water pouring at the other side of the room. He had finished, and had gone to wash his hands. The voices came from farther off.

"Ambrosius' bastard, eh?" The foreigner was still curious. "Who was his mother, then?"

"She was a king's daughter, Southern Welsh, from Maridunum in Dyfed. They say he got the Sight from her. But not his looks; he's a mirror of the late King, more than Uther ever was. Same colouring, black eyes, and that black hair. I remember the first time I saw him, back in Brittany when he was a boy; he looked like something from the hollow hills. Talked like it, too, sometimes; that is, when he talked at all. Don't let his quiet ways fool you; it's more than just book-learning and luck and a knack of timing; there's power there, and it's real."

"So the stories are true?"

"The stories are true," said Gandar flatly. "There. He'll do now. No need to stay with him. Get some sleep. I'll do the rounds myself, and come and take a look at him again before I go to bed. Good night."

The voices faded. Others came and went in the darkness, but these were voices without blood, belonging to the air. Perhaps I should have waited and waked to listen, but I lacked the courage. I reached for sleep and drew it round me like a blanket, muffling pain and thought together in the merciful dark.

When I opened my eyes again it was to darkness lit by calm candle-light. I was in a small chamber with a barrel roof of stone and rough-hewn walls where the once bright paint had darkened and flaked away with damp and neglect. But the room was clean. The floor of Cornish slate had been well scrubbed, and the blankets that covered me were fresh-smelling and thick, and richly worked in bright patterns.

The door opened quietly, and a man came in. At first, against the stronger light beyond the doorway, I could only see him as a man of middle height, broad shouldered and thickly built, dressed in a long plain robe, with a round cap

15

on his head. Then he came forward into the candle-light, and I saw that it was Gandar, the chief physician who travelled with the King's armies. He stood over me, smiling.

"And about time."

"Gandar! It's good to see you. How long have I slept?"

"Since dusk yesterday, and now it's past midnight. It was what you needed. You looked like death when they brought you in. But I must say it made my job a lot easier to have you unconscious."

I glanced down at the hand which lay, neatly bandaged, on the coverlet in front of me. My body was stiff and sore inside its strapping, but the fierce pain had died to a dull aching. My mouth was swollen, and tasted still of blood mingled with the sick-sweet remnants of the drug, but my headache had gone, and the cut on my face had stopped hurting.

"I'm thankful you were here to do it," I said. I shifted the hand a little to ease it, but it was no use. "Will it mend?"

"With the help of youth and good flesh, yes. There were three bones broken, but I think it's clean." He looked at me curiously. "How did you come by it? It looked as if a horse had trodden on you and then kicked your ribs in. But the cut on your face, that was a sword, surely?"

"Yes. I was in a fight."

His brows went up. "If that was a fight, then it wasn't fought by any rules I ever heard of. Tell me—wait, though, not yet. I'm on fire to know what happened—we all are—but you must eat first." He went to the door and called, and presently a servant came in with a bowl of broth and some bread. I could not manage the bread at first, but then sopped a little of it in the broth, and ate that. Gandar pulled a stool up beside the bed, and waited in silence till I had finished. At length I pushed the bowl aside, and he took it from me and set it on the floor.

"Now do you feel well enough to talk? The rumours are flying about like stinging gnats. You knew that Gorlois was dead?"

"Yes." I looked about me. "I'm in Dimilioc itself, I take it? The fortress surrendered, then, after the Duke was killed?"

"They opened the gates as soon as the King got back from Tintagel. He'd already had the news of the skirmish, and the Duke's death. It seems that the Duke's men, Brithael and Jordan, rode to Tintagel as soon as the Duke fell, to take the Duchess the news. But you'd know that; you were there." He stopped short, as he saw the implications. "So that was it! Brithael and Jordan—they ran into you and Uther?"

"Not into Uther, no. They never saw him; he was still with the Duchess. I was outside with my servant Cadal— you remember Cadal?—guarding the doors. Cadal killed Jordan, and I killed Brithael." I smiled, wryly, with my stiff mouth. "Yes, you may well stare. He was well beyond my weight, as you can see. Do you wonder I fought foul?"

"And Cadal?"

"Dead. Do you think otherwise that Brithael would have got to me?"

"I see." His gaze told again, briefly, the tally of my hurts. When he spoke, his voice was dry. "Four men. With you, five. It's to be hoped the King counts it worth the price."

"He does," I said. "Or he will soon."

"Oh, aye, everyone knows that. Give him time only to tell the world that he is guiltless of Gorlois' death, and to get him buried with honour, so that he can marry the Duchess. He's gone back to Tintagel already, did you know? He must have passed you on the road."

"He did," I said dryly. "Within a yard or two."

"But didn't he see you? Or surely—he must have known you were hurt?" Then my tone got through to him. "You

mean he saw you, like that, and left you to ride here alone?"
I could see that he was shocked, rather than surprised. Gandar and I were old acquaintances, and I had no need to tell him what my relationship had been with Uther, even though he was my father's brother. From the very beginning, Uther had resented his brother's love for his bastard son, and had half feared, half despised my powers of vision and prophecy. He said hotly: "But when it was done in his service—"

"Not his, no. What I did, I did because of a promise I made to Ambrosius. It was a trust he left with me, for his kingdom." I left it at that. One did not speak to Gandar of gods and visions. He dealt, like Uther, with things of the flesh. "Tell me," I said, "those rumours you were talking of. What are they? What do people think happened at Tintagel?"

He gave a half-glance over his shoulder. The door was shut, but he lowered his voice. "The story goes that Uther had already been in Tintagel, with the Duchess Ygraine, and that it was you who took him there and put him in the way of entering. They say you changed the King by enchantment into a likeness of the Duke, and got him past the guards and into the Duchess's bedchamber. They say more than that; they say she took him to her bed, poor lady, thinking he was her husband. And that when Brithael and Jordan took her the news of Gorlois' death, there was 'Gorlois' sitting large as life beside her at breakfast. By the Snake, Merlin, why do you laugh?"

"Two days and nights," I said, "and the story has grown already. Well, I suppose that is what men will believe, and go on believing. And perhaps it is better than the truth."

"What is the truth, then?"

"That there was no enchantment about our entry into Tintagel, only disguise, and human treachery."

I told him the story then, exactly as it had happened, with the tale I had given the goat-herd. "So you see, Gandar, I sowed that seed myself. The nobles and the King's advisers must know the truth, but the common folk will find the tale of magic, and a blameless Duchess, better to believe—and, God knows, easier—than the truth."

He was silent for a while. "So the Duchess knew."

"Or we would not have got in," I said. "It shall not be said, Gandar, that this was a rape. No, the Duchess knew."

He was silent again, for rather longer. Then he said, heavily: "Treachery is a hard word."

"It is a true one. The Duke was my father's friend, and he trusted me. It would never have occurred to him that I would help Uther against him. He knew how little I cared for Uther's lusts. He could not guess that my gods demanded that I should help him satisfy this one. Even though I could not help myself, it was still treachery, and we shall suffer for it, all of us."

"Not the King." He said it positively. "I know him. I doubt if the King will feel more than a passing guilt. You are the one who is suffering for it, Merlin, just as you are the one who calls it by its name."

"To you," I said. "To other men this will remain a story of enchantment, like the dragons which fought at my bidding under Dinas Emrys, and the Giants' Dance which floated on air and water to Amesbury. But you have seen how Merlin the King's enchanter fared that night." I paused, and shifted my hand on the coverlet, but shook my head at the question in his face. "No, no, let be. It's better already. Gandar, one other truth about that night must be known. There will be a child. Take it as hope, or take it as prophecy, you will see that, come Christmas, a boy will be born. Has he said when he will marry her?"

19

"As soon as it's decent. Decent!" He repeated the word on a short bark of laughter, then cleared his throat. "The Duke's body is here, but in a day or two they'll carry him to Tintagel to bury him. Then, after the eight days' mourning, Uther is to marry the Duchess."

I thought for a moment. "Gorlois had a son by his first wife. Cador, he was called. He must be about fifteen. Have you heard what is to become of him?".

"He's here. He was in the fight, beside his father. No one knows what has passed between him and the King, but the King gave an amnesty to all the troops that fought against him in the action at Dimilioc, and he has said, besides, that Cador will be confirmed Duke of Cornwall."

"Yes," I said. "And Ygraine's son and Uther's will be King."

"With Cornwall his bitter enemy?"

"If he is," I said wearily, "who is to blame him? The payment may well be too long and too heavy, even for treachery."

"Well," said Gandar, suddenly brisk, gathering his robe about him, "that's with time. And now, young man, you'd better get some more rest. Would you like a draught?"

"Thank you, no."

"How does the hand feel?"

"Better. There's no poison there; I know the feel of it. I'll give you no more trouble, Gandar, so stop treating me like a sick man. I'm well enough, now that I've slept. Get yourself to bed, and forget about me. Good night."

When he had gone I lay listening to the sounds of the sea, and trying to gather, from the god-filled dark, the courage I would need for my visit to the dead.

Courage or no, another day passed before I found the

strength to leave my chamber. Then I went at dusk to the great hall where they had put the old Duke's body. Tomorrow he would be taken to Tintagel for burial among his fathers. Now he lay alone, save for the guards, in the echoing hall where he had feasted his peers and given orders for his last battle.

The place was cold, silent but for the sounds of wind and sea. The wind had changed and now blew from the northwest, bringing with it the chill and promise of rain. There was neither glazing nor horn in the windows, and the draught stirred the torches in their iron brackets, sending them sideways, dim and smoking, to blacken the walls. It was a stark, comfortless place, bare of paint, or tiling, or carved wood; one remembered that Dimilioc was simply the fortress of a fighting man; it was doubtful if Ygraine had ever been here. The ashes in the hearth were days old, the half-burned logs dewed with damp.

The Duke's body lay on a high bier in the center of the hall, covered with his war cloak. The scarlet with the double border of silver and the white badge of the Boar was as I had seen it at my father's side in battle. I had seen it, too, on Uther as I led him disguised into Gorlois' castle and his bed. Now the heavy folds hung to the ground, and beneath them the body had shrunk and flattened, no more than a husk of the tall old man I remembered. They had left his face uncovered. The flesh had sunk, grey as twice-used tallow, till the face was a moulded skull, showing only the ghost of a likeness to the Gorlois I had known. The coins on his eyes had already sunk into the flesh. His hair was hidden by his war helm, but the familiar grey beard jutted over the badge of the Boar on his chest.

I wondered, as I went forward soft-footed over the stone floor, by which god Gorlois had lived, and to which god he had gone in dying. There was nothing here to show. Christians, like other men, put coins on the eyes. I remembered other death-beds, and the press of spirits waiting round them; there was nothing here. But he had been dead three days, and perhaps his spirit had already gone through that bare and windy gap in the wall. Perhaps it had already gone too far for me to reach it and make my peace.

I stood at the foot of his bier, the man I had betrayed, the friend of my father Ambrosius the High King. I remembered the night he had come to ask me for my help for his young wife, and how he had said to me: "There are not many men I'd trust just now, but I trust you. You're your father's son." And how I had said nothing, but watched the firelight stain his face red like blood, and waited my chance to lead the King to his wife's bed.

It is one thing to have the gift of seeing the spirits and hearing the gods who move about us as we come and go; but it is a gift of darkness as well as light. The shapes of death come as clear as those of life. One cannot be visited by the future without being haunted by the past; one cannot taste comfort and glory without the bitter sting and fury of one's own past deeds. Whatever I had thought to encounter near the dead body of the Duke of Cornwall, it would hold no comfort and no peace for me. A man like Uther Pendragon, who killed in open battle and open air, would think no more of this than a dead man dead. But I, who in obeying the gods had trusted them even as the Duke had trusted me, had known that I would have to pay, and in full. So I had come, but without hope.

There was light here from the torches, light and fire. I was Merlin; I should be able to reach him; I had talked with the dead before. I stood still, watching the flaring torches, and waited.

Slowly, all through the fortress, I could hear the sounds

dwindling and sinking to silence as men finally went to rest. The sea soughed and beat below the window, the wind plucked at the wall, and ferns growing there in the crevices rustled and tapped. A rat scuttled and squeaked somewhere. The resin bubbled in the torches. Sweet and foul, through the sharp smoke, I smelled the smell of death. The torchlight winked blank and flat from the coins on the dead eyes.

The time crawled by. My eyes ached with the flame, and the pain from my hand, like a biting fetter, kept me penned in my body. My spirit was pared down to nothing, blind as the dead. Whispers I caught, fragments of thought from the still and sleepy guards, meaningless as the sound of their breathing, and the creak of leather or chime of metal as they stirred involuntarily from time to time. But beyond these, nothing. What power I had been given on that night at Tintagel had drained from me with the strength that had killed Brithael. It had gone from me and was working, I thought, in a woman's body; in Ygraine, lying even now beside the King in that grim and battered near-isle of Tintagel, ten miles to the south. I could do nothing here. The air, solid as stone, would not let me through.

One of the guards, the one nearest me, moved restlessly, and the butt of his grounded spear scraped on the stone. The sound jarred the silence. I glanced his way involuntarily, and saw him watching me.

He was young, rigid as his own spear, his fists white on the shaft. The fierce blue eyes watched me unwinkingly under thick brows. With a shock that went through me like the spear striking I recognized them. Gorlois' eyes. It was Gorlois' son, Cador of Cornwall, who stood between me and the dead, watching me steadily, with hatred.

In the morning they took Gorlois' body south. As soon as he was buried, Gandar had told me, Uther planned to ride back to Dimilioc to rejoin his troops until such time as he could marry the Duchess. I had no intention of waiting for his return. I called for provisions and my horse and, in spite of Gandar's protestations that I was not yet fit for the journey, set out alone for my valley above Maridunum and the cave in the hill which the King had promised should remain, in spite of everything, my own.

3

No one had been inside the cave during my absence. This was hardly to be wondered at, since the people held me in much awe as an enchanter, and moreover it was commonly known that the King himself had granted me the hill Bryn Myrddin. Once I left the main road at the water-mill, and rode up the steep tributary valley to the cave which had become my home, I saw no one, not even the shepherd who commonly watched his flocks grazing the stony slopes.

In the lower reaches of the valley the woods were thick; oaks still rustled their withered leaves, chestnut and sycamore crowded close, fighting for the light, and hollies showed black and glinting between the beeches. Then the trees thinned, and the path climbed along the side of the valley, with the stream running deep down on the left, and to the right slopes of grass, broken by scree, rising sharply to the crags that crowned the hill. The grass was still bleached with winter, but among the rusty drifts of last year's bracken the bluebell leaves showed glossy green, and blackthorn was budding. Somewhere, lambs were crying. That, and the mewing of a buzzard high over the crags, and the rustle of the dead bracken where my tired horse trod, were all the sounds in the valley. I was home, to the solace of simplicity and quiet.

The people had not forgotten me, and word must have gone round that I was expected. When I dismounted in the thorn grove below the cliff and stabled my horse in the shed there I found that bracken had been freshly strewn for bedding, and a netful of fodder hung from a hook beside the door; and when I climbed to the little apron of lawn which lay in front of my cave I found cheese and new bread wrapped in a clean cloth, and a goatskin full of the local thin, sour wine, which had been left for me beside the spring.

This was a small spring, a trickle of pure water welling out of a ferny crack in the rock to one side of the entrance to the cave. The water ran down, sometimes in a steady flow, sometimes no more than a sliding glimmer over the mosses, to drip into a rounded basin of stone. Above the spring the little statue of the god Myrddin, he of the winged spaces of the air, stared from between the ferns. Beneath his cracked wooden feet the water bubbled and dripped into the stone basin, lipping over into the grass below. Deep in the clear water metal glinted; I knew that the wine and bread, like the thrown coins, had been left as much as an offering to the god as to me; in the minds of the simple folk I had already become part of the legend of the hill, their god made flesh who came and went as quietly as the air, and brought with him the gifts of healing.

I lifted down the cup of horn which stood above the spring, filled it from the goatskin, then poured wine for the god, and drank the rest myself. The god would know whether there was more in the gesture than ritual homage. I myself was tired beyond thought, and had no prayer to offer; the drink was for courage, nothing more.

To the other side of the cave entrance, opposite the spring, was a tumble of grass-grown stones, where saplings of oak and mountain ash had seeded themselves, and grew in a thick tangle against the rocky face. In summer their boughs cast a wide pool of shade, but now, though overhanging it, they did nothing to conceal the entrance to the cave. This was a smallish arch, regular and rounded, as if made by hand. I pushed the hanging boughs aside and went in.

Just inside the entrance the remnants of a fire still lay in white ash on the hearth, and twigs and damp leaves had drifted over it. The place smelled already of disuse. It seemed strange that it was barely a month since I had ridden out at the King's urgent summons to help him in the matter of Ygraine of Cornwall. Beside the cold hearth stood the unwashed dishes from the last, hasty meal my servant had prepared before we set out.

Well, I would have to be my own servant now. I put the goatskin of wine and the bundle of bread and cheese on the table, then turned to re-make the fire. Flint and tinder lay to hand where they had always lain, but I knelt down by the cold faggots and stretched out my hands for the magic. This was the first magic I had been taught, and the simplest, the bringing of fire out of the air. It had been taught me in this very cave, where as a child I had learned all I knew of natural lore from Galapas, the old hermit of the hill. Here, too, in the cave of crystal which lay deeper in the hill, I had seen my first visions, and found myself as a seer. "Some day," Galapas had said, "you will go where even with the Sight I cannot follow you." It had been true. I had left him, and gone where my god had driven me; where none but I, Merlin, could have gone. But now the god's will was done, and he had forsaken me. Back there in Dimilioc, beside Gorlois' bier, I had found myself to be an empty husk; blind and deaf as men are blind and deaf; the great power gone. Now, weary though I was, I knew I would not rest until I saw if, here in my magic's birthplace, the first and smallest of my powers was left to me.

I was soon answered, but it was an answer I would not accept. The westering sun was dropping red past the boughs at the cave mouth, and the logs were still unkindled, when finally I gave up, with the sweat running scalding on my body under my gown, and my hands, outstretched for the magic, trembling like those of an old man. I sat by the cold hearth and ate my supper of bread and cheese and watered wine in the chill of the spring dusk, before I could gather even strength enough to reach for the flint and tinder and try with them.

Even this, a task that every wife does daily and without thought, took me an age, and set my maimed hand bleeding. But in the end fire came. A tiny spark flew in among the tinder and started a slow, creeping flame. I lit the torch from it, and then, carrying the flame high, went to the back of the cave. There was something I still must do.

The main cavern, high-roofed, went a long way back. I stood with the torch held high, looking up. At the back of the cave was a slope of rock leading up to a wide ledge, which in its turn climbed into the dark, high shadows. Invisible among these shadows was the hidden cleft beyond which lay the inner cave, the globed cavity lined with crystals where, with light and fire, I had seen my first visions. If the lost power lay anywhere, it lay there. Slowly, stiff with fatigue, I climbed the ledge, then knelt to peer through the low entrance to the inner cave. The flames from my torch caught the crystals, and light ran round the globe. My harp still stood where I had left it, in the center of the crystal-studded floor. Its shadow shot towering up the shimmering walls, and flame sparked from the copper of the string-shoes, but no stir of the air set it whispering, and its own arching shadows quenched the light. I knelt there for a long time, eyes wide and staring, while round me light and shadow shivered and beat. But my eyes ached, empty of vision, and the harp stayed silent.

At length I withdrew, and made my way down into the main cave. I remember that I picked my way slowly, carefully, like a man who has never been that way before. I thrust the torch under the dry wood I had piled for a fire, till the logs caught, crackling; then went out and found my saddle-bags, and lugged them back into the human comfort of the firelight, and began to unpack them.

My hand took a long time to heal. For the first few days it pained me constantly, throbbing so that I was afraid it was infected. During the day this did not matter so much, for there were tasks to do; all that my servant had done for me for so long that I hardly knew how to set about it; cleaning, preparing food, tending my horse. Spring came slowly to South Wales that year, and there was no grazing yet on the hill, so I had to cut and carry fodder for him, and walk farther than I cared to in search of the healing plants I needed. Luckily food for myself was always forthcoming; gifts were left almost daily at the foot of the small cliff below the lawn. It may have been that the country folk had not yet heard that I was out of favour with the King, or it may simply have been that what I had done for them in the way of healing outweighed Uther's displeasure. I was Merlin, son of Ambrosius; or, as the Welsh say it, Myrddin Emrys, the enchanter of Myrddin's Hill; and in another way, I suppose, the priest of the old god of the hollow hill, Myrddin himself. What gifts they would have brought for him they brought now for me, and in his name I accepted them.

But if the days were full enough, the nights were bad. I seemed always wakeful, less perhaps from the pain of my hand than from the pain of my memories: where Gorlois' death chamber had been empty, my own cave was full of ghosts. Not the spirits of the loved dead whom I would have welcomed; but the spirits of those I had killed went past me in the dark with thin sounds like the cry of bats. At least, this is what I told myself. I believe now that I was often touched with fever: the cave still housed the bats that Galapas and I had studied, and it must have been these I heard, passing to and from the cave mouth during the night. But in my memory of this time they are the voices of dead men, restless in the dark.

April went by, wet and chill, with winds that searched you to the bone. This was the bad time, empty except for pain, and idle except for the barest efforts to live. I believe I ate very little; water and fruit and black bread was my staple diet. My clothes, never sumptuous, became threadbare with no one to care for them, and then ragged. A stranger seeing me walking the hill paths would have taken me for a beggar. Days passed when I did little but huddle over the smoking fire. My chest of books was unopened, my harp was left where it stood. Even had my hand been whole, I could have made no music. As for magic, I dared not put myself to the test again.

But gradually, like Ygraine waiting in her cold castle to the south, I slid into a sort of calm acceptance. As the weeks went by my hand healed, cleanly enough. I was left with two stiff fingers, and a scar along the outer edge of the palm, but the stiffness passed with time, and the scar never troubled me. And as time passed the other wounds healed, too. I grew used to loneliness, as I had been accustomed to solitude, and the nightmares ceased. Then as May drew on the winds changed, grew warm, and grass and flowers came springing. The grey clouds packed away, and the valley was full of sunlight. I sat for hours in the sun at the mouth of the cave, reading, or preparing the plants I had gathered, or from time to time watching—but no more than idly—for the approach of a rider which would mean a message. (Even so, I thought, must my old teacher Galapas have sat here many a time in the sunlight, looking down the valley where, one day, a small boy would come riding.) And I built up again my stock of plants and herbs, wandering farther and farther from the cave as my strength came back to me. I never went into the town, but now and again when poor folk came for medicines or for healing, they brought snatches of news. The King had married Ygraine with as much pomp and ceremony as such a hasty union would permit, and he had seemed merry enough since the wedding, though quicker to anger than he used to be, and would have sudden morose fits when folk learned to avoid him. As for the Queen, she was silent, acceding in everything to the King's wishes, but rumour had it that her looks were heavy, as if she mourned in secret. . . .

Here my informant shot a quick sidelong look at me, and I saw his fingers move to make the sign against enchantment. I let him go on, asking no more questions. The news would come to me in its own time.

It came almost three months after my return to Bryn Myrddin.

One day in June, when a hot morning sun was just lifting the mist from the grass, I went up the hill to find my horse, which I had tethered out to graze on the grassland above the cave. The air was still, and the sky was full of singing larks. Over the green mound where Galapas lay buried the black-thorns showed green leaves budding through fading snow-banks of flowers, and bluebells were thick among the fern.

I doubt if I actually needed to tether my horse. I usually carried with me the remnants of the bread my benefactors left for me, so when he saw me coming he would advance to the end of his tether and stand waiting, expectant.

But not today. He was standing at the far stretch of his

31

rope, on the edge of the hill, head up and ears pricked, apparently watching something away down the valley. I walked over to him and, while he nuzzled in my hand for the bread, looked where he had been looking.

From this height I could see the town of Maridunum, small in the distance, clinging to the north bank of the placid Tywy as it wound its way down its wide green valley towards the sea. The town, with its arched stone bridge and its harbour, lies just where the river widens towards the estuary. There was the usual huddle of masts beyond the bridge, and nearer, on the towpath that threaded its way along the silver curves of the river, a slow grey horse towed a grain barge up to the mill. The mill itself, lying where the stream from my own valley met the river, was hidden in woodland; out of these trees ran the old military road which my father had repaired, straight as a die through five open miles, to the barracks near Maridunum's eastern gate.

On this road, perhaps a mile and a half beyond the water-mill, there was a cloud of dust where horsemen skirmished. They were fighting; I saw the flash of metal. Then the group resolved itself, clearer through the dust. There were four mounted men, and they were fighting three to one. The lone man seemed to be trying to escape, the others to surround him and cut him down. At length he burst free in what looked like a desperate bid for escape. His horse, pulled round hard, struck one of the others on the shoulder, and its rider fell, dislodged by a heavy blow. Then the single man, crouched and spurring hard, turned his horse off the road and across the grass, making desperately for the cover afforded by the edge of the woodland. But he did not reach it. The other two spurred after him; there was a short, wild gallop, then they had caught him up, one on each side,

32

and as I watched he was dragged from his horse and beaten to his knees. He tried to crawl away, but he had no chance. The two horsemen circled, their weapons flashing, and the third man, apparently uninjured, had remounted and was galloping to join them. Then suddenly he checked his horse, so sharply that it reared. I saw him fling up an arm. He must have shouted a warning, for the other two, abruptly abandoning their victim, wheeled their beasts, and the three of them galloped off, full stretch, with the loose horse pelting behind them, to be lost to sight eastwards beyond the trees.

Next moment I saw what had startled them. Another group of horsemen was approaching from the direction of the town. They must have seen the retreating trio, but it soon appeared that they had seen nothing of the attack, for they came on at a canter, riding at ease. I watched them as they drew level with the place where the fallen man—injured or dead—must be lying. They passed it without slackening pace. Then they, too, were lost to sight below the woodland.

My horse, finding no more bread, nipped me, then jerked his head away sharply, ears flattened. I caught him by the halter, pulled up the tether, peg and all, and turned his head downhill.

"I stood on this spot once before," I told him, "while a King's messenger came riding to see me and bid me go and help the King to his desire. I had power that day; I dreamed I held the whole world cupped in my hands, shining and small. Well, maybe I've nothing today but the hill I stand on, but that might be a Queen's messenger lying down yonder, with a message still in his pouch. Message or not, he'll need help if he's still alive. And you and I, my friend, have had our fill of idleness. It's time to be doing again."

In a little less than twice the time it would have taken my

33

servant to do the job, I had the horse bridled, and was on my way down the valley. Reaching the mill road, I turned my horse's head to the right, and drove my heels in.

The place where I had seen the horseman fall was near the edge of the woods, where the bushes were thick, a place of bracken and undergrowth and scattered trees. The smell of horses still hung in the air, with the tang of trampled bracken and sweet briar and, foul through it all, the smell of vomit. I dismounted and tethered my horse, then pushed my way forward through the thick growth.

He lay on his face, half hunched as he had crawled and collapsed, one hand still trapped under his body, the other outflung and gripping a tuft of bracken. A youth, lightly built but well grown, fifteen, perhaps, or a little more. His clothes, torn and grimed and bloodstained by the fight and his crawl through the thorns, had been good, and there was a glint of silver on one wrist, and a silver brooch at his shoulder. So they had not managed to rob him, if robbery had been the motive for the attack. His pouch was still at his belt, and fastened.

He made no move as I approached him, so I thought him insensible, or dead. But when I knelt beside him I saw the slight movement as his hand clenched more tightly on the stems of bracken, and I realized that he was exhausted or hurt beyond all caring. If I were one of his murderers come to finish him off, he would lie there and let me.

I spoke gently. "Be easy, I shan't hurt you. Lie still a moment. Don't try to move."

There was no response. I laid careful hands on him, feeling for wounds and broken bones. He flinched from my touch, but made no sound. I satisfied myself soon that no bones were broken. There was a bloodied swelling near the back of his head, and one shoulder was already blackened with

34

bruising, but the worst that I could see was a patch of crushed and bleeding flesh on the hip, which looked—and indeed later proved—to be where a horse's hoof had struck him.

"Come," I said at length, "turn over, and drink this."

He moved then, though wincing from the touch of my arm round his shoulder, and turned slowly round. I wiped the dirt and sickness from his mouth and held my flask to his lips; he gulped greedily, coughed, and then, losing strength again, leaned heavily against me, his head drooping against my chest. When I put the flask back to his mouth he turned his head away. I could feel him using all his strength not to cry out against the pain. I stoppered the flask and put it away.

"I have a horse here. You must try and sit him somehow, and I'll get you home, where I can see to your hurts." Then, when he made no response: "Come now. Let's get you out of this before they decide to come back and finish what they started."

He moved then, abruptly, as if these were the first words that had got through to him. I saw his hand grope down to the pouch at his belt, discover it was still there, and then fall limply away. The weight against my chest sagged suddenly. He had fainted.

So much the better, I thought, as I laid him down gently and went to bring up my horse. He would be spared the painful jolting of the ride, and by the gods' mercy I might have him in bed with his hurts bandaged before he woke. Then in the very act of stooping to lift him again I paused. His face was dirty, grime mingled with bloodstains from scratches and a cut above the ear. Under the mask of dirt and blood the skin was drained and grey. Brown hair, shut eyes, a slack mouth. But I recognized him. It was Ralf,

Ygraine's page, who had let us into Tintagel that night, and who with Ulfin and myself had guarded the Duchess's chamber until the King had had his desire.

I stooped and lifted the Queen's messenger, and heaved his unconscious body across my waiting horse.

4

Ralf did not regain his senses during the journey up to the cave, and only after I had washed and bound his wounds and put him into bed did he open his eyes. He stared at me for a few moments, but without recognition.

"Don't you know me?" I said. "Merlinus Ambrosius. You brought your message safely enough. See." I held up the wallet, still sealed. But his eyes, cloudy and unfocused, slid past it, and he turned his head against the pillow, wincing as he felt the pain from the bruising on the back of his neck. "Very well," I told him, "sleep now. You're in safe hands."

I waited beside him till he drifted back into sleep, then took the wallet and its contents out to my seat in the sunlight. The seal was, as I had expected, the Queen's, and the superscription was mine. I broke the seal and read the letter.

It was not from the Queen herself, but from Marcia, Ralf's grandmother and the Queen's closest confidante. The letter was brief enough, but held all I wanted to know. The Queen was indeed pregnant, and the child would be born in December. The Queen herself—said Marcia—seemed happy to be bearing the King's child, but, where she spoke of me at all, spoke with bitterness, throwing on me the responsibility for her husband Gorlois' death. "She says little, but it is my belief that she mourns in secret, and that even in her great love for the King there will always be the shadow of guilt. Pray God her feeling for the child may not be tainted with it. As for the King, it is seen that he is angry, though he is as ever kind and loving to my lady, and there is no man who doubts but that the child is his. Alas, I could find it in me to fear for the child at the King's hands, if it were not unthinkable that he should so grieve the Queen. Wherefore, Prince Merlin, I beg by this letter to commend to you as your servant my grandson Ralf. For him, too, I fear at the King's hands; and I believe that, if you will take him, service abroad with a true prince is better than here with a King who counts his service as betrayal. There is no safety for him in Cornwall. So pray you, lord, let Ralf serve you now, and after you, the child. For I think I understand what you were speaking of when you said to my lady, 'I have seen a bright fire burning, and in it a crown, and a sword standing in an altar like a cross.' "

Ralf slept until dusk. I had lit the fire and made broth, and when I took it to the back of the cave where he lay I saw his eyes open, watching me. There was recognition in them now, and a wariness that I could not quite understand.

"How do you feel now?"

"Well enough, my lord. I—this is your cave? How did I come here? How did you find me?"

"I had gone up to the hill above here, and from there I saw you being attacked. The men were frightened off, and ran away, leaving you. I went down to get you, and carried you up here on my horse. So you recognize me now, do you?"

"You've let your beard grow, but I'd have known you, my lord. Did I speak to you before? I don't remember anything. I think they hit me on the head."

"They did. How is it now?"

"A headache. But not bad. It's my side"—wincing—"that hurts most."

"One of the horses struck you. But there's no real damage

done; you'll be well enough in a few days. Do you know who they were?"

"No." He knitted his brows, thinking, but I could see the effort hurt him, so I stopped him.

"Well, we can talk later. Eat now."

"My lord, the message—"

"I have it safely. Later."

When I went back to him he had finished the broth and bread, and looked more like himself. He would not take more food, but I made him drink a little wine, and watched the colour come back into his face. Then I drew up a chair, and sat down beside the bed.

"Better?"

"Yes." He spoke without looking at me. He looked down at his hands, nervously plucking at the covers in front of him. He swallowed. "I—I haven't thanked you yet, my lord."

"For what? Picking you up and bringing you here? It was the only way to get your news."

He glanced up at that, and for a startled second I realized that he thought it was no more than the truth. I saw then what there was in that look he had given me; he was afraid of me. I thought back to that night in Tintagel, the gay youth who had dealt so bravely for the King, and so truly with me. But for the moment I let it go. I said:

"You brought me the news I wanted. I've read your grandmother's letter. You know what she tells me in it about the Queen?"

"Yes."

"And about yourself?"

"Yes." He shut his mouth on the syllable, and looked away, sullen, like someone unfairly trapped and held for questioning, who is determined not to answer. It seemed that, whatever Marcia's motives for sending him to me, he

39

himself was far from willing to offer me service. From which I guessed that she had told him nothing about her hopes for the future.

"All right, we'll leave that for the moment. But it seems that somebody wants to harm you, whoever it may be. If those men this morning weren't just roadside cutthroats, it would help to know who they were, and who paid them. Have you no idea who they might have been?"

"No," still mumbling.

"It's of some interest to me," I said mildly. "They might conceivably want to kill me, too."

That startled him out of his resentment. "Why?"

"If you were attacked out of revenge for the part you played at Tintagel, then presumably they will attack me as well. If you were attacked for the message you carried to me, I want to know why. If they were plain thieves, which seems the most likely, then they may still be hereabouts, and I must get a message to the troopers down at the barracks."

"Oh. Yes, I see." He looked disconcerted and slightly ashamed. "But it's true, my lord; I don't know who they were. I—it was of interest to me, too. I've been trying to think, all this time, but I've no idea. There's no clue that I can remember. They didn't wear badges; at least I don't think so . . ." His brows drew together, painfully. "I'd have noticed badges, surely, if they'd had them?"

"How were they dressed?"

"I—I hardly noticed. Leather tunics, I think, and chain-mail caps. No shields, but swords and daggers."

"And they were well mounted. I saw that. Did you hear their speech?"

"Not that I remember. They hardly spoke, a shout or two, that was all. British speech, but I couldn't tell where from. I'm not good at accents."

"There was nothing you can think of that might have marked them for King's men?"

This was probing too near the wound. He went scarlet, but said levelly enough: "Nothing. But is it likely?"

"I wouldn't have thought so," I said. "But kings are queer cattle, and queerest of all when they have bad consciences. Well, then, Cornishmen?"

The flush had ebbed, leaving him if possible more sickly pale than before. His eyes were sullen and unhappy. This was the wound itself; this was a thought he had lived with. "Duke's men, you mean?"

"They told me before I left Dimilioc that the King was to confirm young Cador as Duke of Cornwall. That's one man, Ralf, who will have no love for you. He won't stop to consider that you were the Duchess's man, and were serving her as you were bidden. He is full of hatred, and it might extend to vengeance. One could hardly blame him if it did."

He looked faintly surprised, then in some odd way set at ease by this dispassionate handling. After a bit he said, with an attempt at the same tone: "They might have been Cador's men, I suppose. There was nothing to show it, one way or the other. Maybe I'll remember something." He paused. "But surely, if Cador intended to kill me, he could have cut me down in Cornwall. Why come all the way here? To follow me to you? He must hate you as much."

"More," I said. "But if he had intended to kill me, he knew where to find me; the whole world knows that. And he'd have come before this."

He eyed me doubtfully. Then he appeared to find an explanation for my apparent lack of fear. "I suppose no one would dare come after you here, for fear of your magic?"

"It would be nice to think so," I agreed. There was no point in telling him how thin my defenses were. "Now, that's enough for the moment. Rest again, and you'll find you feel better tomorrow. Will you sleep, do you think? Are you in pain?"

"No," he said, not truthfully. Pain was a weakness he would not admit to me. I stooped and felt for the heart-beat in his wrist. It was strong and even. I let the wrist drop, and nodded at him. "You'll live. Call me in the night if you want me. Good night."

Ralf did not in fact remember anything more next morning that would give a clue to the identity of his attackers, and I forbore for a few days from questioning him further about the contents of Marcia's letter. Then one evening, when I judged he was better, I called him to me. It had been a damp day, and the evening had brought a chill with it, so I had lit a fire, and sat with my supper beside it.

"Ralf, bring your bowl and eat beside me where it's warm. I want to talk to you."

He came obediently. He had somehow managed to mend and tidy his clothes, and now, with the cuts and bruises fading, and with colour back in his face, he was almost himself again, except for a limp where the wound on his hip had not yet mended; and except, still, for his silence, and the sullen shadow of wariness in his face. He limped across and sat where I pointed.

"You said you knew what else was in your grandmother's letter to me besides news of the Queen?" I asked him.

"Yes."

"Then you know she sent you to take service with me, because she feared the King's displeasure. Did the King himself give you any reason to fear him?"

A slight shake of the head. He would not meet my eyes. "Not to fear him, no. But when the alarm came of a Saxon landing on the south coast, and I asked to ride with his men, he would not take me." His voice was sullen and furious. "Even though he took every other Cornishman who had fought against him at Dimilioc. But myself, who had helped him, he dismissed."

I looked thoughtfully at the bent head, the hot averted cheek. This, of course, was the reason for his attitude to me, the wary resentment and anger. He could only see, understandably enough, that through his service to me and the King he had lost his place near the Queen; worse, he had incurred his Duke's anger, had been disgraced as a Cornish subject and banished from his home to a kind of service he disdained.

I said: "Your grandmother tells me little except that she feels you had better seek a career for yourself outside Cornwall. Leave that for a moment; you can't seek anything much until your leg is healed. But tell me, did the King ever say anything to you directly about the night of Gorlois' death?"

A pause, so long that I thought he would not answer. Then he said: "Yes. He told me that I had served him well, and he—he thanked me. He asked me if I wanted a reward. I said no, the service was reward enough. He didn't like that. I think he wanted to give me money, and requite me, and forget it. He said then that I could no longer serve him or the Queen. That in serving him I had betrayed my master the Duke, and that a man who had betrayed one master could betray another."

"Well?" I said. "Is that all?"

"*All?*" His head jerked up at that. He looked startled and contemptuous. "*All?* An insult like that? And it was a lie, you know it was! I was my lady's man, not Duke Gorlois'! I did not betray the Duke!"

"Oh, yes, it was an insult. You can't expect the King to be level-headed yet, when he himself feels as guilty as Judas.

43

He's got to put the betrayal on someone's shoulders, so it's yours and mine. But I doubt if you're in actual danger from him. Even a doting grandmother could hardly call that a threat."

"Who was talking about threats?" said Ralf hotly. "I didn't come away because I was afraid! Someone had to bring the message, and you saw how safe that was!"

It was hardly the tone a servant uses. I hid my amusement and said mildly: "Don't ruffle your feathers at me, young cockerel. No one doubts your courage. I'm sure the King does not. Now, tell me about this Saxon landing. Where? What happened? I've had no news from the south for over a month now."

In a little while he answered me civilly enough. "It was in May. They landed south of Vindocladia. There's a deep bay there, they call it Potters' Bay. I forget its real name. Well, it's outside federated territory, in Dumnonia, and that was against all the agreements the Federates made. You would know that."

I nodded. It is hard to remember now, looking back down the years to the time I write of, Uther's time, that today men hardly remember even the name of Federate. The first of the Federated Saxons were the followers of Hengist and Horsa, who had been called in by King Vortigern as mercenary help to establish him on his stolen throne. When the fighting was done, and the rightful princes Ambrosius and Uther had fled to Brittany, the usurper Vortigern would have dismissed his Saxon mercenaries; but they refused to withdraw, demanding territory where they could settle, and promising, as federated settlers, to fight as Vortigern's allies. So, partly because he dared not refuse them, partly because he foresaw that he might need them again, Vortigern gave them the coastal stretches in the south, from Rutupiae to Vindocladia—the stretch that was called the Saxon Shore.

In the days of the Romans it had been so called because the main Saxon landings had been there; by Uther's time the name had taken on a direr and truer significance. On a clear day you could see the Saxon smoke from London Wall.

It had been from this secured base, and from similar enclaves in the north-east, that the new attacks had come when my father was King. He had killed Hengist and his brother, and had driven the invaders back, some northwards into the wild lands beyond Hadrian's Wall, and others behind their old boundaries, where once again—but this time forcibly—they had been bound by treaty. But a treaty with a Saxon is like writing in water: Ambrosius, not trusting to the prescribed boundaries, had thrown up a wall to protect the rich lands which marched with the Saxon Shore. Until his death the treaty—or the Wall—had held them, nor had they openly joined in the attacks led by Hengist's son Octa and Eosa his kinsman in the early days of Uther's reign; but they were uneasy neighbours: they provided a beach-head for any wandering longships, and the Saxon Shore grew crowded and still more crowded, till even Ambrosius' Wall looked frail protection. And everywhere along the eastern shores raiders came in from the German Sea, some to burn and rape and sail again, others to burn and rape and stay, buying or extorting new territory from the local kings.

Such an attack, now, Ralf was describing to me.

"Well, of course the Federates broke the agreement. A new war-band—thirty ships it was—landed in Potters' Bay, well west of the boundary, and the Federates welcomed them and came out in force to help them. They established a beach-head near the river's mouth and started to push up towards Vindocladia. I think if they had once got to Badon Hill—what is it?"

He broke off, staring at me. There was amazement in his face, and a touch of fear.

"Nothing," I said. "I thought I heard something outside, but it's only the wind."

He said slowly: "You looked for a moment the way you did that night at Tintagel, when you said the air was full of magic. Your eyes went strange, all black and blurred, as if you were seeing something, out there beyond the fire." He hesitated. "Was it prophecy?"

"No. I saw nothing. All I heard was a sound like horses galloping. It was only the wild geese going over in the wind. If it was prophecy, it will come again. Go on. You were speaking of Badon Hill."

"Well, the Saxons can't have known that King Uther was in Cornwall, with all the force he'd brought down to fight Duke Gorlois. He gathered his army and called on the Dumnonians to help him, and marched to drive the Saxons back." He paused, compressing his lips, then finished briefly: "Cador went with him."

"Did he indeed?" I was thoughtful. "You didn't happen to hear what had passed between them?"

"Only that Cador had been heard to say that since he couldn't defend his part of Dumnonia alone he didn't mind fighting alongside the Devil himself, as long as the Saxons could be cleared from the coast."

"He sounds a sensible young man."

Ralf, hot on his grievance, was not listening. "You see, he didn't exactly make peace with Uther—"

"Yes. One gathers that."

"—but he did march with him! And I could not! I went to him, and to my lady, and begged to go, but he wouldn't take me!"

"Well," I said, reasonably, "how could he?"

That stopped him. He stared at me, ready to be angry again. "What do you mean? If *you* think me a traitor—"

"You're the same age as Cador, aren't you? Then try to

46

show as much common sense. Think. If Cador was to go into battle beside the King, then the King, for your sake, could hardly take you. Uther may suffer a few pangs of conscience when he lays eyes on you, but Cador must see you as one of the causes of his father's death. Do you think he would bear you near him, however much he may need the King and his legions? Now do you see why you were left at home, and then sent north to me?"

He was silent. I said, gently: "What's done is done, Ralf. Only a child expects life to be just; it's a man's part to stand by the consequence of his deeds. As we both shall, believe me. So put all this behind you, and take what the gods send. Your life is not over because you have had to leave the court, or even because you have had to leave Cornwall."

There was a longer silence. Then he picked up his empty bowl and mine and got to his feet. "Yes, I see. Well, since for the moment I can't do much else, I'll stay and serve you. But not because I'm afraid of the King, or because my grand-mother wants to get me out of Duke Cador's way. It's because I choose. And indeed"— he swallowed—"I reckon I owe it to you." His tone was neither grateful nor concilia-tory. He stood there like a soldier, stiffly, the bowls clutched to his ribs.

"Then start paying your debt and wash the supper dishes," I said equably, and picked up a book.

He hung on his heel a moment, but I neither spoke nor looked up. He went then, without another word, to draw water from the spring outside.

5

Bruises on the young heal quickly, and Ralf was soon active again, and insistent that he no longer needed doctoring. The wound on his hip, however, gave some trouble, and left him limping for a week or two.

In "choosing" to stay with me, he had made the best of a bad job, since for the time being he was tied to the cave by his injury and by the loss of his horse, but he served me well, mastering what resentment he might yet feel towards me and his new position. He was silent still, but this suited me, and I went quietly about my affairs, while Ralf gradually fell into my ways, and we got along tolerably well together. Whatever he thought of my quarters in the cave, and the menial tasks which between us we had to do, he made it clear that he was a page serving a prince. Somehow, through the days that followed, I found myself relieved, bit by bit, of burdensome work which I had begun to take for granted; I had leisure again to study, to replenish my store of medicines, even to make music. It was strange at first, and then in some way comforting, to lie wakeful in the night and hear the boy's untroubled breathing from the other side of the cave. After a while, I found I was sleeping better; as the nightmares receded, strength and calmness came back; and if power still withheld itself, I no longer despaired of its return.

As for Ralf, though I could see that he still fretted against his exile—to which, of course, he could see no clear end— he was never less than courteous, and as time went on seemed to accept his banishment with a better grace, and either lost or hid his unhappiness in a kind of contentment.

So the weeks went by, and the valley fields yellowed towards harvest, and the message came at last from Tintagel. One evening in August, towards dusk, a messenger came spurring up the valley. Ralf was not with me. I had sent him that afternoon across the hill to the hut where the shepherd, Abba, lived all summer. I had been treating Abba's son Ban, who was simple, for a poisoned foot; this was almost healed, but still needed salves.

I went out to meet the messenger. He had dismounted below the cliff, and now clambered up to the flat alp in front of the cave. He was a young man, spruce and lively, and his horse was fresh. I guessed from this that his message was not urgent; he had taken his time, and come at his ease. I saw him take in my ragged robe and threadbare mantle in one swift, summing glance, but he doffed his cap and went on one knee. I wondered if the salute was for the enchanter, or for the King's son.

"My lord Merlin."

"You are welcome," I said. "From Tintagel?"

"Yes, sir. From the Queen." A quick upward glance. "I came privily, without the King's knowledge."

"So I had imagined, or you would have borne her badge. Get up, man. The grass is damp. Have you had supper?"

He looked surprised. It was not thus, I reckoned, that most princes received their messengers. "Why, no, sir, but I bespoke it at the inn."

"Then I won't keep you from it. I've no doubt it will be better than you'd get here. Well then, your business? You've brought a letter from the Queen?"

"No letter, sir, just the message that the Queen desires to see you."

"Now?" I asked sharply. "Is there anything wrong with her, or with the child she bears?"

"Nothing. The doctors and the women say that all is well. But"—he dropped his eyes—"it seems she has that on her mind which makes her want to talk with you. As soon as possible, she said."

"I see." Then, with my voice as carefully neutral as his: "Where is the King?"

"The King plans to leave Tintagel in the second week of September."

"Ah. So any time after that it will be 'possible' for me to see the Queen."

This was rather more frank than he cared for. He flashed me a glance, then looked at the ground again. "The Queen will be pleased to receive you then. She has bidden me make arrangements for you. You will understand that it will not do for you to be received openly in the castle of Tintagel." Then, in a burst of candour: "You must know, my lord, there is no man's hand in Cornwall but will be against you. It would be better if you came disguised."

"As for that," I said, fingering my beard, "you will see that I'm half disguised already. Don't worry, man, I understand; I'll be discreet. But you'll have to tell me more. She gave no reason for this summons?"

"None, my lord."

"And you heard nothing—no gossip from among the women, things like that?"

He shook his head, then, at the look in my face, added quickly: "My lord, she was urgent. She did not say so, but it must concern the child, what else?"

"Then I will come." I thought he looked shocked. As he lowered his eyes, I said, sharply: "Well, what did you

50

expect? I am not the Queen's man. No, nor the King's either, so there's no need to look scared."

"Whose, then?"

"My own, and God's. But you can go back to the Queen and tell her I will come. What arrangements have you made for me?"

He hurried, relieved, on to his own ground. "There is a small inn at a ford of the river Camel, in the valley about five miles from Tintagel. It is kept by a man called Caw. He is a Cornishman, but his wife Maeve was one of the Queen's women, and he will keep his counsel. You can stay there without fear; they will expect you. You may send messages to Tintagel, if you will, by one of Maeve's sons— it would not be wise to go near the castle until the Queen sends for you. Now for the journey. The weather should still be fine in mid-September, and the seas are usually calm enough, so—"

"If you are about to advise me that it is easier to go by sea, you're wasting your breath," I said. "Has no one ever told you that enchanters can't cross water? At least, not with any comfort. I should be seasick did I so much as cross the Severn River in the ferry. No, I go by road."

"But the main road takes you past the barracks at Caerleon. You might be recognized. And then the bridge at Glevum is guarded by King's troops."

"Very well. I'll take the river crossing, but make it a short one." I knew that he was right. To go by the main road through Caerleon and then by the Glevum Bridge would, even without the prospect of discovery by Uther's troops, put several days on my journey. "I'll avoid the military road. There's a good track along the coast through Nidum; I'll go that way, if you can bespeak me a boat at the mouth of the Ely River?"

"Very well, my lord." And so it was arranged. I would

cross from the Ely to the mouth of the Uxella in the country of the Dumnonii, and from there I would find my way south-west by the tracks, avoiding the roads where I might fall in with Uther's troops or Cador's men.

"Do you know the way?" he asked me. "For the last part, of course, Ralf can guide you."

"Ralf will not be with me. But I can find it. I've been through that country before, and I have a tongue in my head."

"I can arrange for horses—"

"Better not," I said. "We agreed, did we not, that I would be better disguised? I'll use a disguise that has served me before. I'll be a travelling eye doctor, and a humble fellow like that doesn't expect to post with fresh horses all the way. Have no fear, I shall be safe, and, when the Queen wants me, I shall be there."

He was satisfied, and stayed for a while longer answering my questions and giving me what news there was. The King's brief punitive expedition against the coastal raiders had been successful, and the newcomers had been pushed back behind the agreed boundaries of the Federated West Saxons. For the moment things were quiet in the south. From the north had come rumours of tougher fighting where Anglian raiders, from Germany, had crossed the coast near the Alaunus River in the country of the Votadini. This is the country that we of Dyfed call Manau Guotodin, and it is from here that the great King Cunedda came, invited a century ago by the Emperor Maximus, to drive the Irish from Northern Wales and settle there as allies to the Imperial Eagles. These were, I suppose, the first of the Federates; they drove the Irish out, and afterwards remained in Northern Wales, which they called Gwynedd. A descendant of Cunedda held it still; Maelgon, a stark king and a good warrior, as a man would have to be to keep that country in the wake of the great Magnus Maximus.

Another descendant of Cunedda still held the Votadini country: a young king, Lot, as fierce and as good a fighter as Maelgon; his fortress lay near the coast south of Caer Eidyn, in the center of his kingdom of Lothian. It was he who had faced and beaten off the latest attack of the Angles. He had been given his command by Ambrosius, in the hope that with him the kings of the north—Gwalawg of Elmet, Urien of Gore, the chiefs of Strathclyde, King Coel of Rheged—would form a strong wall in the north and east. But Lot, it was said, was ambitious and quarrelsome; and Strathclyde had sired nine sons already and (while they fought like young bull seals each for his square of territory) was cheerfully siring more. Urien of Gore had married Lot's sister and would stand firm, but was, it was said, too close in Lot's shadow. The strongest of them was still (as in my father's time) Coel of Rheged, who held with a light hand all the smaller chiefs and earls of his kingdom, and brought them together faithfully against the smallest threat to the sovereignty of the High Kingdom.

Now, the Queen's messenger told me, the King of Rheged, with Ector of Galava and Ban of Benoic, had joined with Lot and Urien to clear the north of trouble, and for the time being they had succeeded. On the whole the news was cheering. The harvest had been good everywhere, so hunger would not drive any more Saxons across before winter closed the seaways. We should have peace for a time; enough time for Uther to settle any unrest caused by the quarrel with Cornwall and his new marriage, to ratify such alliances as Ambrosius had made, and to strengthen and extend his system of defenses.

At length the messenger took his leave. I wrote no letters,

53

but sent news of Ralf to his grandmother, and a message of compliance to the Queen, with thanks for the gift of money she had sent me by the messenger's hand to provide for my journey. Then the young man rode off cheerfully down the valley towards the good company and the better supper that awaited him at the inn. It remained now for me to tell Ralf.

This was more difficult even than I had expected. His face lit when I told him about the messenger, and he looked eagerly about for the man, seeming very disappointed when he found that he had already gone. Messages from his grandmother he received almost impatiently, but plied me with questions about the fighting south of Vindocladia, listening with such eagerness to all I could tell him of that and the larger news that it was obvious that his forced inaction in Maridunum fretted him far more than he had shown. When I came to the Queen's summons he showed more animation than I had seen in him since he had come to me.

"How long before we set out?"

"I did not say 'we' would set out. I shall go alone."

"*Alone?*" You would have thought I had struck him. The blood sprang under the thin skin and he stood staring with his mouth open. Eventually he said, sounding stifled: "You can't mean that. You can't."

"I'm not being arbitrary, believe me. I'd like to take you, but you must see it isn't possible."

"Why not? You know everything here will be perfectly safe; in any case, you've left it before. And you can't travel alone. How would you go on?"

"My dear Ralf. I've done it before."

"Maybe you have, but you can't deny I've served you well since I've been here, so why not take me? You can't just go to Tintagel—back to where things are happening—and leave me here! I warn you"—he took a breath, eyes blazing, all

54

his careful courtesy collapsing in ruins—"I warn you, my lord, if you go without me, I shan't be here when you come back!"

I waited till his gaze fell, then said mildly: "Have some sense, boy. Surely you see why I can't take you? The situation hasn't changed so much since you had to leave Cornwall. You know what would happen if any of Cador's men recognized you, and everyone knows you round about Tintagel. You'd be seen, and the word would go round."

"I know that. Do you still think I'm afraid of Cador? Or of the King?"

"No. But it's foolish to run into danger when one doesn't need to. And the messenger certainly seemed to think there was still danger."

"Then what about you? Won't you be in danger, too?"

"Possibly. I shall have to go disguised, as it is. Why do you think I've been letting my beard grow all this while?"

"I didn't know. I never thought about it. Do you mean you've been expecting the Queen to send for you?"

"I didn't expect this summons, I admit," I said. "But I know that, come Christmas, when the child is born, I must be there."

He stared. "Why?"

I regarded him for a moment. He was standing near the mouth of the cave, against the sunset, just as he had come in from his trip across the hill to the shepherd's hut. He was still clutching the osier basket which had held the salves. It held a small bundle now, wrapped in a clean linen cloth. The shepherd's wife, who lived across in the next valley, sent bread up weekly to her man; some of this Abba regularly sent on to me. I could see the boy's fists clenched bone-white on the handle of the basket. He was tense, as angry and fretting as a fighting dog held back in the slips. There was something more here, I was sure, than homesickness, or disappointment at missing an adventure.

"Put that basket down, for goodness' sake," I said, "and come in. That's better. Now, sit down. It's time that you and I talked. When I accepted your service, I did not do so because I wanted someone to scour the cooking pots and carry gifts from Abba's wife on baking day. Even if I am content with my life here on Bryn Myrddin, I'm not such a fool as to think it contents you—or would do so for long. We are waiting, Ralf, no more. We have fled from danger, both of us, and healed our hurts, and now there is nothing to do but wait."

"For the Queen's childbed? Why?"

"Because as soon as he is born, the Queen's son will be given to me to care for."

He was silent for a full minute before he said, sounding puzzled: "Does my grandmother know this?"

"I think she suspects that the child's future lies with me. When I last spoke with the King, on that night at Tintagel, he told me he would not acknowledge the child who would be born. I think this is why the Queen has sent for me."

"But . . . not to acknowledge his eldest son? You mean he will send him away? Will the Queen agree? A baby—surely they would never send it to *you*? How could you keep it? And how can you even know it will be a boy?"

"Because I had a vision, Ralf, that night in Tintagel. After you had let us in through the postern gate, while the King was with Ygraine, and Ulfin kept guard outside the chamber, you diced with the porter in the lodge by the postern. Do you remember?"

"How could I ever forget? I thought that night would never end."

I did not tell him that it had not ended yet. I smiled.

"I think I felt the same, while I waited alone in the guard-room. It was then that I saw—was shown—for certain why God had required me to do as I had done, shown for sure that my prophecies had been true. I heard a sound on the stairs, and went out of the guard-room onto the landing. I saw Marcia, your grandmother, coming down the steps towards me from the Queen's room, carrying a child. And though it was only March, I felt the chill of midwinter, and then I saw the stairs and the shadows clear through her body, and knew it was a vision. She put the child into my arms and said, 'Take care of him.' She was weeping. Then she vanished, and the child too, and the winter's chill went with her. But this was a true picture, Ralf. At Christmas I shall be there, waiting, and Marcia will hand the Queen's son into my care."

He was silent for a long time. He seemed awed by the vision. But then he said, practically: "And I? Where do I come into this? Is this why my grandmother told me to stay with you and serve you?"

"Yes. She saw no future for you near the King. So she made sure you would be near his son."

"A baby?" His voice was blank. He sounded horrified, and far from flattered. "You mean that if the King won't acknowledge the child, you'll have to keep it? I don't understand. Oh, I can see why my grandmother concerns herself, and even why you do, but not why she dragged me into it! What sort of future does she think there is in looking after a king's bastard that won't be acknowledged?"

"Not a king's bastard," I said. "A king."

There was silence but for the fluttering of the fire. I had not spoken with power, but with the full certainty of knowledge. He stared, open-mouthed, and shaken.

"Ralf," I said, "you came to me in anger, and you stayed

from duty, and you have served me as well and as faithfully as you knew how. You were no part of my vision, and I don't know if your coming here, or the wounds that held you here with me, were part of God's plan; I have had no message from my gods since Gorlois died. But I do know now, after these last weeks, that there is no one I would sooner choose to help me. Not with the kind of service you have given till now: when this winter comes it isn't a servant I shall need; I shall need a fighting man who is loyal, not to me or to the Queen, but to the next High King."

He was pale, and stammering. "I had no idea. I thought . . . I thought . . ."

"That you were suffering a kind of exile? In a way, we both were. I told you it was a waiting time." I looked down at my hands. It was dark now outside the cave; the sun had gone, and dusk drew in. "Nor do I know clearly what lies ahead, except danger and loss and treachery, and in the end some glory."

He sat quiet, without moving, till I roused myself from my thoughts and smiled at him. "So now, perhaps, you will accept that I don't doubt your courage?"

"Yes. I'm sorry I spoke as I did. I didn't understand." He hesitated, chewing his lip, then sat forward, hands on knees. "My lord, you really don't know why the Queen has sent for you now?"

"No."

"But because you know that your vision of the birth was a true one, you know that you will go safely this time to Cornwall, and return?"

"You could say so."

"Then if your magic is always true, might it not be because I go with you to protect you that you make the journey safely?"

I laughed. "I suppose it's a good quality in a fighting man, never to admit defeat. But can't you see, taking you would only be taking two risks instead of one. Because my bones tell me I shall be safe, it doesn't mean that you will."

"If you can be disguised, so can I. If you even say that we must go as beggars and sleep in the ditches . . . whatever the danger . . ." He swallowed, sounding all at once very young. "What is it to you if I run a risk? *You* are to be safe, you told me so. So taking me can't endanger you, and that's all that matters. Won't you let me take my own risks? Please?"

His voice trailed away. Silence again, and the fire flickering. Time was, I thought, not without bitterness, when I would only have had to watch the flames to find the answer there. Would he be safe? Or would I carry the burden of yet another death? But all that the firelight showed me was a youth who needed to find manhood. Uther had denied it to him; I could not let my conscience do the same.

At length I said heavily: "I told you once that men must stand by their own deeds. I suppose that means I have no right to stop you taking your own risks. Very well, you may come. . . . No, don't thank me. You'll dislike me thoroughly enough before we're done. It will be a damned uncomfortable journey, and before we set out, you'll have work to do that won't suit you."

"I'm used to that," he said, and straightened, laughing. He was shining, excited, the gaiety that I remembered back in his face. "But you don't mean you're going to teach me magic?"

"I do not. But I shall have to teach you a little medicine, whether you like it or not. I shall be a travelling eye doctor; it's a good passport anywhere, and one can pay one's way easily without spending the Queen's gold abroad where questions might be asked. So you will have to be my assistant, and that means learning to mix the salves properly."

"Well, if I must, but God help the patients! You know I can't tell one herb from the other."

"Never fear, I wouldn't let you touch them. You can leave me to select the plants. You'll just prepare them."

"And if any of Cador's men show signs of recognizing us, just try some of my salves on them," he said buoyantly. "Talk about magic, it'll be easy. The eye doctor's skilled assistant will simply strike them blind."

6

We came to the inn at Camelford two days before the middle of September.

The Camel valley is winding, with steep sides clothed with trees. For the last part of the way we followed the track along the waterside. The trees were closely crowded, and the path where we rode was so thickly padded with moss and small, dark-green ferns that our horses' hoofs made no sound. Beside us the river wrangled its way down through granite boulders that glittered in the sun. Around and above us the dense hangers of oak and beech were turning yellow, and acorns crunched among the dead leaves where the horses trod. Nuts ripened in the thickets; the willows trailed amber leaves in the tugging shallows; and wherever the bright sun splashed through the boughs it shimmered on the spiders' webs of autumn furred and glittering, sagging deep with dew.

Our journey had been uneventful. Once south of the Severn and beyond hourly danger of recognition, we had ridden at ease, and in pleasant stages. The weather, as so often in September, was warm and bright, but with a crisp feel to the air that made riding a pleasure. Ralf had been in high spirits all the way, in spite of poor clothes, an undistinguished horse (bought with some of the Queen's gold) and the work he had had to do for me making the washes and ointments with which I largely paid our way. We were only questioned once, by a troop of King's men who came on us just short of Hercules Point. Uther kept the old Roman camp there garrisoned as a strongpoint, and by the purest mischance we fell foul of a scouting party which was making its way home by the moorland track we followed. We were taken to the camp and questioned, though it seemed this was merely a matter of form as, after a cursory look at our baggage, my story was accepted. We were sent on our way with our flasks refilled with the ration wine, the richer for a copper coin given me by a man off duty who followed us out of camp and begged a pot of salve from me.

I found the men's vigilance interesting, and would have liked to know more of the state of affairs in the north, but that would have to wait. To have asked questions here would have attracted attention I did not want. No doubt I would find out what I wished to know from the Queen herself.

"Did you see anyone you knew?" I asked Ralf, as we headed over the moors at a brisk canter away from the gate of the camp.

"None. Did you?"

"I'd met the officer before, a few years ago. His name is Priscus. But he gave no sign of recognizing me."

"I wouldn't have known you myself," said Ralf. "And it isn't just the beard. It's the way you walk, your voice, everything. It's like that night at Tintagel, when you were disguised as the Duke's captain. I'd known him all my life, and I'd have sworn you were he. It's no wonder folks are talking about magic. I thought it was magic myself."

"This is easier," I said. "If you carry a trade or a skill with you men think about that, instead of looking at you too closely."

Indeed, I had troubled very little with disguise. I had bought a new riding cloak, brown, with a hood which could be pulled about my face, and I spoke Celtic with the accent of Brittany. This is a tongue close to the Cornish one, and would be understood where we were going. This, with the beard, and my humble tradesman's bearing, should keep any but my intimates from knowing me. Nothing would part me from the brooch my father had given me, with its royal cipher of the Red Dragon on gold, but I wore it clipped inside the breast of my tunic, and had threatened Ralf with every fate in the Nine Books of Magic if he called me "my lord" even in private.

We reached Camelford towards evening. The inn was a small squat building of daubed stone built where the coast road ran down into the ford. It was at the top of the bank, just clear of flood level. Ralf and I, approaching by the country track along the river, came on it from the rear. It seemed a pleasant place, and clean. Someone had given the stones a wash of red ochre, the colour of the rich earth thereabouts, and fat poultry picked about among the ricks at the edge of a swept yard. A chained dog dozed in the shade of a mulberry tree heavy with fruit. There was a tidy stack of firewood against the byre, and the midden was fully twenty feet from the back door.

As luck would have it, the innkeeper's wife was out at the back with a maidservant, taking in bedding which had been spread over the bushes in the sun. As we approached the dog flew out, barking, at the length of his chain. The woman straightened, shading her eyes against the light, and staring.

She was a young woman, broadly built and lively looking, with a fresh, high colour and prominent light-blue eyes. Her bad teeth and plump figure gave away a rash passion for sweetmeats, and the lively blue eyes spoke even more clearly of other pleasures. They ran now over Ralf, who rode ahead of me, appraised him as likely, but young for it; then, more hopefully, over me, to dismiss me finally as less likely, and probably too poor to pay my shot anyway. Then, as her gaze returned to Ralf, I saw her recognize him. She stiffened, looking quickly back at me. Her mouth fell open, and I thought for an anxious moment that she was going to curtsy, but then she had command of herself. A word sent the maid packing indoors with an armful of bedding, a shrill bidding to the dog drove him back, ears down and growling, into the mulberry shade, then she was greeting us, smiling widely, eyes curious and excited.

"You'll be the eye doctor, likely?"

We drew our horses to a halt in the dust of the yard. "Indeed, mistress. My name is Emrys, and this is my servant Ban."

"We've been expecting you. Your beds is bespoke." Then under her breath as she came close to my horse's shoulder: "You be very welcome, my lord, and Ralf, too. I declare he do look a handspan taller than when I seen him last. Will you be pleased to come in?"

I dismounted and handed the reins to Ralf. "Thank you. It's good to be here; we're both weary. Ralf will look after the horses himself. Now before we go in, Maeve, give me the news from Tintagel. Is all well with the Queen?"

"Yes, indeed, sir, praise be to all the saints and fairies. You need have no worries there, surely."

"And the King? He's still at Tintagel?"

"Aye, my lord, but the word goes that he'll ride out any day now. You'll not have long to bide. You're as safe here as anywhere in Cornwall. We'll have good enough warning of troops moving, and you can hear them on this road a mile off. And never worry about Caw—that's my husband; he's a Duke's man, sure enough, but he'll do nothing to harm my lady, and besides, he always does as I tell him. Leastways, not always. There's some things he don't do near often enough for my liking." This with a burst of cheery laughter. I saw Ralf grinning as he led the horses away, then Maeve, talking loudly about beds and supper-time, and the sore eyes of her

64

youngest which could do with looking at, led me through the back door of the inn.

When I saw her husband later that evening I knew that I need have no fears for his discretion. He was a dry stick of a man, and silent as an oyster. He came in as we were sitting down to supper, stared at Ralf, nodded at me, then went about his business of serving wine without a word spoken. His wife treated him—and all comers—with the same rough, frank kindliness, and saw to it without fuss that we were well served and comfortably housed. It was as good a house of its kind as I have ever been in, and the food was excellent.

Understandably, the inn was always busy, but there was little danger of our being recognized. My character as a travelling healer was not only my pass to people's incurious acceptance; it gave Ralf and me the excuse to be abroad in the countryside. Each day early we would take food and wine with us, and make our way up by one of the deep, densely wooded glens that fed the Camel valley, to the windy upland that lay between Camelford and the sea. Ralf knew all the ways. We would separate, more often than not, and each choose some hidden point of vantage from which he could watch the two roads which Uther and his men might take out of Tintagel. He might turn north-east along the coast for Dimilioc and the camp near Hercules Point, or— if he was making straight for Winchester or the trouble centers along the Saxon Shore—he would follow the valley tracks through Camelford and from there climb south-east to the military road which ran along the spine of Dumnonia. Here on the wind-swept heights the forest thins, and there are great tracts of broken moorland treacherous with bog and watched over by strange stony hills. The old Roman road, crumbling fast in that wild country, but still service-able, runs straight through Isca, into the kinder lands behind Ambrosius' Wall. It was my guess that this latter was the way that Uther would take, and I wanted to see who rode with him. Ralf and I gave it out that I was searching for plants for my medicines, and indeed I came back each evening to my meeting-place with him with a pouch full of roots and berries which did not grow at home, and which I was glad to have. Luckily the weather continued fine, and no one wondered to see us ride abroad. They were too glad to have a doctor staying there who, each evening, would treat any who came to him, and ask no more than they could afford to pay.

So the days went by, serene and still, while we waited for the King to move, and the Queen to send word.

It was a week before he rode out. He went the way I had expected, and I was there watching.

There is a place where the track from Tintagel to Camelford runs straight for some quarter of a mile along the foot of a steeply wooded bank. For the most part the wood is too steep and thickly grown to penetrate, but there were places at the wood's edge open to the sun, stony banks deep in ferns and drifting thistledown, where brambles and bracken grew in thickets over the rocks. The blackthorn bushes were high, and glinting with fruit. Some of the little sloe-plums were still greenish, but most were ready; black bloomed over pale blue with ripeness. There is an extract one can make of the fruit which is sovereign for a flux of the bowels: one of Maeve's children had been suffering in this way, and I had promised a draught that night. It would need no more than a handful, but the fruit was ripe to perfection, and so tempting that I went on gathering. If the berries are crushed and added in a certain way to juniper-wine they make a good drink, rich, astringent and powerful. I had told Maeve of it, and she wanted to try it.

My bag was almost full when I heard, like a soft thunder

in the distance, horses coming steadily along the track below me. I withdrew quickly into the edge of the wood, and watched from hiding. Soon the head of the column came in sight; then the long train of dust, filled with the beat of trotting hoofs, the clash of mail, the coloured glint of pennants, rolled past along the foot of the slope. A thousand, perhaps more. I stood stone-still in the shadow of the trees, and watched them go by.

A horse's length to the front the King rode, and behind him, on his left hand, his standard-bearer carried the Red Dragon. Other colours showed through the dust, but there was no wind to move the banners, and though I strained my eyes the length of the column, I could not swear to most that I saw. Nor did I glimpse the one I was watching for, though it might well have been there. I waited till the last horseman disappeared at a smart trot round a bend in the road, then I made my way to the place where I had arranged to meet Ralf.

He met me halfway, panting. "Did you see them?"

"Yes. Where were you? I sent you to watch the other road."

"I was watching. There was nothing stirring there, nothing at all. I was on my way back here when I heard them, so I ran. I almost missed them—only saw the tail end. It was the King, wasn't it?"

"It was. Ralf, could you pick out the devices? Did you see any that you knew?"

"I saw Brychan, and Cynfelin, but no others from Dyfnaint that I recognized. The men from Garlot were there, and Cernyw, too, I think, and others I thought I knew, but there was too much dust to make sure. They were round that bend before I could get a good sight of them."

"Was Cador there?"

"My lord, I'm sorry, I didn't see."

"No matter. If the others were there from Cornwall, you may be sure he would be. No doubt they'll know at the inn. And had you forgotten that you were not to call me 'my lord,' even when we were alone?"

"I'm sorry . . . Emrys." It was a measure of our new, easier relationship that he should add, with a suspicious meekness: "And had you forgotten that my name is Ban?" Then, laughing as he dodged my cuff at his head: "Do you have to call me after the half-wit?"

"It's the first name that came into my head. It's a king's name too, the King of Benoic, so you can take your choice which was your sponsor."

"Benoic? Where's that?"

"In the north. Come now, we'll get back to the inn. I doubt if the Queen will send before tomorrow, but I've a draught to make tonight, and it's a decoction that takes time. Here, carry these."

I was right; the messenger came next morning. Ralf had gone out down the road to watch for him, and the two of them came back together, with the news that I was to ride to Tintagel immediately for my audience with the Queen.

I had not confessed it to Ralf, nor even hardly admitted it to myself, but I was apprehensive about the coming interview with Ygraine. On that night at Tintagel when the child was conceived I had been certain, in every way a seer can be certain, that the boy who was to be born would be given to me to foster, and that I should be the guardian of a great King. Uther himself, in his bitterness and anger over Gorlois' death, had sworn to reject the "bastard" he had begotten, and from Marcia's letter I knew he was still of the same mind. But in the six long months since that March night I had had no direct message from Ygraine, and no means of knowing whether she would obey her husband, or whether as the time drew near she would find it impossible to face separation from her child. I had gone over in my mind a hundred times all the arguments I might bring to bear, remembering half incredulously the sureness with which I had spoken to her before, and to the King. Indeed my god had been with me then. And in truth, and how bitterly, was he gone from me now. There were even times when, lying wakeful in the night, I saw my sure visions in the past as chances, illusions, dreams fed by desire. I remembered the King's bitter words to me. *"I see now what your magic is, this 'power' you talk of. It is nothing but human trickery, an attempt at statecraft which my brother taught you to like and to play for, and to believe was your mystery. You use even God to gain your ends. 'It is God who tells me to do these things, it is God who exacts the price, it is God who sees that others should pay . . .' For what, Merlin? For your ambition? And who is it pays this debt to God for carrying out your plans? Not you. The men who play your game for you, and pay the price. But you pay nothing."* When I listened to such words as these, heard clearly in the nights when nothing else spoke to me, I wondered if I had read my vision of the future aright, or if everything I had done and dreamed of had been a mockery. Then, thinking of those who had paid with death for my dream, I would wonder if that death had not been kinder than this desert of self-doubt where I lay fixed, waiting in vain for even the smallest of my gods to speak to me. Oh, yes, I paid. Every night of those nine long months I paid.

But now it was day, and I would soon find out what the Queen wanted with me. I remember how restlessly I fidgeted around while Ralf saddled my horse and made ready. Maeve was with the maids in the kitchen, washing the sloes for the wine-making. A pan of them was on the stove, coming to the simmer. It seemed a strange memory to take with me on my visit to the Queen, the smell of sloe wine. Suddenly I found the pungent sweetness intolerable, and made, choking, for the air outside. But then one of the girls came running to ask something about the mixing, and in answering her I forgot my sickness, and then all at once Ralf was at my elbow to summon me, and the three of us—Ralf, the messenger and I—were heading for Tintagel at a hand-gallop through the soft, blowing September noon.

7

It was only a few months since I had last seen Ygraine, but she seemed very much changed. At first I thought this was only the pregnancy; her once-slim body was greatly swollen and, though her face was full of the bloom of health, she had that pinched and shadowy look that women get around the eyes and mouth. But the change was deeper than this; it was in the expression of her eyes, in her gestures, the way she sat. Where before she had seemed young and burning, a wild bird beating her wings against the wires of the cage, now she seemed to brood, wings clipped, gravid, a creature of the ground.

She received me in her own chamber, a long room above the curtain wall, with a deep circular recess where the turret stood at the north-west corner. There were windows in the long wall facing south-west, and through these the sunlight fell freely, but the Queen was sitting by one of the narrow turret windows, through which came the breeze of the soft September afternoon, and the eternal noise of the sea on the rocks below. So much was still here, then, of the Ygraine I remembered. It was like her, I thought, to choose the wind and the sea sounds, rather than the sunlight. But even here, in spite of the light and air, one got the feeling of a cage: this was the room in which the young wife of Gorlois the old Duke had passed those pent years before the fateful trip to London where she had met the King. Now, after that brief flight, she was penned again, by her love for the King, and by the weight of his child. I never loved a woman, except one, but I have pitied them. Now, looking at the Queen, young, beautiful, and with her heart's desire, I pitied her even as I feared her for what she might say to me.

She was alone. I had been led by a chamberlain through the outer room where the women span and weaved and gossiped. Bright eyes looked at me in momentary curiosity, and the chattering was stilled, only to begin again as soon as I had passed. There was no recognition in their faces, only perhaps here and there some disappointment at the sight of so ordinary and humble a fellow. No diversion here. To them I was a messenger, to be received by the Queen in the King's absence; that was all.

The chamberlain rapped on the door of the inner chamber and then withdrew. Marcia, Ralf's grandmother, opened the door. She was a grey-haired woman with Ralf's eyes in a lined and anxious face, but in spite of her age she bore herself as straight as a girl. Though she was expecting me, I saw her eyes rest on me for a moment without recognition, then with a flicker of surprise. Even Ygraine looked startled for a moment, then she smiled and held out her hand.

"Prince Merlin. Welcome." Marcia curtsied to the air somewhere between me and the Queen, and withdrew. I went forward to kneel and kiss the Queen's hand.

"Madam."

She raised me kindly. "It was good of you to come so quickly for such a strange summons. I hope the journey was easy?"

"Very easy. We are well lodged with Maeve and Caw, and so far no one has recognized me, or even Ralf. Your secret is safe."

"I must thank you for taking so much care of it. I promise you I'd not have known you until you spoke."

I fingered my chin, smiling. "As you see, I've been preparing for some time."

"No magic this time?"

"As much as there was before," I said.

She looked at me straightly then, the beautiful dark-blue eyes meeting mine in the way I remembered, and I saw that this was still the old Ygraine, direct as a man, and with the same high pride. The heavy stillness was just an overlay, the milky calm that seems to come on women in pregnancy. Beneath the stillness, the placidity, was the old fire. She spread her hands out. "Looking at me now, do you still tell me that when you spoke to me that night in London, and promised me the King's love, there was no magic there?"

"Not in the ruse that brought the King to you, madam. In what happened after, perhaps."

" 'Perhaps'?" There was a quick lift to her voice that warned me. Ygraine might be a Queen, with mettle as high as a man's, but she was a woman nearing her seventh month. My fears were my own, and must stay my own. I hesitated, searching for words, but she went on quickly, burningly, as if to convince herself across my silence: "When you first spoke with me and told me you could bring the King to me, there was magic there, I know there was. I felt it, and I saw it in your face. You told me that your power came from God, and that in obeying you I was God's creature, even as you were. You said that because of the magic that would bring Uther to me, the kingdom should have peace. You spoke of crowns and altars. . . . And now, see, I am Queen, with God's blessing, and I am heavy with the King's child. Dare you tell me now that you deceived me?"

"I did not deceive you, madam. That was a time full of visions, and a passion of dreams and desires. We are quit of those now, and we are sober, and it is daylight. But magic is here, growing in you, and this time it is fact, not vision. He will be born at Christmas, they tell me."

" 'He'? You sound very sure."

"I am sure."

I saw her press her lips together as if at a sudden spasm of pain, then she looked away from me, down at her hands which lay folded across her belly. When she spoke, she spoke calmly, straight to her hands, or to what they covered. "Marcia told me of the messages she sent to you in the summer. But you must have known, without her telling you, the way my lord the King thinks of this matter."

I waited, but she seemed to expect an answer. "He told me himself," I said. "If he's still of the same mind now as he was then, he won't acknowledge the child as his heir."

"He is still of the same mind." Her eyes came swiftly up to mine again. "Don't misunderstand me, he has not the faintest doubt of me, nor ever had. He knows that I was his from the first moment I saw him, and that from that moment, on one excuse or another, I never lay with the Duke. No, he does not doubt me; he knows the child is his. And for all his high speech"—there was the glimmer of a smile, and suddenly her voice was indulgent, the voice of a woman speaking of her child or of a loved husband—"and for all his rough denials, he knows your power and fears it. You told him a child would come out of that night, and he would trust your word, even if he could not trust mine. But none of this alters the way he feels about it. He blames himself—and you, and even the child—for the Duke's death."

"I know."

"If he had waited, he says, Gorlois would still have died that night, and I would have been Queen, and the child conceived in wedlock, so that no one could question his parentage or call him bastard."

"And you, Ygraine?"

She was silent for a long time. She turned that lovely head of hers and gazed out of the window, where the sea birds swung and tilted, crying, on the wind. I saw, I am not sure

74

how, that her calm was that of a soldier who has won one battle, and rests before the next. I felt my nerves tighten. I did not hold Ygraine lightly, should the battle be with me.

She said, very quietly: "What the King says may well be true. I don't know. But what's done is done, and it is the child who must concern me now. This is why I sent for you." A pause. I waited. She faced me again. "Prince Merlin, I fear for the child."

"At the King's hands?" I asked.

This was too straight, even for Ygraine. Her eyes were cold, and her voice. "This is insolence, and folly, too. You forget yourself, my lord."

"I?" I spoke as coldly. "It is you who forget, madam. If my mother had been wed to Ambrosius when he begot me, Uther would not now be King, nor would I have helped him to your bed to beget the child you carry. There should be no talk of insolence or folly from you to me. I know, who better, what chance there is in Britain for a prince conceived out of wedlock and unacknowledged by his sire."

She had flushed as red as she was pale before. Her eyes dropped from mine, their anger dying. She spoke simply, like a girl. "You are right, I had forgotten. I ask your pardon. I'd forgotten, too, what it was like to talk freely. There is no one here besides Marcia and my lord, and I cannot talk to Uther about the child."

I had been standing all this while; now I turned aside to bring up a chair and set it near her in the turret embrasure. I sat down. Things had changed between us, suddenly, as when a wind changes. I knew then that the battle was not with me, but with herself, her own woman's weakness. She was watching me now as a woman in pain watches her doctor. I said gently: "Well, I am here. And I am listening. What did you send for me to tell me?"

She drew in her breath. When she spoke her voice was

calm, but no more than a whisper. "That if this child is a boy, the King will not allow me to rear him. If it's a girl I may keep her, but a boy so begotten cannot be acknowledged as a prince and legitimate heir, so he must not remain here, even as a bastard." Visibly, she steadied herself. "I told you, Uther does not doubt me. But because of what happened that night, my husband's death, and all the talk of magic, he swears that men may still believe that the Duke and not himself begot this child. There will be other sons, he says, whose begetting no man will question, and among them he will find the heir to the High Kingdom."

"Ygraine," I said, "I know what a heavy thing it is—however it happens—for a woman to lose her child. Perhaps there is no heavier grief. But I think the King is right. The boy should not remain here to be reared as a bastard in times so wild and uncertain. If there should be other heirs, declared and acknowledged by the King, they might count him a danger to themselves, and certainly they would be a danger for him. I know what I'm talking about; this is what happened in my own childhood. And I, as a royal bastard, found fortune as this prince may never find it; I had my father's protection."

A pause. She nodded without speaking, her eyes once again on the hands that lay in her lap.

"And if the child is to be sent away," I said, "it's better that he should be taken straight from the birth chamber, before you have had time even to hold him. Believe me"— I spoke quickly, though she had not moved—"this is true. I'm speaking now as a doctor."

She moistened her lips. "Marcia says the same."

I waited a moment, but she said no more. I started to speak, found my voice come hoarsely, and cleared my throat. In spite of myself, my hands tightened on the arms of my chair. But my voice was calm and steady as I came to the core of the interview. "Has the King told you where the child is to be fostered?"

"No. I told you it wasn't easy to talk to him about it. But when he last spoke of it he said he would take counsel; and he spoke of Brittany."

"*Brittany?*" For all my care, the word came out with a cutting edge. I fought to recover my calm. My hands had clenched on the chair, and I relaxed them and held them still. So, my doubts were real. Oddly enough, the knowledge hardened me. If I must fight the King as well as Ygraine— yes, and my Delphic gods as well—then I would do so. As long as I could see the ground to fight from . . . "So Uther will send him to King Budec?"

"It seems so." She seemed to have noticed nothing strange in my manner. "He sent a messenger a month ago. That was just before I sent to ask you to come. Budec is the obvious choice, after all."

This was true. King Budec of Less Britain was a cousin of the King's. It was he who, some thirty years ago, had taken my father and the young Uther under his protection when the usurper Vortigern murdered their elder brother King Constans, and in his capital of Kerrec they had assembled and trained the army which had won the High Kingdom back from Vortigern. But I shook my head. "Too obvious. If anyone should look for the boy to harm him, they'll guess where to go. Budec can't protect him all the time. Besides—"

"Budec cannot care for my child as he should be cared for!" The words came forcibly, stopping me short, but the interruption was not uncivil. It came almost like a cry. It was plain that she had not heard a word I had said. She was fighting herself, choosing words. "He is old, and besides, Brittany is a long way off, and less secure even than this Saxon-ridden land. Prince Merlin, I—Marcia and I—we think that you—" The hands suddenly twisted together in her

77

lap. Her voice changed. "There is no one else we can trust. And Uther—whatever Uther says, he knows that his kingdom, or any part of it, would be safe in your hands. You are Ambrosius' son, and the child's closest kinsman. Everyone knows your power, and fears it—the child would be safe with you to protect him. It's you who must take him, Merlin!" She was begging me now. "Take him safe, somewhere away from this cruel coast, and rear him for me. Teach him as you were taught, and rear him as a King's son should be reared, and then when he is grown, bring him back and let him take his place as you did, at the next King's side."

She faltered. I must have been staring at her like a fool. She fell quiet, twisting her hands. There was a long silence, filled with the scent of the salt wind and the crying of the gulls. I had not been aware of rising, but I found myself standing at the window with my back to the Queen, staring out at the sky. Below the turret wall the gulls wheeled and mewed in the wind, and far below, at the foot of the black cliff, the sea dashed and whitened. But I saw and heard nothing. My hands were pressed down hard on the stone of the sill, and when at length I lifted them and straightened they showed a mottled bar of bloodless flesh where the stone had bitten in. I began to chafe them, only now feeling the small hurt as I turned back to meet the Queen's eyes. She too had hold of herself again, but I saw strain in her face, and a hand plucked at her gown.

I said flatly: "Do you think you can persuade the King to give him to me?"

"No. I don't think so. I don't know." She swallowed. "Of course I can talk to him, but—"

"Then why send for me to ask me this, if you have no power to sway the King?"

She was white, and her lips worked together, but she kept

78

her head up and faced me. "I thought that if you agreed, my lord, you could—you would—"

"I can do nothing with Uther now. You should know that." Then, in sudden, bitter comprehension: "Or did you send for me as you did last time, hoping for magic to order, as if I were an old spell-wife, or a country druid? I would have thought, madam—" I stopped. I had seen the flinching in her eyes, and the drawn pallor round her mouth, and I remembered what she carried in her. My anger died. I turned up a hand, speaking gently: "Very well. If it can be done, Ygraine, I will do it, even if I have to talk to Uther myself to remind him of his promise."

"His promise? What did he promise you, and when?"

"When he first sent for me, and told me of his love for you, he swore to obey me in anything, if only he could have his way." I smiled at her. "It was meant as a bribe rather than a promise, but no matter, we'll hold it to him as a royal oath."

She began to thank me, but I stopped her. "No, no, keep your thanks. I may not succeed with the King; you know how little he loves me. You were wise to send secretly, and you'll be wiser not to let him know we talked of this together."

"He shan't know from me."

I nodded. "Now, for the child's sake and your own, you must put your fears aside. Leave this to me. Even if we can't move the King, I promise you that wherever the child is fostered, I shall make it my business to watch over him. He will be kept safely, and reared as a King's son should be reared. Will that content you?"

"If it has to, yes."

She drew a long breath then and moved at last, rising from her chair and, still gracefully in spite of her bulk, pacing down the long room to one of the far windows. I

79

made no move to follow her. She stood there for a while with her back to me, in silence. When at length she turned, she was smiling. She lifted a hand to beckon me and I went to her.

"Will you tell me one thing, Merlin?"

"If I can."

"That night when we spoke in London, before you brought the King to me here. You talked of a crown, and a sword standing in an altar like a cross. I have wondered so much about it, thinking . . . Tell me now, truly. Was it my crown you saw? Or did you mean that this child—this boy who has cost so much—that he will be King?"

I should have said to her: "Ygraine, I do not know. If my vision was true, if I was a true prophet, then he will be King. But the Sight has left me, and nothing speaks to me in the night or in the fire, and I am barren. I can only do as you do, and take the time on trust. But there is no going back. God will not waste all the deaths."

But she was watching me with the eyes of a woman in pain, so I said to her: "He will be King."

She bent her head and stood silent for a few moments, watching the sunlight on the floor, not as if thinking, but as if listening to what stirred within her. Then she looked up at me again.

"And the sword in the altar?"

I shook my head. "Madam, I don't know. It has not come yet. If I am to know, I will be shown."

She put out a hand. "One more thing . . ." From something in her voice, I knew that this mattered most to her. Not knowing what was coming, I braced myself to lie. She said: "If I must lose this child . . . Shall I have others, Merlin?"

"That is three things you have asked me, Ygraine."

"You won't answer?"

I had spoken only to gain time, but at the flash of fear and doubt in her eyes I was glad to tell her the truth. "I would answer you, madam, but I do not know."

"How is that?" she asked sharply.

I lifted my shoulders. "That again I cannot answer. Further than this boy you carry, I have not seen. But it seems probable, since he is to be King, that you will have no other sons. Girls, maybe, to bring you comfort."

"I shall pray for it," she said simply, and led the way back to the embrasure. She gestured me to sit. "Will you not take a cup of wine with me now, before you leave? I've received you poorly, I'm afraid, after asking such a journey of you, but I was in torment until I had talked with you. Won't you sit down with me now for a little while, and tell me what the news is with you?"

So I stayed a short while longer and, after I had given her my meager news, I asked where Uther was bound with his troops. She told me that he was heading, not for his capital at Winchester as I had supposed, but northwards to Viroconium, where he had called a council of leaders and petty kings from the north and north-east. Viroconium is the old Roman town which lies on the border of Wales, with the mountains of Gwynedd between it and the threat of the Irish Shore. It was still at this time a market center, and the roads were well maintained. Once out of the Dumnonian Peninsula, Uther could make good speed north by the Glevum Bridge. He might even, if the weather stayed fair and the country quiet, be back for the Queen's lying-in. For the moment, Ygraine told me, the Saxon Shore was quiet; after Uther's victory at Vindocladia the invaders had retired on the hospitality of the federated tribes. There was no clear news from the north, but the King (she told me) feared some kind of concerted action there in the spring between the Picts of Strathclyde and the invading Angles: the meeting of the Kings at Viroconium had been called in an attempt to thrash out some kind of united plan of defense.

"And Duke Cador?" I asked her. "Does he stay here in Cornwall, or go on to Vindocladia to watch the Saxon Shore?"

Her answer surprised me. "He is going north with the King, to the council."

"Is he indeed? Then I'd better guard myself." At her quick look I nodded. "Yes, I shall go straight to the King. Time grows short, and it's luck for me that he's travelling north. He's bound to take his troops by the Glevum Bridge, so Ralf and I can cross by the ferry and get there before him. If I intercept him north of the Severn, there's nothing to show him that I ever left Wales."

Soon after that I took my leave. When I left her she was standing by the window again. Her head was held high, and the breeze was ruffling her dark hair. I knew then that when the time came the child would not be taken from a weeping and regretful woman, but from a Queen, who was content to let him go to his destiny.

Not so with Marcia. She was waiting for me in the anteroom, bursting with questions, regrets, and anger against the King which she barely smothered into discretion. I reassured her as best I could, swore several times on every god in every shrine and hollow hill in Britain that I would do my utmost to get possession of the child and keep him safe, but when she started to ask me for spells for protection in childbed, and to talk of wet-nurses, I left her talking, and made for the door.

Forgetting herself in her agitation, she followed me and grabbed my sleeve. "And did I tell you? The King says she must have his own physician, a man he can trust to put the right stories about afterwards, and say nothing about where the poor mite goes for fostering. As if it wasn't more important that my lady should be properly looked after! Give any doctor enough gold, and he'd swear his own mother's life away, everybody knows that."

"Certainly," I said gravely. "But I know Gandar well, and there's no one better. The Queen will be in good hands."

"But an army doctor! What can he know about child-birth?"

I laughed. "He served with my father's army in Brittany for a long time. Where there are fighting men, there are also their women. My father had a standing army in Brittany of fifteen thousand men, encamped. Believe me, Gandar has had plenty of experience."

With that she had to be content. She was talking again about wet-nurses when I left her.

She came to the inn that night, cloaked and hooded, and riding straight as a man. Maeve led her to the room her family shared, drove out everyone—including Caw—who was still awake, then took Ralf in to talk to his grandmother. I was in bed before she left.

Next morning Ralf and I set out for Bryn Myrddin, with a flask or two of sloe wine to cheer us on our way. To my surprise, Ralf seemed every bit as cheerful as he had been on the way south. I wondered if, after the brief spell back in the scene of his childhood, service with me had begun to look like freedom. He had heard all the news from his grandmother; he told it me as we rode; most of it was what I had learned already from the Queen, with some court gossip added which was entertaining but hardly informative, except for the talk which was inevitably going round about Uther's rejection of the child.

Ralf, to my secret amusement, seemed as anxious now as Marcia for me to get custody of the baby.

"If the King refuses, what will you do?"

"Go to Brittany to talk to King Budec."

"Do you think he'll let you stay with the prince?"

"Budec is my kinsman too, remember."

"Well, but would he risk offending King Uther? Would he keep it secret from him?"

"That I can't tell you," I said. "If it had been Hoel, now —Budec's son—that would be different. He and Uther always fought like dogs after the same bitch."

I did not add that the description was in fact more accurate than was decent. Ralf merely nodded, chewing (we had stopped on a sunny hillside to eat), and reached for a flask. "Have some of this?" He was offering me the sloe wine.

"God of green grapes, boy, no! It won't be ready to drink for a year. Wait till next harvest's ripe, and open it then."

But he insisted, and unstoppered the flask. It certainly smelled odd and, he admitted, tasted worse. When I suggested, not unkindly, that Maeve had probably made a mistake and given him the medicine for the flux, he spat the mouthful out on the grass, then asked me a little stiffly what I was laughing at.

"Not at you. Here, let me taste the stuff. . . . Well, there's nothing in it that there shouldn't be; but I must have been thinking of something else when they asked me about the mixing. No, I was laughing at myself. All these months— these years, even—hammering at heaven's doors to get what? A baby and a wet-nurse. If you insist on staying with me, Ralf, the next few years will certainly bring new experiences for both of us."

He merely nodded; he was busy pursuing present anxieties.

"If we have to go to Brittany, you mean we might have to stay disguised like this? For *years?*" He flicked with a contemptuous finger at the coarse stuff of his cloak.

"That will depend. Not quite like this, I hope. Hold step till you reach your bridges, Ralf."

His face showed me that this was not how enchanters were expected to talk. They built their own bridges, or flew across without them. "Depend on the King, you mean? Must you seek him out? My grandmother says, if it's put about that the baby's stillborn, it could be handed to you secretly, and the King never know."

"You forget. Men must know if a prince is born. How else, when Uther dies, can they be brought to accept him?"

"Then what are you going to do, my lord?"

I shook my head, not answering. He took my silence for refusal to tell him, and accepted it with no more questions. For my part, I had perforce to take my own advice about crossing bridges; I was waiting to see a way over. With the Queen won, the harder half of the game was played; now I must plan how best to deal with the King—whether to seek his consent openly, or go first to Budec. But as we sat finishing our meal I was not thinking overmuch about Brittany, or the King, or even the child; I was content to rest in the sun and let the time go over. What had just happened at Tintagel had happened without my contriving. Something was moving; there was a kind of breathing brightness in the air, the wind of God brushing by, invisible in sunlight. Even for men who cannot see or hear them, the gods are still there, and I was not less than a man. I had not the arrogance—or the hardihood—to test my power again, but I put on hope, as a naked man welcomes rags in a winter storm.

8

The weather held, so we went easily, taking care not to tread too closely on the heels of Uther's force; if we were caught west of the Uxella marshes—or indeed south of the Severn at all—it would be only too obvious where we had been. Uther usually moved fast, and there was nothing to delay him here in settled country, so we followed cautiously, waiting until his army should be clear of the southern end of the Severn ferry. If we were lucky with the ferry and, once we were across the Severn, made good speed northwards, we should be able (having apparently just come innocently for the purpose from Maridunum) to fall in with the troops on their way up the Welsh border, and try to have speech with the King.

On the way south we had avoided the main road, but had used the pack tracks which run near the coast, winding in and out of the valleys. Now, since we dared not fall too far behind Uther, we kept as closely as we dared to the straight route along the ridges, but avoiding the paved road where the posting stations might be left guarded in the army's wake.

We were even more careful than we had been formerly. After we had left the shelter of Maeve's roof we sought out no more inns. Indeed, the ways we went boasted of no inns even had we looked for them; we lodged where we could—in wood-cutters' cabins, sheep shelters, even once or twice in the lee of a stack of bracken cut for bedding—and blessed the mild weather. It was wild country through which we went. There are high ridged stretches of moorland, where heather grows among the granite tors, and the land is good to feed nothing except the sheep and the wild deer; but just below the rocky spine of the land the forest begins. On the uplands the trees grow sparsely, raked by the wind, already in early autumn half scoured of leaves. But lower, in every dip and valley, the forest is dense, of trees crowded and hugely grown, impassable with undergrowth as toughly woven as a fisherman's net. Here and there, unnoticed until you stumble across them, are crags and bouldered screes of rock thickly clothed with thorn and creeper, invisible and deadly as a wolf trap. Even more dangerous are the stretches of bog, some black and slimy, some innocent and green as a meadow, where a man on horseback can sink from sight as easily and almost as quickly as a spoon sinking into a bowl of gruel. There are secret ways through these places, known to the beasts and the forest dwellers, but mostly men shun them. At night the soft ground flickers with marshlights and strange dancing flames which, men say, are the souls of the wandering dead.

Ralf had known the ways in his own country, but once we struck the low-lying marshy forests through which the Uxella and its tributaries flow towards the Severn we had to go more cautiously, relying on information from the people of the forest, charcoal-burners and woodmen, and once or twice a solitary hermit or holy man who offered us a night's shelter in some cave or woodland shrine. Ralf seemed to enjoy the rough travel and rougher lodging, and even the danger that seemed to lie about us in forest and track, and the threat of the army so few miles ahead. Both of us grew daily more unkempt and more like the roles we had assumed. It might be said that our disguise was more necessary here even than in Tintagel; woe betide the King's messenger or merchant who rides off the guarded road in these parts, but the poor are received kindly, vagrants or holy men with nothing to steal, and Ralf and I, as poor travelling healers, met welcome everywhere. There was nowhere we could not buy food and shelter with a copper penny and a pot of medicine. The marsh folk always need medicine, living as they do at the edge of the fetid bogland, with agues and swollen joints and the fear of fever. They build their huts right at the borders of the scummed pools, just clear of the deep black mud at the edge, or even set them on stilts right over the stagnant water. The huts crack and rot and fall to pieces every year, and have to be patched each spring, but in spring and autumn the flocks of travelling birds fly down to drink, in summer the waters are full of fish and the forest of game, and in winter the folk break the ice and lie in wait for the deer to come and drink. And always the place is loud with frogs; I have eaten these many times in Brittany, and it is true that they make a good meal. So the folk of the marshes cling to their stinking cabins, and eat well and drink the standing water, and die of the fever and the flux; nor do they fear the walking fires which haunt the marsh at night, for these are the souls of men they knew.

We were still twelve miles short of the ferry, and it was growing dusk, when the first hint of trouble came. The oak forests had given way to a lighter woodland of birch and alder, the trees crowding so closely to the sides of the track that we had to lie low on the horses' necks to avoid the whipping branches. Though there had been no rain the ground was very soft, and now and again our horses' hoofs splashed deep in the black mire. Soon, somewhere near us, I smelled the marsh, and before long through the thinning trees we could see the dull glimmer of the bog pools reflecting the last light from the sky. My horse stumbled, floundering, and Ralf, who was riding ahead of me, checked and put a quick hand to my rein. Then he pointed ahead.

Ahead of us, a different light pricked the dusk: the steady, dull yellow of candle or rushlight. The hut of a marsh dweller. We rode towards it.

The dwelling was not set over the water, but the ground was very wet, and was no doubt flooded in bad weather, for the hut was raised on piles, and approached by a narrow causeway of logs sawn short and jammed together across a ten-foot moat of mud.

A dog barked. I could see a man, a shadow against the dully lit interior of the hut, peering out at us. I hailed him. The marsh dwellers speak a tongue of their own, but they understand the Celtic of the Dumnonii.

"My name is Emrys. I'm a travelling doctor, and this is my servant. We're making for the ferry at Uxella. We came by the forest because the King's army is on the road. We're looking for shelter, and can pay for it."

If there was one thing the poor folk of these parts understood, it was the need for a man to keep out of the way of troops on the march. In a few moments a bargain was struck, the dog was hauled back into the hut and tied up, and I was picking my way gingerly across the slippery logs, leaving Ralf to tend the horses and tether them on the driest piece of ground he could find.

Our host's name was Nidd; he was a short, agile-looking fellow with black hair and a black bristle of beard. His shoulders and arms looked immensely strong, but he limped badly from a leg which had been broken, then set by guesswork and left to knit crooked. His wife, who was probably little more than thirty, was white-haired and bent double on herself with rheumatism; she looked and moved like an old woman, and her face was drawn into tight lines round a toothless mouth. The hut was cramped and foul-smelling, and I would rather have slept in the open, but the evening had turned chilly, and neither Ralf nor I wished to spend a night out in the sodden forest. So when we had had our fill of black bread and broth we accepted the space of floor offered us, and prepared to lie down wrapped in our cloaks, and take what rest we could. I had mixed a potion for the woman, and she was already asleep, huddled against the other wall under a pile of skins, but Nidd made no move to join her. He went instead to the doorway, peering again into the night, as if expecting someone. Ralf's eyes met mine, and his brows lifted; his hand moved towards his dagger. I shook my head. I had heard the light, quick footsteps on the causeway. The dog made no sound, but his tail beat the floor. The curtain of rough-tanned deerhide was pushed aside from the doorway, and a boy came running in, his mouth one huge grin in a filthy face. He stopped short when he saw Ralf and me, but his father said something in patois and the boy, still eyeing us curiously, dumped the bundle of faggots he carried on the table and undid the thong that held it together. Then, with a swift wary look at me, he pulled from the middle of the faggots a dead fowl, a few strips of salted pork, a bundle which he shook out to reveal a pair of good leather trews, and a well-sharpened knife of the kind issued to the soldiers of the King's armies.

I approached the table, holding out my hand. The man stood watchful, but made no move, and after a moment the boy dropped the knife into my palm. I weighed it in my hand, considering. Then I laughed and dropped it point down, to the table. It stuck there beside the fowl, quivering.

"You've had good hunting tonight, haven't you? That's easier than waiting for the wild duck to flight in at dawn. So, the King's army lies nearby? How near?"

The boy merely stared, too shy to answer, but with the help of his father I got the information bit by bit.

It was not reassuring. The army had made camp barely five miles away. The boy had lurked in a tree at the forest's edge, watching his chance to steal food, and had overheard scraps of talk among the men who had gone in among the trees to relieve themselves. It seemed, if the boy had rightly understood what he had heard, that though the main body of the army would no doubt head on its way in the morning, a troop was to be detached and sent directly to Caerleon, with a message for the commander there. They would obviously go by the quickest way, the river crossing. They would certainly commandeer whatever boats were available.

I looked at Ralf. He was already fastening his cloak. I nodded, and turned to Nidd.

"We must go, I'm afraid. We must get to the ferry before the King's troops, and no doubt they'll ride at first light. We'll have to leave now. Can the boy guide us?"

The boy would do anything, it seemed, for the copper penny I gave him, and he knew all the ways through the marsh. We thanked our host, left the fee and medicines we had promised, and were soon on our way, with the boy— whose name was Ger—at my horse's head.

There were stars, and a quarter moon, but hazed over with fitful cloud. I could barely see the path, but the boy never hesitated. He seemed able to see even in the dark under the trees. The beasts trod softly enough on the forest floor, but the boy made no sound at all.

It was difficult to tell, what with the dark, the bad going and the winding track, what kind of distance we were covering. It seemed a long time before the trees dwindled and thinned, and the way stretched clearer ahead of us. As the moon grew stronger, the clouds diffusing her pale light, I could see more clearly. We were still in the marsh; water gleamed on either hand, islanded with blackness. Underfoot mud pulled and sucked at the horses' hoofs. Rushes swished and rustled shoulder high. There was a noise of frogs everywhere, and now and again a splash as something took to the water. Once, with a clap and a call and a flash of white, a feeding bird shot off not a yard in front of my horse's hoofs, and, had it not been for the boy's hand on the reins, I must have been unseated and thrown into the water. After that my horse picked his way nervously, starting even at the faint sucking sounds from the pools where the marshlights flickered and bubbles popped under the wisps of vapour which hung and floated over the water. Here and there, sticking up black out of the bog, was the stripped skeleton of a tree.

It was a strange, dead-looking landscape, and smelling of death. From Ralf's silence, I knew that he was afraid. But our guide, at my horse's head, plodded on through the wandering mists and the wisps of fire that were the souls of his fathers. The only sign he gave was when, at a fork in the track, we passed a hollow tree, a thick trunk twice the height of a man, with a gaping hole in the bark, and inside this a greenish glow that, with the help of the moonlight, faintly lit a crouching shape of eyes, mouth, and crudely carved breasts. The old goddess of the crossways, the Nameless One, who sits staring from her hollowed log like the owl who is her creature; and in front of her, decaying with the greenish glow that folk call enchanter's light, an offering of fish, laid in an oyster shell. I heard Ralf's breath go in, and his hand flickered in a defensive gesture. The boy Ger, without even looking aside, muttered the word under his breath, and held straight on.

Half an hour later, from the head of a rise of solid ground, we saw the wide, moonlit stretch of the estuary, and smelled salt on the clean and moving air.

Down by the shore where the ferry plied there was a red glimmer of light, the flame of the cresset on the wharf. The road to it, clear in the moonlight, crossed the ridge not far from us and ran straight downhill to the shore. We drew rein, but when I turned to thank the boy I found that he had already vanished, melting back into the darkness as silently as one of the wandering marshlights fading. We headed our weary horses down towards the distant glimmer.

When we reached the ferry we found that our luck had deserted us as swiftly and as decisively as our guide. The cresset burned on its post at the strip of shingle where the ferry beached, but the ferry was not there. Straining my ears, I thought I heard, above the ripple of water, the splashing of oars some way out on the estuary. I gave a hail, but got no reply.

"It looks as if he expects to come back to this side soon," said Ralf, who had been exploring. "There's a fire in the hut, and he's left the door open."

"Then we'll wait inside," I said. "It's not likely the King's troops will set out before cock-crow. I can't imagine his message to Caerleon is as urgent as that, or he'd have sent a rider posting last night. See to the horses, then come in and get some rest."

The ferryman's hut was empty, but the remains of a fire still glowed in the ring of stones that served for a hearth. There was a pile of dry kindling beside it, and before long a comforting tongue of flame licked up through the wood and set the turf glowing. Ralf was soon dozing in the warmth, while I sat watching the flames and listening for the return of the ferry.

But the sound that roused me was not the sound of a keel grating on shingle; it was the soft and distant thudding of a troop of horse coming at the canter.

Before my hand could reach Ralf's shoulder to shake him awake, he was on his feet.

"Quick, my lord, if we ride fast along the shingle—the tide's not full yet—"

"No. They'd hear us, and in any case the horses are too tired. How far away would you say they were?"

He was at the door in two strides, his head slanted, listening. "Half a mile. Less. They'll be here in a few minutes. What are you going to do? We can't hide. They'll see the horses, and the country's open as a map in the sand."

This was true. The road down which the horsemen were coming ran straight up from the shore to the head of the ridge. To right and left of it lay the marshlands, glinting with water, and white with mist. Behind us the estuary stretched glimmering, throwing back the moonlight.

"What you can't run from, you must face," I said. "No, not like that"—as the boy's hand went to his sword—"not against King's men, and we wouldn't stand a chance anyway. There's a better way. Get the bags, will you?"

I was already stripping off my stained and ragged tunic. He threw me a doubtful look, but ran to obey. "You won't get away with that doctor disguise again."

"I don't intend to try. When fate forces your hand, Ralf, go with it. It looks as if I may get to see the King sooner than I'd hoped to."

"Here? But you—he—the Queen—"

"The Queen's secret will be safe. I've been thinking how to deal with this if it happened. We'll let them think we've just come south from Maridunum, hoping to see the King."

"But the ferryman? If they check with him?"

"It could be awkward, but we'll have to chance it. Why should they, after all? Even if they do, I can deal with it. Men will believe anything of the King's enchanter, Ralf, even that he could cross the estuary on a cloud, or ford it knee high at flood-tide."

While we were talking he had unstrapped one of the saddle-bags and pulled out of it the decent dark robe and stitched doeskin boots I had worn for my interview with the Queen, while I bent over the bucket of water by the door and swilled the weariness of the journey and the stench of the marshlander's hut off my face and hands. *When fate forces you*, I had said to Ralf. I felt my blood running fast and light with the hope that this stroke—ill luck we had thought it—might be the first cold, dangerous touch of the god's hand.

When the troop rode up, halting with a clatter and slither of shingle in front of the ferryman's hut, I was standing waiting for them in the open doorway, with the firelight behind me, and the bright moonlight catching the royal Dragon at my shoulder.

Behind me in the shadows I heard Ralf mutter thankfully: "Not Cornwall's men. They won't know me."

"But they'll know me," I said. "That's Ynyr's badge. They're Welshmen from Guent."

The officer was a tall man, with a thin hawk face and a white scar twisting the corner of his mouth. I did not remember him, but he stared, saluted, and said: "By the Raven himself! How came you here, sir?"

"I must have words with the King. How far away is his camp?"

As I spoke, a kind of ripple of movement went among the troop, horses fidgeting and one suddenly rearing as if curbed too nervously. The officer snapped something over his shoulder, then turned back to me. I heard him swallow before he answered me.

"Some eight miles off, sir."

There was something more here, I thought, than surprise at finding me in this deserted place, and the awe that I was accustomed to meeting among common men. I felt Ralf move up close behind me to my shoulder. A half-glance showed me the sparkle in his eyes; show Ralf danger, and he came alive.

The officer said abruptly: "Well, my lord, this has saved us something. We were on the way to Caerleon. We had the King's orders to find you and bring you to him."

I caught the sharp intake of Ralf's breath. I thought fast, through a sudden quickening of the heart. This explained the soldiers' reaction; they thought the King's enchanter must have had magical foreknowledge of the King's will. On a plainer level, it settled the matter of the ferryman; if this troop was an escort for me, they would not now need to cross the ferry. Ralf could buy the man's silence when I had gone with the troops. I would not risk taking the boy back within reach of Uther's displeasure.

There was no harm in driving the point home. I said pleasantly: "So I have saved you the trip to Bryn Myrddin. I'm glad. Where did the King plan to receive me? At Viroconium? I didn't think he meant to lie at Caerleon."

"Nor does he," said the man. I could hear the effort of control, but his voice was hoarse, and he cleared his throat. "You—you knew the King was travelling north to Viroconium?"

"How not?" I asked him. From the edge of my eye I saw the nods and head-turning among the men that also asked *How not?* "But I had a mind to talk to him sooner than that. Did he charge you with a letter for me?"

"No, sir. Instructions to take you to him, that was all." He leaned forward in the saddle. "I think it was on account of the message he got last evening from Cornwall. Ill news, I think, though he told no one what it was. He seemed angry. Then he gave the order to fetch you."

He waited, looking down at me as if I would be sure to know the contents of the message.

I was only too afraid that I did. Someone had recognized us, or made a guess, and sent to tell the King. The messenger could easily have passed us on the road. So, whatever was to happen between Uther and myself, I had to get Ralf out of danger first. And although I was not afraid for the Queen at Uther's hands, there were others—Maeve, Caw, Marcia, the child himself. . . . The skin on my nape stung and roused like a dog's that smells danger. I took a long, steadying breath and looked about me. "You have a spare horse? My beast is weary and must be led. My servant will rest here, and go back at first light with the ferry, to make ready for me at home. The King will no doubt see me escorted there when my business with him is done."

The officer's voice, apologetic but definite, cut across Ralf's furious whisper of dissent. "If it please you, sir, you will both come. Those were my orders. We have horses. Shall we ride?"

At the lift of his hand the men were already moving forward to close us round. There was nothing to be done. He had his orders, and I would risk more by arguing than by obeying. Besides, every minute's delay might bring the ferry back. I had heard nothing, but the fellow must have seen the soldiers' torches, and might even now be heading back for custom.

A trooper came up with the spare horses and took our own beasts in hand. We mounted. The officer barked an order, and the troop wheeled and fell in behind us.

We were barely two hundred paces from the shore when I heard, clear behind me, the sound of a boat's bottom grating on shingle. No one else paid any attention. The officer was busy telling me about the council to be held in the north, and behind me I could hear Ralf's voice, gay and amused, promising the troopers "a skin of sloe wine, the best stuff you ever tasted. A recipe of my master's. It's what they give you with the rations now in Caerleon, so you'll see what you've missed. That's what comes of sending messages for a wizard, who knows everything that's happened before it's even happened at all. . . ."

The King was abed when we arrived at the camp, and we were lodged—and guarded—in a tent not far from his. We said nothing to each other that could not be overheard. And, danger or no danger, it was the most comfortable lodging we had had since we left the inn at Camelford. Ralf was soon asleep, but I lay wakeful, watching the empty dark, listening to the little wind which had sprung up throwing handfuls of rain against the walls of the tent, and telling myself: "It must happen. It must happen. The god sent me the vision. The child was given to me." But the dark stayed empty, and the wind swept the tent walls and withdrew into silence, and nothing came.

I turned my head on its uneasy pillow, and saw dimly the shine of Ralf's eyes, watching me. But he turned over without speaking, and soon his breathing slackened again into sleep.

9

The King received me alone, soon after dawn.

He was armed and ready for the road, but bareheaded. His helmet with its gold circlet lay on a stool beside his chair, and his sword and shield stood propped against the box which held the travelling altar of Mithras that he always carried with him. The tent was hung with skins and worked curtains, but it was chilly, and draughts crept everywhere. Outside were the sounds of the army breaking camp. I could hear the snap and flutter of the Dragon standard by the entrance.

He greeted me briefly. His face still wore the bleak expression I remembered, empty of friendliness, but I could see neither anger nor enmity there. His look was cool and summing, his voice brisk.

"You and your Sight have saved me a little trouble, Merlin."

I bent my head. If he asked no questions I need answer none. I came to the point. "What do you want with me?"

"Last time we spoke together I was harsh with you. I have since thought that this was perhaps unworthy of a king to whom you had just done a service."

"You were bitter at the Duke's death."

"As to that, he fought against his King. Whatever the circumstances, he raised a sword to me, and he died. It's done, and it is past. We, you and I, are left with the future. This is what concerns me now."

"The child," I said, assenting.

The blue eyes narrowed. "Who sent you the news? Or is this still the Sight?"

"Ralf brought the news. When he left your court, he came to me. He serves me now."

He considered that for a moment, his brows drawing together, then smoothing as he found no harm in it. I watched him. He was a tall man, with reddish hair and beard, and a fair, high-coloured skin that made him look younger than his years. It was just over a year, I thought, since my father had died and Uther had lifted the Pendragon standard. Kingship had steadied him; I could see discipline in his face as well as the lines drawn there by passion and temper, and kingship along with his victories clothed him like a cloak.

He moved a hand, dismissively, and I knew that Ralf need fear him no longer. "I said the past was past, but there is one thing I must ask you. On that night in Tintagel when this child was begotten, I bade you keep away from me and trouble me no more. Do you remember?"

"I remember."

"And you replied that you would not trouble me again, that I should not need your service again. Was this foresight, or only anger?"

I said quietly: "When I spoke, I spoke the words that came to me. I thought they were foresight. All the words I spoke and the things I did throughout that night I took as if they came straight from the gods. Why do you ask? Have you sent for me now to command service of me?"

"To ask it, rather."

"As a prophet?"

"No. As a kinsman."

"Then I'll tell you, as a kinsman, that it was not prophecy that night, nor was it anger, sir, but only grief. I was grieving for my servant's death, and for the deaths of Gorlois and his companions. But now, as you say, the past is past. If I can serve you, you have only to command me."

But, I thought, as I waited for him to speak, if it was no prophecy, then none of that night was God's and He never spoke to me. No, I had told the truth when I said that Uther would have no need of my service; it had not been Uther whom I served that night; it was not Uther I would serve now. I remembered the words of the other King, my father: "*You and I between us, Merlin, we will make such a king as the world has never known.*" It was the dead King, and the one still unborn, who commanded me.

If there had been any hesitation in my manner, Uther had not noticed it. He nodded, then set his elbow on his knee and his chin on his fist and thought for a while, frowning.

"There is one other thing I said that night. I told you that I would not acknowledge the child begotten then. I spoke in anger, but now I speak coldly, after taking thought and counsel, and I tell you, Merlin, that I'm still of the same mind."

He seemed to expect an answer, but I was silent. He went on, half irritably: "Don't misunderstand me, I don't doubt the Queen. I believe her when she tells me that she never lay with Gorlois after he brought her to London. The child is mine, yes, but he cannot be my heir, nor can he be reared in my house. If the child is a girl, then none of this matters, but if it is a boy it would be folly to rear him as heir to the High Kingdom, when men will only have to count on their fingers to say that Gorlois begot him of his wife Ygraine, half a month before the High King married her." He looked at me. "You must know this as well as I do, Merlin. You have lived in kings' houses. There will always be those who doubt his birth, so there will always be those who would try to pull him off the throne in favour of men with a 'better claim,' and God knows there will always be claims in plenty. And the best claims will be those of my other sons. So, even brought up as my bastard at my court, the child is dangerous. He may try to come at the kingship by the deaths of my other children. By the Light, this is not unknown. I will not have my house a battleground. I must beget myself another son, an undoubted heir, conceived in wedlock to the satisfaction of all men, and reared at my side when the kingdom is settled and the Saxon wars are over. Do you accept this?"

"You are the King, Uther, and the child's father."

It was hardly an answer, but he nodded as if I had agreed. "There is more. This child is not only dangerous, he'll be a victim of danger. If men can say that he was not mine, that he must have been begotten by Gorlois on Ygraine his wife, then it follows that he is the true son of the Duke of Cornwall, with a claim on the younger son's portion of the lands which Cador holds, now that I've confirmed him as Duke in his father's place. You see? King's son or Duke's, Cador is bound to be the child's enemy, and there are some who'd follow him quickly enough."

"Is Cador loyal to you?"

"I trust him." He gave a short laugh. "So far. He's young, but hard-headed. He wants Cornwall, and he won't risk anything that could lose it—yet. But later, who knows? And when I am gone . . ." He let it hang. "No, Cador is not my enemy, but there are others who are."

"Who?"

"God knows, but what king was ever without them? Even Ambrosius . . . they're still saying he died of poison. I know you told me this was not true, but even so I have Ulfin taste my food. Ever since I took Octa and Eosa prisoner, they've been the storm center for every disaffected leader who

thinks he can see his way to a crown like Vortigern's—
backed with Saxon forces, and paid for with British lives
and lands. But what else can I do? Let them go, to raise
the Federates against me? Or kill them, and give their sons
in Germany a grievance to be wiped out in blood? No, Octa
and his cousin are my hostages. Without them, Colgrim and
Badulf would have been here long since, and the Saxon
Shore would have burst its bounds and be lapping at Ambrosius' Wall. As it is, I'm buying time. You can't tell me
anything, Merlin? Have you heard anything, or seen?"

He was not asking for prophecy; Uther looked askance
and white-eyed at things of the Otherworld, like a dog that
sees the wind. I shook my head.

"Of your enemies? Nothing, except that when Ralf came
to me after leaving your court, he was set upon, and nearly
killed. The men had no badge. They may have thought he
was your messenger, or perhaps the Queen's. Troops from
the barracks hunted the woods, but found no trace of them.
More than that, I've heard nothing. But be sure that if I ever
learn anything I will tell you."

He gave a brief nod, then went on, slowly, choosing his
words. His manner was abrupt, almost reluctant. For myself, my mind was spinning, and I had to fight to hold myself
calm and steady. We were coming now onto the battleground, but it must be a very different battle from the one
I had planned for. "You and I," he had said. He would
hardly have sent for me unless I was to have some concern
in the child's future.

He was going over the same ground that Ygraine and I
had covered. ". . . so you see why, if the child is a boy, he
cannot stay with me, yet if I send him away, he is beyond
my power to protect. But protection he must have. Bastard
or no, he is my child and the Queen's, and if we have no

other sons he must one day be declared my heir to the High Kingdom." He turned up a hand. "You see where this leaves me. I must consign him to a guardian who will keep him in safety for the first few years of his life . . . at least until this torn kingdom is settled and safe, and in the hands of strong and loyal allies, and my own declared heirs."

He waited again for my agreement. I nodded, then said, carefully neutral: "Have you chosen this guardian?"

"Yes. Budec."

So the Queen had been right, and the decision was made. But still he had sent for me. I held myself still and said, so flatly that it sounded indifferent: "It was the obvious choice."

He shifted in his chair and cleared his throat. I saw with some surprise that he was uneasy, nervous even. He even looked half pleased at my commendation of his choice. The knowledge steadied me. I realized that I had been so single-minded—so wrapped in what I had believed was my and the child's driving fate—that I had seen Uther falsely as the enemy. He was not so concerned: the plain fact was that Uther was a war-leader harassed perpetually by the strife in and around his borders, working desperately against time to patch a dam here, a sea-wall there, against the piling flood-water; and to him this affair of the child, though it might prove one day vitally important, was now little but a rub in the way of major issues, something he wanted out of the way and delegated. He had spoken without emotion, and indeed had set the thing out fairly enough. It was possible that he had sent for me, genuinely, to ask my advice, as his brother had been used to do. In which case . . . I wetted dry lips, and schooled myself to listen quietly, an adviser with a man beset by trouble.

He was speaking again, something about a letter. The message which had come yesterday. He pointed to the stool beside him where the parchment lay, crumpled as if he had thrown it down in anger. "Did you know about this?"

I picked the letter up and smoothed it out. It was brief, a message from Brittany, that had been sent to the King at Tintagel and brought here after him. King Budec had fallen sick of a fever, it said, during the summer. He had seemed on the way to recovery, then, towards the end of August, he had quite suddenly died. The letter finished with protestations of formal friendship from the new king, Hoel, Uther's "devoted cousin and ally . . ."

I looked up. Uther had sat back in his chair, shifting a fold of the scarlet mantle over his arm. Everything seemed quite still. Outside, the wind had dropped. The sounds of the camp came from far away, faintly. Uther's chin was sunk on his chest, and he was watching me with a mixture of worry and impatience.

I was noncommittal. "This is heavy news. Budec was a good man and a good friend."

"Heavy enough, even if it had not destroyed my plans. I was preparing to send messages even when this letter came. Now I can't see my way clear. Have they told you that I go to a council of kings at Viroconium?"

"Audagus told me." Audagus was the officer who had escorted us from the ferry.

He threw out a hand. "Then you see how much I want to turn aside to deal with this. But it must be dealt with now. This is why I sent for you."

I flicked the seal with a forefinger. "You won't send the child to Hoel, then? He swears himself your devoted cousin and ally."

"He may be my devoted cousin and ally, but he's also a—" Uther used a phrase that became a soldier rather than a king in council. "I never liked him, nor he me. Oh, Mithras knows he would never mean harm to a son of mine, but he's not the man his father was, and he might not be able to protect the boy from his ill-wishers. No, I'll not send him to Hoel. But what other court can I send him to? Reckon it for yourself." He told over a few names, all powerful men, all of them kings whose lands lay in the southern part of the country, behind the Wall of Ambrosius. "Well? Do you see my problem? If he goes to one of the nobles or petty kings here in safe country he could still be in danger from an ambitious man; or worse, become a tool of treachery and rebellion."

"So?"

"So I come to you. You are the only man who can steer me between these clashing rocks. On the one hand, the child must be sworn and acknowledged my own, in case there is no other heir. On the other, he must be taken away out of danger for himself and the kingdom, and brought up in ignorance of his birth until the time comes when I send for him." He turned over a hand on his knee and asked me as simply as he had asked me once before: "Can you help me?"

I answered him as simply. The bewilderment, the confused whirl of thought, settled suddenly into a pattern, like coloured leaves blown down into a tapestry on the grass when the spinning wind drops still. "Of course. You need wreck no part of your kingdom on either of these rocks. Listen, and I will tell you how. You told me you had 'taken counsel.' Other men, then, know of your plans to send the boy to Budec?"

"Yes."

"Have you spoken to anyone of this letter, and your doubts of Hoel?"

"No."

"Good. You will give it out that your plan stays as formerly, and that the boy will go to Hoel's court at Kerrec. You will write to Hoel requesting this. Have someone make all arrangements to send the boy with his nurse and attendants as soon as the weather allows. See that it is given out that I will accompany him there myself."

He was frowning, intent, and I could see protest in his face, but he made none. He said merely: "And?"

"Next," I said, "I must be at Tintagel for the birth. Who is her physician?"

"Gandar." He seemed about to say something more, then changed his mind and waited.

"Good. I'm not suggesting I should attend her." I smiled. "In view of what I shall suggest, that might lead to some rather dangerous rumours. Now, will you be there yourself for the lying-in?"

"I shall try, but it's doubtful."

"Then I shall be there to attest the child's birth, as well as Gandar and the Queen's women, and whoever you can appoint. If it is a boy, the news will be sent to you by beacon, and you will declare him your son by the Queen, and, in default of a son begotten in wedlock, your heir until another prince shall be born."

He took some time over that, frowning, and obviously reluctant to commit himself. But it was only the conclusion of what he had himself said to me. Finally he nodded and spoke a little heavily: "Very well. It is true. Bastard or not, he is my heir until I get another. Go on."

"Meantime the Queen will keep her chamber, and once he has been seen and sworn to, the child will be taken back to the Queen's apartments and kept there, seen only by Gandar and the women. Gandar can arrange this. I myself will leave openly, by the main gate and the bridge. Then after dark I shall go down secretly to the postern gate on the cliff, to receive the child."

"And take him where?"

"To Brittany. No, wait. Not to Hoel, nor by the ship

which everyone will be watching. Leave that part of it to me. I shall take him to someone I know in Brittany, on the edge of Hoel's kingdom. He will be safe, and well cared for. You have my word for it, Uther."

He brushed that aside as if there had been no need for me to say it. He was already looking lighter, glad to be relieved of a care that must, among the weighty cares of the kingdom, seem trivial, and—with the child still only a weight in a woman's womb—unreal. "I'll have to know where you take him."

"To my own nurse, who reared me and the other royal children, bastard and true alike, in the nurseries at Maridunum. Her name is Moravik, and she's a Breton. After the sack by Vortigern she went home to her people. She has married since. While the child is sucking, I can think of no better place. He won't be looked for in such a humble home. He will be guarded, but better than that, he will be hidden and unknown."

"And Hoel?"

"He will know. He must. Leave Hoel to me."

Outside a trumpet sounded. The sun was growing stronger, and the tent was warm. He stirred, and flexed his shoulders, as a man does when he lays off his armour. "And when men find that the child is not on the royal ship, but has vanished? What do we tell them?"

"That for fear of the Saxons in the Narrow Sea the prince was sent, not by the royal ship, but privily, with Merlin, to Brittany."

"And when it is found he is not at Hoel's court?"

"Gandar and Marcia will swear to it that I took the child safely. What will be said I can't tell you, but there's no one who will doubt me, or that the child is safe as long as he's under my protection. And what my protection means you know. I imagine that men will talk of enchantments and vanishings, and wait for the child to reappear when my spells are lifted."

He said prosaically: "They're more like to say the ship foundered and the child is dead."

"I shall be there to deny it."

"You mean you won't stay with the boy?"

"I must not, not yet. I'm known."

"Then who will be with him? You said he would be guarded."

For the first time I hesitated fractionally. Then I met his eyes. "Ralf."

He looked startled, then angry, then I saw him thinking back past his anger. He said slowly: "Yes. I was wrong there, too. He will be true."

"There is no one truer."

"Very well, I am content. Make what arrangements you please. It's in your hands. You of all men in Britain will know how to protect him." His hands came down hard on the arms of his chair. "So, that is settled. Before we march today I shall send a message to the Queen telling her what I have decided."

I thought it wise to ask: "Will she accept it? It's no easy thing for a woman to bear, even a queen."

"She knows my decision, and she will do as I say. There's one thing, though, where she'll have her way; she wants the child baptized a Christian."

I glanced at the Mithras altar against the tent wall. "And you?"

He lifted his shoulders. "What does it matter? He will never be King. And if he were, then he would pay service where he had to, in the sight of the people." A hard, straight look. "As my brother did."

If it was a challenge I declined it, saying merely: "And the name?"

"Arthur."

The name was strange to me, but it came like an echo of something I had heard long before. Perhaps there had been Roman blood in Ygraine's family . . . The Artorii; that would be it. But that was not where I had heard the name. . . .

"I'll see to it," I said. "And now, with your permission, I'll send the Queen a letter, too. She'll lie the easier for being assured of my loyalty."

He nodded, then stood up and reached for his helmet. He was smiling, a cold ghost of the old malicious smile with which he had baited me when I was a child. "It's strange, isn't it, Merlin the bastard, that I should talk so easily of trusting the body of my own ill-begotten son to the one man in the kingdom whose claim to the throne is better than his? Are you not flattered?"

"Not in the least. You'd be a fool if you didn't know by now that I have no ambitions towards your crown."

"Then don't teach my bastard any, will you?" He turned his head, shouting for a servant, then back to me. "And none of your damned magic, either."

"If he's your son," I said dryly, "he won't take very kindly to magic. I shall teach him nothing except what he has the need and the right to know. You have my word on it."

On that we parted. Uther would never like me, nor I him, but there was a kind of cold mutual respect between us, born of our shared blood and the different love and service we had given to Ambrosius. I should have known that he and I were linked in this as closely as the two sides of the same counter, and that we would move together whether we willed it or not. The gods sit over the board, but it is men who move under their hands for the mating and the kill.

I should have known; but I had been so used to God's

voice in the fire and stars that I had forgotten to listen for it in the counsels of men.

Ralf was waiting, alone in the guarded tent. When I told him the result of my talk with the King, he was silent a long time. Then he said: "So it will all happen, just as you said it would. Did you expect it to come like this? When they brought us here last night, I thought you were afraid."

"I was, but not in the way you mean."

I expected him to ask how, but oddly, he seemed to understand. His cheek flushed and he busied himself over some detail of packing. "My lord, I have to tell you . . ." His voice was stifled. "I have been very wrong about you. At first I—because you are not a man of war, I thought—"

"You thought I was a coward? I know."

He looked up sharply. "You knew? You didn't mind?" This, obviously, was almost as bad as cowardice.

I smiled. "When I was a child among budding warriors, I grew used to it. Besides, I have never been sure myself how much courage I have."

He stared at that, then burst out: "But you are afraid of nothing! All the things that have happened—this journey— you'd have thought we were riding out on a summer morning, instead of going by paths filled with wild beasts and outlaws. And when the King's men took us—even if he is your uncle, that's not to say you'd never be in danger from him. Everyone knows the King's unchancy to cross. But you just looked cold as ice, as if you expected him to do what you wanted, just as everyone does! You, afraid? You're not afraid of anything that's real."

"That's what I mean," I said. "I'm not sure how much courage is needed to face human enemies—what you'd call 'real'—knowing they won't kill you. But foreknowledge has its own terrors, Ralf. Death may not lie just at the next corner, but when one knows exactly when it will come, and how . . . It's not a comfortable thought."

"You mean you do know?"

"Yes. At least, I think it's my death that I see. At any rate it is darkness, and a shut tomb."

He shivered. "Yes, I see. I'd rather fight in daylight, even thinking I might die perhaps tomorrow. At least it's always 'perhaps tomorrow,' never 'now.' Will you wear the doeskin boots for riding, my lord, or change them now?"

"Change them. Thank you." I sat down on a stool and stretched out a foot for him. He knelt to pull off my boots. "Ralf, there is something else I must tell you. I told the King you were with me, and that you would go to Brittany to guard the child."

He looked up at that, struck still. "You told him *that?* What did he say?"

"That you were a true man. He agreed, and approved you."

He sat back on his heels, my boots in his hands, gaping at me.

"He has had time to think, Ralf, as a king should think. He has also had time—as kings do—to still his conscience. He sees Gorlois now as a rebel, and the past as done with. If you wish to go back into his service he will receive you kindly, and give you a place among his fighting men."

He did not answer, but stooped forward again and busied himself fastening my boots. Then he got to his feet and pulled back the flap of the tent, calling to a man to bring up the horses. "And hurry. My lord and I ride now for the ferry."

"You see?" I said. "Your own decision this time, freely given. And yet who can say it is not as much a part of the pattern as the 'chance' of Budec's death?" I got to my feet, stretching, and laughed. "By all the living gods, I'm glad that things are moving now. And gladder for the moment of one thing more than any other."

"That you're to get the child so easily?"

"Oh, that, of course. No, I really meant that now at last I can shave off this damnable beard."

10

By the time Ralf and I reached Maridunum my plans, so far as could be at this stage, were made. I sent him by the next ship to Brittany, with letters of condolence to Hoel, and with messages to supplement the King's. One letter, which Ralf carried openly, merely repeated the King's request that Hoel should give shelter to the baby during his infancy; the other, which Ralf was to deliver secretly, assured Hoel that he would not be burdened with the charge of the child, nor would we come by the royal ship or at the time ostensibly fixed. I begged his assistance for Ralf in all the arrangements for the secret journey at Christmas that I planned. Hoel, easy-going and lazy by nature, and less than fond of his cousin Uther, would be so relieved, I knew, that he would help Ralf and myself in every way known to him.

With Ralf gone, I myself set out for the north. It was obvious that I would not be able to leave the baby too long in Brittany; the refuge with Moravik would serve for a while, till men's interest died down, but after that it might be dangerous. Brittany was the place (as I had said to the Queen) where Uther's enemies would look for the child; the fact that the child was not—had never been—at his publicly declared refuge at Hoel's court might make them believe that the talk of Brittany had been nothing but a false trail. I would make certain that no real trail would lead them to Moravik's obscure village. But this was only safe as long as the boy was an infant. As soon as he grew and began to go about, some query or rumour might start. I knew how easily this could happen, and for the child of a poor house to be so cared for and guarded as must happen here, it would be very easy for some question to start a rumour, and a rumour to grow too quickly into a guess at the truth.

More than this, once the child was weaned from women and the nursery, he would have to be trained, if not as a young prince, then as a young noble and a warrior. It was obvious that Bryn Myrddin, on no count, could be his home: he must have the comfort and safety of a noble house around him. In the end I had thought of a man who had been a friend of my father's, and whom I had known well. His name was Ector, styled Count of Galava, one of the nobles who fought under King Coel of Rheged, Uther's most considerable ally in the north.

Rheged is a big kingdom, stretching from the mountainous spine of Britain right to the western coast, and from the Wall of Hadrian in the north clear down to the plain of Deva. Galava, which Ector held under Coel, lies about thirty miles in from the sea, in the north-west corner of the kingdom. Here there is a wild and mountainous tract of country, all hills and water and wild forest; in fact, one of the names it goes by is the Wild Forest. Ector's castle lies on the flat land at the end of one of the long lakes that fill these valleys. There was in past time a Roman fortress there, one of a chain on the military road running from Glannaventa on the coast to join the main way from Luguvallium to York. Between Galava and the port of Glannaventa lie steep hills and wild passes, easily defended, and inland is the well-guarded country of Rheged itself.

When Uther had talked of fostering the child in some safe castle he had thought only of the rich, long-settled lands inside Ambrosius' Wall, but even without his fears of the nobles' loyalty, I would have counted that country dangerous; these were the very lands that the Saxons, immured along the Shore, coveted most dearly. It was these lands which, I guessed, they would fight for first and most bitterly. In the north, in the heart of Rheged, where no one would look for him and where the Wild Forest itself would guard him, the boy could grow up as safely as God would allow, and as freely as a deer.

Ector had married a few years back. His wife was called Drusilla, of a Romano-British family from York. Her father, Faustus, had been one of the city magistrates who had defended the city against Hengist's son Octa, and had been one of those urgent to advise the Saxon leader to yield himself to Ambrosius. Ector himself was fighting at the time in my father's army. It was in York that he had met Drusilla, and had married her. They were both Christians, and this was possibly why their paths and Uther's had not often crossed. But I, along with my father, had been to Faustus' house in York, and Ambrosius had there taken part in many long discussions about the settlement of the northern provinces.

The castle at Galava was well protected, being built on the site of the old Roman fort, with the lake before it, and a deep river on the one hand, and the wild mountains near. It could be approached only from the open water, or by one of the easily watched and defended valley passes. But it did not have the air of a fortress. Trees grew near it, now rich with autumn, and there were boats out and men fishing where the river flowed deep and still through its sedgy flatlands. The green meadows at the waters' head were full of cattle, and there was a village crowded under the castle walls as there had been in the Roman Peace. Two full miles beyond the castle walls lay a monastery, and so secluded were the valleys that right up on the heights above the tree-line, where the land stretched bare of all but short grass and stones, one saw the strange little blue-fleeced sheep that breed in Rheged, with some shepherd boy cheerfully braving the wolves and fierce hill foxes with the protection of a stick and a single dog.

I travelled alone, and quietly. Though the hated beard had gone, and with it the heavy disguise, I managed the journey unnoticed and unrecognized, and came to Galava towards late afternoon on a bright, crisp October day.

The great gates were wide open, giving on a paved yard where men and boys were unloading a wagon of straw. The oxen stood patiently, chewing their cud; near them a lad was watering a pair of sweating horses. Dogs barked and skirmished, and hens pecked busily among the fallen straw. There were trees in the yard, and to either side of the steps up to the main door someone had planted beds of marigolds, which blazed orange and yellow in the late sunshine. It looked like a prosperous farm rather than a fortress, but through an open door I could see the rows of freshly burnished weapons, and from behind one of the high walls came shouted orders and the clash of men drilling.

I had barely paused between the posts of the archway when the porter was barring my way and asking my business. I handed him my Dragon brooch, wrapped in a small pouch, and bade him take it to his master. He came hurrying back to the gate within minutes, and the chamberlain, puffing in his wake, showed me straight in to Count Ector.

Ector was not much changed. He was a man of medium height, growing now into middle age; if my father had lived they would have been of an age now, I reckoned, which made him something over forty. He had a brown beard going grey, and brown skin with the blood springing healthily beneath it. His wife was more than ten years younger; she was tall, a statuesque woman still in her twenties, reserved and a little shy, but with smoky-blue eyes that belied her cool manner and distant speech. Ector had the air of a contented man.

He received me alone, in a small chamber where spears

and bows stood stacked against the walls, and the hearth was four deep in deer-hounds. The fire was heaped as high as a funeral pyre with pine logs blazing, and small wonder, for the narrow windows were unglazed and open to the brisk October air, and the wind whined like another hound in the bowstrings that were stacked there.

He gripped my arms with a bearlike welcome, beaming. "Merlinus Ambrosius! Here's a pleasure indeed! What is it, two years? Three? There's been water under the bridge, aye, and stars fallen, since we last met, eh? Well, you're welcome, welcome. I can't think of any man I'd rather see under my roof! You've been making a name for yourself, haven't you? The tales I've heard tell . . . Well, well, but you can tell me the truth of it yourself. God's sweet death, boy, you get more like him by the day! Thinner, though, thinner. You look as if you've seen no red meat for a year. Come, sit down by the fire now, and let me send for supper before we talk."

The supper was enormous and excellent, and would have served me ten times over. Ector ate enough for three, and pressed me to finish the rest. While we ate we exchanged news. He had heard of the Queen's pregnancy, and spoke of it, but for the moment I let it go, and asked him instead what had happened at Viroconium. Ector had attended the King's council there, and was but newly returned home.

"Success?" he asked, in reply to my question. "It's hard to say. It was well attended. Coel of Rheged, of course, and all from these lands"—he named half a dozen neighbours— "except Riocatus of Verterae, who sent to say he was sick."

"I gather you didn't believe it?"

"When I believe anything that jackal says," said Ector forcibly, "I'm a spit-licker too. But the wolves were there, all of them, so the scavengers hardly matter."

"Strathclyde?"

"Oh, aye, Caw was there. You know the Picts in the

western half of his land have been giving trouble—when haven't they given trouble, come to that? But for all Caw's Pictish himself, he'll co-operate with any plan that'll help him keep control of that wild territory of his, so he was well disposed to the idea of the council. He'll help, I'm sure of it. Whether he can control that pack of sons he's sired is another matter. Did you know that one of them, Heuil, a wild young blackguard scarcely old enough (you'd have thought) to lift a spear, took one of Morien's girls by force last spring when she was on her way to the monastery her father had promised her to since birth? He lifted his spear to *her* easily enough; by the time her father got the news she was over the border with him, and in no condition for any monastery, however broad-minded." He chuckled. "Morien cried rape, of course, but everyone was laughing, so he made the best of it. Strathclyde had to pay, naturally, and he and Morien sat on opposite benches at Viroconium, and Heuil wasn't there at all. Ah, well, but they agreed to sink their differences. King Uther managed it well enough, so what between Rheged and Strathclyde, there's half the northern frontier solid for the King."

"And the other half?" I asked. "What about Lot?"

"Lot?" Ector snorted. "That braggart! He'd swear allegiance to the Devil and Hecate combined if it would get him a few more acres for himself. He cares no more for Britain than that hound by the hearthstone. Less. He and his wild brood of brothers sitting on that cold rock of theirs. They'll fight when it pays them, and that's all." He fell silent, scowling at the fire, poking with a foot at the hound nearest him; it yawned with pleasure, and flattened its ears. "But he talks well, and maybe I'm blackguarding him. Times are changing, and even barbarians like Lot ought to be able to see that unless we band together with a strong oath, and keep it, it'll be the Flood Year all over again."

He was not referring to an actual flood, but to the year of the great invasion a century ago, when the Picts and Saxons, joined with the Scots from Ireland, poured across Hadrian's Wall with axe and fire. Maximus commanded then, in Segontium. He drove them back and broke them, and won for Britain a time of peace, and for himself an empire and a legend.

I said: "Lothian is a key to the defense that Uther's planning, even more than Rheged or Strathclyde. I'd heard tell—I don't know if it's true?—that there are Angles settled on the Alaunus, and that the strength of the Anglian Federates south of York along the Abus has doubled since my father's death?"

"It's true." He spoke heavily. "And south of Lothian there's only Urien on the coast, and he's another carrion crow, picking at Lot's leavings. Nay, that may be another one I'm doing an injustice to. He's married to Lot's sister, when all's done, so he'd be bound to cry the same way. Talking of which—"

"Talking of what?" I asked, as he paused.

"Marriage." He scowled, then began to grin. "If it wasn't so plaguy dangerous, it would be funny. You knew Uther had a bastard girl, I forget her name, she must be seven or eight years old?"

"Morgause. Yes, I remember her. She was born in Brittany."

Morgause was a sideslip of Uther's by a girl in Brittany who had followed him to Britain hoping, I suppose, for marriage, since she was of good family, and the only woman, so far as anyone knew then for certain, who had borne him a child. (It had always been a matter of amazement, and a good deal of private and public conjecture among Uther's troops, how he managed to avoid leaving a train of bastards

120

in his wake like seedlings following the sower down a furrow. But this girl was, to public knowledge, the only one. And I believe to Uther's knowledge, too. He was a fair man and a generous one, and no girl had suffered any loss worse than maidenhead through him.) He had acknowledged the child, kept both child and mother at one of his houses, and after the mother's marriage to a lord of his household, had taken the girl into his own. I had seen her once or twice in Brittany, a thin pale-haired girl with big eyes and a mouth folded small.

"What about Morgause?" I asked.

"Uther was casting out feelers for marrying her to Lot, come the time she'll be ready for bedding."

I cocked an eyebrow at him. "And what did Lot think about that?"

"Eh, you'd have laughed to watch him. Black as a wolverine at the suggestion that Uther's byblow was good enough, but careful to keep his talk sweet in case there's no other daughter born in the right bed now the King's wedded. Bastards—and their mates—have inherited kingdoms before now. Saving your presence, of course."

"Of course. Lot casts his eyes as high as that, then?"

He gave a short nod. "High as the High Kingdom itself, you can take my word for it."

I digested that, frowning. I had never met Lot; he was at this time scarcely older than myself—somewhere in his early twenties—and though he had fought under my father, his path and mine had not crossed. "So Uther wants to tie Lothian to him, and Lot wants to be tied? Whether it's for his own ambition or not, it means surely that Lot will fight for the High King when the time comes? And Lothian is our main bulwark against the Angles and the other invaders from the north."

"Oh, aye, he'll fight," said Ector. "Unless the Angles offer him a better bribe than Uther does."

"Do you mean that?" I was alarmed. Ector, for all his bluff ways, was a shrewd observer, and few men knew more about the changing shifts of power along our shores.

"Maybe I was putting it a trifle high. But for my money Lot's unscrupled and ambitious, and that's a combination that spells danger to any overlord who can't placate him."

"How is he with Rheged?" I was thinking of the child to be lodged here perhaps at Galava, with Lot east by north across the Pennines.

"Oh, friends, friends. As good friends as two big hounds each with his own full platter of meat. No, it's not yet a matter for concern, and may never be. So forget it, and drink up." He drank deeply himself, set down his cup and wiped his mouth. Then he fixed me with a sharp and curious eye. "Well? You'd better get to it, boy. You didn't come all this way for a good supper and a brattle with an old farmer. Tell me how I can serve Ambrosius' son?"

"It is Ambrosius' nephew you will be serving," I said, and told him the rest. He heard me out in silence. For all his warmth and heartiness, there was nothing impulsive or over-quick about Ector. He had been a cold-brained and calculating officer; a valuable man in any circumstance, from a pitched fight to a long and careful siege. After a sharp glance of surprise and a lift of the brows when I spoke of the King's decision and my guardianship of the child, he listened without moving and without taking his eyes off me.

When I had finished, he stirred. "Well . . . I'll say one thing to start with, Merlin; I'm glad and proud you should have come to me. You know how I felt about your father. And to tell you the truth, boy"—he cleared his throat, hesitated, then looked away into the fire as he spoke—"it always sorrowed my heart that you yourself were a bastard. And that's between these four walls, I don't have to tell you. Not that Uther's made a bad shot at being High King—"

"A far better shot than I'd ever have made," I said, smiling. "My father used to say that Uther and I, between us, shared out some of the qualities of a good king. It was a dear dream of his that some day, between us, we might fashion one. And this is the one." Then, as his head went up, "Oh, I know, a baby not yet born. But all the first part has happened as I knew it must happen: a child begotten by Uther and given to me to raise. I know this is the one. I believe he will be such a king as this poor country has never had before, and may never see again."

"Your stars tell you this?"

"It has been written there, certainly, and who writes among the stars but God?"

"Well, God grant it is so. There's coming a time, Merlin, maybe not next year, or for five years, or even for ten, but it is coming—when the Flood Year will come again, and pray God that this time there's a king here to raise the sword of Maximus against it." He turned his head sharply. "What's that? That sound?"

"Only the wind in the bowstrings."

"I thought it was a harp sounding. Strange. What is it, boy? Why do you look so?"

"Nothing."

He looked at me doubtfully for a moment longer, then grunted and fell silent, and behind us the long humming stretched out, a cold music, something from the air itself. I remembered how, as a child, I had lain watching the stars and listening for the music which (I had been told) they made as they moved. This must, I thought, be how it sounded.

A servant came in then with logs to replenish the fire, and the sound died. When he had gone, and the door had shut behind him, Ector spoke again in quite a different tone. "Well, I'll do it, of course, and proud to. You're right; in the next few years I can't see that Uther will have much time for him, and for that matter he'd be hard put to it to keep the child safe. Tintagel might have done, but as you say, there's Cador there . . . Does the King know that you've come to me?"

"No. Nor will I tell him, yet."

"Indeed?" He thought it over for a moment, frowning a little. "Do you think he'll be content with that?"

"Possibly. I don't know. He didn't press me too hard about Brittany. I think that just now he wants as little to do with it as need be. The other thing is"—I smiled a little wryly—"the King and I have a truce declared, but I wouldn't bank on its staying that way; and out of sight, out of mind. If I'm to have anything to do with the child's teaching, then it had better be at a fair distance from the High King."

"Aye, I've heard that, too. It's never a wise thing to help kings to their heart's desire. Will the boy be a Christian?"

"The Queen wants it, so he'll be baptized in Brittany if I can arrange it. He's to be called Arthur."

"You'll stand for him?"

I laughed. "I believe the fact that I was never baptized myself puts me out of the running."

His teeth showed. "I forgot you were a pagan. Well, I'm glad to hear about the boy. There'd have been a peck of trouble else."

"Your wife, you mean? She's so devout?"

"Poor lass," he said, "she has nothing else since our second died. There'll be no more, they say. In fact it will be God's mercy if we take this boy into our house; my son Cei's a headstrong little ruffian for all he's only three, and the women spoil him. It will be good to have the second child. What did you say his name was to be? Arthur? You'll leave this with me to talk over with Drusilla? Though there's no question, she'll be as glad as I am to have him. And I can tell you that she's close-mouthed enough, for all she's a woman. He'll be safe with us."

"I was sure of it. It doesn't need the stars to tell me that." But when I began to thank him, he cut me short.

"Well, then, that's settled. We can talk over the details later. I'll speak with Drusilla tonight. You'll stay a while, of course?"

"Thank you, but I can't—no longer than it takes to rest myself and my horse. I have to be at Tintagel again in December, and before that I must be home when Ralf gets back from Brittany. There's a lot to be arranged."

"A pity. But you'll be back. I'll look forward to it." He grinned, stirring the hounds again. "I'll enjoy seeing you installed as tutor to the household, or whatever you think will give you some claim on the boy. And I own I should like to see Cei licked into shape. Maybe he'll mind his manners with you, if he thinks he can be turned into a toad for disobeying you."

"Bats are my speciality," I said, smiling. "You are very good, and I'll never be out of your debt. But I'll find a place of my own."

"Look, boy, Ambrosius' son doesn't wander the country-side looking for a home while I have four walls and a fireplace to offer him. Why not here?"

"Because I might be recognized, and where Merlin is for the next few years, men will look for Arthur near him. No, I must stay unknown. A household as big as this is too risky, and, with all my thanks to you, four walls are not always the best shelter for such as me."

"Ah, yes. A cave, isn't it? Well, there are a few here-abouts, they tell me, if you turn the wolves out first. Well, you know your own business. But tell me, what of the

125

Queen? You didn't say where she stood in this? What woman would let her first child be taken from the bed where she bore him, and never try to see him again or make herself known to him?"

"The Queen herself sent for me secretly, and asked me to take him. She has suffered, I know, but it's the King's will, and she knows that it's more than a whim born of anger; she sees the dangers as well as he. And she is a queen before she is a woman." I added, carefully: "I think that the Queen is not a woman for a family, any more than Uther is a family man. They are man and woman for each other, and outside their bed they are King and Queen. It may be that in the future Ygraine will wonder, and ask questions; but that is with the future. For the moment she is content to let him go."

After this we talked on, late into the night, arranging as far as we could the details of the time ahead. Arthur would be left in Brittany until he was three or four years old, then at a safe time of year Ralf would bring him across from Brittany to Ector's home.

"And you?" asked Ector. "Where will you be?"

"Not in Brittany, for the same reason that I can't live here. I shall vanish, Ector. It's a talent that magicians have. And when I do appear again, it will be somewhere that draws men's eyes away from Brittany and Galava." When he questioned me further, I laughed, and refused to enlighten him.

"Truth to tell, my plans are not yet fixed. Now, I've kept you out of your bed for long enough. Your wife will be wondering what sort of mystery man you have been closeted with all these hours. I'll make my apologies when you present me in the morning."

"And I'll make my own now," he said, getting to his feet. "But that's one apology I enjoy making. You miss a lot, you know, Merlin—but then you can't know."

"I know," I said.

"You do? Then you must think it's worth it, life without women?"

"For me, yes."

"Well, then, come this way to your cold bed," he said, and held the door for me.

11

The boy was born on the eve of Christmas, an hour before midnight.

Just before the birth I and the two nobles appointed as witnesses were called into the Queen's chamber, where Gandar attended with Marcia and other women of the Queen's household. One of these was a girl called Branwen who had lately been brought to bed of a dead child; she was to be the child's wet-nurse. When all was done, the baby washed and swaddled, and the Queen sleeping, I took my leave and rode out of the castle and along the track towards Dimilioc. As soon as the lights of the gate-house were out of view I turned my horse aside down the steep path into the valley which runs from the high fields above the headland down to the shore.

The castle at Tintagel is built on a promontory of rock, or near-island, a crag jutting up out of the fearsome seas, which is joined to the cliffs of the mainland only by a narrow causeway. To either side of this causeway the cliffs drop away sheer to small bays of rock and shingle tucked in under the cliff. From one of these a path, narrow and precarious, and passable only on a receding tide, leads up the face of the cliff to a small gate let into the roots of the castle wall. This is the postern, the secret entrance to the castle. Inside is a narrow stairway of stone leading up to the private door of the royal apartments.

Halfway up the steep stairway was a broad landing, and a guard-room. Here I was to wait, until the child was judged fit to be taken abroad into the winter's cold. There were no guards: months past, the King had had the postern sealed, and the guard-room's other door, giving on the main part of the castle, had been built up. For tonight the postern gate had been opened, but no porter manned it; only Ulfin the King's man, and Valerius, his friend and trusted officer, waited there to let me in. Valerius took me up to the guard-room, while Ulfin went out down the path into the bay to take my horse. Ralf was not with me. He had gone to ensure that the Breton ship was waiting as it had promised, and he was also to bring horses and to keep watch each night in the bay below the secret path.

I waited for two days and nights. There was a pallet in the guard-room, and Ulfin himself had kindled a fire to banish the disused chill of the place, and from time to time brought food and fuel, and the news from above stairs. He would have waited on me if I had let him; he was grateful still for some kindness I had shown to him in the past, and I think the King's disfavour had distressed him. But I sent him back to his post at the Queen's door, and spent the waiting time alone.

At the other side of the landing, in the outer wall of the castle and opposite the guard-room door, was another door leading out onto a narrow, level platform skirted waist-high by a battlement. It was not overlooked by any of the castle windows, and below it, between the castle wall and the sea, was an apron of grass sloping down to the edge of the sheer cliffs. In summer the place was alive with nesting sea birds, but now, in midwinter, it was barren and crisp with frost. From below, incessantly, came the suck and hush and thud of the winter sea.

Each day, at dawn and sunset, I walked out to this platform to see if the weather had changed. But for three days there was no change. The air was cold, and below me the grass, grey with rime, was barely distinguishable in the thick mist that held the whole place shrouded, from the invisible sea below the invisible cliffs to the pale blur where the winter sun fought to clear the sky. Below the blanket of mist the sea was quiet, as quiet as it ever is on that raging coast. And every midnight, before I slept, I went out into the icy dark and looked upwards for the stars. But there was only the blank pall of the mist.

Then on the third night, the wind came. A small wind from the west, that crept across the battlements and in under the doors and set the flames fluttering blue round the birch logs. I stood up, listening. I had a hand to the latch of the door when I heard a sound, in the quiet, from the head of the stairway. The door to the Queen's apartments had opened and shut again, gently. I opened the door and looked upwards.

Someone was coming softly down the stairs; a woman, shrouded in a mantle, carrying something. I stepped out onto the landing, and the light from the guard-room door came after me, firelight and shadow.

It was Marcia. I saw the tears glisten on her cheeks as she bent her head over what lay in her arms. A child, wrapped warm against the winter night. She saw me and held her burden out to me. "Take care of him," she said. "Take care of him, as God loves him and you."

I took the child from her. Inside the woollen wrappings I caught the glint of cloth of gold. "And the token?" I asked. She handed me a ring. It was one I had often seen on Uther's hand, made of gold, enclosing a stone of red jasper with a dragon crest carved small. I slipped it on my own finger, and saw her instinctive movement of protest, stilled as she remembered who I was.

I smiled. "For safekeeping only. I shall put it away for him."

"My lord prince . . ." She bent her head. Then she threw

a quick glance over her shoulder to where the girl Branwen, hooded and cloaked, was coming down the stairway, with Ulfin behind her carrying a pack with her effects. Marcia turned back to me swiftly and laid a hand on my arm. "You will tell me where you are taking him?" It was a plea, whispered.

I shook my head. "I'm sorry. It's better that no one should know."

She was silent, her lips working. Then she straightened herself. "Very well. But you promise me that he will be safe? I'm not asking you as a man, or even as a prince. I'm asking you from your power. He will be safe?"

So Ygraine had said nothing, even to Marcia. Marcia's guess at the future was still only a guess. But in the days to come both these women would feel the bitter need for each other's confidence. It would be cruel to leave the Queen isolated with her knowledge and her hopes. It is not true that women cannot keep secrets. Where they love, they can be trusted to death and beyond, against all sense and reason. It is their weakness, and their great strength.

I met Marcia's eyes full for a moment. "He will be King," I said. "The Queen knows it. But for the child's sake, you will tell no one else."

She bent her head again, without replying. Ulfin and Branwen were beside us. Marcia leaned forward gently and drew back a fold of the shawl from the child's face. The baby was sleeping. The eyelids, curiously full, lay over the shut eyes like pale shells. There was a thick down of dark hair on his head. Marcia stooped and kissed him lightly on the head. He slept on, undisturbed. She pulled the fold of wool back to shelter him, then with gentle expert hands settled the bundle closer into my arms. "So. Hold his head so. You will be careful going down the path?"

"I will be careful."

She opened her mouth to speak again, then shook her head quickly, and I saw a tear slide from her cheek to fall on the child's shawl. Then she turned abruptly away, and started back up the stairs.

I carried the baby down the secret path. Valerius went ahead, with his sword drawn and ready, and behind me, with Ulfin's arm to help her, came Branwen. As we reached the bottom and stepped on the grating pebbles, Ralf's shadow detached itself from the immense darkness of the cliffs, and we heard his quick, relieved greeting, and the tread of hoofs on the shingle.

He had brought a mule for the girl, tough and sure-footed. He settled her in the saddle, then I handed the baby up to her, and she folded him close in the warmth of her cloak. Ralf vaulted to the back of his own horse and took the mule's rein in hand. I was to lead the pack-mule. This time I planned to travel as an itinerant singer—a harper is free of kings' courts where a drug-peddler is not—and my harp was strapped to the mule's saddle. Ulfin gave me the lead-rein, then held my gelding for me; it was fresh, and anxious to be moving and warm itself. I said my thanks and farewells, then he and Valerius started back up the cliff path. They would seal the postern again behind them.

I turned my horse's head into the wind. Ralf and the girl had already put their mounts to the bank. I saw the dim shapes pause above me, waiting, and the pale oval of Ralf's face as he turned back to watch me. Then his arm went out, pointing.

"Look!"

I turned.

The mist was lifting, drawing back from a sparkling sky. Faintly, high over the castle promontory, grew a hazy moon of light. Then the last cloud blew clear, billowing before the west wind like a sail blowing towards Brittany, and in its wake, blazing through the sparkle of the lesser stars, grew the great star that had lit the night of Ambrosius' death, and now burned steady in the east for the birth of the Christmas King.

We set spurs to our horses and rode for the ship.

12

The wind stayed fair for Brittany, and we came in sight of the Wild Coast at dawn on the fifth day. Here the sea is never quiet; the cliffs, high and dangerous, towered black with the early light behind them and the teeth of the sea gnawing white at the base; but once round Vindanis Point the seas flattened and ran calmer, and I was even able to leave my cabin in time to watch our arrival at the wharf south of Kerrec which my father and King Budec had built years back when the invasion force was being assembled here.

The morning was still, with a touch of frost and a thin mist pearling the fields. The country hereabouts is flat, field and moorland stretching inland where the wind scours the grass with salt, and for miles nothing grows but pine and wind-bitten thorn. Thin streams wind between steep mudbanks down to the bays and inlets that bite everywhere into the coast, and at low tide the flats teem with shellfish and are loud with the cries of wading birds. For all its dour seeming it is a rich country, and had provided a haven not only for Ambrosius and Uther when Vortigern murdered their brother the King, but for hundreds of other exiles who fled from Vortigern and the threat of the Saxon Terror. Even then, they found parts of the country already peopled by the Celts of Britain. When the Emperor Maximus, a century before, had marched on Rome, those British troops who survived his defeat had straggled back to the refuge of this friendly land. Some had gone home, but a great many had remained to marry and settle; my kinsman, King Hoel, came of one such family. The British had indeed settled in such numbers that men called the peninsula Britain also, dubbing it Less Britain, as their homeland was known as Greater Britain. The language spoken here was still recognizably the same as that of home, and men worshipped the same gods, but the memories of older gods still visibly held the land, and the place was strange. I saw Branwen gazing out over the ship's rail with wide eyes and wondering face, and even Ralf, who had travelled here before as my messenger, had a look of awe as we drew nearer the wharf and saw, beyond the huts and the piles of casks and bales, the first ranks of the standing stones.

These line the fields of Less Britain, rank on rank, like old grey warriors waiting, or armies of the dead. They have stood there, men say, since time began. No one knows why, or how they came there. But I had long known that they were raised, not by giants or gods or even enchanters, but by human engineers whose skill lives on only in song. These skills I learned, when as a boy I lived in Brittany, and men called it magic. For all I know they may be right. One thing is certain, though men's hands lifted the stones, and are long since dust under their roots, the gods they served still walk there. When I have gone between the stones at night, I have felt eyes on my back.

But now the sun was up, gilding the granite surfaces, and throwing the shadows of the stones slanting blue across the frost. The wharf-side was already busy; carts stood ready for loading, and men and boys ran about the business of tying up and unloading the ship. We were the only passengers, but no one cast more than a glance at the travellers in their decent, sober clothes; the musician with the harp in his baggage and his wife and baby beside him, with his servant in attendance. Ralf had lifted the baby from Branwen's arms, and supported her as she trod gingerly down the gangplank. She was silent and pale, and leaned heavily on him. I saw, as he bent over her, how—suddenly, it seemed—he had grown from boy to man. He would be turned sixteen now, and though Branwen was perhaps a year older than he, Ralf might well be taken for her husband, rather than I. He looked brisk and bright, sleek as a springtime cockerel in his neat new clothes. He was the only one of our party, I thought sourly, feeling the wharf tilt and sway under me as if it had still been the heaving deck, who had weathered the passage well.

The escort he had arranged was waiting for us. Not the escort of troops which King Hoel had wanted to provide, but simply a mule litter for Branwen and the child, with a muleteer and one other man, who had brought horses for Ralf and myself. This man came forward now to greet me. From his bearing I judged him to be an officer, but he was not in uniform, and there was nothing to show that the escort came from the King. Nor apparently had the officer been told anything about us, beyond the fact that we were to be led into town and housed there until the King should send for us.

He greeted me civilly, but without the courtesies of rank. "You are welcome, sir. The King sends his greetings, and I am here to escort you into town. I trust you had a good voyage?"

"They tell me so," I said, "but neither I nor the lady are inclined to believe them."

He grinned. "I thought she looked a little green. I know how she feels. I'm not a great one for the sea, myself. And you, sir? Can you ride as far as the town? It's little more than a mile."

"I can try," I said. We exchanged courtesies while Ralf helped Branwen into the litter and drew the curtains against the morning chill. As she settled herself into the warmth the baby woke and began to cry. He had very good lungs, had Arthur. I suppose I must have winced. I saw a gleam of amusement in the officer's face, and said dryly:

"Are you married?"

"Yes, indeed."

"I used to think sometimes what I might be missing. Now I begin to know."

He laughed at that. "One can always escape. It's the best reason I know for being a soldier. Will you mount, sir?"

He and I rode side by side on the way into the town. Kerrec was a sizeable settlement, half civil, half military, walled and moated, clustered round a central hill where the King's stronghold lay. Near the ramp which led up to the castle gate was the house where my father had lived during his years of exile, while he and King Budec assembled and trained the army which had invaded Britain to claim it back for him, her rightful King.

And now, perhaps, her next and greater King was here at my side, still yelling lustily, muffled in a litter, and being carried over the wooden bridge that spanned the moat, and in through the gate of the town.

My companion was silent beside me. Behind us the others rode at ease; they chatted among themselves, the sound of their voices and the sharp clop of the horses' hoofs on the cobbles and the jingling of bits sounding loud in the still and misty daybreak. The town was just waking. Cocks crowed from yards and middens; here and there doors were opened and women, shawled against the cold, could be seen moving with pails or armfuls of kindling to start the day's work.

I was glad of my companion's silence as I looked about me. Even in the five years since I had left it the place seemed to have changed completely. I suppose one cannot pull a standing army out of a town where it has been built and trained for years, and not leave an echoing shell. The army, indeed, had been mainly quartered outside the walls, and the camps had long since been dismantled and gone back to grassland. But in the town, though King Budec's own troops remained, the orderly bustle and the air of purpose and expectancy which had characterized the place in my father's time had gone. In the street of the engineers, where I had served my apprenticeship with Tremorinus, there were a few workshops open and already clanging in the early dawn, but the air of high purpose had gone with the crowd and the clamour, and something almost like desolation had taken its place. I was glad that the way to our lodging did not pass my father's house.

We were lodged with a decent couple, who made us welcome; Branwen and the baby were carried straight off to some women's fastness, while I was shown to a good room where a fire blazed and breakfast was spread waiting beside it. A servant carried the baggage in, and would have stayed to wait on me, but Ralf dismissed him and served the meal himself. I bade him eat with me, and he did so, cheerful and brisk as if the last week or so had been spent holidaying, and when we had done asked if I wanted to go out to explore the town. I gave him leave, but said that I would stay within doors. I am a strong man, and do not readily tire, but it takes more than a mile on dry land and a good breakfast to dispel the grinding sickness and exhaustion of a winter voyage. So I bade Ralf merely see to it that Branwen and the child were comfortable, and, after he had gone, composed myself to rest and wait for the King's summons.

It came at lamplighting, and Ralf with it, wide-eyed, with a robe over his arm of soft combed wool dyed a rich dark blue, with a border worked in gold and silver thread.

"The King sent this for you. Will you wear it?"

"Certainly. It would be an insult to do anything else."

"But it's a prince's robe. People will wonder who you are."

"Not a prince's, no. A singer's robe of honour. This is a civilized country, Ralf, like my own. It's not only princes and soldiers who are held in high esteem. When will King Hoel receive me?"

"In an hour's time, he says. He will receive you alone, before you sing in the hall. What are you laughing at?"

"King Hoel being cunning from necessity. There's only one catch about going as a singer to Hoel's court; he happens to be tone deaf. But even a tone deaf king will receive a travelling singer, to get his news. So he receives me alone. Then if the barons in his hall want to hear me, he doesn't have to sit through it."

"He sent that harp along, though." Ralf nodded to the instrument which stood shrouded near the lamp.

"He sent it, yes, but it was never his; it's my own." He looked at me in surprise. I had spoken more curtly than I had meant to. All day the silent harp had stood there, untouched, but speaking to me of memories, of most, indeed, that I had ever had of happiness. As a boy here in Kerrec, in my father's house, I had played it almost nightly. I added: "It was one I used here, years ago. Hoel's father must have kept it for me. I don't suppose it's been touched since I last played it. I'd better try it before I go. Uncover it, will you?"

A scratch at the door then heralded a slave with a ewer of steaming water. While I washed, and combed my hair, then let the slave help me into the sumptuous blue robe, Ralf uncovered the harp and set it ready.

It was bigger than the one I had brought with me. That was a knee harp, easy to transport; this was a standing harp, with a greater range and a tone which would reach the corners of a King's hall. I tuned it carefully, then ran my fingers over the strings.

To remember love after long sleep; to turn again to poetry after a year in the market place, or to youth after resignation to drowsy and stiffening age; to remember what once you thought life could hold, after telling over with muddied and calculating fingers what it has offered; this is music, made after long silence. The soul flexes its wings, and, clumsy as any fledgling, tries the air again. I felt my way, groping back through the chords, for the passion that slept there in the harp, exploring, testing as a man tests in the dark ground which once he knew in daylight. Whispers, small jags of sound, bunches of notes dragged sharply. The wires thrilled, catching the firelight, and the long running chords lapsed into the song.

There was a hunter at the moon's dark
Who sought to lay a net of gold in the marshes.
A net of gold, a net heavy as gold.
And the tide came in and drowned the net,
Held it invisible, deep, and the hunter waited,
Crouching by the water in the moon's dark.

They came, the birds flighting the dark,
Hundred on hundred, a king's army.
They landed on the water, a fleet of ships,
Of king's ships, proud with silver, silver masted,
Swift ships, fierce in battle,
Crowding the water in the moon's dark.

The net was heavy beneath them, hidden,
    waiting to catch them.
But he lay still, the young hunter, with idle hands.

Hunter, draw in your net. Your children
    will eat tonight,
And your wife will praise you, the cunning hunter.

He drew in his net, the young hunter,
    drew it tight and fast.
It was heavy, and he drew it to shore, among the reeds.
It was heavy as gold, but nothing was there but water.
There was nothing in it but water, heavy as gold,
And one grey feather,
From the wing of a wild goose.

They had gone, the ships, the armies,
into the moon's dark.

And the hunter's children were hungry,
and his wife lamented.
But he slept dreaming, holding the wild goose feather.

King Hoel was a big, thick-bodied man in his middle thirties. During the time I had spent in Kerrec—from my twelfth to my seventeenth year—I had seen very little of him. He had been a lusty and dedicated fighting man, while I was only a youth, and busy with my studies in hospital and workshop. But later he had fought with my father's troops in Greater Britain, and there we had come to know and to like one another. He was a man of big appetites and, as such men often are, good natured and tending to laziness. Since I had last seen him he had put on flesh, and his face had the flush of good living, but I had no doubt he would be as stalwart as ever in the field.

I started by speaking of his father King Budec and the changes that had come, and we talked for a while of past times.

"Ah, yes, those were good years." He stared, chin on fist, into the fire. He had received me in his private chamber, and after we had been served with wine, had dismissed the servants. His two deer-hounds lay stretched on the skins at his feet, dreaming still of the chase they had had that day. His hunting spears, freshly cleaned, stood against the wall behind his chair, their blades catching the firelight. The King stretched his massive shoulders, and spoke wistfully. "I wonder, when will such years come again?"

"You are talking of the fighting years?"

"I am talking of Ambrosius' years, Merlin."

"They will come again, with your help now." He looked

puzzled, then startled, and uneasy. I had spoken prosaically enough, but he had caught the implications. Like Uther, he was a man who liked everything normal, open and ordinary. "You mean the child? The bastard? After all we've heard about it, he'll be the one to succeed Uther?"

"Yes. I promise you."

He fidgeted with his cup, and his eyes slid away from mine. "Ah, yes. Well, we shall keep him safely. But tell me, why the secrecy? I had a letter from Uther asking me openly enough to care for the boy. Ralf couldn't tell me much more than was in the letters he brought. I'll help, of course, every way I can, but I don't want a quarrel with Uther. His letter to me made it pretty clear that this boy's only his heir in default of a better claim."

"That's true. Don't be afraid, I don't want a quarrel, either, between you and Uther. One doesn't throw a precious morsel down between two fighting-dogs and expect it to survive. Until there is a boy with what Uther calls a better claim, he's as anxious as I am to keep this one safe. He knows what I'm doing, up to a point."

"Ah." He cocked an eye at me, intrigued. I had been right about him. He might be well disposed towards Britain, but he was not above doing a quietly back-handed turn to Britain's King. "Up to what point?"

"The time when the baby is weaned, and grown enough to need men's company and to be taught men's arts. Four years, perhaps, or less. After that I shall take him back from you, and he must go home to Britain. If Uther asks where he is, he will have to be told, but until he does—well, there's no need to seek him out, is there? Myself, I doubt if Uther will question you at all. I think he would forget this child if he could. In any case, if there is blame, it is mine. He put the boy in my charge, to rear as I thought fit."

"But will it be safe to take him back? If Uther's sending him here now because of enemies at home, are you sure it will be better then?"

"It's a risk that will have to be taken. I want to be near the child as he grows. It should be in Britain, and therefore it must be in secret. There are bad times coming, Hoel, for us all. I cannot yet see what will happen, beyond these facts; that this boy—this bastard if you like—will have enemies, even more than Uther has. You call him bastard; so will other men with ambition. His secret enemies will be more deadly even than the Saxons. So he must be hidden until the time comes for him to take the crown, and then he must take it with no cast of doubt, and be raised King in the sight of all Britain."

" 'He must be?' You have seen things, then?" But before I could answer he shied quickly away from the strange ground, and cleared his throat. "Well, I'll keep him safe for you, as well as I may. Just tell me what you want. You know your own business, always did. I'll trust you to keep me right with Uther." He gave his great laugh. "I remember how Ambrosius used to say that your judgment in matters of policy, even when you were a youngling, was worth ten of any bedroom emperor's." My father, naturally, had said no such thing, and in any case would hardly have said it to Hoel, who had a fair reputation himself as a lover, but I took it as it was intended, and thanked him. He went on: "Well, tell me what you want. I confess I'm puzzled. . . . These enemies you talk of, won't they guess he's in Brittany? You say Uther made no secret of his plans, and when the time comes for the royal ship to sail and it's seen that you and the child aren't on it, won't they simply think he was sent over earlier, and search first for him here in Brittany?"

"Probably. But by that time he'll be disposed of in the

place I've arranged for him, and that's not the kind of place where Uther's nobles would think of looking. And I myself will be gone."

"What place is that? Am I to know?"

"Of course. It's a small village near your boundary, north, towards Lanascol."

"What?" He was startled, and showed it. One of the hounds stirred and opened an eye. "North? At the edge of Gorlan's land? Gorlan is no friend to the Dragon."

"Nor to me," I said. "He's a proud man, and there is an old score between his house and my mother's. But he has no quarrel with you?"

"No, indeed," said Hoel fervently, with the respect of one fighting man for another.

"So I believed. So Gorlan isn't likely to make forays into the edge of your territory. What's more, who would dream that I would hide the child so near him? That with all Brittany to choose from, I'd leave him within bowshot of Uther's enemy? No, he'll be safe. When I leave him, I'll do so with a quiet mind. But that's not to say I'm not deeply in your debt." I smiled at him. "Even the stars need help at times."

"I'm glad to hear it," said Hoel gruffly. "We mere kings like to think we have our parts to play. But you and your stars might make it a bit easier for us, perhaps? Surely, in all that great forest north of here, there must be safer places than the very edge of my lands?"

"Possibly, but it happens that I have a safe house there. The one person in both the Britains who'll know exactly what to do with the child for the next four years, and will care for him as she would for her own."

"She?"

"Yes. My own nurse, Moravik. She's a Breton born, and after Maridunum was sacked in Camlach's war she left South Wales and went home. Her father owned a tavern north of

144

here at a place called Coll. Since he'd grown too old for work, a fellow called Brand kept it for him. Brand's wife was dead, and soon after Moravik returned home she and Brand married, just to keep things right in the sight of God . . . and, knowing Moravik, I'm not just talking about the inn's title deeds. . . . They keep the place still. You must have passed it, though I doubt if you'd ever stop there—it stands where two streams join and a bridge crosses them. Brand's a retired soldier of your own, and a good man—and in any case will do as Moravik bids him." I smiled. "I never knew a man who didn't, except perhaps my grandfather."

"Ye—es." He still sounded doubtful. "I know the village, a handful of huts by the bridge, that's all. . . . As you say, hardly a likely place to hunt a High King's heir. But an inn? Isn't that in itself a risk? With men—Gorlan's, too, since it's a time of truce—coming and going from the road?"

"So, no one will question your messengers or mine. My man Ralf will stay there to guard the boy, and he'll need to stay abreast of news, and get messages to you from time to time, and to me."

"Yes. Yes, I see. And when you take the child there, what's your story?"

"No one will think twice about a travelling harper plying his trade on a journey. And Moravik has put a story round that will explain the sudden appearance of Ralf and the baby and his nurse. The story, if anyone questions it, will be that the girl, Branwen, is Moravik's niece, who bore a child to her master over in Britain. Her mistress cast her from the house, and she had no other place to go, but the man gave her money for the passage to her aunt's house in Brittany, and paid the travelling singer and his man to escort her. And the singer's man, meanwhile, will decide to leave his master and stay with the girl."

"And the singer himself? How long will you stay there?"

"Only as long as a travelling singer might, then I'll move on and be forgotten. By the time anyone even thinks to look farther for Uther's child, how can they find him? No one knows the girl, and the baby is only a baby. Every house in the country has one or more to show."

He nodded, chewing it over this way and that, and asked a few more questions. Finally he admitted: "It will serve, I suppose. What do you want me to do?"

"You have watchers in the kingdoms that march with yours?"

He laughed shortly. "Spies? Who hasn't?"

"Then you'll hear quickly enough if there's any hint of trouble from Gorlan or anyone else. And if you can arrange for some quick and secret contact with Ralf, should it be necessary—?"

"Easy. Trust me. Anything I can do, short of war with Gorlan . . ." He gave his deep chuckle again. "Eh, Merlin, it's good to see you. How long can you stay?"

"I'll take the boy north tomorrow, and with your permission will go unescorted. I'll come back as soon as I see all is safe. But I'll not come here again. You might be expected to receive a travelling singer once, but not actually to encourage him."

"No, by God!"

I grinned. "If this weather holds, Hoel, could the ship stay for me for a few days?"

"For as long as you like. Where do you plan to go?"

"Massilia first, then overland to Rome. After that, eastwards."

He looked surprised. "You? Well, here's a start! I'd always thought of you being as fixed as your own misty hills. What put that into your head?"

"I don't know. Where do ideas come from? I have to lose myself for a few years, till the child needs me, and this seemed to be the way. Besides, there was something I heard."

I did not tell him that it had only been the wind in the bowstrings. "I've had a mind lately to see some of the lands I learned about as a boy."

We talked on then for a while. I promised to send letters back with news from the eastern capitals, and, as far as I could, I gave him points of call to which he would send his own tidings and Ralf's about Arthur.

The fire died down and he roared for a servant. When the man had been and gone—

"You'll have to go and sing in the hall soon," said Hoel. "So if we've got all clear, we'll leave it at that, shall we?" He leaned back in his chair. One of the hounds got to its feet and pushed against his knee, asking for a caress. Over the sleek head the King's eyes gleamed with amusement. "Well now, you've still to give me the news from Britain. And the first thing you can do is to tell me the inside story of what happened nine months ago."

"If you in your turn will tell me what the public story is."

He laughed. "Oh, the usual stories that follow you as closely as your cloak flapping in the wind. Enchantments, flying dragons, men carried through the air and through walls, invisibly. I'm surprised, Merlin, that you take the trouble to come by ship like an ordinary man, when your stomach serves you so ill. Come now, the story."

It was very late when I got back to our lodging. Ralf was waiting, half asleep in the chair by the fire in my room. He jumped up when he saw me, and took the harp from me.

"Is all well?"

"Yes. We go north in the morning. No, thank you, no wine. I drank with the King, and they made me drink again in the hall."

"Let me take your cloak. You look tired. Did you have to sing to them?"

"Certainly." I held out a handful of silver and gold pieces,

147

and a jewelled pin. "It's nice to think, isn't it, that one can earn one's keep so handsomely? The jewel was from the King, a bribe to stop me singing, otherwise they'd have had me there yet. I told you this was a cultured country. Yes, cover the big harp. I'll take the other with me tomorrow." Then as he obeyed me: "What of Branwen and the baby?"

"Went to bed three hours since. She's lying with the women. They seem very pleased to have a baby to look after." He finished on a note of surprise which made me laugh.

"Did he stop crying?"

"Not for an hour or two. They didn't seem to mind that, either."

"Well, no doubt he'll start again at cock-crow, when we rouse them. Now go to bed and sleep while you can. We start at first light."

13

There is a road leading almost due north out of the town of Kerrec, the old Roman road which runs straight as a spear-cast across the bare, salty grassland. A mile out of town, beyond the ruined posting station, you can see the forest ahead of you like a slow tidal wave approaching to swallow the salt flats. This is a vast stretch of woodland, deep and wild. The road spears straight into it, aiming for the big river that cuts the country from east to west. When the Romans held Gallia there was a fort and settlement beyond the river, and the road was built to serve it; but now the river marks the boundary of Hoel's kingdom, and the fort is one of Gorlan's strongholds. The writ of neither king runs far into the forest, which stretches for countless hilly miles, covering the rugged center of the Breton peninsula. What traffic there is keeps to the road; the wild land is served only by the tracks of charcoal-burners and wood-cutters and men who move secretly outside the law. At the time of which I write the place was called the Perilous Forest, and was reputed to be magic-bound and haunted. Once leave the road and plunge into the tracks that twist through the tangled trees, and you could travel for days and hardly see the sun.

When my father had held command in Brittany under King Budec, his troops had kept order even in the forest, as far as the river where King Budec's land ended and King Gorlan's began. They had cut the trees well back to either side of the road, and opened up some of the subsidiary tracks, but this had been neglected, and now the saplings and the bushes had crowded in. The paved surface of the road had long since been broken by winter, and here and there it crumbled off into patches of iron-hard mud that in soft weather would be a morass.

We set out on a grey, cold day, with the wind tasting faintly of salt. But though the wind blew damp from the sea it brought no rain with it, and the going was fair enough. The huge trees stood on either hand like pillars of metal, holding a weight of low, grey sky. We rode in silence, and after a few miles the thickly encroaching growth of the underwood forced us, even on this road, to ride in single file. I was in the lead, with Branwen behind me, and Ralf in the rear leading the pack-mule. I had been conscious for the first hour or so of Ralf's tension, the way his head turned from side to side as he watched and listened; but we saw and heard nothing except the quiet winter life of the forest; a fox, a pair of roe deer, and once a shadowy shape that might have been a wolf slipping away among the trees. Nothing else; no sound of horses, no sign of men.

Branwen showed no hint of fear. When I glanced back I saw her always serene, sitting the neat-footed mule stolidly, with an unmoved calm that held no trace of uneasiness. I have said little about Branwen, because I have to confess that I remember very little about her. Thinking back now over the span of years, I see only a brown head bent over the baby she carried, a rounded cheek and downcast eyes and a shy voice. She was a quiet girl who—though she talked easily enough to Ralf—rarely addressed me of her own will, being painfully in awe of me both as prince and enchanter. She seemed to have no inkling of any risk or danger in our journey, nor did she seem stirred—as most girls would have been—by the excitement of travelling abroad to a new country. Her imperturbable calm was not due to confidence in myself or Ralf; I came to see that she was meek and biddable to the point of stupidity, and her devotion to the baby was such as to blind her to all else. She was the kind of woman whose only life is in the bearing and rearing of children, and without Arthur she would, I am sure, have suffered bitterly over the loss of her own baby. As it was, she seemed to have forgotten this, and spent the hours in a kind of dreamy contentment that was exactly what Arthur needed to make the discomforts of the journey tolerable.

Towards noon we were deep in the forest. The branches laced thick overhead, and in summer would have shut out the sky like a pitched shield, but above the bare boughs of winter we could see a pale and shrouded point of light where the sun struggled to be through. I watched for a sheltered place where we could leave the road without showing too many traces, and presently, just as the baby woke and began to fret, saw a break in the undergrowth and turned my horse aside.

There was a path, narrow and winding, but in the sparse growth of winter it was passable. It led into the forest for a hundred paces or so before it divided, one path leading on deeper among the trees, the other—no more than a deer-trod —winding steeply up to skirt the base of a rocky spur. We followed the deer-trod. This picked its way through fallen boulders tufted with dead and rusty fern, then led upwards round a stand of pines, and faded into the bleached grass of a tiny clearing above the rock. Here, in a hollow, the sun came with a faint warmth. We dismounted, and I spread a saddle-cloth in the most sheltered spot for the girl, while Ralf tethered the horses below the pines and threw down feed from the hay nets. Then we sat ourselves down to eat. I sat at the lip of the hollow, with my back against a tree, a post from which I could see the main path running below the rock. Ralf stayed with Branwen. It had been a long time since we had broken our fast, and we were all hungry. The baby, indeed, had begun to yell lustily as the mule scrambled up the steep path. Now he found his cries stifled against the girl's nipple, and fell silent, sucking busily.

The forest was very quiet. Most wild creatures lie still at noon. The only thing moving was a carrion crow, which flapped heavily down onto a pine above us, and began to caw. The horses finished their feed and dozed, hip-shotten, heads low. The baby still fed, but more slowly, drowsing into milky sleep. I leaned back against the stem of the tree. I could hear Branwen murmuring to Ralf. He said something, and I heard her laugh, then through the murmur of the two young voices I caught another, distant, sound. Horses, at the trot.

At my word the boy and girl fell abruptly silent. Ralf was on his feet in the blink of an eye, and kneeling beside me to watch the path below. I signed Branwen to stay where she was. I need not have troubled; she had turned a wondering look on us, then the baby hiccupped, and she held him to her shoulder, patting him, all her attention on him again. Ralf and I knelt at the edge of the clearing, watching the path below.

The horses—there were two of them by the sound of it—could not be wood-cutters' beasts nor the slow train of the charcoal-burners. Trotting horses, in the Perilous Forest, meant only one thing, trouble. And travellers who carried, as we did, gold for the baby's keep were quarry for any outlaws and disaffected men. Hampered as we were by Branwen and Arthur, both fighting and flight were impossible. Nor was it easy, with the baby, to keep silent and let danger pass by so closely. I had made it clear to Ralf that whatever happened he was to stay with the girl and, at the least hint of danger, leave it to me to devise some way of drawing the danger away. Ralf had protested, mutinied, then finally seen the sense of it and sworn to obey.

So now when I whispered, "Only two, I think. If they don't come up this way, they'll not see us. Get to the horses. And for God's sake tell the girl to keep the baby quiet," he merely nodded, melting back from my side. He stooped to whisper to Branwen, and I saw her nod placidly, shifting the child to her other breast. Ralf slipped like a shadow among the pines where the horses stood. I waited, watching the path.

The riders were approaching. There was no other sound except the crow, still cawing high in the pine tree. Then I saw them. Two horses, trotting single file; poor beasts, heavy bred and none too well fed by the look of them, careless how they put their feet, and having to be hauled up by their cursing riders at every hole or root across the path. It was a fair enough guess that the men were outlaws. They were as unkempt as their beasts, and looked half savage, and dangerous. They were dressed in what looked like old uniforms, and on the arm of one of them was a dirty badge, half torn away. It looked like Gorlan's. The fellow in the rear rode carelessly, lolling in the saddle as if half drunken, but the man in front pricked at the alert, as such men learn to do, his head moving from side to side like that of a questing dog. He held a bow at the ready. Through the rotten leather of the sheath at his thigh I saw the long knife, burnished to a killing point.

They were almost below me. They were passing. There had been no sound from the baby, nor from our horses, hidden among the pines. Only the carrion crow, balancing high in the sunshine, scolded noisily.

I saw the fellow with the bow lift his head. He said something over his shoulder, in a thick accent I could not catch. He grinned, showing a row of rotten teeth, then lifted his bow, notched it, and sent an arrow whizzing into the pine. It hit. The crow shot upwards off the bough with a yell, then fell, transfixed. It landed within two paces of Branwen and the child, flapped for a second or two, then lay still.

As I dodged back and ran for the pines I heard both men laughing. Now the marksman would come to retrieve his arrow. Already I could hear him forcing his beast through the underbrush. I picked up the arrow, crow and all, and flung it out over the edge of the hollow. It landed down among the boulders. From the path the man could not have seen where the bird fell; it was a chance that he might believe it had fluttered there, and would ride no farther. I saw Branwen's eyes, startled and wondering, as I ran past her. But she did not stir, and the baby slept at her breast. I gave her a sign which was meant to convey reassurance, approval, and warning all in one, and ran for my horse.

Ralf was holding the beasts quiet, heads together, muffling eyes and nostrils with his cloak. I paused beside him, listening. The outlaws were coming on. They must not have seen the crow; they came on without pausing, making for the pines.

I seized my sorrel's bridle from Ralf, and turned it to mount. The horse circled, treading the dry stalks and snapping twigs. I heard the sudden clatter and tramp as the outlaws dragged their beasts to a standstill. One of them said, "Listen!" in Breton, and there was the rasp of metal as weapons came hissing out. I was in the saddle. My own sword was out. I pulled the sorrel's head round, and had opened my mouth to shout when I heard another cry from the path, then the same voice yelling "Look! Look there!" and my horse reared sharply back on its haunches as something broke out of the bushes beside me and went by so close that it almost brushed my leg.

It was a hind, white against the winter forest. She scudded through the pines like a ghost, bounded along the top of the hollow where we had lain, stood poised for a moment in view at the edge, then vanished down the steep, boulder-strewn slope, straight into the path of the two outlaws. I heard shouts of triumph from below, the crack of a whip, the sudden thud and flurry of hoofs as the men wrenched their horses back to the path and lashed them to a gallop. They were giving hunting calls. I jumped from the saddle, threw the sorrel's reins to Ralf, and ran back to my place above the rock. I reached it in time to see the two of them going back full tilt the way they had come. Ahead of them, dimly seen for a moment, like a scud of mist through the bare trees, fled the white hind. Then the laughter, the hunting cries, the hammer of hard-driven horses, echoed plunging back through the forest, and was gone.

14

The river which marks the boundary of Hoel's kingdom flows right through the heart of the forest. In places it cuts a deep gorge between overhanging banks of trees, and everywhere in the central part of the forest the land is seamed by small, wild valleys where tributary streams wind or tumble into the main. But there is a place, almost in the center of the forest, where the river valley is wider and more gentle, forming a green basin where men have tilled the fields, and over the years have cut back the forest to make grazing land round the small settlement called Coll, which in Breton means the Hidden Place. Here there had been, in past times, a Roman transit camp on the road from Kerrec to Lanascol. All that remained of this now was the squared outline where the original ditch had been dug beside the tributary. Here lay the village. On two sides of it the stream made a natural defense or moat; for the rest, the Roman ditch had been cleared and widened, and filled with water. Inside this were steep defensive earthworks, crowned with palisades. The bridge had been a stone one in Roman times; the piles still stood and were spanned now with planking. Though the village lay near Gorlan's border, it was accessible from it only through the narrow pass cut by the river, and there the road had crumbled almost back to the original rocky path that wolves and wild men had used before the Romans ever came. Coll was well named.

Brand's tavern lay just inside the gate. The main street of the village was little more than a dirty alley floored unevenly with cobbles. The inn stood a little way back from this, on the right. It was a low building, roughly built of stone, with mortar slapped haphazardly into the gaps. The outbuildings round the yard were no more than wattle huts, daubed with mud. The roof was newly thatched, with good close work of reeds held down by a net of rope weighted with heavy stones. The door was open, as the door of an inn should be, with a heavy curtain of skins hung across the opening to keep the weather out. Through the chimney hole at one end rose a sluggish column of smoke that smelled of peat.

We arrived at dusk when the gates were closing. Everywhere mingled with the peat smoke came the smells of supper cooking. There were few people about; the children had been called in long since, and the men were home at their supper. Only a few hungry-looking dogs skulked here and there; an old woman hurried past with a shawl held over her face and a fowl squawking under her other arm; a man led a yoke of weary oxen along the street. I could hear the clink of a smith's anvil not far away, and smell the sharp fume of burned hoofs.

Ralf eyed the inn dubiously. "It looked better in October, on a sunny day. It's not much of a place, is it?"

"All the better," I said. "No one will come looking in a place like this for the son of the King of Britain. Go in now and play your part, while I hold the horses."

He pushed aside the curtain and went in. I helped Branwen dismount, and settled her on one of the benches beside the door. The baby woke, and began to whimper, but almost immediately Ralf came out again, followed by a big, burly man and a boy. The man must be Brand himself; he had been a fighting man and still bore himself like one, and I saw the puckered seam of an old wound across the back of one hand.

He hesitated, uncertain how to greet me. I said quickly: "You'll be the innkeeper? I'm Emrys the singer, who was to

157

bring your wife's niece along with us, with the baby. You're expecting us, I believe?"

He cleared his throat. "Indeed, indeed. You're most welcome. My wife's been looking for you this week past." He saw the boy staring, and added sharply: "What are you waiting for? Take the horses round the back."

The boy darted to obey. Brand, ducking his head at me and indicating the door of the inn with a gesture that was half invitation, half salute, said: "Come in, come in. Supper's cooking." Then, doubtfully, "It's mighty rough company we get here, but maybe—"

"I'm used to rough company," I said tranquilly, and preceded him through the door.

This was not a time of year for much coming and going on the roads, so the place was not crowded. There were some half-dozen men, dimly seen in a room lit only by one tallow candle and the light from the peat fire. The talk hushed as we went in, and I saw the looks at the harp I carried, and the whisper that went round. Nobody spared a glance for the girl carrying the baby. Brand said, a shade too quickly: "On through there. That far door, behind the fire." Then the door shut behind us, and there in the back room stood Moravik, fists on her hips, waiting to greet us.

Like everyone else whom one has not seen since childhood, she had shrunk. When I had last seen her I had been a boy of twelve, and tall for my age. Even then she had seemed much bigger than I was, a creature of bulk and commanding voice, surrounded by the aura of authority and infallible decisions left over from the nursery. Now she came no higher than my collar-bone, but she still had the bulk and the voice, and—I was to find—the authority. Though I had turned out to be the favoured son of the High King of all Britain, I was still, obviously, the wayward small boy from her first nursery.

Her first words were characteristic. "And a fine time of night to come, with the gates just shutting! You could have been out in that forest all night, and a precious lot there'd have been left of you by morning, what with the wolves, and worse, that lives out there. And damp, too, I shouldn't wonder—sweet saints and stars preserve us, look at your cloak! Get it off this minute, and come to the fire. There's a good supper cooking, special for you. I remember all the things you like, and I never thought to see you sitting at my table again, young Merlin, not after that night when the place burned down round you, and there was nothing to be found of you in the morning but a few burned bones in your room." Then suddenly she came forward with a rush and had hold of me. There were tears on her face. "Eh, Merlin, little Merlin, but it's good to see you again."

"And you, Moravik." I embraced her. "I swear you must have got younger every year since you left Maridunum. And now you're putting me in your debt again, you and your good man here. I'll not forget it, and neither will the King. Now, this is Ralf, my companion, and this"—drawing the girl forward—"is Branwen, with the child."

"Eh, the baby! The good Goddess save us all! What with seeing you, Merlin, I'd forgotten all about him! Come near the fire, girl, don't stand there in the draught. Come to the fire, and let me see him . . . Eh, the lamb, the bonny lamb. . . ."

Brand touched my arm, grinning. "And now, what with seeing *him*, she'll forget everything else, my lord. It's lucky she got the supper ready for you before she got a sight of the baby. Sit you down here. I'll serve you myself."

Moravik had made a rich mutton stew, satisfying and very hot. The mutton of the Breton salt flats is as good even as anything we get in Wales. There were dumplings with the stew, and good new bread hot from the oven. Brand brought a

159

jug of red wine, very much better than anything we can make at home. He waited on us while Moravik busied herself with Branwen and the baby, whose whimpering had broken now into lusty crying, only to be stilled by Branwen's breast. The fire blazed and crackled, the room was warm and smelled of good food and wine, the firelight traced the shape of the girl's cheek, and the baby's head. I became conscious of someone watching me, and turned my head to see Ralf's eyes on my face. He opened his mouth as if to speak, but at that moment some clamour from the outer room made Brand set the wine-jug down on the table, excuse himself quickly to me, and hurry out. He left the door slightly ajar. Beyond it I could hear voices raised in what sounded like persuasion or argument. Brand answered, quietly, but the clamour persisted.

He came back into the room, looking worried, and shut the door behind him. "My lord, there's those outside who saw you come in, and saw you'd a harp with you. Now, well, it's only natural, my lord, they want a song. I tried to argue them out of it, said you were tired, and had come a long way, but they insisted. Said they'd pay for your supper, between them, if the song was a good one."

"Well," I said, "why not let them?"

His mouth dropped open. "But—sing to them? You?"

"Don't you hear anything in Brittany?" I asked him. "I really am a singer. And it wouldn't be the first time I've earned my fee."

From her place near Branwen beside the fire, Moravik looked up quickly. "Here's a new start! Potions and such I knew about, learned from that old hermit above the mill, and even magic—" crossing herself. "But music? Who taught you?"

"Queen Olwen taught me the notes," I said, adding, to

Brand, "That was my grandfather's wife, a Welsh girl who sang like a laverock. Then later when I was here in Brittany with Ambrosius I learned from a master. You may have heard him, perhaps? An old blind singer, who had travelled and made music in every country in the world."

Brand nodded as if he knew the man I spoke of, but Moravik looked doubtfully at me, tut-tutting, and shaking her head. I suppose no one who has reared a boy from babyhood, and not seen him since his twelfth year, ever thinks he can be a master at anything. I grinned at them. "Why, I played in front of King Hoel, back there in Kerrec. Not that he's anything of a judge, but Ralf has heard me, too. Ask him, if you think I can't earn my supper."

Brand said doubtfully: "But you'll not want to be singing to the likes of them, my lord?"

"Why not? A travelling minstrel sings where he's hired to sing. And that's what I am, while I'm in Less Britain." I got to my feet. "Ralf, bring me the harp. Finish the wine yourself, and then get to bed. Don't wait for me."

I went out into the tavern's public room. This had filled up now; there were about twenty men there, crowded in the smoky warmth. When I went in there were shouts of "The singer, the singer!" and "A tale, a tale!"

"Make room for me then, good people," I said. A stool was vacated for me near the fire, and someone poured me a cup of wine. I sat down and began to tune the harp. They fell still, watching me.

They were simple folk, and such folk like tales of marvels. When I asked them what they would have, they asked for this tale and that of gods and battles and enchantments, so in the end—my mind, I think, on the child sleeping in the next room—I gave them the story of Macsen's Dream. This is as much a tale of magic as any of the rest, though its

161

hero is the Roman commander Magnus Maximus, who was real enough. The Celts call him Macsen Wledig, and the legend of Macsen's Dream was born in the singing valleys of Dyfed and Powys, where every man claims Prince Macsen as his own, and the stories have gone from mouth to mouth until, if Maximus himself appeared to tell them the truth, no one would believe him. It's a long story, the Dream, and every singer has his own version of it. This is the one I sang that night:

Macsen, Emperor of Rome, went hunting, and being tired in the heat of the day lay down to sleep on the banks of the great river that flows towards Rome, and he dreamed a dream.

He dreamed that he journeyed along the river towards its source, and came to the highest mountain in the world; and from there followed another fair flowing river through the rich fields and broad woodlands till he reached the mouth of the river, and there at its mouth was a city of turrets and castles crowded round a fair harbour. And in that harbour lay a ship of gold and silver with no man on board, but with all sails set and shivering to the wind out of the east. He crossed a gangplank made of the white bone of a whale, and the ship sailed.

And soon, after a sunset and a sunset, he came to the fairest island of all the world, and leaving the ship, he traversed the island from sea to sea. And there on the western shore he saw an island at hand across a narrow strait. And on the near shore where he stood was a fair castle, with an open gate. Then Macsen entered the castle and found himself in a great hall with golden pillars, and walls dazzling with gold and silver and precious stones. In that hall two youths sat playing chess on a silver board, and near them an old man in an ivory chair carved chessmen for them out of crystal. But Macsen had no eyes for all this splendour. More beautiful than silver and ivory and precious stones was a maiden, who sat still as a queen in her golden chair. The moment the Emperor saw her he loved her, and, raising her, he embraced her and begged her to be his wife. But in the very moment of the embrace he woke, and found himself in the valley outside Rome, with his companions watching him.

Then Macsen leaped to his feet and told his dream; and messengers were sent the length and breadth of the world, to find the land he had traversed, and the castle with the beautiful maiden. And after many months, and a score of false journeys, one man found them, and came home to tell his master. The island, most beautiful in all the world, was Britain, and the castle by the western sea was Caer Seint, by Segontium, and the island across the shining strait was Mona, isle of druids. So Macsen journeyed to Britain, and found everything just as he had dreamed it, and requested the hand of the maiden from her father and her brothers, and made her his Empress. Her name was Elen, and she bore Macsen two sons and a daughter, and in her honour he built three castles, in Segontium, Caerleon and Maridunum, which was called Caer Myrddin in honour of the god of high places.

Then, because Macsen stayed in Britain and forgot Rome, they made a new emperor in Rome, who set his standard on the walls and defied Macsen. So Macsen raised an army of the Britons, and, with Elen and her brothers at his side, set out for Rome; and he conquered Rome. Thereafter he stayed in Rome, and Britain saw him no more, but Elen's two brothers took the British forces back to their homes, and to this day the seed of Macsen Wledig reigns in Britain.

When I had done, and the last note had hummed away to nothing in the smoky stillness, there was a roar of applause, cups thumping on the tables, and rough voices calling for more music, and more wine. Another cupful was pressed on me, and while I drank and rested before singing again, the men went back to talking among themselves, but softly, lest they disturb the singer's thoughts.

It was as well they could not guess at them; I was wondering what they would do if they knew that the last and latest scion of Maximus lay sleeping on the other side of the wall. For this part of the legend, at least, was true, that my father's family was descended straight from Maximus' marriage with the Welsh princess Elen. The rest of the legend, like all such tales, was a kind of dreaming distortion of the truth, as if an artist, reassembling a broken mosaic from a few worn and random fragments, rebuilt the picture in his own shimmering new colours, with here and there the pieces of the old, true picture showing plain.

The facts were these. Maximus, a Spaniard by birth, had commanded the armies in Britain under his general Theodosius at a time when Saxons and Picts were raiding the coasts constantly, and the Roman province of Britain looked like crumbling to its fall. Between them the commanders repaired the Wall of Hadrian, and held it, and Maximus himself rebuilt and garrisoned the great fortress at Segontium in Wales, and made it his headquarters. This is the place that is called Caer Seint by the British; it is the "fair castle" of the Dream, and here it must have been that Maximus met his Welsh Elen, and married her.

Then in the year that Ector had called the Flood Year it was Maximus (though his enemies denied him the credit) who after months of bitter fighting drove the Saxons back and constructed the provinces of Strathclyde and Manau Guotodin, buffer states, in whose shelter the people of Britain—his people—might live in peace. Already "Prince Macsen" to the folk of Wales, he was declared Emperor by his troops, and so might have remained, but for the events everyone knows of which took him abroad to avenge his old general's murder, and thereafter to march on Rome itself.

He never came back; here again the Dream is true; but not because he conquered Rome and stayed to rule it. He was defeated there, and later executed, and though some of the British forces who had gone with him came home and pledged themselves to his widow and his sons, the brief peace was over. With Maximus dead the Flood came again, and this time there was no sword to stop it.

Small wonder, in the dark years that followed, that the short stretch of Maximus' victorious peace should appear to men like a lost age as golden as any the poets sing. Small wonder that the legend of "Macsen the Protector" had grown and grown until his power compassed the earth, and in their dark times men spoke of him as of a god-sent saviour. . . .

My thoughts went back to the baby sleeping in the straw. I lifted the harp again, and when they hushed for me, sang them another song:

> *There was a boy born,*
> *A winter king.*
> *Before the black month*
> *He was born,*
> *And fled in the dark month*
> *To find shelter*
> *With the poor.*
>
> *He shall come*
> *With the spring*
> *In the green month*
> *And the golden month*
> *And bright*
> *Shall be the burning*
> *Of his star.*

"And did you earn your supper?" asked Moravik.

"Plenty to drink, and three copper coins." I laid them on

the table and put the leather bag containing the King's gold beside them. "That's for your care of the child. I'll send more when it's needed. You'll not regret this, you and Brand. You've nursed kings before, Moravik, but never such a king as this one will be."

"What do I care for kings? That's nought but a bonny bairn, that should never have been set to such a journey in this weather. He should be home in his own nursery, and you can tell your King Uther that from me! Gold, indeed!" But the leather bag had vanished into some fastness of her skirt, and the coins with it.

"He's come to no harm on the journey?" I asked quickly.

"None that I can see. That's a good, strong boy, and like to flourish as well as any of my children. He's abed now, and those two young things with him, poor children, so keep your voice down and let them sleep."

Branwen and the child lay on a pallet in the far corner of the room, away from the fire. Their bed was underneath the flight of rough wooden steps which led up to a platform, like a small loft such as they use for hay in kings' stables. Indeed there was hay stacked there, and our beasts had been led in from the yard at the back, and were tethered now under the loft. A donkey, which I suppose was Brand's own, stood near them in the straw.

"Brand brought yours in," said Moravik. "There isn't much room, but he daren't leave them outside in the byre. That sorrel of yours with the white blaze, someone might know it for King Hoel's own, and there'd be questions asked that weren't too easy to answer. I've put you up above, and the boy. It's maybe not what you're used to, but it's soft, and it's clean."

"It'll be fine. But don't send me to bed yet, please, Moravik. May I stay up and talk to you?"

"Hm. Send you to bed, indeed! Aye, you always did look meek and talk soft, and you doing exactly as you wanted all the time. . . ." She sat down by the fire, spreading her skirts, and nodded to a stool. "Well, now, sit down and let me look at you. Mercy me, and here's a change! Who'd ever have thought it, back there in Maridunum, with hardly a decent rag to your name, that you'd turn out a son of the High King himself, and a doctor and a singer . . . and the sweet saints only know what else besides!"

"A magician, you mean?"

"Well, that never surprised me, the way I heard you'd been running off to the old man at Bryn Myrddin." She crossed herself, and her hand closed on an amulet at her neck. I had seen it glinting in the firelight; it was hardly a Christian symbol. So Moravik still hedged herself around with every talisman she could find. In this she was like most of the folk bred in the Perilous Forest, with its tales of old haunt-ings, and things seen in the twilight and heard in the wind. She nodded at me. "Aye, you always were a queer lad, with your solitary ways, and the things you'd say. Always knew too much, you did. I thought it was with listening at doors, but it seems I was wrong. 'The King's prophet,' they tell me you're called now. And the doings I've heard about, if the half of them's to be believed, which I doubt they're not . . . Well, now, tell me. Tell me everything."

The fire had burned low, almost to ash. There was silence from the next room now; the drinkers had either gone home, or settled to sleep. Brand had climbed the ladder an hour since, and snored softly beside Ralf. In the corner beside the dozing beasts, Branwen and the child slept, unmoving.

"And now here's this new start," said Moravik softly. "This baby here, you tell me he's the son of the High King,

Uther himself, that won't own to him. Why do you have to take it on yourself to look after him? I'd have thought there's others he might ask, that could do it easier."

"I can't answer for King Uther," I said, "but for myself, you might say the child was a trust left to me by my father, and by the gods."

"The gods?" she asked sharply. "What talk is this for a good Christian man?"

"You forget, I was never baptized."

"Not even yet? Aye, I remember the old King would have none of it. Well, that's no concern of mine now, only of your own. But this child here, is he christened?"

"No. There's been no time. If you want to, then have him christened."

" 'If you want to'? What way is that to talk? What 'gods' were you talking of just now?"

"I hardly know. They—he—will make himself known in his own good time. Meanwhile have the boy christened, Moravik. When he leaves Brittany he's to be reared in a Christian household."

She was satisfied. "As soon as may be. I'll see him right with the dear Lord and his saints, trust me for that. And I've hung the vervain charm over his crib, and seen the nine prayers said. The girl says his name's Arthur. What sort of a name is that?"

"You would say Artos," I told her. This is a name meaning "Bear" in Celtic. "But don't call him by that name here. Give him some other name that you can use, and forget the other."

"Emrys, then? Ah, I thought that would make you smile. I'd always hoped that one day there'd be a child I could call after you."

"No, after my father Ambrosius, as I was called." I tried the names over to myself, in Latin and then in the Celtic tongue. *"Artorius Ambrosius, last of the Romans . . . Artos Emrys, first of the British . . ."* Then aloud to Moravik, smiling: "Yes, call him so. Once, long ago, I foretold it, the coming of the Bear, a king called Arthur, who would knit past and future. I had forgotten, till now, where I had heard the name before. Christen him so."

She was silent for a few minutes. I saw her quick eyes searching my face. "In trust to you, you said. A king such as there hasn't been before. He will be King, then? You swear he will be King?" Then suddenly: "Why do you look like that, Merlin? I saw you look the same way a while back when the girl put the child to her breast. What is it?"

"I don't know . . ." I spoke slowly, my eyes on the last glimmer of fire where the burned logs hollowed round a red cave. "Moravik, I have done what I have done because God—whichever god he is—drove me to do it. Out of the dark he told me that the child which Uther begot of Ygraine that night at Tintagel would be King of all Britain, would be great, would drive the Saxons out of our shores and knit our poor country into a strong whole. I did nothing of my own will, but just for this, that Britain might not go down into the dark. It came to me whole, out of the silence and the fire, and as a certainty. Then for a time I saw nothing and heard nothing, and wondered if, in my love for my father and my father's land, I had been led astray, and had seen vision where there was nothing but hope and desire. But now, see, there it lies, just as the god told me." I looked at her. "I don't know if I can make you understand, Moravik. Visions and prophecies, gods and stars and voices speaking in the night . . . things seen cloudy in the flames and in the stars, but real as pain in the blood, and piercing the brain like ice. But now . . ." I paused again. ". . . now it is no longer a god's voice or a vision, it is a small human child with lusty lungs, a baby like any other baby, who cries, and

169

sucks milk, and soaks his swaddling clothes. One's visions do not take account of this."

"It's men who have visions," said Moravik. "It's women who bear the children to fulfill them. That's the difference. And as for that one there"—she nodded towards the corner —"we shall see what we shall see. If he lives—and why should he not live, he's strong enough?—if he lives he has a good chance to be King. All we can do now is see that he makes a man. I'll do my part as you've done yours. The rest is with the good God."

I smiled at her. Her sturdy common sense seemed to have lifted a great weight from me. "You're right. I was a fool ever to doubt. What will come, will come."

"Then sleep on that."

"Yes. I'll go to bed now. You have a good man there, Moravik. I'm glad of it."

"Between us, boy, we'll keep your little King safely."

"I'm sure of that," I said, and after we had talked a little longer I climbed the ladder to bed.

That night I dreamed. I was standing in a field I knew near Hoel's town of Kerrec. It was a place of ancient holiness, where once a god had walked and I had seen him. In my dream I knew that I had come in the hope of seeing him again.

But the night was empty. All that moved was the wind. The sky arched high, bright with indifferent stars. Across its black dome, soft through the glitter of the fiercer stars, lay the long track of light they call the Galaxy. There was no cloud. About me stretched the field, just as I remembered it, bitten by the wind and sown by the sea's salt, with bare thorn trees hunched along the banks, and, solitary in the center, a single giant stone. I walked towards it. In the scattered light of the stars I cast no shadow, nor was there a shadow by the stone. Only the grey wind blurring the grass, and behind the stone the faint drifting of the stars that is not movement, but the heavens breathing.

Still the night was empty. My thoughts arrowed up into the shell of silence, and fell back spent. I was trying, with every grain of skill and power which I had fought and suffered for, to recall the god whose hand had been over me then, and whose light had led me. I prayed aloud, but heard no sound. I called on my magic, my gift of eyes and mind that men called the Sight, but nothing came. The night was empty, and I was failing. Even my human vision was failing, night and starlight melting into a blur, like something seen through running water. . . .

The sky itself was moving. The earth held still, but heaven itself was moving. The Galaxy gathered and narrowed into a shaft of light, then froze still as a stream in the bite of winter. A shaft of ice—no, a blade, it lay across the sky like a king's sword, with the great jewels blazing in the hilt. Emerald I saw, topaz, sapphires, which in the tongue of swords mean power and joy and justice and clean death.

For a long time the sword lay there, still, like a weapon newly burnished, waiting for the hand which will lift and wield it. Then, of itself, it moved. Not as a weapon is lifted in battle, or in ceremony, or sport. But as a blade slides home to its housing it slid, how gently, down towards the standing stone, dropping into it as a sword slips resting into its scabbard.

Then there was nothing but the empty field and the whistling wind, and a grey stone standing.

I woke to the darkness of the inn room, and a single star, small and bright, showing through a gap above the rafters. Below me the beasts breathed sweet breath, while all around were the snores and stirrings of the sleepers. The place smelled warmly of horses and peat smoke and hay and mutton stew.

I lay unmoving, flat on my back, watching the little star. I hardly thought about the dream. Vaguely, I remembered that there had been talk of a sword, and now this dream . . . But I let it pass me. It would come. I would be shown. God was back with me; time had not lied. And in an hour or two it would be morning.

BOOK II

THE SEARCH

1

The gods, all of them, must be accustomed to blasphemy. It is a blasphemy even to question their purposes, and to wonder, as I had done, who they were or if they even existed is blasphemy itself. Now I knew my god was back with me, that his purpose was working, and though I still saw nothing clearly, I knew that his hand would be over me when the time was right, and I would be guided, driven, shown—it did not matter which, nor in what form he came. He would show me that, too. But not yet. Today was my own. The dreams of the night had vanished with the stars that made them. This morning the wind was only the wind, and the sunlight nothing but light.

I do not think I even looked back. I had no fear for Ralf or the child. The Sight may be an uncomfortable thing to possess, but foreknowledge of catastrophe relieves the possessor of the small frets of day to day. A man who has seen his own old age and bitter end does not fear what may come to him at twenty-two. I had no doubts about my own safety, or the boy's whose sword I had seen—twice now—drawn and shining. So I was free to dread nothing worse than the next sea voyage, which took me, suffering but alive, to the port of Massilia on the Inland Sea, and landed me there on a bright February day which, in Britain, we would have called summer.

Once there, it did not matter who saw me and reported meeting me. If it should be noised abroad that Prince Merlin had been seen in Southern Gaul, or Italy, then perhaps

Uther's enemies would watch me for a while, hoping for a lead to the vanished prince. Eventually they would give up and search elsewhere, but by that time the trail would be cold. In Kerrec the visit of the inconspicuous singer would be forgotten, and Ralf, quietly anonymous in the forest tavern, would be able to come and go without fear between Coll and the castle at Kerrec, with news of the child's progress for Hoel to transmit to me. So, once landed in Massilia, and recovered from my voyage, I set about making open preparations for my journey eastwards.

With no need this time for disguise, I travelled in comfort, if not in princely style. Appearances had never troubled me; a man makes his own; but I had friends to visit, and if I could not do them honour, at least I must not shame them. So I hired a body-servant and bought horses and baggage mules and a slave to look after them, and set off for my first destination, which was Rome.

The road out of Massilia is a straight, sun-beaten ribbon of white dust running along the shore where the villages built by Caesar's veterans crouch among their carefully tended olive groves and vines. We set out at sunrise with our horses' shadows long behind us. The road was still dewed, and the air smelled of dung and peppery cypress and the smoke of the early fires. Cockerels crowed and curs ran out yapping at our horses' heels. Behind me the two servants talked, low voiced, not to intrude on me. They seemed decent men; the freeman, Gaius, had seen service before, and came to me well recommended. The other, Stilicho, was the son of a Sicilian horse-dealer who had cheated himself into debt and sold his son to pay it. Stilicho was a thin, lively youth with a cheerful eye and unquenchable spirits. Gaius was solemn and efficient, and more conscious of my dignity than I had ever been myself. When he discovered my royal status he took on an aura of pomp which amused me, and impressed Stilicho into silence for almost twenty minutes. I believe that thereafter it was continually used as a threat or a bribe for service. Certainly, whatever means the two of them employed, I was to find my journey almost a miracle of smoothness and comfort.

Now, as my horse pricked his ears at the morning sun, I felt my mood lift to meet the growing brilliance. It was as if the griefs and doubts of the last year streamed back from me like my horse's shadow. As I set off eastwards with my little train I was for the first time in my life free; free of the world in front of me, and free of the obligations at my back. Until this moment I had lived always towards some goal; I had sought for and then served my father, and after his death had waited in grief until, with Arthur, my servitude might start again. Now the first part of my work was done; the boy was safe and, as my gods and my stars could be trusted, he would remain so. I was still young, and facing the sun, and, call it solitude or call it freedom, I had a new world in front of me and a span of time ahead when at last I could travel the lands of which as a boy I had been taught so much, and which I had longed to see.

So in time I came to Rome, and walked on the green hills between the cypresses, and talked with a man who had known my father when he was the age I was now. I lodged in his house, and wondered how I had ever thought my father's house in Kerrec a palace, or seen London as a great city, or even a city at all. Then from Rome to Corinth, and overland through the valleys of the Argolid where goats grazed the baked summer hills, and people lived, wilder than they, among the ruins of cities built by giants. Here at last I saw stones greater even than those in the Giants' Dance, lifted and set just as the songs had told me, and as I travelled farther east I saw lands yet emptier with giant stones standing in desert sunlight, and men who lived as simply as roving wolf-packs, but who made songs as easily as the birds, and as marvellously as the stars moving in their courses. Indeed, they know more about the movements of the stars than any other men; I suppose their world is made up of the empty spaces of the desert and the sky. I spent eight months with a man near Sardis, in Maeonia, who could calculate to a hair's breadth, and with whose help I could have lifted the Giants' Dance in half the time had it been twice as great. Another six months I spent on the coast of Mysia, near Pergamum, in a great hospital where sick men flock for treatment, rich and poor alike. I found much that was new to me there in the art of healing; in Pergamum they use music with the drugs to heal a man's mind through dreams, and his body after it. Truly the god must have guided me when he sent me to learn music as a child. And all the time, on all my journeys, I learned smatterings of strange tongues, and heard new songs and new music, and saw strange gods worshipped, some in holy places, and some in manners we would call unclean. It is never wise to turn aside from knowing, however the knowing comes.

Through all this time I rested, steady and secure, in the knowledge that, back there in the Perilous Forest in Brittany, the child grew and thrived in safety.

Messages from Ralf came occasionally, sent by King Hoel to await me at certain prearranged ports of call. This way I learned that, as soon as might be, Ygraine was pregnant again. She was delivered in due time of a daughter, who was called Morgian. By the time I read them, the letters were of course long out of date, but as far as the boy Arthur was concerned I had my own more immediate source of reassurance. I watched, in the way I have, in the fire.

It was in a brazier lit against the chill of a Roman evening that I first watched Ralf make the journey through the forest to Hoel's court. He travelled alone and unremarked, and when he set out again in the misty dark to make for home he was not followed. In the depths of the forest I lost him, but later the smoke blew aside to show me his horse safely stabled, and Branwen smiling in the sun- lit yard with the baby in her arms. Several times after that I watched Ralf's journey, but always smoke or darkness seemed to gather and lie like mist along the river, so that I could not see the tavern, or follow him through the door. It was as if, even from me, the place was guarded. I had heard it said that the Perilous Forest of Brittany was spell- bound land; I can affirm that this is true. I doubt if any magic less potent than mine could have spied through the wall of mist that hid the inn. Glimpses I had, no more than that, from time to time. Once, fleetingly, I saw the baby playing among a litter of puppies in the yard while the bitch licked his face and Brand looked on, grinning, till Moravik burst scolding out of her kitchen to snatch the child up, wipe his face with her apron, and vanish with him indoors. Another time I saw him perched aloft on Ralf's horse while it was drinking at the trough, and yet again astride the saddle in front of Ralf, hanging on to the mane with both hands while the beast trotted down to the river's edge. I never saw him closely, or even clearly, but I saw enough to know that he thrived and grew strong.

Then, when he was four years old, the time came when Ralf was to take him from the Forest's protection and seek Count Ector's.

The night his ship set sail from the Small Sea of Morbihan I was lying under a black Syrian sky where the stars seem to burn twice as big and ardent as the stars at home. The fire I watched was a shepherd's, lit against the wolves and moun- tain lions, and he had given me its hospitality when my servants and I were benighted crossing the heights above Berytus. The fire was stacked high with wind-dried wood, and blazed fiercely against the night. Somewhere beyond it I could hear Stilicho talking, then the rough mutter of the shepherd, and laughter shushed by Gaius' grave tones, till the roar and crackling of the fire drowned them. Then the pictures came, fragmentary at first, but as clear and vivid as the visions I had had as a boy in the crystal cave. I watched the whole journey, scene by scene, in one night's vision, as you can dream a lifetime between night and morning. . . .

This was my first clear sight of Ralf since I had parted from him in Brittany. I hardly knew him. He was a tall young man now, with the look of a fighter, and an air of decision and responsibility that gave him weight and sat well on him. I had left it to Hoel's and his discretion whether or not an armed escort would be needed to convoy his "wife and child" to the ship: in the event they played safe, though it was obvious that the secret was still our own. Hoel had contrived that a wagon-load of goods should be dispatched through the forest under the escort of half a dozen troopers; when it set off back towards Kerrec and the wharf where the ship lay, what more natural than that the young man and his family should travel back to Kerrec with the return load—I never saw what was in those corded bales—using its protection for themselves? Branwen rode in the wagon, and so, in the end, did Arthur. It looked to me as if he had already outgrown women's care; he would have spent all his time with the troopers, and it took Ralf's authority to make him ride concealed in the wagon with Branwen, rather than on the saddle-bow at the head of the troop. After the little party had reached the ship and embarked safely, four of the troop took ship along with Ralf, apparently convoying those precious bales to their destination. So the ship set sail. Light glittered on the firelit sea, and the little ship had red sails which spread against a breezy sky of sunset, till they dwindled and vanished small in the blowing fire.

It was in a blaze of sunrise, perhaps lit only by the Syrian flames, that the ship docked at Glannaventa. I saw the ropes made fast and the party cross the gangplank to be met by Ector himself, brown and smiling, with a full-armed body of men. They bore no badge. They had brought a wagon for the cargo, but as soon as they were clear of the town the wagon was left to follow, while out of it came a litter for Branwen and Arthur, and then the party rode as fast as might be for Galava, up the military road through the mountains which lie between Ector's castle and the sea. The road climbs through two steep passes with between them a low-lying valley sodden with marsh, which is flooded right through till late spring. The road is bad, broken by storm and torrents and winter frosts, and in places where the hillsides had slipped in flood time the road has vanished, and all that remains of it are the ghosts of the old tracks that were there before the Romans came. Wild country and a wild road, but straight going on a May day for a body of well armed men. I watched them trotting along, the litter swinging between its sturdy mules, through flame-lit dawn and firelit day, till suddenly with evening the mist rolled down dark from the head of the pass, and I saw in it the glitter of swords that spelled danger.

Ector's party was clattering downhill from the second summit, slowing to a walk at a steep place where crags crowded the edge of the road. From here it was only a short descent to the broad river valley and the good flat road to the waterhead where the castle stands. In the distance, still lit by evening, were the big trees and the blossoming orchards and the gentle green of the farmlands. But up in the pass among the grey crags and the rolling mist it was dark, and the horses slipped and stumbled on a steep scree where a torrent drove across the way and the road had collapsed into the water's bed. The rush of water must have blanketed all other sound from them. No one saw, dim behind the mist, the other men waiting, mounted and armed.

Count Ector was at the head of the troop, and in the middle of it, surrounded, the litter lurched and swung between its mules with Ralf riding close beside it. They were approaching the ambush; were beside it. I saw Ector's head turn sharply, then he checked his horse so suddenly that it tried to rear and instead plunged, slipping on the scree as Ector's sword flashed out and his arm went up. The troopers, surrounding the litter as best they might on the rushing slope, stood to fight. At the moment of clashing, shouting attack I saw what none of the troop appeared yet to have seen, other shadows riding down out of the mist beyond the crags.

I believe I shouted. I made no sound, but I saw Ralf's head go up like a hound's at his master's whistle. He yelled, wheeling his horse. Men wheeled with him, and met the new attack with a crash and flurry that sent sparks up from the swords like a smith's hammer from the anvil.

I strained my eyes through the visionary firelight to see who the attackers were. But I could not see. The wrestling, clashing darkness, the sparkling swords, the shouting, the wheeling horses—then the attackers vanished into the mist as suddenly as they had come, leaving one of their number dead on the scree, and carrying another bleeding across a saddle.

There was nothing to be gained by pursuing them across mountains thick with the misty twilight. One of the troopers picked up the fallen man and flung him across a horse. I saw Ector point, and the trooper searched the body looking, apparently, for identification, but finding none. Then the guard

formed again round the litter, and rode on. I saw Ralf, sur-
reptitious, winding a rag round his left arm where a blade
had hacked in past the shield. A moment later I saw him,
laughing, stoop in the saddle to say through the curtains of
the litter: "Well, but you're not grown yet. Give it a year
or two, and I promise you we'll find you a sword to suit
your size." Then he reached to pull the leather curtains of
the litter close. When I strained my sight to see Arthur,
smoke blew grey across the scene and the shepherd called
something to his dog, and I was back on the scented hillside
with the moon coming out above the ruins of the temple
where nothing remains now of the Goddess but her night-
owls brooding.

So the years passed, and I used my freedom in travels
which I have told of in other places; there is no room for
them here. For me they were rich years, and lightly borne,
and the god's hand lay gently on me, so that I saw all I
asked to see; but in all the time there was no message, no
moving star, nothing to call me home.

Then one day, when Arthur was six years old, the message came to me near Pergamum, where I was teaching
and working in the hospital.

It was early spring, and all day rain had been falling like
whips on the streaming rock, darkening the white limestone
and tearing ruts in the pathway which leads down to the
hospital cells by the sea. I had no fire to bring me the vision,
but in that place the gods stand waiting by every pillar, and
the air is heavy with dreams. This was only a dream, the
same as other men's, and came in a moment of exhausted
sleep.

A man had been carried in late in the night, with a leg
badly gashed and the life starting to pump out of the great
vein. I and the other doctor on duty had worked over him

for more than three hours, and afterwards I had gone out into the sea to wash off the blood which had gushed thick and then hardened on me. It was possible that the patient would live; he was young, and slept now with the blood staunched and the wound safely stitched. I stripped off my soaked loin-cloth—that climate allows one to work near naked on the bloodier jobs—swam till I was clean, then stretched on the still warm sand to rest. The rain had stopped with evening, and the night was calm and warm and full of stars.

It was no vision I had, but a kind of dream of wakefulness. I lay (as I thought) open-eyed, watching, and watched by, the bright swarm. Among that fierce host of stars was one distant one, cloudy, its light faint among the others like a lamp in a swirl of snow. Then it swam closer, closer still, till its clouded air blotted out the brighter stars, and I saw mountains and shore, and rivers running like the veins of a leaf through the valleys of my own country. Now the snow swirled thicker, hiding the valleys, and behind the snow was the growl of thunder, and the shouting of armies, and the sea rose till the shore dissolved, and salt ran up the rivers and the green fields bleached to grey, and blackened to desert with their veins showing like dead men's bones.

I woke knowing that I must go back. It was not yet, the flood, but it was coming. By the next snow-time, or the next, we would hear the thunder, and I must be there, between the King and his son.

2

I had planned to go home by Constantinopolis, and letters had already gone ahead of me. Now I would have preferred to take a quicker way, but the only ship I could get was one plying north close inshore towards Chalcedon, which lies just across the strait from Constantinopolis. Arrived here, delayed by freakish winds and uncertain weather, luck still seemed against me; I had just missed a westbound ship, they told me, and there was no other due to leave for a week or more. From Chalcedon the trade is mostly small coastbound craft; the bigger shipping uses the great harbour of Constantinopolis. So I took the ferry over, not averse, in spite of the need I felt for haste, to seeing the city of which I had heard so much.

I had expected the New Rome to surpass the old Rome in magnificence, but found Constantine's city a place of sharper contrasts, with squalor crowding close behind the splendour, and that air of excitement and risk which is breathed in a young city looking forward to prosperity, still building, spreading, assimilating, and avid to grow rich.

Not that the foundation was new; it had been capital of Byzantium since Byzas had settled his folk there a thousand years before; but it was almost a century and a half now since the Emperor Constantine had moved the heart of the empire eastwards, and started to build and fortify the old Byzantium and call it after himself.

Constantinopolis is a city marvellously situated on a tongue of land which holds a natural harbour they call the Golden

Horn, and rightly; I had never imagined such a traffic of richly laden ships as I saw in the brief crossing from Chalcedon. There are palaces and rich houses, and government buildings with corridors like a maze and the countless officials employed by the government coming and going like bees in a hive. Everywhere there are gardens, with pavilions and pools, and fountains constantly gushing; the city has an abundance of sweet water. To the landward side Constantine's Wall defends the city, and from its Golden Gate the great thoroughfare of the Mese runs, magnificently arcaded through most of its length, through three fora decorated with columns, to end at the great triumphal arch of Constantine. The Emperor's immense church dedicated to the Holy Wisdom sits high over the walls that edge the sea. It was a magnificent city, and a splendid capital, but it had not the air of Rome as my father had spoken of it, or as we had thought of it in Britain; this was still the East, and the city looked to the East. Even the dress, though men wore the Roman tunic and mantle, had the look of Asia, and, though Latin was spoken everywhere, I heard Greek and Syrian and Armenian in the markets, and once beyond the arcades of the Mese you might have supposed yourself in Antioch.

It is a place not easy to picture, if one has never been beyond Britain's shores. Above everything it was exciting, with an air full of promise. It was a city looking forward, where Rome and Athens and even Antioch had seemed to be looking back; and London, with its crumbling temples and patched-up towers and men always watching with their hands to their swords, seemed as remote and near as savage as the ice-lands of the northmen.

My host in Constantinopolis was a connection of my father's, distant, but not too distant to let him greet me as cousin. He was descended from one Adean, brother-in-law of Maximus, who had been one of Maximus' officers and had followed him on the final expedition to Rome. Adean had been wounded outside Rome and left for dead, but rescued and nursed back to health by a Christian family. Later he had married the daughter of the house, turned Christian, and though he never took service with the Eastern Emperor (being content with the pardon granted him through his father-in-law's intercession) his son entered the service of Theodosius II, made a fortune at it, and was rewarded with a royally connected wife and a splendid house near the Golden Horn.

His great-grandson bore the same name, but pronounced it with the accent of Byzantium: Ahdjan. He was still discernibly of Celtic descent, but looked, you might say, like a Welshman gone bloodless by being drawn too high towards the sun. He was tall and thin, with the oval face and pale skin, and the black eyes set straight, that you see in all their portraits. His mouth was thin-lipped, bloodless too; the court servant's mouth, close-lipped with keeping secrets. But he was not without humour, and could talk wisely and entertainingly, a rarity in a country where men—and women—argue perpetually about matters of the spirit in terms of the more than stupid flesh. I had not been in Constantinopolis half a day before I found myself remembering something I had read in a book of Galapas': "If you ask someone how many obols a certain thing costs, he replies by dogmatizing on the born and unborn. If you ask the price of bread, they answer you, the Father is greater than the Son, and the Son is subordinate to Him. If you ask is my bath ready, they answer you, the Son has been made out of nothing."

Ahdjan received me very kindly, in a splendid room with mosaics on the walls and a floor of golden marble. In Britain, where it is cold, we put the pictures on the floor and hang thick coverings over walls and doors; but they do things differently in the East. This room glittered with colour; they use a lot of gold in their mosaics, and with the faintly uneven surface of the tesserae this has the effect of glimmering movement, as if the wall-pictures were tapestries of silk. The figures are alive, and full of colour, some of them very beautiful. I remembered the cracked mosaic at home in Maridunum, which as a child I had thought the most wonderful picture in the world; it had been of Dionysos, with grapes and dolphins, but none of the pictures was whole, and the god's eyes had been badly mended, and showed a cast. To this day I see Dionysos with a squint. One side of Ahdjan's room opened to a terrace where a fountain played in a wide marble pool, and cypress and laurel grew in pots along the balustrade. Below this the garden lay, scented in the sun, with rose and iris and jasmine (though it was hardly into April) competing with the scent of a hundred shrubs, and everywhere the dark fingers of cypress, gilded with tiny cones, pointing straight at the brilliant sky. Below the terraces sparkled the waters of the Horn, as thickly populated with ships as a farm pond at home is with water-beetles.

There was a letter waiting for me, from Ector. After Ahdjan and I had exchanged greetings, I asked his leave, then unrolled and read it.

Ector's scribe wrote well, though in long periods which I knew were a gloss on what that forthright gentleman had actually said. But the news, sorted out from the poetry and the perorations, bore out what I already knew or suspected. In more than guarded phrases he conveyed to me that Arthur (for the scribe's sake he wrote of "the family, Drusilla and both the boys") was safe. But for how long "the place" might be safe, said Ector, he could not guess, and went on to give me the news as his informers reported it.

The danger of invasion, always there but for the last few

years sporadic, had begun to grow into something more formidable. Octa and Eosa, the Saxon leaders defeated by Uther in the first year of his reign, and kept prisoner since then in London, were still safely held; but lately pressure had been brought to bear—not only by the Federates, but by some British leaders who were afraid of the growing discontent along the Saxon Shore—on King Uther to free the Saxon princes on terms of treaty. Since he had refused this, there had been two armed attempts to release them from prison. These had been punished with brutal severity, and now other factions were pressing Uther to kill the Saxon leaders out of hand, a course he was apparently afraid to take for fear of the Federates. These, firmly ensconced along the Shore, and crowding too close for comfort even to London, were again showing threatening signs of inviting reinforcements from abroad, and pressing up into the rich country near Ambrosius' Wall. Meanwhile there were worse rumours: a messenger had been caught, and under torture had confessed, that he carried tokens of friendship from the Angles on the Abus in the east, to the Pictish kings of the wild land west of Strathclyde. But nothing more, added Ector, than tokens; and he personally did not think that trouble could yet come from the north. Between Strathclyde and the Abus, the kingdoms of Rheged and Lothian still stood firm.

I skimmed through the rest, then rolled up the letter. "I must go straight home," I told Ahdjan.

"So soon? I was afraid of it." He signed to a servant, who lifted a silver flagon from a bowl of snow, and poured the wine into glass goblets. Where the snow had come from I did not know; they have it carried by night from the hilltops, and stored underground in straw. "I'm sorry to lose you, but when I saw the letter, I was afraid it might be bad news."

"Not bad yet, but there will be bad to come." I told him what I could of the situation, and he listened gravely. They understand these things in Constantinopolis. Since Alaric the Goth took Rome, men's ears are tuned to listen for the thunder in the north. I went on: "Uther is a strong king and a good general, but even he cannot be everywhere, and this division of power makes men uncertain and afraid. It's time the succession was made sure." I tapped the letter. "Ector tells me the Queen is with child again."

"So I had heard. If this is a boy he'll be declared the heir, won't he? Hardly a time for a baby to inherit a kingdom, unless he had a Stilicho to look after his interests." He was referring to the general who had protected the empire of the young Emperor Honorius. "Has Uther anyone among his generals who could be left as regent if he were killed?"

"For all I know they'd be as likely to kill as to protect."

"Well, Uther had better live, then, or allow the son he's already got to be his legitimate heir. He must be—what? Seven? Eight? Why cannot Uther do the sensible thing and declare him again, with you to become regent if the King should be killed during the boy's minority?" He looked at me sideways over his glass. "Come, Merlin, don't raise your brows at me like that. The whole world knows you took the child from Tintagel and have him hidden somewhere."

"Does the world say where?"

"Oh, yes. The world spawns solutions the way that pool yonder spawns frogs. The general opinion is that the child is safe in the island of Hy-Brasil, nursed by the white paps of nine queens, no less. It's no wonder he flourishes. Or else that he is with you, but invisible. Disguised perhaps as a pack-mule?"

I laughed. "How would I dare? What would that make Uther?"

"You'd dare anything, I think. I was hoping you'd dare tell me where the boy is, and all about him . . . No?"

I shook my head, smiling. "Forgive me, but not yet."

He moved a hand gracefully. They understand secrets, too, in Constantinopolis. "Well, at least you can tell me if he's safe and well?"

"I assure you of it."

"And will succeed, with you as regent?"

I laughed, shook my head, and drained my wine. He signalled to the slave, who was standing out of hearing, and the man hurried to refill my glass. Ahdjan waved him away. "I've had a letter, too, from Hoel. He tells me that King Uther has sent men in search of you, and that he doesn't speak of you with kindness, though everyone knows how much he owes you. There are rumours, too, that even the King himself does not know where his son is hidden, and has spies out searching. Some say the boy is dead. There are also those who say that you keep the young prince close for your own ambitious ends."

"Yes," I agreed equably, "there would be some who say that."

"You see?" He threw out a hand. "I try to goad you into speaking, and you are not even angry. Where another man would protest, would even fear to go back, you say nothing, and—I'm afraid—decide to take ship straight for home."

"I know the future, Ahdjan, that's the difference."

"Well, I don't know the future, and it's obvious you won't tell me, but I can make my own guess at the truth. What men are saying is just that truth twisted: you keep the boy close because you know he must one day be King. You can tell me this, though. What will you do when you get back? Bring him out of hiding?"

"By the time I get back the Queen's child should be born," I said. "What I do must depend on that. I shall see Uther, of course, and talk to him. But the main thing, as I see it, is to let the people of Britain know—friend and enemy alike—

that Prince Arthur is alive and thriving, and will be ready to show himself beside his father when the time comes."

"And that's not yet?"

"I think not. When I reach home I hope I shall see more clearly. With your leave, Ahdjan, I'll take the first ship."

"As you will, of course. I shall be sorry to lose your company."

"I regret it, too. It's been a happy chance that brought me after all to Constantinopolis. I might have missed seeing you, but I was delayed by bad weather and lost the ship I should have got at Chalcedon."

He said something civil, then looked startled as he saw the implications. "Delayed? You mean you were on your way home already? Before you saw the letter? You knew?"

"No details. Only that it was time I was home."

"By the Three!" For a moment I had seen the Celt looking out of his eyes, though it was the Christian god that he swore by; they only have one other oath in Constantinopolis, and that is "By the One," and they fight to the death over them. Then he laughed. "By the Three! I wish I'd had you beside me last week in the Hippodrome! I lost a cool thousand on the Greens—a sure thing, you'd have sworn, and they ran like three-legged cows. Well, it seems that whatever prince has you to guide him, he's lucky. If *he* had had you, I might have had an empire today, instead of a respectable government post—and lucky to get that without being a eunuch besides."

He nodded as he spoke at the great mosaic on the main wall of the room behind us. I had noticed it already, and wondered vaguely at the Byzantine strain of melancholy which decorates a room with such scenes instead of the livelier designs one sees in Greece and Italy. I had already observed, in the entrance hall, a crucifix done life-size with mourning figures and Christian devices all round it. This, too, was an execution, but a noble one, on the battlefield. The sky was dark, done with chips of slate and lapis hammered into clouds like iron, with among them the staring heads of gods. The horizon showed a line of towers and temples with a crimson sun setting behind. It seemed meant to be Rome. The wide plain in front of the walls was the scene of the battle's end: to the left the defeated host, men and horses dead or dying on a field scattered with broken weapons; to the right the victors, clustered behind the crowned leader, and bathed in a shaft of light descending from a Christ poised in blessing above the other gods. At the victor's feet the other leader knelt, his neck bared to the executioner's blade. He was lifting both arms towards his conqueror, not for mercy, but in formal surrender of the sword which lay across his hands. Below him, in the corner of the picture, was written *Max*. On the right, below the victor, were stamped the words *Theod. Imp.*

"By the One!" I said, and saw Ahdjan smile; but he could not have known what had brought me so quickly to my feet. He rose gracefully and followed me to the wall, obviously pleased at my interest.

"Yes, Maximus' defeat by the Emperor. Good, isn't it?" He smoothed a hand over the silken tesserae. "The man who did it can't have known much of the ironies of war. In spite of all this, you might say it came out even enough in the end. That hang-dog fellow on the left behind Maximus is Hoel's ancestor, the one who took the remnants of the British contingent home. This holy-looking gentleman shedding blood all over the Emperor's feet is my great-great-grandfather, to whose conscience and good business sense I owe both my fortune and the saving of my soul."

I hardly listened. I was staring at the sword in Maximus' hand. I had seen it before. Glowing on the wall behind Ygraine. Flashing home to its scabbard in Brittany. Now here, the third time, imaged in Maximus' hand outside the walls of Rome.

Ahdjan was watching me curiously. "What is it?"

"The sword. So it was his sword."

"What was? Have you seen it, then?"

"No. Only in a dream. Twice, I've seen it in dreams. Now here for the third time, in a picture . . ." I spoke half to myself, musing. Sunlight, striking up off the pool on the terrace, sent light rippling across the wall, so that the sword shimmered in Macsen's hands, and the jewels in its hilt showed green and yellow and vivid blue. I said, softly: "So that is why I missed the ship at Chalcedon."

"What do you mean?"

"Forgive me, I hardly know. I was thinking of a dream. Tell me, Ahdjan, this picture . . . Are those the walls of Rome? Maximus wasn't murdered at Rome, surely?"

"Murdered?" Ahdjan, speaking primly, looked amused. "The word on our side of the family is 'executed.' No, it wasn't at Rome. I think the artist was being symbolic. It happened at Aquileia. You may not know it; it's a small place near the mouth of the Turrus River, at the northern end of the Adriatic."

"Do ships call there?"

His eyes widened. "You mean to go?"

"I would like to see the place where Macsen died. I would like to know what became of his sword."

"You won't find that at Aquileia," he said. "Kynan took it."

"*Who?*"

He nodded at the picture. "The man on the left. Hoel's ancestor, who took the British back home to Brittany. Hoel could have told you." He laughed at my expression. "Did you come all this way for that piece of information?"

"It seems so," I said. "Though until this moment I didn't

know it. Are you telling me that Hoel has that sword? It's in Brittany?"

"No. It was lost long since. Some of the men who went home to Greater Britain took his things with them; I suppose they would have taken his sword to give his son."

"And?"

"That's all I know. It's a long time ago and all it is now is a family tale, and the half of it's probably not true. Does it matter so much?"

"Matter?" I said. "I hardly know. But I've learned to look close at most things that come my way."

He was watching me with a puzzled look, and I thought he would question me further, but after a short hesitation he said merely: "I suppose so. Will you walk out now into the garden? It's cooler. You looked as if your head hurt you."

"That? It was nothing. Someone playing a lyre on the terrace down there. It isn't in tune."

"My daughter. Shall we go down and stop her?"

On the way down he told me of a ship due to leave the Horn in two days' time. He knew the master, and could bespeak me a passage. It was a fast ship, and would dock at Ostia, whence I would certainly find a vessel plying westwards.

"What about your servants?"

"Gaius is a good man. You could do worse than employ him yourself. I freed Stilicho. He's yours if he'll stay, and he's a wizard with horses. It would be cruelty for me to take him to Britain; his blood's as thin as an Arabian gazelle's."

But when the morning came Stilicho was there at the quayside, stubborn as the mules he had handled with such skill, his belongings in a stitched sack, and a cloak of sheepskin sweltering round him in the Byzantine sun. I argued with him, traducing even the British climate, and my simple

195

way of living which he might find tolerable in a country where the sun shines, but would be hardship itself in that land of icy winds and wet. But, seeing finally that he would have his way even if he paid his own passage with the money I had given him as a parting gift, I gave way.

To tell the truth I was touched, and glad to have his company on the long voyage home. Though he had had none of Gaius' training as a body-servant, he was quick and intelligent, and had already shown skill in helping me with plants and medicines. He would be useful, and besides, after all these years away life at Bryn Myrddin looked a little lonelier than it had used to, and I knew well that Ralf would never come back to me.

3

It was late summer when I reached Britain. Fresh news met me on the quay, in the person of one of the King's chamberlains, who greeted me with passionate relief, and such a total absence of surprise that I told him: "You should be in my business."

He laughed. He was Lucan, whom I had known well when my father was King, and he and I were on terms. "Soothsaying? Hardly. This is the fifth ship I've met. I own I expected you, but I never thought to see you so soon. We heard you went east a long while back, and we sent messengers, hoping to reach you. Did they find you?"

"No. But I was already on my way."

He nodded, as if I had confirmed his thoughts. He had been too close to my father, Ambrosius, to question the power that guided me. "You knew the King was sick, then?"

"Not that, no. Only that the times were dangerous, and I should get home. Uther ill? That's grave news. What's the sickness?"

"A wound gone bad. You knew he's been seeing to the rebuilding of the Saxon Shore defenses, and training the troops there himself? Well, an alarm was raised about longships up the Thames—they'd been seen level with Vagniacae—too near London for comfort. A small foray, nothing serious, but he was first into it as usual, and got a cut, and the wound didn't heal. This was two months since, and he's still in pain, and losing flesh."

"Two months? Hasn't his own physician been attending him?"

"Indeed yes. Gandar's been there from the beginning."

"And he could do nothing?"

"Well," said Lucan, "according to him the King was mending, and he says—along with the other doctors who've been consulted—that there's nothing to fear. But I've watched them conferring in corners, and Gandar looks worried." He glanced at me sideways. "There's a kind of uneasiness—you might even call it apprehension—infecting the whole court, and it's going to be hard to keep it contained there. I don't have to tell you, it's a bad time for the country to doubt if their leader's going to be fit to lead them. In fact, rumours have started already. You know the King can't have the bellyache without a scare of poison; and now they whisper about spells and hauntings. And not without reason; the King looks, sometimes, like a man who walks with ghosts. It was time you came home."

We were already moving along the road from the port. The horses had been there ready saddled at the quayside, and an escort waiting; this more for ceremony than for safety; the road to London is well-travelled and guarded. It occurred to me that perhaps the armed men who rode with us were there, not to see that I came to the King unharmed, but that I came there at all.

I said as much dryly, to Lucan. "It seems the King wants to make sure of me."

He looked amused, but only said with his courtier's smoothness: "Perhaps he was afraid that you might not care to attend him. Shall we say that a physician who fails to cure a king does not always add to his reputation."

"Does not always survive, you mean. I trust poor Gandar's still alive?"

"So far." He paused, then said neutrally: "Not that I'm

much of a judge, but I'd have said it's not the King's body that lacks a cure, but his mind."

"So it's my magic that's wanted?" He was silent. I added: "Or his son?"

His eyelids drooped. "There are rumours about him, too."

"I'm sure there are." My voice was as bland as his. "One piece of news I did hear on my travels, that the Queen was pregnant again. I reckon she should have been brought to bed a month ago. What is the child?"

"It was a son, stillborn. They say that it was this sent the King out of his mind, and fevered his wound again. And now there are rumours that the eldest son is dead, too. In fact some say he died in infancy, that there is no son." He paused. His gaze fixed on his horse's ears, but there was the faintest of queries in his voice.

"Not true, Lucan," I said. "He's alive, a fine boy, and growing fast. Don't be afraid, he'll be there when he's needed."

"Ah." It was a long exhalation of relief. "Then it's true he's with you! This is the news that will heal the kingdom, if not the King. You'll bring the boy to London now?"

"First I must see the King. After that, who knows?"

A courtier knows when a subject has been turned, and Lucan asked no more questions, but began to talk of more general news. He told me in more detail what I had already learned from Ector's letters; Ector had certainly not exaggerated the situation. I took care not to ask too many questions about the possible danger in the north, but Lucan spoke of it himself, of the manning of strongpoints north of Rheged along the old line of Hadrian's Wall, and then of Lot's contribution to the defense of the north-east. "He's making hard going of it. Not because the raids are bad— the place has been quiet lately—but perhaps because of that very fact. The small kings don't trust Lot; they say he's a hard man and niggardly with spoils, and cares little for any interests except his own. When they see there's no fighting to be done yet, and nothing to win, they desert him wholesale and take their men home to till the fields." He made a sound of contempt, as near to a snort as a courtier ever gets. "Fools, not to see that whether they like their commander or not, they'll have no fields to till, nor families to till them for, unless they fight."

"But Lot's whole interest lies in his alliances, especially to the southward. I suppose that that with Rheged is safe enough? Why do his allies distrust him? Do they suspect him of lining his own nest at their expense? Or perhaps of something worse?"

"That I can't tell you." His voice was wooden.

"Is there no one else Uther can appoint as commander in the north?"

"Not unless he goes himself. He can't demote Lot. His daughter is promised to him."

I said, startled: "His daughter? Do you mean that Lot accepted Morgause after all?"

"Not Morgause, no," said Lucan. "I doubt that marriage wasn't tempting enough for Lothian, for all the girl's turned out such a beauty. Lot's an ambitious man, he'd not dangle after a bastard when there was a true-born princess to be had. I meant the Queen's daughter; Morgian."

"*Morgian?* But she can hardly be five years old!"

"Nevertheless, she's promised, and you know that's binding between kings."

"If I don't, who should?" I said dryly, and Lucan knew what I was thinking of: my own mother who had borne me to Ambrosius with no bond but a promise made in secret; and my father who had let the promise bind him as securely as a ceremonial oath.

We came in sight of London Wall then, and the traffic

of the morning market thronged about us. Lucan had given me plenty to think about, and I was glad when the escort closed up, and he was silent, and left me to my thoughts.

I had expected to find Uther attended, and about some at least of his affairs, but he was still keeping his own chamber, and alone.

As I was led through the antechambers towards his room I saw nobles, officers and servants all waiting, and there was an apprehensive quiet about the crowded rooms which told its own tale. Men conferred in small groups, low-voiced and worried, the servants looked nervous and edgy, and in the outer corridors, where merchants and petitioners waited, there was the patient despondency of men who have already passed the point of hope.

Heads turned as I went through, and I heard the whisper run ahead of me like wind through a waste land, and a Christian bishop, forgetting himself, said audibly: "God be praised! Now we'll see the spell lifted." One or two men whom I knew started forward with warm greetings, and a spate of questions ready, but I smiled and shook my head and went through with no more than a quick word. And since with kings one can never quite rule out the thought of malice or murder, I checked the faces that I knew: somewhere in this crowd of armed and jewelled lords there might be one who would not welcome my return to the King's side; someone who watched for Uther to fail before his son was grown; someone who was Arthur's enemy, and therefore mine.

Some of them I knew well, but even these, as I greeted them, I studied. The leaders from Wales, Ynyr of Guent, Mador and Gwilim from my own country of Dyfed. Not Maelgon himself from Gwynedd, but one of his sons, Cunedda. Beside them, with a handful of their countrymen,

Brychan and Cynfelin from Dyfnaint, and Nentres of Garlot, whom I had watched ride out with Uther from Tintagel. Then the men from the north; Ban of Benoic, a big, handsome man so dark that he might have been, like Ambrosius and myself, a descendant of the Spaniard Maximus. Beside Ban stood his cousin from Brittany, whose name I could not recall. Then Cadwy and Bors, two of the petty kings from Rheged, neighbours of Ector's; and another neighbour, Arrak, one of the numerous sons of Caw of Strathclyde. These I marked carefully, recalling what I knew of them. Nothing of importance yet, but I would remember, and watch. Rheged himself I did not see, nor Lot; it was to be assumed that their affairs in the north were more pressing even than the King's illness. But Urien, Lot's brother-in-law, was here, a thin, red-haired man with the light-blue eyes and high colour of temper; and Tudwal of Dinpelydr, who ran with him; and his blood-brother Aguisel, of whose private doings in his cold fortress near Bremenium I had heard strange tales.

There were others I did not know, and these I scanned briefly as I passed them. I could find out later who they were, from Lucan, or from Caius Valerius, who stood over near the King's door. Beside Valerius was a young man I thought I should recognize; a strongly built, sunburned man of twenty or so, with a face that I found faintly familiar. I could not place him. He watched me from his stance near Uther's doorway, but he neither spoke nor made any sign of greeting. I said under my breath to Lucan: "The man near the door, by Valerius. Who is he?"

"Cador of Cornwall."

I knew it now, the face I had last seen watching by Gorlois' body in the midnight hall of Dimilioc. And with the same look; the chill blue eyes, the frowning bar of brows, the warrior's face grown with the years more than ever like his father's and every whit as formidable.

Perhaps I need look no further. Of all those present he had most reason to hate me. And he was here, though Lucan had told me he was commander of the Irish Shore. In Rheged's absence, and Lot's, I supposed that he was the nearest there to Uther, except only myself.

I had to pass within a yard of him to get to the door of the King's room. I held his eyes deliberately, and he returned my look, but neither saluted nor bent his head. The blue eyes were cold and impassive. Well, I thought, as I greeted Valerius beside him, we should see. No doubt I could find out from Uther why he was here. And how much, if the King failed to recover, the young Duke stood to gain.

Lucan had gone in to tell the King of my arrival. Now he came out again and beckoned me forward. On his heels came Gandar. I would have paused to speak with him, but he shook his head quickly.

"No. He wants you to go straight in. By the Snake, Merlin, I'm glad to see you! But have a care . . . There, he's calling. A word with you later?"

"Of course. I'll be grateful."

There was another, peremptory call from inside the room. Gandar's eyes, heavy with worry, met mine again briefly as he stood aside to let me pass. The servant shut the door behind us and left me with the King.

4

He was up, and dressed in a house robe open at the front, with beneath it a tunic girded by a jewelled belt with a long dagger thrust through. His sword, the King's sword Falar, lay across its hangers below the gilded dragon that climbed the wall behind the bed. Though it was still summer there had been through the night a chill breeze from the north, and I was glad—my blood thin, I suppose, from my travels—to see a brazier glowing red on the empty hearth, with chairs set near.

He came quickly across the room to greet me, and I saw that he limped. As I answered his greeting I studied his face for signs of the sickness or distraction that I had been led to expect. He was thinner than before, with new lines to his face which made him look nearer fifty than forty (which was his age), and I saw that drawn look under the eyes which is one of the signs of long-gnawing pain or sleeplessness. But apart from the slight limp he moved easily enough, and with all the restless energy I remembered. And his voice was the same as ever, strong and quick with arrogant decision.

"There's wine there. We will serve ourselves. I want to talk to you alone. Sit down."

I obeyed him, pouring the wine and handing him a goblet. He took it, but set it down without drinking, and seated himself across from me, pulling the robe about his knees with an abrupt, almost angry gesture. I noticed that he did not look at me, but at the brazier, at the floor, at the goblet, anywhere not to meet my eyes. He spoke with the same abruptness, wasting no time on civilities about my journey. "They will have told you that I have been ill."

"I understood you still were," I said. "I'm glad to see you on your feet and so active. Lucan told me about the skirmish at Vagniacae; I understand it's about two months now since you were wounded?"

"Yes. It was nothing much, a spear glancing, not deep. But it festered, and took a long time to heal."

"It's healed now?"

"Yes."

"Does it still pain you?"

"No."

He almost snapped the word, pushing himself suddenly back in his chair to sit upright with his hands clenched on the arms, and his eyes on mine at last. It was the hard blue gaze I remembered, showing nothing but anger and dislike. But now I recognized both look and manner for what they were, those of a man driven against his will to ask help where he had sworn never again to ask it. I waited.

"How is the boy?"

If the sudden question surprised me, I concealed it. Though I had told Hoel and Ector that the King need only be told of the child's whereabouts if he demanded to know, it had seemed wise to send reports from time to time—couched in phrases that no one but the King would understand—of the boy's health and progress. Since Arthur had been at Galava the reports had gone to Hoel, and thence to Uther; nothing was to pass directly between Galava and the King. Hoel had written to me that, in all the years, Uther had made no direct enquiry about the boy. It was to be inferred that now he had no idea of his son's whereabouts.

I said: "You should have had a report since the last one I saw. Has it not come?"

"Not yet. I wrote myself a month ago to ask Hoel where the boy was. He has not replied."

"Perhaps his answer went to Tintagel, or to Winchester."

"Perhaps. Or perhaps he is not prepared to answer my question?"

I raised my brows. "Why not? It was always understood, surely, that the secrecy should not extend to you. Has he refused to answer you before?"

He said coldly, disconcerted and covering it: "I did not ask. There has been no need before."

This told me something beyond what I already knew. The King had only felt the need to locate Arthur since the Queen's last miscarriage. I had been right in thinking that, if she had given him other sons, he would have preferred to forget the "bastard" in Brittany. It also told me something I did not like: if he felt a need for Arthur now, this summons might be to tell me that my guardianship was ended before it had really begun.

To give myself time, I ignored what he had just said. "Then depend upon it, Hoel's answer is on its way. In any case it doesn't matter, since I am here to answer you instead."

His look was still stony, allowing no guesses. "They tell me you have been abroad all these years. Did you take him with you?"

"No. I thought it better to keep away from him till the time came when I could be of use to him. I made sure of his safety, then after I had left Brittany I kept close touch." I smiled slightly. "Oh, nothing that your spies could have seen . . . or any other man's. You know I have ways of my own. I took no risks. If you yourself have no inkling now of his whereabouts, you may be sure that no one else has."

I saw from the brief flicker in his eyes before the lids veiled them that I had guessed rightly: messages and constant reports of my movements had been sent back to him. No

206

doubt, wherever he could, he had had me watched. It was no more than I expected. Kings live by information. Uther's enemies had probably watched me, too, and perhaps the King's own informants might have picked up some kind of lead to them. But when I asked him about this, he shook his head. He was silent for a while, following some private track of his own. He had not looked at me again. He reached for the goblet at his elbow, but not to drink; he fidgeted with it, turning it round and round where it stood. "He'll be seven years old now."

"Eight this coming Christmas, and strong for his age and well doing. You need have no fears for him, Uther."

"You think not?" Another flash, of bitterness stronger than any anger. In spite of my outward calmness I felt a violent moment of apprehension: if, contrary to appearances, the King's sickness was in fact mortal, what chance would the boy have at the head of this kingdom now, with half the petty kings (I saw Cador's face again) at his throat? And how was even I to know, through the light and the smoke, what the god's smile portended?

"You think not?" said the King again. I saw his finger-bones whiten where he held the goblet, and wondered that the thin silver did not crush. "When we last spoke together, Merlin, I asked a service of you, and I have no doubt it has been faithfully performed. I believe that service has almost reached its end. No, listen to me!" This though I had not spoken, nor even taken breath to speak. He talked like a man in a corner, attacking before he is even in danger. "I don't have to remind you what I said to you before, nor do I have to ask if you obeyed me. Wherever you have kept the boy, however you have trained him, I take it he is ignorant of his birth and standing, but that he is fit to come to me and stand before all men as a prince and my heir."

The blood ran hot under my skin in a flush I could feel.

"Are you trying to tell me that you think the time has come?"

I had forgotten to school my voice. The silver goblet went back on the table with a rap. The angry blue eyes came back to me. "A king does not 'try to tell' his servants what they must do, Merlin."

I dropped my eyes with an effort and slowly, deliberately unclenched the apprehension that gripped me, the way one levers open the jaws of a fighting dog. I felt his angry stare on me, and heard the breath whistle through his pinched nostrils. Make Uther really angry, and it might take me years to fight my way back to the boy's side. I was aware in the silence that he shifted in his chair as if in sudden discomfort. In a breath or two I was able to look up and say: "Then supposing you tell me, King, whether you sent for me to discuss your health, or your son. Either way, I am still your servant."

He stared at me in rigid silence, then his brow slowly cleared, and his mouth relaxed into something like amusement. "Whatever you are, Merlin, you are hardly that. And you were right; I am trying to tell you something, something which concerns both my health and my son. By the Scorpion, why can I not find the words? I have sent for you not to demand my son of you, but to tell you that, if your healing skill fails me now, he must needs be King."

"You told me just now that you were healed."

"I said the wound was healed. The poison has gone, and the pain, but it has left a sickness behind it of a kind that Gandar cannot cure. He told me to look to you."

I remembered what Lucan had told me about the King who walked with ghosts, and I thought of some of the things I had seen at Pergamum. "You don't look to me like a man who is mortally ill, Uther. Are you speaking of a sickness of the mind?"

He didn't answer that, but when he spoke, it was not in the voice of a man changing the subject. "Since you were abroad, I have had two more children by the Queen. Did you know that?"

"I heard about the girl Morgian, but I didn't know about this last stillbirth until today. I'm sorry."

"And did this famous Sight of yours tell you that there would be no more?" Suddenly, he slammed the goblet down again on the table beside his chair. I saw that the silver had indeed dented under his fingers' pressure. He got to his feet with the violence of a thrown spear. I could see then that what I had taken for energy was a kind of drawn and dangerous tightness, nerves and sinews twanging like bowstrings. The hollows under his cheekbones showed sharp as if something had eaten him empty from within. "How can anyone be a King who is less than a man?" He flung this question at me, and then strode across the room to the window, where he leaned his head against the stone, looking out at the morning.

Now at last I understood what he had been trying to tell me. He had sent for me once before, to this very room, to tell me how his love for Ygraine, Gorlois' wife, was eating him alive. Then, as now, he had resented having to call upon my skill; then, as now, he had shown this same feverish and tightly drawn force, like a bowstring ready to snap. And the cause had been the same. Ambrosius had once said to me, "If he would think with his brains instead of his body sometimes he'd be the better for it." Until this matter of Ygraine, Uther's violent sexual needs had served his ends—not only of pleasure and bodily ease, but because his men, soldiers like himself, admired the prowess which, if not boasted of, was at any rate unconcealed. To them it was a matter for envy, amusement and admiration. And to Uther himself it was more than bodily satisfaction; it was an affirmation of self, a pride which was part of his own picture of himself as a leader.

He still neither moved nor spoke. I said: "If you find it hard to talk to me, would you rather I consulted with your other doctors first?"

"They don't know. Only Gandar."

"Then with Gandar?"

But in the end he told me himself, pacing up and down the room with that quick, limping stride. I had risen when he did, but he motioned me back impatiently, so I stayed where I was, turned away from him, leaning back in my chair beside the brazier, knowing that he walked up and down the room only because he would not face me as he talked. He told me about the raid at Vagniacae and the defending party he had led, and the sharp bitter skirmish on the shingle. The spear thrust had taken him in the groin, not a deep wound but a jagged one, and the blade had not been clean. He had had the cut bound up, and, because it did not trouble him overmuch, had disregarded it; on a new alarm about a Saxon landing in the Medway, he had followed this up immediately, taking no rest until the menace was over. Riding had been uncomfortable, but not very painful, and there had been no warning until it was too late that the wound had begun to fester. In the end even Uther had to admit that he could no longer sit his horse, and he had been carried in a litter back to London. Gandar, who had not been with the troops, had been sent for, and under his care, slowly, the poison had dried up, and the festering scars healed. The King still limped slightly where the muscles had knitted awry, but there was no pain, and everything had seemed to be set for full recovery. The Queen had been all this time at Tintagel for her lying-in, and as soon as he was better himself, Uther made ready to go to her. Apparently quite recovered, he had ridden to Winchester, where he had halted his party to hold a council. Then, that night, there had been a girl—

Uther stopped talking abruptly, and took another turn of the room, which sent him back to the window. I wondered if he imagined I had thought him faithful to the Queen, but it had never occurred to me. Where Uther was, there had always been a girl.

"Yes?" I said.

And then at last the truth came out. There had been a girl and Uther had taken her to bed, as he had taken so many others in passing but urgent lust. And he found himself impotent.

"Oh, yes"—as I began to speak—"it has happened before, even to me. It happens to us all at times, but this should not have been one of the times. I wanted her, and she was skillful, but I tell you there was nothing—nothing. . . . I thought that perhaps I was weary from the journey, or that the discomfort of the saddle—it was no more than discomfort—had fretted me overmuch, so I waited there in Winchester to rest. I lay with the girl again, with her and with others. But it was no use, not with any of them." He swung away from the window then and came back to where I sat. "And then a messenger came from Tintagel to say that the Queen had been brought to bed early, of a stillborn prince." He was looking down at me, almost with hatred. "That bastard you hold for me. You've always been sure, haven't you, that he would be King after me? It seems you were right, you and your damned Sight. I'll get no other children now."

There was no point in commiseration, and he would not have wanted it from me. I said merely: "Gandar's skill in surgery is as great as mine. You can have no reason to doubt it. I will look at you if you wish, but I should like to talk to Gandar first."

"He has not your way with drugs. There is no man living who knows more about medicine. I want you to make me some drug that will bring life back to my loins. You can do this, surely? Every old woman swears she can concoct love potions—"

"You've tried them?"

"How could I try them without telling every man in my army—yes, and every woman in London—that their King is impotent? And can you hear the songs and stories if they knew this about me?"

"You are a good king, Uther. People don't mock that. And soldiers don't mock the men who lead them to victory."

"How long can I do that, the way I am? I tell you I am sick in more than body. This thing eats at me . . . I cannot live as half a man. And as for my soldiers—how would you like to ride a gelding into battle?"

"They'd follow you even if you rode in a litter, like a woman. If you were yourself, you would know that. Tell me, does the Queen know?"

"I went on from Winchester to Tintagel. I thought that, with her . . . but . . ."

"I see." I was matter of fact. The King had told me enough, and he was suffering. "Well, if there is a drug that will help you, be sure I shall find it. I learned more of these things in the East. It may be that this is only a matter of time and treatment. We have seen this happen too often to think of it as the end. You may yet get another son to supplant the 'bastard' I hold for you."

He said harshly: "You don't believe that."

"No. I believe what the stars tell me, if I have read them rightly. But you can trust me to help you as best I can: whatever happens, it's with the gods. Sometimes their ways seem cruel; who knows this better than you and I? But there is something else I have seen in the stars, Uther; whoever succeeds you, it will not be yet. You'll fight and win your own battles for a few years to come."

From his face, I knew then that he had feared worse things than his impotence. I saw, from the lightening of his look, that the cure of mind and body might well have begun. He came back to his chair, sat, and picking up the goblet, drained it, and set it down.

"Well," he said, and smiled for the first time, "now I shall be the first to believe the people who say that the King's prophet never lies. I shall be glad to take your word on this. . . . Come, fill the cups again, Merlin, and we'll talk. You have a lot to tell me; I can listen now."

So we talked for a while longer. When I began to tell him what I knew of Arthur, he listened calmly and with deep attention; I realized from the way he spoke that for some time now he must, whether consciously or not, have been pinning his hopes on his eldest born. I told him where the boy was now, and to my relief he raised no objections; indeed, after a few questions and a pause for thought he nodded approvingly.

"Ector is a good man. I might have thought of him myself, but as you know I was telling over the kings' courts, and never spared a thought for such as he. Yes, it will do . . . Galava is a good place, and safe. . . . And by the Light Himself, if the treaties I have made in the north hold good, I shall see that it remains so. And what you tell me about the boy's status there, and training . . . It will do well. If blood and training tell, he'll be a good fighter and a man whom men can trust and follow. We must see that Ector gets the best master-at-arms in the country."

I must have made a slight movement of protest, because he smiled again. "Oh, never fear, I can be secret too. After all, if he is to have the most illustrious teacher in the land, then the King must try to match him. How do you propose to get yourself up there to Galava, Merlin, without having half Britain follow you looking for magic and medicines?"

I answered with something vague. My public coming to London had served its purpose; already the buzz would have gone out that Prince Arthur was alive and thriving. As to my next disappearance, I did not yet know how or when it must be done; I could hardly think beyond the fact that the King had accepted all my plans, and that there was no question of Arthur's being removed from my care. I suspected that, as before, it was a decision taken with relief; once I had gone to my secret post at Galava, the King would forget me more readily than ever would the good folk at Maridunum.

He was speaking of it now. Unless the need came sooner, he said, he would send for the boy when he was grown—fourteen or so, and ready to lead a troop—and present him publicly, ratifying the young prince as his heir.

"Providing still that I have no other," he added, with a flash of the old hard look, and dismissed me to go and talk with Gandar.

5

Gandar was waiting for me in the room which had been allotted to me. While I had been talking with the King my baggage had been brought from the ship, and unpacked by my servant Stilicho. I showed Gandar the drugs I had brought with me, and after we had talked the King's case over, suggested that he send an assistant to study their use and preparation with me over the next few days, before I left London. If he had no one whom he could sufficiently trust to tend the King and be silent about it, I would lend him Stilicho.

At his look of surprise, I explained. As I have said, Stilicho had discovered a fair talent for preparing the dried plants and roots I had brought with me from Pergamum. He could not read, of course, but I put signs on the jars and boxes, and to begin with allowed him to handle only the harmless ones. But he proved reliable, and oddly painstaking for so lively a boy. I have learned since that men of his race have this facility with plants and drugs, and that the little kings of that country dare not eat even an unblemished apple without a taster. I was pleased to have found a servant who could be of use to me in this way, and had taught him a good deal. I would have been sorry to leave him behind in London, so was relieved when Gandar replied that he had an assistant he could trust, who should be sent to me as soon as I was ready.

I started work immediately. At my request Stilicho had been given a small chamber to himself, with a charcoal stove, and a table, and the various bowls and implements he needed. The room adjoined my own, with no door between, but I had had a double thickness of curtain hung across the doorway. Stilicho had by no means come to terms with the British summer, and kept his room at eruption point with heat.

It was about three days before I found a formula which promised some help for the King, and sent a message to Gandar. He, gasping before he had fairly got through the curtains, came himself, but instead of the assistant I expected he brought a girl with him, a young maiden whom I recognized after a moment as Morgause, the King's bastard daughter. She could be no more than thirteen or fourteen, but she was tall for her age, and it was true that she was beautiful. At that age many girls only show promise of beauty; Morgause had the thing itself, and even I, who am no judge of women, could see that this might be a beauty to send men mad. Her body was slight with a child's slenderness, but her breasts were full and pointed and her throat round as a lily stem. Her hair was rosy gold, streaming long and unbound over the golden-green robe. The large eyes that I remembered were gold-green too, liquid and clear as a stream running over mosses, and the small mouth lifted into a smile over kitten's teeth as she dropped a deep reverence to me.

"Prince Merlin." It was a demure child's voice, little more than a whisper. I saw Stilicho glance round from his work, then stand staring.

I gave her my hand. "They told me you had grown into a beauty, Morgause. Some man will be fortunate. You're not contracted yet? Then all the men in London have been slow."

The smile deepened, folding itself into dimples at the corner of her mouth. She did not speak. Stilicho, catching my glance, bent over his work again, but not, I thought, with quite the concentration it required.

"Phew," said Gandar, fanning himself. I could see the sweat already beading his broad face. "Do you have to work in a tepidarium?"

"My servant comes from a more blessed corner of the earth than this. They breed salamanders in Sicily."

"More blessed, you call it? I'd die in an hour."

"I'll have him bring the things out into my chamber," I offered.

"No need, for me. I'll not stay. I only came to present you my assistant, who will care for the King. Aye, you may well look surprised. You'll hardly believe me, but this child here is skilled already with drugs. Seems she had a nurse in Brittany, one of their wise women, who taught her the gathering and drying and preparing, and since she came over here she's been eager to learn more. But an army medical unit didn't seem quite the place for her."

"You surprise me," I said dryly. The girl Morgause had moved near the table where Stilicho was working, and bent her graceful little head towards him. A tress of the rose-gold hair brushed his hand. He labelled two jars at random, both wrongly, before he recovered himself and reached for a knife to melt the seals again.

"So," said Gandar, "when she heard the King needed drugs, she asked to look after them. She's practised enough, no fear of that, and the King has consented. For all she's young, she knows how to keep her counsel, and who better to care for him and keep his secrets than his own daughter?"

It was a good idea, and I said so. Gandar himself, though nominally the King's chief physician, had charge of the army medical teams. Until this recent wounding the King had hardly needed his personal care, and in any action or threat of it Gandar's place would be with the army. In Uther's present predicament his own daughter, so fortunately skilled, would answer very well.

"She's more than welcome to learn all she can here." I turned to the girl. "Morgause, I've distilled a drug which I think will help the King. I've copied out the formula for you here—can you make it out? Good. Stilicho has the ingredients, if he'll take time to label them correctly . . . Now, I'll leave him to show you how to compound the medicine. If you give him half an hour to get his apparatus out of this steam bath—"

"No need, for me," she said in a demure echo of Gandar. "I like the heat."

"Then I'll leave you," said Gandar with relief. "Merlin, will you come and sup with me tonight, or are you with the King?"

I followed him out into the cool airiness of my own room. From beyond the curtain came the murmur, hesitant with shyness, of the servant's voice, and an occasional soft question from the girl.

"It'll be all right, you'll see," said Gandar. "No need to look so doubtful."

"Was I? Not about the medicine, at any rate, and I'll take your word for the girl's skill."

"In any case, you'll surely stay a little while, and see how she does?"

"Certainly. I don't want to be too long in London, but I can give it a few days. You'll be here yourself?"

"Yes. But there's been such a marked change in him even in these last three days since you came, that I can't see he'll need me in attendance much longer."

"Let's hope it continues," I said. "To tell you the truth, I'm not much troubled . . . Certainly not for his general health. And for the impotence—if he gets ease and sleep, his mind may stop tormenting his body, and the condition may right itself. This seems to be happening already. You know how these things go."

"Oh, aye, he'll mend"—he glanced towards the curtained door and dropped his voice—"as far as need be. As to whether we can get the stallion back to the stand again, I can't see that it matters, now that we know there's a prince safe, and growing, and likely for the crown. We'll get him out of his distemper, and if by God's grace and the drugs you brought he lives to fight . . . and stays king of the pack—"

"He'll do that."

"Well . . ." he said, and let it go. I may say here that the King did in fact mend rapidly. The limp disappeared, he slept well and put on flesh, and I learned some time later from one of his chamberers that, although the King was never again the Bull of Mithras that his soldiers had laughed over and admired, and though he fathered no more children, he took certain satisfactions in his bed, and the unpredictable violences of his temper declined. As a soldier he was soon, again, the single-minded warrior who had inspired his troops and led them to victory.

When Gandar had gone, I went back into the boy's room to find Morgause slowly conning over the paper I had given her, while Stilicho showed her, one by one, the simples for distillation, the powders for sleeping draughts, the oils for massage of the pulled muscles. Neither of them saw me come in, so I watched for a few minutes in silence. I could see that Morgause missed nothing, and that, though the boy still watched her sideways and tended to shy from her beauty like a colt from fire, she seemed as oblivious of his sex as a princess should be of a slave.

The heat of the room was making my head ache. I crossed

quickly to the table. Stilicho's monologue stopped short, and the girl looked up and smiled.

I said: "You understand it all? Good. I'll leave you now with Stilicho. If there's anything you want to know that he can't tell you, send for me."

I turned then to give instructions to the boy, but to my surprise Morgause made a quick movement towards me, laying a hand on my sleeve.

"Prince—"

"Morgause?"

"Must you really go? I—I thought you would teach me, you yourself. I want so much to learn from you."

"Stilicho can teach you all you need to know about the drugs the King will want. If you wish, I will show you how to help him over the pain of the tightened muscles, but I should have thought his bath-slave would do that better."

"Oh, yes, I know. I wasn't thinking of things like that: it's easy enough to learn what is needed for the King's care. It was—I had hoped for more. When I asked Gandar to bring me to you, I had thought—I had hoped—"

The sentence died and she drooped her head. The rose-gold hair fell in a gleaming curtain to hide her face. Through it, as through rain, I saw her eyes watching me, thoughtful, meek, childlike.

"You had hoped—?"

I doubt if even Stilicho, four paces away, heard the whisper. "—that you might teach me a little of your art, my lord Prince." Her eyes appealed to me, half hopeful and half afraid, like a bitch expecting to be whipped.

I smiled at her, but I knew my manner was stiff and my voice over-formal. I can face an armed enemy more easily than a young girl pleading like this, with a pretty hand on my sleeve, and her scent sweet on the hot air like fruit in a sunny orchard. Strawberries, was it, or apricots. . . ? I said quickly: "Morgause, I've no art to teach you that you cannot learn as easily from books. You read, don't you? Yes, of course you do, you read the formula. Then learn from Hippocrates and Galen. Let them be your masters; they were mine."

"Prince Merlin, in the arts I speak of you have no master."

The heat of the room was overpowering. My head hurt me. I must have been frowning, because she came close with a gentle dipping movement, like a bird nestling, and said rapidly, pleadingly: "Don't be angry with me. I've waited so long, and I was so sure that the chance had come. My lord, all my life I have heard people speak of you. My nurse in Brittany—she told me how she used to see you walking through the woods and by the seashore, gathering the cresses and roots and the white berries of the thunder-bough, and how sometimes you went with no more sound than a ghost, and no shadow even on a sunny day."

"She was telling stories to frighten you. I am a man like other men."

"Do other men talk to the stars as if they were friends in a familiar room? Or move the standing stones? Or follow the druids into Nemet and not die under the knife?"

"I did not die under the druids' knife because the arch-druid was afraid of my father," I said bluntly. "And when I was in Brittany I was hardly a man, and certainly not a magician. I was a boy then, learning my trades as you are learning yours. I was barely seventeen when I left there."

She seemed hardly to have heard. I noticed how still she was, the long eyes shadowed under the curtaining hair, the narrow white hands folded below her breast against the green gown. She said: "But you are a man now, my lord, and can you deny that you have worked magic here in Britain?

Since I have been here with my father the King, I have heard you spoken of as the greatest enchanter in the world. I have seen the Hanging Stones, which you lifted and set in their place, and I have heard how you foretold Pendragon's victories and brought the star to Tintagel, and made the King's son vanish away to the isle of Hy-Brasil—"

"So you heard that here, too, did you?" I tried for a lighter tone. "You'd better stop, Morgause, you're scaring my servant, and I don't want him running off, he's too useful."

"Don't laugh at me, my lord. Do you deny that you have the arts?"

"No, I don't deny it. But I couldn't teach you the things you want to know. Certain kinds of magic you can learn from any adept, but the arts which are mine are not mine to give away. I could not teach them to you, even if you were old enough to understand them."

"I could understand them now. I already have magic—such magic as young maids can learn, no more. I want to follow you and learn from you. My lord Merlin, teach me how to find power like yours."

"I've told you it isn't possible. You will have to take my word for that. You are too young. I'm sorry, child. I think that for power like mine you will always be too young. I doubt if any woman could go where I go and see what I see. It is not an easy art. The god I serve is a hard master."

"What god? I only know men."

"Then learn from men. What I have of power I cannot teach you. I have told you it is not my gift."

She watched me without comprehension. She was too young to understand. The light from the stove glimmered on the lovely hair, the wide, clever brows, the full breasts, the small, childish hands. I remembered that Uther had offered her to Lot, and that Lot had rejected her in favour of the young half-sister. I wondered if Morgause knew; and, compassionately, what would become of her.

I said gently: "It's true, Morgause. He only lends his power for his own ends. When they are achieved, who knows? If he wants you, he will take you, but don't walk into the flames, child. Content yourself with such magic as young maids can use."

She began to speak, but we were interrupted. Stilicho had been heating something in a bowl over the burner, and was no doubt so busy straining to hear what was being said that he let the bowl tilt, and some of the liquid spilled onto the flames. There was a hiss and a spitting, and a cloud of herb-smelling steam billowed thick between me and the girl, obscuring her. Through it I saw her hands, those still hands, moving quickly to fan the pungent mist away from her eyes. My own were watering. Vision blurred and glittered. The pain in my head blinded me. The movement of the small white hands through the steam was weaving a pattern like a spell. The bats went past me in a cloud. Somewhere near me the strings of my harp whimpered. The room shrank round me, chilled to a globe of crystal, a tomb . . .

"I'm sorry, master. Master, are you ill? Master?"

I shook myself awake. My vision cleared. The steam had thinned, and the last of it was wisping away through the window. The girl's hands were still again, folded as before; she had shaken her hair back, and was watching me curiously. Stilicho had lifted the bowl from the burner, and peered at me across it, anxious and scared.

"Master, it's one you mix yourself. You said there was no harm in it . . ."

"No harm at all. But another time, watch what you're doing." I looked down at the girl. "I'm sorry, did I frighten you? It's nothing, a headache, I get them sometimes. Sudden, and soon gone. Now I must go. I leave London at the end of the week. If you need my help before then, send to me and I shall be glad to come." I smiled, and reached out a hand to touch her hair. "No, don't look so downcast, child. It's a hard gift to have, and not for young maids."

She curtsied to me again as I went out, the small lovely face hidden once more behind the curtaining hair.

6

I think this was the only time in my life that I saw Bryn
Myrddin not as the home I was eager to reach, but as a
mere halting place on a journey. And once I had arrived in
Maridunum, instead of welcoming the familiar quiet of the
valley, the company of my books, the time to think and to
work with my music and my medicines, I found myself fretting to be away, all my being straining northwards to where
the boy lived who was to be my life from this time on.

All I knew of him, apart from the cryptic reassurances
which had come to me through Hoel and Ector, was that he
was healthy and strong, though smaller for his age than Cei,
Ector's own son, had been. Cei was eleven years old now, to
Arthur's eight, and as familiar to my visions as the young
prince. I had watched Arthur scuffling with the older boy,
riding a horse that to my coward's eye looked far too big
for him, playing at swordsmanship with staves, and then with
swords: I suppose these must have been blunted, but all I
saw was the dangerous flash of the metal, and here, though
Cei had the strength and the longer reach, I could see that
Arthur was quick as a sword himself. I watched the pair of
them fishing, climbing, racing through the edge of the Wild
Forest in a vain bid to escape Ralf who (with the help of
Ector's two most trusted men) rode guard on Arthur at all
times, day or night. All this I watched in the fire, in the
smoke or the stars, and once where there were none of these
and the message was straining to be through, in the side of a
precious crystal goblet which Ahdjan was displaying to me

in his palace by the Golden Horn. He must have wondered at my sudden inattention, but probably put it down to indigestion after one of his lavish meals, which to an Eastern host is rather a compliment than otherwise.

I could not even be sure that I should recognize Arthur when I saw him, nor could I tell what kind of boy he had grown to be. Daring I could see, and gaiety, and stubborn strength, but of his real nature I could be no judge; visions may fill the mind's eye, but it takes blood to engage the heart. I had not even heard him speak. Nor had I as yet any clear idea how to enter his life when I did reach the north country, but every night of my journey from London to Bryn Myrddin I walked outside under the stars, searching for what they had to tell me, and always the Bear hung there straight ahead of me, glittering, speaking of the dark north and cool skies and the smell of pines and mountain water.

Stilicho's reaction when he saw the cave where I lived was not what I expected. When I had left home to go on my travels, since I was to be away for so long, I had hired help to look after the place for me. I had left money with the miller on the Tywy, asking him to send one of his servants up from time to time; it was apparent that this had been done, for the place was clean, dry and well provisioned. There was even fresh bedding for the horses, and we had barely dismounted before the girl from the mill came panting after us up the track with goats' milk and fresh bread and five or six newly caught trout. I thanked her, and then, because I would not let Stilicho clean the fish at the holy well, asked her to show him where the runaway water trickled down below the cliff. While I checked over my sealed jars and bottles, making sure that the lock on my chest was untouched and that the books and instruments within were undamaged, I could hear the two young voices outside still clacking busily as the mill wheel, with a good deal of laughter

226

as each tried to make the other understand the foreign tongue.

When at length the girl went and the boy came in with the fish neatly gutted and split ready for roasting, he seemed happily prepared to find the place as convenient and comfortable as any of the houses we had stayed in on my travels. At first I put this down in some amusement to the compensation he had just discovered, but I found later that he had in fact been born and reared in just such a cave in his own country, where people of the lower sort are so poor that the owners of a well-placed and dry cavern count themselves lucky, and often have to fight like foxes to keep their den to themselves. Stilicho's father, who had sold him with rather less thought than one would give to an unwanted puppy, had been well able to spare him out of a family of thirteen; his room in the cave had been more valuable than his presence. As a slave, his quarters had been in the stables, or more usually out in the yard, and even since he had been in my service I was aware that I had lodged in places where the grooms were worse housed than the horses. The chamber he had occupied in London was the first he had ever had to himself. To him my cave on Bryn Myrddin was spacious and even luxurious, and now it promised further pleasures which did not often come the way of a young slave in the sharp competition of the servants' quarters.

So he settled in cheerfully, and word soon got round that the enchanter was back in his hill, and the folk came for drugs, and paid as they had always done with food and comforts. The miller's girl, whose name was Mai, seized every opportunity to come up the valley with food from the mill, and sometimes with the people's offerings which she brought for them. Stilicho, in his turn, made a practice of calling at the mill every time he went down to the town for me. And before very long it appeared that Mai had made him welcome in every way known to her. One night when I could

227

not sleep I went out onto the lawn beside the holy well to look at the stars, and heard, in the night's quiet, the horses moving and stamping restlessly in their shed below the cliff. It was a night bright with stars and a white scythe of a moon, so I did not need a torch, but called softly to Stilicho to follow me and trod quickly down to the thorn grove to find out what was disturbing the beasts. It was only when I saw, through the half-opened door, the two young bodies coupling in the straw, that I realized Stilicho was there before me. I withdrew without being seen, and went back to my own bed to think.

A few days later when I talked to the boy, and told him that I planned to go north soon, but wanted no one to know of it, so would leave him behind to cover my retreat, he was enthusiastic, and fervent in protestations of faithfulness and secrecy. I was sure I could trust him; another gift he had besides his facility with drugs, he was a marvellous liar. I am told that this, too, is a gift of his people. My only fear was that he might lie too well, like his horse-trading father, and cheat himself and me into trouble. But it was a risk I had to take, and I judged him too loyal to me, and too happy in his life at Bryn Myrddin, to put it at risk. When he asked (trying not to sound too eager) when I would be gone, I could only tell him that I was waiting for a time, and a sign. As always, he accepted what I said, simply and without question. He would as soon have questioned a priestess mouthing in her shrine—they hold the Old Religion in Sicily—or Hephaistos himself when he breathed flame from the mountains. I had found that he believed every tale the people told of me, and would have shown no surprise if I had vanished in a puff of smoke or conjured gold from thin air. I suspected that, like Gaius, he made the most of his status as my servant; certainly Mai was terrified of me, and could not be persuaded to set foot beyond the thorn grove. Which was just as well for the plans I had in mind.

It was no magic sign that I was waiting for. If I had been certain it was safe, I would have set off for the north soon after I had reached home from London. But I knew that I would be watched. Uther would almost certainly continue to have me spied upon. There was no danger in this—not, that is, from the King; but if one man can buy a spy's loyalty, so can another, and there must be many others who, even only for curiosity, would be watching me. So I curbed my impatience, stayed where I was, and went about my business, waiting for the watchers to show themselves.

One day I sent Stilicho down with the horses to the forge at the edge of the town. Both animals had been shod for the journey from London, and though normally the shoes would have been removed before winter, I wanted my own mare left shod in preparation for my journey. Her girth buckles, too, were in need of repair, so Stilicho had ridden down, and was to do some errands in the town while the smith looked after the animals.

It was a day of frost, dry and still, but with the kind of thick sky that cuts the rays from the sun and lets it hang red and cold and low. I went over the hilltop to the hut of Abba the shepherd. His son Ban, the simpleton, had cut his hand a few days ago on a stake, and the wound had festered. I had cut the swelling and bound it with salve, but I knew that Ban could be trusted no more than a bandaged dog, and would worry the thing off if it hurt him.

I need not have troubled; the bandage was still in place, and the wound healing fast and neatly. Ban—I have noticed this with simple folk—mended like a child or a wild animal. Which was just as well, since he was one of those men who can hardly pass a week without injuring themselves in some way. After I had tended the hand I stayed. The hut was in a sheltered part of the valley, and Abba's sheep were all in fold. As sometimes happens, there were early lambs due, though it was only December. I stayed to help Abba with a hard lambing where the simpleton's hand would not have served him. By the time the twin lambs were curled, dry and sleeping, on Ban's knee near the fire, with the ewe watching nearby, the short winter's day had drawn to a red dusk. I took my leave, and walked home over the hilltop. The way took me across my own valley higher up, and it was dark when I reached the pine wood above the cave. The sky had cleared, the night was still and brightly starred, with a blurred moon throwing blue shadows on the frost. And shadows I saw, moving. I stopped dead, and stood to watch.

Four men, on the flat lawn outside my cave. From the thorn thicket below the cliff came the movement and clink of their tethered horses. I could hear the mutter of the men's voices as they huddled together, conferring. Two of them had swords in their hands.

Every moment the moonlight strengthened and fresh stars showered out into the frosty sky. Far away at the foot of the valley I heard the bark of a dog. Then, faintly, the clip of hoofs coming at a gentle pace. The intruders below me heard it, too. One of them gave a low command, and the group turned and made at speed for the path which would take them down to the grove.

They had barely reached the head of the path when I spoke from directly above them. "Gentlemen?"

You would have thought I had fallen straight from heaven in a chariot of flame. I suppose it was alarming enough, to be addressed out of the dark by a man they thought they had just heard riding up the valley some half-mile away. Besides, any man who sets out to spy on a magician starts more than half terrified, and ready to believe any marvel. One of them cried out in fear, and I heard a stifled oath from the leader. In the starlight their faces, upturned, looked grey as the frost.

I said: "I am Merlin. What do you want with me?"

There was a silence, in which the hoof-beats came nearer, quickening as the horses scented home and supper. I caught a movement below me as if they were half minded to turn and run. Then the leader cleared his throat. "We come from the King."

"Then put up your foolish swords. I will come down."

When I reached them I saw they had obeyed me, but their hands hovered not far from their weapons, and they huddled close together.

"Which of you is the leader?"

The biggest of them stepped forward. He was civil, but with truculence behind it. He had not relished that moment of fear. "We were waiting for you, Prince. We bring messages from the King."

"With swords drawn? Well, you are only four to one, after all."

"Against enchantment," said the man, nettled.

I smiled. "You should have known that my enchantment would never work against King's men. You could have been sure of your welcome." I paused. Their feet shuffled in the frost. One of them muttered something, half curse, half invocation, in his own dialect. I said: "Well, this is hardly the place to talk. My home is open to all comers, as you see. Why did you not kindle the fire and light the lamps and wait for me in comfort?"

More shuffling. They exchanged glances. No one answered. Clearly where we stood the scuffled frost showed their tracks up to the cave mouth. So, they had been inside. "Well," I said, "be welcome now."

I crossed to the holy well where the wooden image of the

god stood, barely visible in its dark niche. I lifted down the cup, poured for him and drank. I invited the leader with a gesture. He hesitated, then shook his head. "I am a Christian. What god is that?"

"Myrddin," I said, "the god of high places. This was his hill before it was mine. He lends it to me, but he watches it still."

I saw the movement I had been waiting for among the men. Hands were behind backs as they made the sign against enchantment. One of them, then another, came forward to take the cup, drink, and spill for the god. I nodded at them. "It does not do to forget that the old gods still watch from the air and wait in the hollow hills. How else did I know you were here?"

"You knew?"

"How not? Come in." I turned in the cave mouth, holding back the boughs that half screened the entrance. None of them moved, except the leader, and he took one step only, then hesitated. "What's the matter?" I asked him. "The cave is empty, isn't it? Or isn't it? Did you find something amiss when you went in, that you are afraid to tell me?"

"There was nothing amiss," said the leader. "We didn't go in—that is—" He cleared his throat, and tried again. "Yes, we went inside, only a pace over the threshold, but—" He stopped. There was muttering, and more glances, and I heard, "Go on, tell him, Crinas."

Crinas started again. "The truth is, sir—"

His story was a long time coming, with many hesitations and promptings, but I got it in the end, still waiting in the cave mouth with the troopers standing round in a half circle, like wary cattle.

It seemed they had come to Maridunum a day or so before, waiting their chance to ride up to the cave unobserved. They had had orders not to approach me openly, for fear that other watchers (whose presence the King suspected) might waylay them and take from them any message I might put into their hands.

"Yes?"

The man cleared his throat. This morning, he said, they had seen my mare tethered outside the smithy, saddled and shod. When they asked the smith where I was he told them nothing, leaving them to assume that I was somewhere in the town, with business to pursue that would keep me until the mare was ready. They had imagined that whoever else was watching me would be staying near me in the town, so had seized the chance and ridden up to the cave.

Another pause. They could see nothing in that darkness, but I could feel they were straining to guess my reactions to their story. I said nothing, and the man swallowed, and ploughed on.

The next part of the story had, at least, the ring of truth. During their wait in Maridunum they had asked, among other idle-sounding questions, the way to the cave. Be sure they had been told, with nothing spared about the holiness of the place, and the power and awesomeness of its owner. The people of the valley were very proud of their enchanter, and my deeds would lose nothing in the telling. So the men had ridden up the valley half afraid already.

They had found, as they expected, a deserted cave. The frost outside held the lawn blank and printless. All that had met them was the silence of the winter hills, broken only by the trickle of the spring. They had lit a torch and peered in through the entrance; the cave was orderly but empty, and the ashes were cold. . . .

"Well?" I asked, as Crinas stopped.

"We knew you were not there, sir, but there was a feeling about the place . . . When we called out there was no reply, but then we heard something rustling in the dark. It seemed

233

to come from the inner cave, where the bed is with the lamp beside it—"

"Did you go in?"

"No, sir."

"Or touch anything?"

"No, sir," he said quickly. "We—we did not dare."

"It's just as well," I said. "And then?"

"We looked all about us, but there was no one. But all the time, that sound. We began to be afraid. There had been stories . . . One of the men said you might be there watching, invisible. I told him not to be a fool, but indeed there was a feeling . . ."

"Of eyes in one's back? Of course there was. Go on."

He swallowed. "We shouted again. And then—they came down out of the roof. The bats, like a cloud."

We were interrupted then. Stilicho had reached the grove and seen the troopers' horses tied there. I heard the shed door slam shut on our horses, then the boy came racing up the twisting pathway and across the flat grass, dagger in hand.

He was shouting something. Moonlight caught the blade of the long knife, held low and level, ready to stab. Metal rasped as the men whirled to defend themselves. I took two swift strides forward, pushing them aside, and bore down hard on the boy's knife hand, bringing him up short.

"No need. They're King's men. Put up." Then, as the others put their weapons back: "Were you followed, Stilicho?"

He shook his head. He was trembling. A slave is not trained to arms like a free man's son. Indeed, it was only since we had come to Bryn Myrddin that I had let him carry a knife at all. I let him go, and turned back to Crinas. "You were telling me about the bats. It sounds to me as if you had let the stories trouble you overmuch, Crinas. If you disturbed the bats, they might certainly alarm you for a moment, but they are only bats."

"But that was not all, my lord. The bats came down, yes, out of the roof, somewhere in the dark, and went past us into the air. It was like a plume of smoke, and the air stank. But after they had gone by us we heard another sound. It was music."

Stilicho, standing close to me, stared from them to me, wide-eyed in the dusk. I saw they were making the sign again.

"Music all around us," said the man. "Soft, like whispering, running round and round the wall of the cave in an echo. I'm not ashamed, my lord, we came out of that cave, and we did not dare go in again. We waited for you outside."

"With swords drawn against enchantment. I see. Well, there is no need to wait longer in the cold. Will you not come in now? I assure you that you will not be harmed, so long as you do not raise a hand against me or my servant. Stilicho, go in and kindle the fire. Now, gentlemen? No, don't try to go. Remember you have not yet given me the King's message."

Finally, between threats and reassurance, they came in, treading very softly indeed, and not speaking above a whisper. The leader consented to sit with me, but none of the others would come in as far, preferring to sit between the fire and the mouth of the cave. Stilicho hurried to warm wine with spices, and hand it round.

Now that they were in the light I could see that they were not dressed in the uniform of the King's regular troops; there was neither badge nor blazon to be seen; they might be taken for the armed troops of any petty leader. They certainly carried themselves like soldiers, and though they paid Crinas no obvious deference, it was apparent that there was some difference of rank between them.

I surveyed them. The leader sat stolidly, but the others fidgeted under my gaze, and I saw one of them, a thin, smallish man with black hair and a pale face, still surreptitiously making the sign.

At length I spoke: "You have come, you tell me, with messages from the King. Did he charge you with a letter?"

Crinas answered me. He was a big man, reddish fair, with light eyes. Some Saxon blood, perhaps; though there are red Celts as fair as this. "No, sir. Only to convey his greetings, and ask after his son's welfare."

"Why?"

He repeated my question in apparent surprise. "Why, my lord?"

"Yes, why? I have been gone from the court four months. In that time the King has had reports. Why should he send you now, and to me? He knows the child is not here. It seems obvious"—I lingered on the word, looking from one to the other of the armed men—"that he could not be safe here. The King also knew that I would wait at Bryn Myrddin for a while before I left to join Prince Arthur. I expect to be spied on, but I find it hard to believe that he sent you with such a message."

The three beyond the fire looked at one another. A broad fellow with a red, pimpled face shifted his sword-belt forward nervously, his hand playing unthinkingly with the hilt. I saw Stilicho's eyes on him; then he moved round with the wine-jug to stand nearby.

Crinas held my eyes for a moment in silence, then nodded. "Well, sir, all right. You've smoked us out. I didn't hope to get away with a thin tale like that, not with you. It was all I could think of at a jump, when you surprised us like that."

"Very well. You are spies. I still want to know why?"

He lifted his broad shoulders. "You know, sir, who better, what kings are. It wasn't for us to question when we were told to come here and look the place over without letting you see us." Behind him the others nodded, agreeing anxiously. "And we did no harm, my lord. We never came into the cave. That much was true."

"No, and you told me why not."

He turned up a hand. "Well, sir, I don't say but you do right to be angry. I'm sorry. This isn't our normal business, as you'll guess, but orders are orders."

"What were you ordered to find out?"

"Nothing special, just ask around, and take a look at the place, and find out when you were going." A quick look sideways, to see how I was taking it. "It was my understanding that there was a lot you hadn't told the King, and he wanted to find out. Did you know he had you followed from the minute you left London?"

Another grain of truth. "I guessed it," I said.

"Well, there you are." He managed to say it as if it explained everything. "It's a way kings have, trusting nobody and wanting to know everything. It's my belief—if you'll excuse me for saying it, my lord—"

"Go on."

"I think the King didn't believe what you told him about where you were keeping the young prince. Maybe he thought you'd shift him, and keep him hidden, like before. So he sent us on the quiet, hoping we'd find some clue."

"Perhaps. Wanting knowledge is a disease of kings. And speaking of that, is there any worsening of the King's health which might have made him suddenly anxious for news?"

I saw, as clearly as if he had said it, that he wished he had thought of this himself. He hesitated, then decided that where it could be told, the truth was safer. "As to that, my lord, we've no information, and I've not seen him myself lately. But they say the sickness has passed, and he's back in the field."

This tallied with what I had been told. I said nothing for a while, but watched them thoughtfully. Crinas drank, with an assumption of ease, but his eyes on me were wary. At length I said: "Well, you have done as you were bidden, and found out what the King wanted. I am still here, and the child is not. The King must trust me for the rest. As for when I am going, I will tell him in my own good time."

Crinas cleared his throat. "That's an answer we'd sooner not take, sir." His voice came over-loud, like a braggart's, but he was not bluffing. The others shared his fear, but without his measure of courage; though this was no comfort to me; I knew that frightened men are dangerous. One of the troopers—the small fellow with black eyes shifting in a face pale with nerves—leaned forward and plucked at his leader's sleeve. I caught the mutter of, "Better go. Don't forget who he is . . . Quite enough now . . . Make him angry."

I said crisply: "I am not angry. You are doing your duty, and it is not your fault if the King trusts no one, but must have each story ratified twice over. You may tell him this" —I paused as if for thought, and saw them craning—"that his son is where I told him, safe and thriving, and that I am only waiting for good weather to make the voyage."

"*Voyage?*" Crinas asked sharply.

I lifted my brows. "Come now. I thought all the world knew where Arthur was. In any case, the King will understand."

One of the men said hoarsely: "Yes, we knew, but it was only a whisper. Then it's true about the island?"

"Quite true."

"Hy-Brasil?" asked Crinas. "That's a myth, my lord, saving your presence."

"Did I give it a name? I am not responsible for the whispers. The place has many names, and enough stories are told about it to fill the Nine Books of Magic . . . And every man who sees it sees something different. When I took Arthur there—"

I paused to drink, as a singer wets his throat before touching the chords. The three in front of me were all attention now. I did not look at Crinas, but spoke past him, giving my voice the tale-teller's extra pitch and resonance.

"You all know that the child was handed to me three nights after he was born. I took him to a safe place, then when the time was right and the world quiet, I carried him westwards, to a coast I know. There, below the cliffs, is a bay of sand where the rocks stand up like the fangs of wolves, and no boat or swimmer can live when the tide is breaking round them. To right and left of the bay the sea has driven arches through the cliff. The rocks are purple and rose-coloured and pale as turquoise in the sun, and on a summer's evening when the tide is low and the sun sinking, men see on the horizon land that comes and goes with the light. It is the Summer Isle, which (they say) floats and sinks at the will of heaven, the Island of Glass through which the clouds and stars can be seen, but which for those who dwell there is full of trees and grass and springs of sweet water . . ."

The pale-faced man was straining forward, open-mouthed, and I saw the shoulders of another shift under his woollen cloak as if with cold. Stilicho's eyes were like shield-bosses.

". . . It is the Isle of Maidens, where kings are carried at their endings. And there will come a day—"

"My lord! I have seen it myself!" That the pale man should interrupt a prophet apparently on the point of prophecy showed a nerve scraped raw. "I have seen it myself! When I was a boy I saw it! Clear, as clear as the Cassiterides on a fair day after rain. But it seemed an empty land."

"It is not empty. And it is not only there when men like

you can see it. It can be found even in winter, for those who know how to find it. But there are not many who can travel to it and then return."

Crinas had listened without moving, his face expressionless. "Then he's on Cornish land?"

"You know it too?"

There was no hint of mockery in my voice, but he said with a snap: "I do not," and set down his empty cup and made ready to rise. I saw his hand go to his sword-belt. "Is this the message we have to take back to the King?"

At a movement of his head the others rose with him. Stilicho set the wine-jug down with a clatter, but I shook my head at him and laughed. "It would go hard with you, I think, if that were all. And hard with me, to have fresh spies set on me. For all our sakes, I'll set his mind at rest. Will you bear a letter back to London for me?"

Crinas stood still a moment, his eyes fast on mine. Then he relaxed, his thumb hooking harmlessly in his belt. When I heard his breath of relief I knew how near he had been to questioning me further in the only way he knew. "Willingly, sir."

"Then wait a while longer. Sit down again. Fill their cups, Stilicho."

The letter to Uther was brief. I began by asking after his health, then wrote that, according to my private sources of information, the prince was well. As soon as the spring came, I told him, I intended to travel and see the boy myself. Meantime I would watch him in my own way, and send the King all the news there was.

After I had sealed the message I took it back into the outer cave. The men had been talking quickly among themselves in undertones, while Stilicho hovered with the wine-jug. They broke off as I came in, and got to their feet. I handed the letter to Crinas.

"Anything else I have to say is in that letter. He will be satisfied." I added: "Even if your mission did not work out precisely to orders, you have nothing to fear from the King. Leave me now, and the god of going watch you on your way."

They went at last, perhaps not so grateful as they might have been for my parting invocation. As they hurried out across the frost I saw the quick sidelong glances into the shadows, and the hunching of cloaks close round their shoulders as if the night were breathing on their backs. As they passed the holy well every one of them made a sign, and I do not think that the last—Crinas'—was the sign of the Cross.

7

The sound of their horses' hoofs dwindled down the valley track. Stilicho came racing back from the cliff above the grove.

"They've all gone." His eyes were wide, dilated not only with the frosty dark. "My lord, I thought they were going to kill you."

"It was possible. They were brave men, and they were frightened. It's a risky combination, especially as one of them was a Christian."

He was on to that as quickly as a house dog on to a rat. "Meaning he didn't believe you?"

"Meaning just that. He was sure he didn't believe me, but he wouldn't have staked anything on its being a lie. Now find me some food, Stilicho, will you? It doesn't matter what, but hurry, and put together what you can for a journey. I'll see to my clothes myself. Is the mare ready?"

"Why, yes, lord, but—you're going tonight?"

"As soon as I can. This is the chance I have been waiting for. They've shown themselves, and by the time they find that the trail I gave them is false I shall be gone—vanished to the island beyond the west. . . . Now, you know what to do; we've talked of it many times."

This was true. We had planned that, when I went, Stilicho would remain at Bryn Myrddin, fetching and carrying supplies as usual, keeping up for as long as he could the illusion that I was still at home. I had built up a store of medicines, and for some time now had let him compound the simpler ones himself and dispense them to the poor folk who came up the valley, so they would not suffer by my absence, and it would be a little time before anyone would raise a question. We might not gain much time in this way, but I should gain enough. Once I was across the nearer hills and had reached the valley tracks in the forest, I would be hard indeed to follow.

So now Stilicho merely nodded, and ran to do as I bade him. In a very short time food was ready, and while I ate he packed together what I would need for the journey. I could see he was bursting with questions, so I let him talk. I could talk to him haltingly in his own tongue, but mainly he got along with his fluent but heavily accented Latin. Since we had left Constantinopolis most of his natural lively spirits had flowed in my direction; he had to talk to someone, and it would have been cruelty to insist on the silent respect which Gaius had tried to instill. Besides, this is not my way. So, as he hurried about his tasks, the questions came eagerly.

"My lord, if that man Crinas didn't really believe in the Isle of Glass, and he had to have the information about the prince, why did he go away?"

"To read my letter. He thinks the truth will be in that."

His eyes widened. "But he'll never dare open a letter to the King! Did you write the truth in it?"

I raised my brows at him. "The truth? Don't you believe in the Isle of Glass, either?"

"Oh, yes. Everyone knows about that." He was solemn. "Even in Sicily we knew of the invisible island beyond the west. But that's not where you're going now, I'd stake anything on that!"

"Why so sure?"

He gave me a limpid look. "You, lord? Across the Western Sea? In winter? I'll believe anything, but not that! If you could use magic instead of a ship, we'd have journeyed more

243

easily in the Middle Sea. Do you remember the storm off Pylos?"

I laughed. "With no magic but mandragora . . . Too well, I remember it. No, Stilicho, I gave nothing away in the letter. That letter will never get to the King. They weren't King's men."

"Not King's men?" He paused, open-mouthed, to stare, then remembered himself and stooped again over the saddlebag he was packing. "How do you know? Did you know them?"

"No. But Uther doesn't use troops to spy; how could he hope to keep them secret? These are troops, sent—as Crinas told me—to ask questions in the market and the taverns in Maridunum, and then to search this place while we were out of it, and find, if not the prince, some clue to him. They weren't even spies. What spy would dare go back to his master and say he had been discovered, but had been given a letter to carry for his victim, with the information in it? I tried to make it easy for them, and it's possible they think they deceived me, but in any case they had to take the chance and get their hands on the letter. I give Crinas best, he's a quick thinker. When I caught them at it, he did well enough. It wasn't his fault that the other man gave him away."

"What do you mean, lord?"

"The small man with the pale face. I heard him say something in his own tongue. I doubt if Crinas heard it. He was speaking in Cornish. So later I spoke of the Isle of Glass, and described the bay, and he knew of that, too, and the Cassiterides. They are islands off the Cornish coast, ones in which even Crinas must believe."

"Cornish?" asked the boy, trying the word.

"From Cornwall, in the south-west."

"Queen's men, then?" Stilicho had not spent all his time

in London in the stillroom with Morgause. He listened almost as much as he talked, and had regaled me continually since we left Uther's court with what "they" were saying about every subject under the sun. "They said she was still in the south-west after the last lying-in."

"That's true. And she might use Cornishmen for secret work, but I think not. Neither the King nor the Queen keep Cornish troops close to them these days."

"There are Cornish troops at Caerleon. I heard it in the town."

I looked up sharply. "Are there indeed? Under whom?"

"I didn't hear. I could find out." He was looking at me eagerly, but I shook my head.

"No. The less you know about it, the better. Leave it now. They'll stop watching me for the length of time it takes to read that letter, and by the time they find someone who can read Greek—"

"Greek?"

"The King has a Greek secretary," I said blandly. "I didn't see why I should make it easy. And I doubt if they know I suspect them. They'll be in no hurry. Besides, I put something in the letter to make them think I would stay here until spring."

"Will they come back?"

"I doubt it. What are they to do? Come back to tell me they read the King's letter, and are not King's men? As long as they think I'm here, they will be afraid to do that, in case I report to the King. They dare not kill me, and they dare not let me find out who they are. They will keep away. As it is, the next time you go into Maridunum, see that a message is sent to the garrison commander to watch for these Cornishmen, and tell him to report what has happened to the King. We may as well use his spies to guard us from the others. . . . There, I've finished. You've packed the food? Fill the flask now, will you? Meanwhile, if anyone does come up here, what is your story?"

"That you have been out daily on the hillside, and that you went last towards Abba's valley, and that I think you must be staying to help him with the sheep." He looked up doubtfully. "They won't believe me."

"Why not? You're an accomplished liar. Be careful, you're spilling that wine."

"A prince help with the sheep? It's not very likely."

"I've done stranger things," I said. "They'll believe you. In any case, it's true. Where do you think I got the blood-stains on my old cloak today?"

"Killing someone, I thought."

He was quite serious. I laughed. "That doesn't happen often, and usually by mistake."

He shook his head in unbelief, and stoppered the wine. "If those men had drawn swords on you, my lord, would you have stopped them with magic?"

"I hardly needed magic, with your dagger so ready. I haven't thanked you yet for your courage, Stilicho. It was well done."

He looked surprised. "You're my master."

"I bought you for money, and gave you back the freedom you were born with. What sort of a debt is that?"

He merely looked without understanding, and presently said: "There, all's ready, lord. You will want your thick boots, and the sheepskin cloak. Shall I get Strawberry ready while you dress?"

"In a moment," I said. "Come here. Look at me. I have promised you that you will be safe here. This is true; I have seen no danger coming, not for you. But once I am clear away, if you are afraid, go down to the mill and stay there."

"Yes, lord."

"Don't you believe me?"

"Yes."

"Then why are you afraid?"

He hesitated, swallowing. Then he said: "The music they spoke of, lord. What was it? Was it really from the gods?"

"In a way. My harp speaks sometimes, of itself, when the air moves. I think that's what they heard and, because they were guilty, they were afraid."

He glanced over to the corner where the big harp stood. I had had it sent across from Brittany, and since I had come home had used it constantly, restoring the other to its place. "That one? How could it, lord, muffled like that against the air?"

"No, not that one. That harp stays dumb until I touch it. I meant the little one I travelled with. I made it myself, here in this cave with Galapas the magician to help me."

He wetted his lips. You could see that this was hardly a re-assurance. "I've not seen it since we got home. Where do you keep it?"

"I was going to show you anyway, before I left. Come, boy, there's no need for you to fear it. You've carried it yourself a thousand times. Now, get me a torch, and come and see."

I led him to the back of the main chamber. I had never shown him the crystal cave, and, because I kept my chest of books and my table across the rough rock-slope that led to the ledge, he had never climbed that way and found it. Now I motioned him to help me shift the table, and holding the torch high, mounted to the shadowy ledge where the crystal cave lay hidden. I knelt down at the entrance and beckoned him forward beside me.

The torch in my hand threw firelight, glimmering through moving smoke, round the globed walls of crystal. Here as a boy I had seen my first visions in the leap and flash of moving flame. Here I had seen myself begotten, the old King dead, the tower of Vortigern built on water, the dragon of Ambrosius leaping to victory. Now the globe was empty but for the harp which stood there, with its shadow thrown clear round the sparkling walls.

I glanced down at the boy's face. Awe was stirring in it, even at the empty globe and the empty shadows.

"Listen," I said. I said it loudly, and as my voice stirred the still air the harp whispered, and the music ran humming round and round the crystal walls.

"I was going to show you the cave," I said. "If ever you want to hide, hide here. I did myself, as a boy. Be sure the gods will watch over you, and you will be safe. Where safer, than right in God's hand, in his hollow hill? Now, go and see to Strawberry. I'll bring the harp down myself. It's time I was gone."

When morning came I was fifteen miles away, riding north through the oak forest which lies along the valley of the Cothi. There is no road there, only tracks, but I knew them well, and I knew the glass-blowers' hut deep in the wood. At this time of the year it would be empty.

I and my mare shared its shelter half that December day. I watered her at the stream, and threw fodder that I had brought into a corner of the hut. I myself was not hungry. There was something else for me to feed on; that deep excited feeling of lightness and power which I recognized. The time had been right, and something lay ahead of me. I was on my way.

I drank a mouthful of wine, wrapped myself warmly in Abba's sheepskins, and fell asleep as soundly and thoughtlessly as a child.

I dreamed again of the sword, and I knew, even through the dream, that this came straight from the god. Ordinary dreams are never so clear; they are jumbles of desires and fears, things seen and heard, and felt though unknown. This came clear, like a memory.

I saw the sword close for the first time, not vast and dazzling, like the sword of stars over Brittany, or dim and fiery as it had shimmered against the dark wall in Ygraine's chamber. It was just a sword, beautiful in the way of a weapon, with the jewels on the hilt set in gold scrollwork, and the blade glimmering and eager, as if it would fight of itself. Weapons are named for this; some are eager fighters, some dogged, some unwilling; but all are alive.

This sword was alive; it was drawn, gripped in the hand of an armed man. He was standing by a fire, a camp fire lit apparently in the middle of a darkened plain, and he was the only person to be seen in all that plain. A long way behind him I saw, dim against the dark, the outline of walls and a tower. I thought of the mosaic I had seen in Ahdjan's house, but it was not Rome this time. The outline of the tower was familiar, but I could not remember where I had seen it, nor even be sure that I had not seen it only in dreams.

He was a tall man, cloaked, and the dark cloak fell in a long heavy line from shoulder to heel. The helmet hid his face. His head was bent, and he held the sword naked across his hands. He was turning it over and over, as if weighing its balance, or studying the runes on the blade. The firelight flashed and darkened, flashed and darkened, as the blade turned. I caught one word, KING, and then again, KING, and saw the jewels sparking as the sword turned. I saw then that the man had a circle of red gold on his helmet, and that his cloak was purple. Then as he moved the firelight lit the ring on his finger. It was a gold ring carved with a dragon.

I said: "Father? Sir?" but, as sometimes happens in dreams, I could make no sound. But he looked up. There were no eyes under the peak of the helmet. Nothing. The hands that held the sword were the hands of a skeleton. The ring shone on bone.

He held the sword out to me, flat across the skeleton hands. A voice that was not my father's said: "Take it." It was not a ghost's voice, or the voice of bidding that comes with vision: I have heard these, and there is no blood in them; it is as if the wind breathed through an empty horn. This was a man's voice, deep and abrupt and accustomed to command, with a rough edge to it such as comes from anger, or sometimes from drunkenness; or sometimes, as now, from fatigue.

I tried to move, but I could not, any more than I could speak. I have never feared a spirit, but I feared this man. From the blank of shadow below the helmet came the voice again, grim, and with a faint amusement, that crept along my skin like the brush of a wolf's pelt felt in the dark. My breath stopped and my skin shivered. He said, and now I clearly heard the weariness in the voice: "You need not fear me. Nor should you fear the sword. I am not your father, but you are my seed. Take it, Merlinus Ambrosius. You will find no rest until you do."

I approached him. The fire had dwindled, and it was almost dark. I put my hands out for the sword, and he reached to lay it across them. I held still, though my flesh shrank from touching his bony fingers; but they were not there to touch. As the sword left his grip it fell, through his hands and through mine, and between us to the ground. I knelt, groping in the darkness, but my hand met nothing. I could feel his breath above me, warm as a living man's, and his cloak brushed my cheek. I heard him say: "Find it. There is no one else who can find it." Then my eyes were open and it was full noon, and the strawberry mare was nuzzling at me where I lay, with her mane brushing my face.

8

December is certainly no time for travelling, especially for one whose business does not allow him to use the roads. The winter woods are open and clear of undergrowth, but there are many places in the remoter valleys where there is no clear going save along the stream-side, and that is tortuous and rough, and the banks are apt to be dangerously broken— or even washed right away—with floods and bad weather. Snow, at least, I was spared, but on the second day out of Bryn Myrddin the weather worsened to a cold wind with flurries of sleet, and there was ice in all the ways.

Going was slow. On the third day, towards dusk, I heard wolves howling somewhere up near the snow-line. I had kept to the valleys, travelling in deep forest still, but now and again where the forest thinned I had caught glimpses of the hilltops, and they were white with fresh snow. And there was more to come; the air had the smell of snow, and the soft cold bite on one's cheek. The snow would drive the wolves down lower. Indeed, as dark drew in and the trees crowded closer I thought I saw a shadow slipping away between the trunks, and there were sounds in the underbrush which might have been made by harmless creatures such as deer or fox; but I noticed that Strawberry was uneasy; her ears flattened repeatedly, and the skin on her shoulders twitched as if flies were settling there.

I rode with my chin on my shoulder and my sword loose in its sheath. "*Mevysen*"—I spoke to my Welsh mare in her own language—"when we find this great sword that Macsen

Wledig is keeping for me, you and I will no doubt be invincible. And find it we must, it seems. But just at the moment I'm as scared of those wolves as you are, so we'll go on till we find some place that's defensible with this poor weapon and my poorer skill, and we'll sit the night out together, you and I."

The defensible place was a ruinous shell of a building deep in the forest. Literally a shell; it was all that remained of a smallish erection the shape of a kiln, or a beehive. Half of it had fallen away, leaving the standing part like an egg broken endways, the curving half-dome backed against the wind and offering some sort of protection from the intermittent sleet. Most of the fallen masonry had been removed—probably stolen for building stone—but there was still a ragged rampart of broken stuff behind which it was possible to take shelter, and conceal myself and the mare.

I dismounted, and led her in. She picked her way between the mossed stones, shook her wet neck, and was soon settled quietly enough with her nosebag, under the dry curve of the dome. I set a heavy rock on the end of her rope, then pulled the dead fronds of some fern from a dry corner under the wall, dried her damp hide with it, and covered her. She seemed to have lost her fears, and munched steadily. I made myself as comfortable as I could with one saddle-bag for a dry seat, and what remained to me of food and wine. I would have dearly liked to light a fire, as much against the wolves as for comfort, but there might be other enemies than wolves looking for me by now, so, with my sword ready to hand, I huddled into my sheepskins and ate my cold rations and fell at last into a waking doze which was the nearest to sleep that danger and discomfort would allow.

And dreamed again. No dream, this time, of kings or swords or stars moving, but a dream half-waking, broken

252

and uneasy, of the small gods of small places; gods of hills and woods and streams and crossways; the gods who still haunt their broken shrines, waiting in the dusk beyond the lights of the busy Christian churches, and the dogged rituals of the greater gods of Rome. In the cities and the crowded places men have forgotten them, but in the forests and the wild hill country the folk still leave offerings of food and drink, and pray to the local guardians of the place who have dwelled there time out of mind. The Romans gave them Roman names, and let them be; but the Christians refuse to believe in them, and their priests berate the poorer folk for clinging to the old ways—and no doubt for wasting offerings which would do better at some hermit's cell than at some ancient holy place in the forest. But still the simple folk creep out to leave their offerings, and when these vanish by morning, who is to say that a god has not taken them?

This, I thought, dreaming, must be such a place. I was in the same forest, and the apse of stone where I sat was the same, even to the rampart of mossed boulders in front of me. It was dark, and my ears were filled with the roaring of the upper boughs where the night wind poured across the forest. I heard nothing approaching, but beside me the mare stirred and breathed gustily into the fodder-bag, and lifted her head, and I looked up to see eyes watching me from the darkness beyond the rampart.

Held by sleep, I could not move. In equal silence, and very swiftly, others came. I could discern them only as shadows against the cold darkness; not wolves, but shadows like men; small figures appearing one by one, like ghosts, and with no more sound, until they ringed me in, eight of them, standing shoulder to shoulder across the entrance to my shelter. They stood there, not moving or speaking, eight small shadows, as much part of the forest and the night as the gloom cast by the trees. I could see nothing except—when high over the bare trees a cloud swept momentarily clear of the winter stars—the gleam of watching eyes.

No movement, no word. But suddenly, without any conscious change, I knew I was awake. And they were still there.

I did not reach for my sword. Eight to one is not a kind of odds that makes sense, and besides, there are other ways to try first. But even those I never got a chance to use. As I moved, taking breath to speak, one of them said something, a word that was blown away in the wind, and the next thing I knew I was being thrown back forcibly against the wall behind me, while rough hands forced a gag into my mouth, and my hands were pulled behind my back and the wrists bound tightly together. They half lifted, half dragged me out of the walled shelter, and flung me down outside with my back against the bruising stones that formed the rampart. One of them produced flint and iron, and after a long struggle managed to set light to the twist of rag stuck in a cracked ox horn which did duty as a torch; the thing burned sullenly with a feeble and stinking light, but with its help they set to work to hunt through the saddle-bags, and examine the mare herself with careful curiosity. Then they brought the torch to where I sat with two of them standing over me and, thrusting the reeking rag almost into my face, examined me much as they had done the mare.

It seemed clear from the fact that I was still alive that they were not simple robbers; indeed, they took nothing from the saddle-bags, and though they disarmed me of sword and dagger, they did not search me further. I began to fear, as they looked me over closely with nods and grunted comments of satisfaction, that they had actually been looking for me. But in that case, I thought, if they had wanted to know my destination, or had been paid to find it out, they would have done better to stay invisible, and follow me. No doubt

I would have led them in the end to Count Ector's doorstep.

Their comments told me nothing about their business with me, but they did tell me something as important: these men spoke in a tongue I had never heard before, but all the same I knew it; the Old Tongue of the Britons, which my master Galapas had taught me.

The Old Tongue has still something the same form as our own British language, but the people who speak it have for so long lived away from other men that their speech has altered, adding its own words and changing its accent until now it takes study and a good ear to follow it at all. I could hear the familiar inflections, and here and there a word recognizable as the Welsh of Gwynedd, but the accent had changed, slurred and strange through five hundred years of isolation, with words surviving that had long fallen out of use in other dialects, and sounds added like the echoes of the hills themselves, and of the gods and wild creatures that dwell there.

It told me who these men must be. They were the descendants of those tribesmen who had, long since, fled to the remoter hills, leaving the cities and the cultivable lands to the Romans, and after them to Cunedda's federates from Guotodin, and had roosted, like homeless birds, in the high tracts of the forest where living was scarce and no better men would dispute it with them. Here and there they had fortified a hilltop and held it, but in most cases any hill that could be so fortified was desirable to conquerors, so was eventually stormed or starved out and taken. So, hilltop by hilltop, the remnants of the unconquered had retreated, till there was left to them only the crags and caves and the bare land which the snow locked in winter. There they lived, seen by none except by chance, or when they wished it. It was they, I guessed, who crept down by night to take the offerings from the country shrines. My waking dream had been true enough. These, perhaps, were all who could be seen by living eyes, of the dwellers in the hollow hills.

They were talking freely—as freely as such folk ever do—not knowing I could understand them. I kept my eyelids lowered, and listened.

"I tell you, it must be. Who else would be travelling in the forest on a night like this? And with a strawberry mare?"

"That's right. Alone, they said, with a red roan mare."

"Maybe he killed the other, and stole the mare. He's hiding, that's certain. Why else lie out here in winter without a fire, and the wolves coming down this low?"

"It's not the wolves he's afraid of. Depend on it, this is the man they were wanting."

"And paying for."

"They said he was dangerous. He didn't look it to me."

"He had a sword drawn ready."

"But he never picked it up."

"We were too quick for him."

"He had seen us. He had time. You shouldn't have taken him like that, Cwyll. They didn't say take him. They said find him and follow him."

"Well, it's too late now. We've taken him. What do we do? Kill him?"

"Llyd will know."

"Yes. Llyd will know."

They did not speak as I have reported it, but in snatches one across the other, brief phrases bandied to and fro in that strange, sparse language. Presently they left me where I lay between my two guards, and withdrew a short distance. To wait, I supposed, for Llyd.

Some twenty minutes later he came, with two companions; three more shadows suddenly no longer part of the forest's blackness. The others crowded round him, talking and pointing, and presently he seized the torch—which was now little more than a singed rag smelling of pitch—and strode towards me. The others crowded after.

They stood in a half circle round me as they had stood before. Llyd held the torch high, and it showed me my captors, not clearly, but enough to know them again. They were small men, dark-haired, with surly lined faces beaten by weather and hard living to a texture like gnarled wood. They were dressed in roughly tanned skins, and breeches of thick, coarse-woven cloth dyed the browns and greens and murreys that you can make with the mountain plants. They were variously armed, with clubs, knives, stone axes chipped to a sheen, and—the one who had given the orders until Llyd came—with my sword.

Llyd said: "They have gone north. There is no one in the forest to hear or see. Take the gag out."

"What's the use?" It was the fellow holding my sword who spoke. "He doesn't know the Old Tongue. Look at him. He does not understand. When we spoke just now of killing him he did not look afraid."

"What does that tell us except that he is brave, which we know already? A man attacked and tied as he is might well be expecting death, but there is no fear in his eyes. Do as I say. I know enough to ask him his name and where he is bound for. Take out the gag. And you, Pwul, and Areth, see if you can find dry stuff to burn. Let us have good light to see him by."

One of the two beside me reached for the knot, and got the gag loosened. It had cut my mouth at the corner, and was foul with blood and spittle, but he thrust it into his pouch. Theirs was a degree of poverty that wasted nothing. I wondered how much "they" had offered to pay for me. If Crinas and his followers had tracked me this far and set the hill-dwellers to watch me and discover where I was bound, Cwyll's hasty action had spoiled that plan. But it had also spoiled mine. Even if they decided now to let me go, so that they could follow me in secret, my journey was fruitless. Forewarned though I was, I could never elude these watchers. They see everything that moves in the forest, and they can send messages as quickly as the bees. I had known all along that the forest would be full of watchers, but normally they stay out of sight and mind their own concerns. Now I saw that my only hope of reaching Galava unbetrayed was to enlist them. I waited to hear what their leader had to say.

He spoke slowly, in bad Welsh. "Who are you?"

"A traveller. I go north to the house of an old friend."

"In winter?"

"It was necessary."

"Where . . ." He searched for the words. ". . . where do you come from?"

"Maridunum."

This, it appeared, tallied with what "they" had told them. He nodded. "Are you a messenger?"

"No. Your men have seen what I carry."

One of them said quickly, in the Old Tongue: "He carries gold. We saw it. Gold in his belt, and some stitched in the mare's girth."

The leader regarded me. I could not read his face; it was about as transparent as oak bark. He said over his shoulder, without taking his eyes off me: "Did you search him?" He was speaking his own language.

"No. We saw what was in his pouch when we took his weapons."

"Search him now."

They obeyed him, not gently. Then they stood back and showed him what they had found, crowding to look by the light of the meager torch. "The gold; look how much. A brooch with the Dragon of the King's house. Not a badge;

258

feel the weight, it is gold. A brand with the Raven of Mithras. And he rides from Maridunum towards the north, and secretly." Cwyll pulled my cloak again across the exposed brand and stood up. "It must be the man the soldiers told us about. He is lying. He is the messenger. We should let him go and follow him."

But Llyd spoke slowly, staring down at me. "A messenger carrying a harp, and the sign of the Dragon, and the brand of the Raven? And he rides alone out of Maridunum? No. There is only one man it can be; the magician from Bryn Myrddin."

"Him?" This was the man who held my sword. It went slack, suddenly, in his grasp, and I saw him swallow and take a fresh grip. "Him, the magician? He is too young. Besides, I have heard of that magician. They say he is a giant, with eyes that freeze you to the marrow. Let him go, Llyd, and we will follow him, as the soldiers asked us."

Cwyll said, uncomfortably: "Yes, let him go. Kings are nothing to us, but a magician is unchancy to harm."

The others crowded close, curious and uneasy.

"A magician? They said nothing about that, or we would never have touched him."

"He's no magician, see how he's dressed. Besides, if he knew magic, he could have stopped us."

"He was asleep. Even enchanters have to sleep."

"He was awake. He saw us. He did nothing."

"We gagged him first."

"He is not gagged now, and see, he says nothing."

"Yes, let him go, Llyd, and we will get the money the soldiers offered. They said they would pay us well."

More mutters, and nods of assent. Then one man said, thoughtfully: "He has more on him than they offered us."

Llyd had not spoken for some time, but now he broke angrily across the talk. "Are we thieves? Or hirelings to give information for gold? I told you before, I will not blindly do as the soldiers asked us, for all their money. Who are they that we, the Old Ones, should do their work? We will do our own. There are things here that I should like to know. The soldiers told us nothing. Perhaps this man will. I think there are great matters afoot. Look at him; that is no man's messenger. That is a man who counts among men. We will untie him, and talk. Light the fire, Areth."

While he had been talking the two he had bidden had brought together a pile of boughs and fallen stuff, and built a pyre ready for lighting. But there could have been no dry twig in the forest that night. Though the sleet showers had stopped some while back, all was dripping wet, and the ground felt spongy as if it must be soaked right to the earth's center.

Llyd made a sign to the two who guarded me. "Untie his hands. And one of you, bring food and drink."

One of them hurried off, but the other hesitated, fingering his knife. Others crowded round, arguing. Llyd's authority, it seemed, was not that of a king, but of an accepted leader whose companions have the right to query and advise. I caught fragments of what they were saying, and then Llyd clearly: "There are things we must know. Knowledge is the only power we have. If he will not tell us of his own will, then we shall have to make him. . . ."

Areth had managed to set the damp stuff smouldering, but it gave neither heat nor light, only an intermittent gusting of smoke, acrid and dirty, which blew into all quarters as the wind wandered, making the eyes smart and choking the breath.

It was time, I thought, that I made an end. I had learned enough. I said, clearly, in the Old Tongue: "Stand back from the fire, Areth."

There was a sudden complete silence. I did not look at

260

them. I fixed my eyes on the smoking logs. I blotted out the bite of my bound wrists, the pain of my bruises, the discomfort of my soaked clothes. And, as easily as a breath taken and then released on the night air, the power ran through me, cool and free. Something dropped through the dark, like a fire arrow, or a shooting star. With a flash, a shower of white sparks that looked like burning sleet, the logs caught, blazing. Fire poured down through the sleet, caught, gulped, billowed up again gold and red and gloriously hot. The sleet hissed in onto the fire, and, as if it had been oil, the fire fed on it, roaring. The noise of it filled the forest and echoed like horses galloping.

I took my eyes from it at last, and looked about me. There was no one there. They had vanished as if they had indeed been spirits of the hills. I was alone in the forest, lying against the tumbled rocks, with the steam rising already from my drying clothes, and the bonds biting painfully into my wrists.

Something touched me from behind. The blade of a stone knife. It slid between the flesh of my wrists and the ropes, sawing at my bonds. They gave way. Stiffly, I flexed my shoulders and began to chafe the bruised wrists. There was a thin cut, bleeding, where the knife had caught me. I neither spoke nor looked behind me, but sat still, chafing my wrists and hands.

From somewhere behind me a voice spoke. It was Llyd's. He spoke in the Old Tongue.

"You are Myrddin called Emrys or Ambrosius, son of Ambrosius the son of Constantius who sprang from the seed of Macsen Wledig?"

"I am Myrddin Emrys."

"My men took you in error. They did not know."

"They know now. What will you do with me?"

"Set you on your journey when you choose to go."

"And meanwhile question me, and force me to tell you of the grave matters that concern me?"

"You know we can force you to do nothing. Nor would we. You will tell us what you wish, and go when you wish. But we can watch for you while you sleep, and we have food and drink. You are welcome to what we have to offer."

"Then I accept it. Thank you. Now, you have my name. I have heard yours, but you must give it to me yourself."

"I am Llyd. My ancestor was Llyd of the forests. There is no man here who is not descended from a god."

"Then there is no man here who need fear a man descended from a king. I shall be glad to share your supper and talk with you. Come out now, and share the warmth of my fire."

The food was part of a cold roast hare, with a loaf of black bread. They had venison, fresh killed, the result of tonight's foray; this they kept for the tribe, but thrust the pluck into the fire to roast, and along with it the carcass of a black hen and some flat uncooked cakes that looked, and smelled, as if they had been mixed with blood. It was an easy guess where these and the hare had been picked up; one sees such things at every crossways stone in that part of the country. It is no blasphemy in these people to take the wayside sacrifices: as Llyd had said to me, they consider themselves descended from the gods and entitled to the offerings; and indeed, I see no harm in it. I accepted the bread, and a piece of venison heart, and a horn of the strong sweet drink they make themselves from herbs and wild honey.

The ten men sat round the fire, while Llyd and I, a little apart from them, talked.

"These soldiers," I said, "who wanted me followed. What sort of men were they?"

"Five men, soldiers fully armed, but with no blazon."

"Five? One of them red-haired, big, in a brown jerkin and a blue cloak? And another on a pied horse?" This was the only horse recognizable to Stilicho, who had glimpsed its white patches in the murk of the grove. They must have had a fifth man, left on watch at the foot of the valley. "What did they say to you?"

But Llyd was shaking his head. "There was no man such as you describe, nor any such horse. The leader was a fair man, thin as a hay-fork, with a beard. They asked us only to watch for a man on a strawberry roan mare, who rode alone, on business that they had no knowledge of. But they said their master would pay well to know where he went."

He threw the bone he had been gnawing over his shoulder, wiped his mouth, and met my eyes straightly. "I said I would not ask your business, but tell me this much, Myrddin Emrys. Why is the son of the High King Ambrosius and the kin of Uther Pendragon hiding alone in the forest while Urien's men hunt him, wishing him ill?"

"*Urien's men?*"

There was deep satisfaction in his voice. "Ah. Some things your magic will not tell you. But in these valleys, no one moves but we know of it. No one comes here but he is marked and followed until we know his business. We know Urien of Gore. These men were his, and spoke the tongue of his country."

"Then you can tell me about Urien," I said. "I know of him; a small king of a small country, brother by marriage to Lot of Lothian. There is no reason that I know why he should hunt me. I am on King's business, and Urien has no quarrel with me or with the King. He and his brother of Lothian are allies of Rheged and of the King. Has Urien, then, become the creature of some other man? Duke Cador?"

"No. Only of King Lot."

I was silent. The fire roared and above us the forest stirred and ruffled. The wind was dying. I was thinking savagely. That Crinas and his gang were Cador's I had no doubt; now it seemed that there had been other spies from the north, watching and waiting, and that somehow they had stumbled across my trail. Urien, Lot's jackal. And Cador. Two of Uther's most powerful allies, his right hand and his left; and the moment the King began to fail they had spies out looking for the prince. . . . The pattern broke and re-formed as a reflection in a pool re-forms after a rock has been thrown into it; but not the same pattern; the rock is there in the center, changing everything. King Lot, the betrothed of Morgian the High King's daughter. King Lot.

I said at length: "I heard you say these men had ridden on north. Were they going straight to report to Urien, or still trying to find and follow me?"

"To follow you. They said they would cast farther north to find some trace of you. If they find none they will seek us out at a place we arranged with them."

"And will you meet them there?"

He spat sideways, not troubling to answer.

I smiled. "I shall go on tomorrow. Will you guide me to a path that the troopers will not know?"

"Willingly, but to do that I must know where you are making for."

"I am following a dream I had," I told him. He nodded. These folk of the hills find this reasonable. They work by instinct like animals, and they read the skies and wait for portents. I thought for a minute, then asked him: "You spoke of Macsen Wledig. When he left these islands to go to Rome, did any of your people go with him?"

"Yes. My own great-grandfather led them under Macsen."

"And came back?"

"Indeed."

"I told you I had had a dream. I dreamed that a dead

king spoke to me, and told me that before I could raise the living one I had a quest to fulfill. Did you ever hear what became of Macsen's sword?"

He threw up a hand in a sign I had never seen before. But I recognized what it was, a strong sign against strong magic. He muttered to himself, some rune in words I did not know, then, hoarsely, to me: "So. It has come. Arawn be praised, and Bilis, and Myrddin of the heights. I knew these were great matters. I felt it on my skin as a man feels the rain falling. So this is what you seek, Myrddin Emrys?"

"This is what I seek. I have been East, and was told there that the sword, with the best of the Emperor's treasure, came back to the West. I think I have been led here. Can you help me further?"

He shook his head slowly. "No. Of that matter I knew nothing. But there are those in the forest who can help you. The word was handed down. That is all I can tell you."

"Your great-grandfather said nothing?"

"I did not say that. I will tell you what he said." He dropped into the singsong voice that the tale-tellers use. I knew he would give me the exact words; these people hand words down from generation to generation, changeless and as precisely worked as the chasing on a cup. "The sword was laid down by a dead Emperor, and shall be lifted by a living one. It was brought home by water and by land, with blood and with fire, and by land and water shall it go home, and lie hidden in the floating stone until by fire it shall be raised again. It shall not be lifted except by a man rightwise born of the seed of Britain."

The chanting stopped. The others round the fire had stopped their talking to listen; I saw eyes glint white, and hands move in the ancient sign. Llyd cleared his throat, spat again, and said gruffly: "That's all. I told you it would be no help."

265

"If I am to find the sword," I said, "help will come, no fear of that. And now I know I am getting near to it. Where the song is, the sword cannot be far away. And after I have found it . . . I think you know where I am going."

"Where else should Myrddin Emrys be going, secretly and on a winter journey, except to the Prince's side?"

I nodded. "He is beyond your territory, Llyd, but not beyond the eyes of your people. Do you know where he is?"

"No. But we will."

"I'm content that you should. Watch me if you wish, and when you see where I am going, watch him for me. This is a king, Llyd, who will deal as justly with the Old Ones of the hills as ever he does with the kings and bishops who meet in Winchester."

"We will watch him for you."

"Then I shall go north, as I was going before, and wait for guidance. Now, with your permission, I should like to sleep."

"You will be safe," said Llyd. "At first light we will see you on your way."

9

The way they showed me was a path no better and no worse than I had followed hitherto, but it was easier to follow by the secret signs they told me of, and it was shorter even than keeping to the road. There were sudden twists and ascents to narrow passes which, without the signs, I would not have suspected of holding a way through. I would ride up some narrow, tree-filled gorge with an apparently solid wall of mountain straight ahead, and the sound of a torrent swelling and echoing between the rocks; but always, when I reached it, there was the pass, narrow and often dangerous, but clear, leading through some (till now) invisible cleft into the steep descent beyond. So for two days more I journeyed, seeing no one, resting little, and keeping myself and the mare alive on what the Old Ones had given me.

On the morning of the third day the mare cast a shoe. As luck would have it we were in easy ground, a ridge of smooth sheep-turf between valley and valley, deserted at this season, but smooth going. I dismounted, and led Strawberry along the ridge, scanning the valleys below me for signs of a road, or the smoke of a settlement. I knew roughly where I was now; though mist and snowstorms veiled the higher crests, I had seen, when they lifted, the white top of the great Snow Hill which holds up the winter sky. I had ridden this way before by the road, and recognized the shape of some of the nearer hills. I was sure that I had not far to travel to find a road, and a smith.

I had considered trying, myself, to remove Strawberry's

other three shoes, but the going had been hard as iron, and if I had not kept her shod, she would have been lame long since. Besides, we were running out of food, and there was none to find in the winter ways. I must take the risk of being seen and recognized.

It was a still clear day of frost. At about noon I saw the smoke of a village, and a few minutes later the gleam of water in the valley below it. I turned the mare's head downhill. We went gently down under the shelter of sparsely set oaks, whose boughs still held a rustle of dead leaves. Soon I could see, below ahead of us through the bare trunks, the grey glitter of the river sliding between its banks.

Just above it I halted the mare at the edge of the oak wood. No movement, no sound, except the noisy river which drowned even the distant sound of barking dogs that marked the village.

I was certain that I was now not far from the course of the road. My best hope for a forge was where road and river met. Such places are generally near a ford or a bridge. Keeping just within the edge of the oak wood, I led Strawberry gently on towards the north.

So we journeyed for another hour or so, when suddenly the valley took a turn to the north-west, and there ahead of me, joining it from a neighbour valley, ran the open belt of green that spoke of a road. And I could hear, clear on the winter's stillness, the metallic clang of a hammer.

There was no sign of the settlement, but where the road met the river the woods were very thick, and I knew that any village in these parts would be built on some hillock or rising ground from which men might defend themselves. The smith, in his solitary forge down by the water, need have no such fears. Such men are too useful, and have nothing worth the taking, and besides, there is still about them some of the old awe that hangs over the places where roads and waters meet.

The smith himself might indeed have been another of the Old Ones. He was a small man, bent by his trade, but immensely broad of shoulder, with arms knotted with muscle and covered with a pelt as thick as a bear's. His hands, broad and cracked, were almost as black as his hair.

He looked up from his work as my shadow fell across the doorway. I greeted him, then tied the mare to a ring by the door and sat down to wait, glad of the heat of the fire which was being blown to a blaze by a boy in a leather apron. The smith answered my greeting, with a sharp stare from under his brows, then without pausing in the rhythm of his work, went back to his hammering. He was making a share. With a hiss of steam and the gradual dulling of the strokes, the share slowly greyed and cooled to its cutting edge. The smith muttered something to the boy at the bellows, who let the air run out, then, picking up the water bucket, left the forge. The smith, setting down his hammer, straightened and stretched. He hooked a wine skin down from the wall and drank, then wiped his mouth. The expert eyes ran over the mare. "Did you bring the shoe?" I had half expected him to speak the Old Tongue, but it was plain Welsh. "Otherwise it'll take more time than you like to spare, I dare say. Or will I just take the other three off?"

I grinned. "And pay me for them?"

"I'd do it for nothing," said the smith, showing a black-toothed grin.

I handed him the cast shoe. "Put this back on and there's a penny in it for you."

He took the thing and examined it, turning it slowly in those horny hands. Then he nodded, and picked up the mare's foot.

"Going far?"

Part of a smith's payment was, of course, whatever news his customers could give him. I had expected this, and had a story ready. He rasped and listened, while the mare stood quietly between us, head down and ears slack. After a while the boy came back with a full bucket and tipped water into the tub. He had taken a long time, and he breathed as if he had been hurrying. If I thought about it at all, I imagined that he had seized, boy-like, the opportunity to spend as long over the errand as he could, and had had to hurry back. The smith made no comment, other than to grunt at him to get back to his bellows, and soon the fire roared up, and the shoe began to glow to red heat.

I suppose I should have been more alert, though to be here at all was a risk I had had to take. And there had been a chance that the troopers asking for the rider with the strawberry mare had not passed this way. But it seemed that they had.

What with the roar of the furnace and the clanging hammer I heard nothing of any approach, just saw, suddenly, the shadows between me and the doorway, then the four men standing there. They were all armed, and they all held their weapons ready, as if they were fully prepared to use them. Two of them held spears, none the less deadly for being home-made, one had a woodsman's hacking knife, its blade honed to a bright edge that would go through living oak, and the fourth held, with some expertness, a Roman short sword.

The last one was the spokesman. He greeted me civilly enough, while the smith held his hammering, and the boy stared.

"Who are you, and where are you bound for?"

I answered him in his own dialect, and without moving from where I sat. "My name is Emrys, and I am travelling

270

north. I have had to come out of my way because, as you see, my mare has cast a shoe."

"Where are you from?"

"From the south, where we do not send armed men against a stranger who passes through our village. What are you afraid of, coming four to one?"

He growled something, and the two with the spears grounded them, shuffling their feet. But the swordsman stood firm.

"You speak our language too well to be a stranger. I think you are the man we have been told to look for. Who are you?"

"No stranger to you, Brychan," I said calmly. "Did you get that sword at Kaerconan, or did we take it when we cut Vortigern's troops to pieces at the crossroads by Bremia?"

"Kaerconan?" The sword-point wavered and fell. "You fought there, for Ambrosius?"

"I was there, yes."

"And at Bremia? With Duke Gorlois?" The point dropped completely. "Wait, you said your name was Emrys? Not Myrddin Emrys, the prophet that won the battle for us, and then doctored our hurts? Ambrosius' son?"

"The same."

The men of my race do not easily bend the knee, but as he slid his sword back into his belt and showed his blackened teeth in a wide grin of pleasure, the effect was the same. "By all the gods, so it is! I didn't know you, sir. Put your weapons up, you fools, can't you see he's a prince, and no meat of ours?"

"Small blame to them if they can't see any such thing," I said, laughing. "I'm neither prince nor prophet now, Brychan, *braud*. I'm travelling secretly, and I need help . . . and silence."

"You shall have anything we can give you, my lord." He

271

had caught my involuntary glance towards the smith and the staring boy, and added quickly: "There's no man here will say a word, look you. No, nor boy neither."

The boy nodded, swallowing. The smith said gruffly: "If I'd known who you were—"

"You'd not have sent your boy scampering off to take the news to the village?" I said. "No matter. If you are a King's man as Brychan is, I can trust you."

"We are all King's men here," said Brychan harshly, "but if you were Uther's worst enemy, instead of his brother's son and the winner of his battles, I would help you, and so would my kinsmen and every man in these parts. Who was it saved this arm of mine after Kaerconan? It's thanks to you that I was able to carry this sword against you today." He clapped the hilt at his belt. I remembered the arm; one of the Saxon axes had driven deep into the flesh, hacking a collop of muscle and laying the bone bare. I had stitched the arm and treated it; whether it was the virtue of the medicine, or Brychan's faith in anything "the King's prophet" might do, the arm had healed. A great part of its strength was gone for ever, but it served him. "And as for the rest of us," he finished, "we're all your men, my lord. You're safe here, and your secrets with you. We all know where the future of these lands lies, and that's in your hands, Myrddin Emrys. If we'd known you were the 'traveller' those soldiers were seeking, we'd have held them here till you came—aye, and killed them if you'd so much as nodded your head." He gave a fierce look round him, and the others nodded, muttering their agreement. Even the smith grunted some sort of assent, and brought his hammer clanging down as if it was an axe on an enemy's neck.

I said something to them, of thanks and acknowledgement. I was thinking that I had been out of the country too long; for too long had been talking with statesmen and lords and

princes. I had begun to think as they were thinking. It was not only the nobles and the fighting kings who would help Arthur to the high throne and maintain him there; it was the folk of Britain, rooted in the land, feeding it and drawing life from it like its own trees, who would lift him there and fight for him. It was the faith of the people, from the high lands to the low, that would make him High King of all the realms and islands in a full sense which my father had dreamed of but had been unable to achieve in the short time allowed him. It had been the dream, too, of Maximus, the would-be emperor who had seen Britain as the foremost in a yoke of nations pulling the same way against the cold wind from the north. I looked at Brychan with his disabled arm, as his kinsmen, poor men of a poor village they would die to defend, at the smith and his ragged boy, and thought of the Old Ones keeping faith in their cold caves with the past and the future, and thought: this time it will be different. Macsen and Ambrosius tried it with force of arms, and laid the paving stones. Now, God and the people willing, Arthur will build the palace. And then, suddenly: that it was time I left courts and castles and went back into the hills. It was from the hills that help would come.

Brychan was speaking again. "Will you not come to the village with us now, my lord? Leave the smith here to finish your mare, and come yourself up to my house, and rest and eat and give us your news. We are sharp set, all of us, to know why troopers should come seeking you, with money in their hands, and as urgent about it as if there was a kingdom at stake."

"There is. But not for the High King."

"Ah," he said. "They would have had us believe they were King's troops, but I thought they were not. Whose, then?"

"They serve Urien of Gore."

The men exchanged glances. Brychan's look was bright

with intelligence. "Urien, eh? And why should Urien pay for news of you? Or maybe it was news of Prince Arthur he'd be paying for?"

"The two are the same," I said, nodding. "Or soon will be. He wants to know where I am going."

"So he can follow you to the boy's hiding-place. Yes. But how would that profit Urien of Gore? He's a small man, and not likely to get bigger. Or—wait, I have it, of course. It would profit his kinsman, Lot of Lothian?"

"I think so. I've been told that Urien is Lot's creature. You may be sure he is working for him."

Brychan nodded, and said slowly: "And King Lot is promised to a lady that's like to be Queen if Arthur dies. So he's paying troops to find where the boy is kept? My lord, that adds up to something I don't like the smell of."

"Nor I. We may be wrong, Brychan, but my bones tell me we are right. And there may be others besides Lot and Urien. Were these men the only ones? You had no Cornishmen pass this way?"

"No, my lord. Rest easy, if any others come this way, they'll get no help." He gave a short bark of laughter. "I'd trust your bones sooner than most men's pledged word. We'll see no danger follows you to the little prince. . . . If any pursuit of you comes through Gwynedd we'll see that it bogs down as surely as a stag's scent fails when he takes to water. Trust us, my lord. We're your men, as we were your father's. We know nothing of this prince you hold in your hand for us, but if he's yours, and you tell us to follow him and serve him, then, Myrddin Emrys, we'll be his men as long as we can hold swords. That's a promise, and it's for you that we make it."

"Then I'll accept it for him, and give you my thanks." I got to my feet. "Brychan, it would be better if I did not come to the village with you, but there is something you

could do for me now, if you will. I need food for the next few days, and wine for my flask, and fodder for the mare. I have money. Could you get these for me?"

"Nothing easier, and you can put away your money. Did you take money of me when you mended my arm? Give us an hour, and we'll get all you want, and no word said. The boy can come with us—folk are used to seeing him bring goods down to the forge. He'll bring what you need."

I thanked him again, and we talked for a little longer, while I gave him what news there was from the south; then they took their leave. It is a matter of fact that, then or at any time, none of them, down to the boy, said a word to any man about my visit.

The boy had not yet returned from the village when the smith finished his job. I paid him his fee and commended him on his work. He took this as no more than his due, and, though he must have heard all that had passed between Brychan and me, showed no awe of me. Indeed, I have never seen why any man skilled in his trade, and surrounded by the articles of his craft, should be in awe of princes. Their task differs, that is all.

"Which way do you ride?" he asked me. Then, as I hesitated: "I told you not to fear me. If that magpie Brychan and his brothers can be silent, then so can I. I serve the road and all men on it, and I'm no more a King's man than any smith who is bound to serve the road, but I spoke to Ambrosius once. And my grandfather's grandfather, why, he shod the horse of the Emperor Maximus himself." He mistook the reason for the look on my face. "Aye, you may well stare. That's a long time ago. But even then, my granda told me, this anvil had been worked by father and son and father and son further back than the oldest man in the village could remember. Why, it's said hereabouts that the first smith who set up his iron here had been taught his trade by Weland

Smith himself. So who else would the Emperor come to? Look."

He pointed at the door, which was set wide open, back against the wall. It was made of oak, adzed smooth as beaten silver, and age and weather had so bleached and polished it that its surface was bone pale, meshed and rippled like grey water. From a hook nearby hung a bag of iron nails, and then a rack of branding irons. All over the silky wood of the door were the scars of brands where the generations of smiths had tried them as they were fashioned.

An *A* caught my eye, but the brand was new, still charred and black. Beneath it and overlaid by it was some sign that looked like a bird flying; then an arrow, and an eye, and one or two cruder signs scrawled in with red-hot metal by idle jesters waiting for the smith to finish a job. But to one side, clear of them all, faded so that they were only dark silver on light, were the letters *M.I.* Just below these was a deeper scar on the door, a half-moon indented, with the marks of nails. It was at this that the smith was pointing. "They say that's where the Emperor's stallion kicked out, but I don't believe it. When I and mine handle a horse, be he the wildest stallion straight off the hills, he doesn't kick. But that, there, above it, that's true enough. That brand was made here, for the horses Macsen Wledig took east with him, the time he killed the King of Rome."

"Smith," I said, "that is the only part of your legend that is false. The King of Rome killed Maximus, and took his sword. But the men of Wales brought it back here to Britain. Was the sword made here, too?"

He was a long time replying, and I felt my heart quicken as I waited. But at last he said, reluctantly: "If it was, I have never heard of it." It was obvious that it had cost him a struggle not to add the sword to the forge's credit, but he had told me the truth.

"I was told," I said, "that somewhere in the forest is a man who knows where the Emperor's sword is hidden. Have you heard of this, or do you know where I can find it?"

"No, how should I? They say there is a holy man a long way north of here who knows everything. But he lives north of the Deva, in another country."

"That is the way I was riding," I said. "I shall seek him out."

"Then if you don't want to meet yon soldiers, don't go by the road. Six miles north of here there's a crossroads, where the road for Segontium heads west. Keep by the river from here, and it'll take you clear across the corner till the west-bound road crosses it."

"But I'm not going to Segontium. If I bear too far to the west—"

"You leave the river where it meets the road again. Straight across from the ford the track runs up into the forest, through a shaw of hollies, and after that it's plain enough to see. It'll carry you on northwards, and never a glimpse of a road you'll see till you reach the Deva. If you ask the ferryman there about the holy man in the Wild Forest, he'll tell you the way. You go by the river. It's a good track, and impossible to miss."

I have found that people never say this unless, in fact, the way is very easy to miss. However, I said nothing and, the boy arriving at that moment with the provisions, helped him stow them. As we did so he whispered: "I heard what he said, lord. Don't listen to him. It's a bad track to follow, and the river's high. Stay with the road."

I thanked him and gave him a coin for his pains. He went back to his bellows, and I turned to take my leave of the smith, who had vanished into some dark and cluttered recess at the back of the smithy. I could hear the clattering of metal, and his whistling between his broken teeth. I called

277

out above it. "I'm on my way now. My thanks." Then my breath caught in my throat. Suddenly, back in the dark clutter behind the chimney, the newly leaping flame had lit the outline of a face.

A stone face; a familiar face once seen at every crossways. One of the first Old Ones, the god of going, the other Myrddin whose name was Mercury, or Hermes, lord of the high roads and bearer of the sacred snake. As one born in September, he was mine. He lay back now, the old Herm who had once stood out in the open watching the passers-by, head propped against the wall, the moss and lichen on him long since dried to powdered grey. Clearly under the blurred and fretted lines of carving I recognized the flat face rimmed with beard, the blank eyes as oval and bulging as grapes, the hands clasped across the belly, the once protruding genitals smashed and mutilated.

"If I had known you were there, Old One," I said, "I would have poured the wine for you."

The smith had reappeared at my elbow. "He gets his rations, never fear. There's none who serves the road would dare neglect him."

"Why did you bring him in?"

"He never stood here. He was at the ford I told you of, where the old track that they call Elen's Causeway crossed the river Seint. When the Romans built their new road to Segontium they put their post station right in front of him. So he was brought here, I never heard how."

I said slowly: "At the ford you told me of? Then I think I must go that way after all." I nodded to the smith, then raised a hand in salute to the god. "Go with me now," I said to him, "and help me find this way—which it is impossible to miss."

He went with me for the first part of the way; indeed, so

long as the track clung to the river's bank it could hardly be missed. But towards late afternoon, when the dim winter sun hung low to its setting, a mist began to gather and hang near the water, thickening with dusk into a damp and blinding fog. It might have been possible to follow the sound of water, though under the mist this was misleading, sometimes loud and near at hand, at others muted and deceivingly distant; but where the river took a bend, the track cut straight across, and twice, following this, I found myself astray and picking a way through the deep forest with no sign or sound of the river. In the end, astray for the third time, I dropped the reins on Strawberry's neck, and let her pick her own way, reflecting that, ironically, had I risked the road I would have been safe enough. I would have heard the troopers approaching, and have been safe from their eyes had I withdrawn only a few yards into the fog-bound forest.

There must be a moon above the low-lying mist. This drifted like lighted cloud, not solid, but rivers of vapour with dark between, banks of pale stuff clinging round the trees like snow. Through it, hiding and showing, the gaunt trees laced their black boughs overhead. Underfoot the forest floor was thick as velvet and as quiet to walk on.

Strawberry plodded steadily on, without hesitation, following some path unseen to me, or some instinct of her own. Now and again she pricked her ears, but at something I could neither hear nor see, and once she checked and flung up her head sideways, coming as near as she ever did to shying, but before I could pick up the reins again, she slacked her ears, dropped her head, and quickened her pace along the invisible line of her choosing. I let her alone. Whatever was drifting past us in the misty silence, it would do us no harm. If this was the way—and I was sure now that it was—we were protected.

An hour after full dark, the mare carried me softly out of

the trees, across a hundred paces or so of flat ground, and came to a halt in front of a looming square of blackness that could only be a building. There was a water trough outside. She lowered her head, blew, and began to drink.

I dismounted and pushed open the door of the building. It was the posting station the smith had told me of, empty now and half derelict, but apparently still in use by travellers such as myself. In one corner a pile of half-charred logs showed where a fire had been lit recently, and in another stood a bed made from some tolerably clean planks laid across stones to raise it from the draught. It was rough comfort, but better than some we had had. I fell asleep within the hour to the sound of Strawberry's munching, and slept deeply and dreamlessly till morning.

When I woke, it was in the dusk of dawn, the sun not yet up. The mare dozed in her corner, slack-hipped. I went out to the trough for water to wash with.

The mist had gone, and with it the milder air. The ground was grey with frost. I looked about me.

The posting station stood a few paces back from the road which ran straight as a spear from east to west through the forest. Along this line the woodland had been cleared when the Romans made the road, the trees felled and the undergrowth hacked down a hundred paces back to either side from the gravelled way. Now saplings had grown up again and the low growth was thick and tangled, but still, near where I stood, I thought I could see under it the line of the old track that had been there before the Romans came. The river, smooth here and quiet-running, slid over the ruins of the causeway that took the road through it, hock deep. Beyond this, at the farther edge of the cleared land, I could see, black against the grey winter oaks, the shaw of holly which marked my road to the north.

Satisfied, I cracked the wafer of ice on the water of the trough and washed. As I did so, behind me the sun came up between the trees in the red of a cold dawn. Shadows grew and sharpened, barring the stiff grass. The frost sparkled. Light grew, like the smith's furnace under the bellows. When I turned, the sun, low and dazzling, blazed into my eyes, blinding me. The winter trees stood black and unbodied against a sky like a forest fire. The river ran molten.

There was something between me and the river, a tall shape, massive and yet insubstantial against the blaze, standing knee deep in the underbrush at the edge of the road. Something familiar, but familiar in another setting, of darkness, and strange places, and outland gods. A standing stone.

For a sharp moment I wondered if I was still asleep, and this was my dream again. I put up an arm against the light and narrowed my eyes under it, peering.

The sun came clear of the tree-tops. The shadow of the forest moved back. The stone stood clear against the sparkling frost.

It was not after all a standing stone. Nothing strange at all, or out of place. It was an ordinary milestone, perhaps two cubits taller than was normal, but bearing only the usual inscription to an emperor, and below this the message: A. SEGONTIO. M . P . XXII.

When I approached it I saw the reason for its height; instead of being sunk in the turf it had been mounted on a squared plinth of stone. A different stone. The plinth where the Herm had stood? I stooped to push the frosted grass aside. The red sunlight struck the stone, showing a mark on the plinth that might have been an arrow. Then I saw what it was: the remains of some ancient writing, the ogam letters blurred and worn till they showed like the fletching on a shaft, and a barbed head pointing westwards.

Well, I thought, why not? The signs were simple, but

messages do not always come from the gods beyond the stars. My god had spoken to me before in ways as small as this, and I had told myself only yesterday to look low as well as high for the things of power. And here they were—a cast horseshoe, a word from a wayside smith, and some scratches on a stone—conspiring to turn me aside from my northern journey and take me westwards to Segontium. I thought again, why not? Who knew but that the sword might really have been made down at the forge yonder, and chilled in the Seint River, and that after his death they had carried it home to his wife's country, where she lodged still with his infant son? Somewhere in Segontium, the Caer Seint of Macsen Wledig, the King's Sword of Britain might lie, waiting to be lifted in fire.

10

The inn I stayed at in Segontium was a comfortable one, at the edge of the town, but not serving the main highway. A few travellers lodged there, but the place mostly served food and drink to the local men who attended the market, or who were on their way with goods down to the port.

The place had seen better days, having been built to serve the soldiers at the vast barracks above the town. It must have stood there, at the least, for a couple of hundred years; originally it had been well built of stone, with one handsome room, almost a hall, where a vast fireplace stood, and oaken beams as solid as iron held up the roof. The remains of the benches and the stout tables were still there, stained and burned, and here and there hacked where the daggers of drunken legionaries had carved their names, along with other things less respectable. It was a marvel that anything remained. some of the stone had been pillaged, and once at least the inn had been burned by raiders from Ireland, so that now the stone oblong of the hall was all that remained, and the blackened beams held up a roof of thatch instead of tiles. The kitchen was no more than a lean-to of daubed wattle behind the great fireplace.

But there was a big fire of logs blazing, and a smell of good ale, with bread baking in the oven outside; and a shed with decent bedding and fodder for the mare. I saw her warm and groomed and fed before I went into the inn myself to bespeak a bed-place and a meal.

At that time of year the port was all but closed to traffic;

few travellers were on the roads, and men did not stay out late drinking, but got themselves home to their beds soon after dusk. No one looked curiously at me, or ventured a question. The inn was quiet early, and I went to bed and slept soundly.

In the morning it was fine, with one of those glittering sharp days that December sometimes throws down like bright gold among the lead of winter's coinage. I breakfasted early, looked in at the mare, then left her resting and went out on foot.

I turned east, away from the town and the port, along the river's bank where, on rising ground about half a mile above the town, stood the remains of Segontium Roman fortress. Macsen's Tower stands just outside it, a little way down the hill. Here the High King Vortigern had lodged his men when my grandfather the King of South Wales had ridden up from Maridunum with his train to talk with him. I, a boy of twelve, had been with them, and on that journey had discovered for the first time that the dreams of the crystal cave were true. Here, in this wild and quiet corner of the world, I had first felt power, and found myself as a seer.

That had been a winter journey, too. As I walked up the weedy road towards the gateway set between its crumbling towers, I tried to conjure again the colours of cloaks and banners and bright weapons where now, in the blue shadows of morning, lay only the unprinted frost.

The vast complex of buildings was deserted. Here and there on the naked and fallen masonry the black marks of fire told their story. Elsewhere you could see where men had taken the great stones, stripping the very paving from the streets and carrying it off for their own building. There were dry thistles in the window spaces, and young trees rooted on the walls. A well-shaft gaped, choked with rubble. The cisterns brimmed with rain water, which slopped out through the grooves on the edge where men had sharpened their swords. No, there was nothing to see. The place was empty, even of ghosts. The winter sun shone down on a wide and crumbling waste land. The silence was complete.

I remember that as I walked through the shells of the buildings I was thinking, not of the past, not even of my present quest, but practically, as Ambrosius' engineer, of the future. I was weighing up the place as Tremorinus the chief engineer and I had been used to do: shifting this, repairing that, making the towers good, abandoning the north-easterly blocks to make good the west and south . . . Yes, if Arthur should ever need Segontium . . .

I had come to the top of the rise, the center of the fort where the Commandant's house—Maximus' house—had stood. It was as derelict as the rest. The great door still hung on rotting hinges, but the lintel was broken and sagging, and the place was dangerous. I went cautiously inside. In the main chamber there was daylight spilling through gaps in the roof, and piles of rubble half hid the walls where paint still showed, flaked and dark with damp. In the dimness I could see the remains of a table—too massive to take away, and not worth chopping for kindling—and behind it the shredded remnants of leather hangings on the wall. A general had sat here once, planning to conquer Rome, as formerly Rome had conquered Britain. He had failed, and died, but in failing he had sown the seeds of an idea which after him another king had picked up. "It will be one country, a kingdom in its own right," my father had said, "not merely a province of Rome. Rome is going, but for a while at least, we can stand." And through this came the memory of another voice, the voice of the prophet who sometimes spoke through me: "And the kingdoms shall be one Kingdom, and the gods one God."

It would be time to listen to those ghostly voices when a

general sat there once again. I turned back into the bright morning stillness. Where, in this waste land, was the end of my quest?

From here you could see the sea, with the small crowded houses of the port, and across from this the druids' isle that is called Mona, or Von, so that the people call the place Caer-y-n'ar Von. To the other side, behind me, reared the Snow Hill, Y Wyddfa, where if a man could climb and live among the snows, he would meet the gods walking. Against its distant whiteness showed, dark and ruined, the remains of Macsen's Tower. And suddenly, from this new angle, I saw it afresh. The tower of my dream; the tower in the picture on Ahdjan's wall . . . I left the Commandant's house and walked quickly out of the fortress gate towards it.

It stood in a wilderness of tumbled stones, but I knew that near it, dug into the side of the little valley beyond the gate, and running in almost beneath the tower itself, was the temple of Mithras; and on the thought I found that my feet had led me, with no will of my own, down the path which led to the Mithraeum door.

There were steps here, cracked and slippery. Halfway down the flight one tread thrust upwards vertically, half blocking the stairway, and at the foot was a pile of mud and shards, fouled by rats and prowling dogs. The place stank of damp and dirt and some ancient noisomeness that might have been spilled blood. On the ruined wall above the steps some roosting birds had whitened the stones; the dung was greening over now with slime. A jackdaw's perch, perhaps? A raven of Mithras? A merlin? I trod cautiously forward over the slimy flags, and paused in the temple doorway.

It was dark, but some sunlight had followed me in, and there was enough light from a hole broken in the roof somewhere, so that I could see dimly. The temple was as filthy and forlorn as the stairway that led to it. Only the strength of the vaulted roof had saved the place from falling in under the weight of the hillside above. The furnishings had gone long since, the braziers, benches, carvings; this, like the scoured ruin overhead, was a shell empty of its tenant. The four lesser altars had been broken and defaced, but the central altar stood there still, fixed and massive, with its carved dedication to the unconquered god, MITHRAE INVICTO, but above the altar, in the apse, axe and hammer and fire had obliterated the story of the bull and the conquering god. All that remained of the picture of the bull-slaying was an ear of wheat, down in one corner, its carving still sharp and new and miraculously unspoiled. The air, sour with the smell of some fungus, caught at the lungs.

It seemed fitting to say a prayer to the god departed. As I spoke aloud, something in the echo of my voice came, not like an echo, but an answer. I had been wrong. The place was not yet empty. It had been holy, and was stripped of its holiness; but something was still held down to that cold altar. The sour smell was not the smell of fungus. It was unlit incense, and cold ashes, and unsaid prayers.

I had been his servant once. There was no one here but I. Slowly, I walked forward into the center of the temple, and held out my open hands.

Light, and colour, and fire. White robes and chanting. Fires licking upwards like light blowing. The bellow of a dying bull and the smell of blood. Outside somewhere the sun blazing and a city rejoicing to welcome its new king, and the sound of laughter and marching feet. Round me incense pouring heavy and sweet, and a voice that said through it, calm and small: "Throw down my altar. It is time to throw it down."

I came to myself coughing, with the air round me swirling

thick with dust, and the sound of a crash still echoing round and round the vaulted chamber. The air trembled and rang. At my feet lay the altar, hurled over on its back into the curve of the apse.

I stared, dazed still and with swimming sight, at the hole it had torn in the floor where it had stood. My head sang with the echo; the hands I held stiffly before me were filthy, and one of them showed a bleeding gash. The altar was heavy, of massive stone, and in my right mind I would never have laid hands to it; but here it lay at my feet, with the echo of its fall dying in the roof, followed by the whisper of settling masonry as the crumbled pavement began to slide down into the hole where the altar had stood.

Something showed in the depths of the hole: a hard straight edge and a corner too sharp for stone. A box. I knelt down and reached for it.

It was of metal, and very heavy, but the lid lifted easily. Whoever had buried it had trusted the god's protection rather than a lock. Inside, my hands met canvas cloth, long rotten, which tore; then inside that again, wrappings of oiled leather. Something long and slender and supple; here at last it was. Gently, I took the wrappings off the sword and held it naked across my hands.

A hundred years since they had put it here, those men who had made their way back from Rome. It shone in my hands, as bright and dangerous and beautiful as on the day it had been made. It was no wonder, I thought, that already in that hundred years it had become a thing of legend. It was easy to believe that the old smith, Weland himself, who was old before the Romans came, might have made this last artifact before he faded with the other small gods of wood and stream and river, into the misty hills, leaving the crowded valleys to the bright gods of the Middle Sea. I could feel the power from the sword running into my palms, as if I held them in water where lightning struck. *Whoso takes this sword from under this stone is rightwise King born of all Britain* . . . The words were clear as if spoken, bright as if carved on the metal. I, Merlin, only son of Ambrosius the King, had taken the sword from the stone. I, who had never given an order in battle, nor led so much as a troop; who could not handle a war stallion, but rode a gelding or a quiet mare. I, who had never even lain with a woman. I, who was no man, but only eyes and a voice. A spirit, I had said once, a word. No more.

The sword was not for me. It would wait.

I wrapped the beautiful thing up again in the filthy wrappings, and knelt to replace it. I saw that the box was deeper than I had thought; there were other objects there. The rotten canvas had fallen away to show the shape, gleaming in the dimness, of a wide-mouthed dish, a krater such as I had seen on my travels in countries east of Rome. It seemed to be of red gold, studded with emeralds. Beside it, still half muffled in wrappings, gleamed the bright edge of a lance-head. The rim of a platter showed, crusted with sapphire and amethyst.

I leaned forward to lay the sword back in its place. But before I could do it, without any warning, the heavy lid of the box fell shut with a crash. The noise set the echoes drumming again, and brought down with it a cascade of stone and plaster from the apse and the crumbling walls above. It happened so quickly that in the single moment of my own sharp recoil the box, hole and all had vanished from view under the rubble.

I was left kneeling there in the choking cloud of dust, with the shrouded sword held fast in my filthy and bleeding hands. From the apse, the last of the carving had vanished. It was only a curved wall, showing blank, like the wall of a cave.

11

The ferryman at the Deva knew the holy man of whom the smith had spoken. It seemed he lived in the hills above Ector's fortress, at the edge of the great tract of mountain land they call the Wild Forest. Though I no longer felt myself to need the hermit's guidance, it would do no harm to talk to him, and his cell—a chapel, the ferryman called it—lay on my way, and might give me lodging until I considered how best to present myself at Count Ector's gates.

Whether or not the possession of the sword had in fact carried power with it, I travelled fast and easily, and with no more alarms. A week after leaving Segontium we—the mare and I—cantered easily along the green margin of a wide, calm lake, making for a light which showed pale in the early dusk, high as a star among the trees on the other shore.

It was a long way round the lake, and it was full dark when at last I trotted the tired mare up the forest track into a clearing and saw, against the soft and living darkness of the forest, the solid wedge of the chapel roof.

It was a smallish oblong building set back against the trees at the far side of a large clearing. All round the open space the pines stood in a dark and towering wall, but above was a roof of stars, and beyond the pines, on every side, the glimmer of the snow-clad heights that cupped this corrie high in the hills. To one side of the clearing, in a basin of mossy rock, stood a still, dark pool; one of those springs that well up silently from below, for ever renewing itself without sound. The air was piercingly cold, and smelled of pines.

There were mossed and broken steps leading up to the

chapel door. This was open, and inside the building the light burned steadily. I dismounted and led the mare forward. She pecked against a stone, her hoof rapping sharply. You would have thought that anyone living in this solitary place would have come out to investigate, but there was no sound, no movement. The forest hung still. Only, far overhead, the stars seemed to move and breathe as they do in the winter air. I slipped the mare's bridle off over her ears, and left her to drink at the well. Gathering my cloak round me, I trod up the mossy steps, and entered the chapel.

It was small, oblong in shape, with a highish barrel roof; a strange building to find in the wild heart of the forest, where at most one might have expected a rough-built hut, or at least a cave, or dwelling contrived among the stones. But this had been built as a shrine, a holy place for some god to dwell in. The floor was of stone flags, clean and unbroken. In the center, opposite the door, stood the altar, with a thick curtain of some worked stuff hung behind it. The altar itself was covered with a clean, coarse cloth, on which stood the lighted lamp, a simple, country-made thing which nevertheless gave a strong and steady light. It had recently been filled with oil, and the wick was trimmed and unsmoking. To one side of the altar, on the step, was a stone bowl of the kind I had seen used for sacrifice; it had been scoured white, and held sweet water. To the other side stood a lidded pot of some dark metal, pierced, such as the Christians use to burn incense. The air of the chapel still held, faintly, the sweet gummy smell. Three bronze lamps, triple-branched, stood unlit against a wall.

The rest of the chapel was bare. Whoever kept it, whoever had lighted the lamp and burned the incense, slept elsewhere.

I called aloud: "Is anyone there?" and waited for the echoes to run up into the roof and die. No answer.

My dagger was in my hand; it had sprung there without conscious thought on my part. I had met this kind of situation before, and it had only meant one thing; but that had been in Vortigern's time, the time of the Wolf. Such a man as this hermit, living alone in a solitary place, trusted to the place itself, its god and its holiness, to protect him. It should have been enough, and in my father's time had certainly been so. But things had changed, even in the few years since his death. Uther was no Vortigern, but it seemed sometimes that we were sliding back to the time of the Wolf. The times were wild and violent, and filled with alarms of war; but more than this, faiths and loyalties were changing faster than men's minds could grow to apprehend them. There were men about who would kill even at the altar's horns. But I had not thought there were any such in Rheged, when I chose it for Arthur's sanctuary.

Struck by an idea, I stepped carefully past the altar and drew back the edge of the curtain. My guess had been right; there was a space behind the curtain, a semicircular recess which was apparently used as storage room; dimly the lamplight showed a clutter of stools and oil jars and sacred vessels. At the back of the recess a narrow doorway had been cut in the wall.

I went through. It was here, obviously, that the keeper of the place lived. There was a small square chamber built on the end of the chapel, with a low window deeply recessed, and another door giving, presumably, straight on the forest. I felt my way across in the dimness and pushed the door open. Outside the starlight showed me the rampart of pine trees crowding close, and to one side a lean-to shed, with its overhanging roof sheltering a stack of fuel. Nothing else.

Leaving the door wide, I surveyed what I could see of the room. There was a wooden bed with skins and blankets piled on it, a stool, and a small table with a cup and platter where the remains of a meal lay half-eaten. I picked up the cup; it was half full of thin wine. On the table a candle had burned down into a mess of tallow. The smell of the dead candle still hung there, mixed with the smell of the wine and the dead embers on the hearth. I put a finger to the tallow; it was still soft.

I went back into the chapel. I stood by the altar, and shouted again. There were two windows, one to either side, high in the wall; they were unglazed, open on the forest. If he was not too far away, he would surely hear me. But again there was no reply.

Then, huge and silent as a ghost, a great white owl swept in through one window and sailed across the lamplit space. I caught a glimpse of the cruel beak, the soft wings, the great eyes, blind and wise, then it was gone with no more sound than a spirit makes. It was only the *dillyan wen*, the white owl which haunts every tower and ruin in the country, but my flesh crept on my bones. From outside came the long, sad, terrible cry of the owl, and after it, like an echo, the sound of a man moaning.

Without his moaning I would not have found him till daylight. He was robed and hooded in black, and he lay face down under the dark trees at the edge of the clearing, beyond the spring. A jug fallen from his hand showed what his errand had been. I stooped and gently turned him over.

He was an old man, thin and frail, with bones that felt as brittle as a bird's. When I had made sure that none was broken, I picked him up in my arms and carried him back indoors. His eyes were half open, but he was still unconscious; in the lamplight I could see how one side of his face was dragged down as if a statuary had run his hand down suddenly over the clay, blurring the outline. I put him into his bed, wrapped warm. There was kindling left by the hearth, and what looked like a winter-stone ready among the ashes. I brought more fuel, then made fire and, when the stone was warm, drew it out, wrapped it in cloth, and put it to the old man's feet. For the moment there was nothing more that could be done for him, so after I had seen to the mare I made a meal for myself, then settled by the dying fire to watch through the rest of the night.

For four days I tended him, while none came near except the forest creatures and the wild deer, and at night the white owl haunting the place as if it waited to convoy his spirit home.

I did not think he could recover; his face was fallen in and grey, and I had seen the same blue tinge round the mouths of dying men. From time to time he seemed to come half to the surface, to know I was beside him. At such times he was restless always, fretting, I understood, about the care of the shrine. When I tried to talk to him and reassure him, he seemed not to understand, so in the end I drew back the curtains that parted the room from the shrine, so that he might see the lamp still burning in its place on the altar.

It was a strange time for me, by day tending the chapel and its keeper, and by night snatching sleep while I watched the sick man and waited for his restless muttering to make sense. There was a small store of meal and wine in the place, and with the dried meat and raisins left in my pack, I had sufficient food. The old man could scarcely swallow; I kept him alive on warm wine mixed with water, and a cordial I made for him from the medicines I carried. Each morning I was amazed that he had lived through the night. So I stayed, tending the place by day, and by night spending long hours beside him watching, or else in the chapel where the smell of incense slowly faded and the sweet air of the pines floated in and set the flame of the lamp aslant in its well of oil.

Now when I look back on that time it is like an island in moving waters. Or like a dreaming night which gives rest and impetus between the hard days. I ought to have been impatient to get on with my journey, to meet Arthur and to talk with Ralf again and arrange with Count Ector how best, without betraying either of us, I might enter the fabric of Arthur's life. But I troubled myself with none of these things. The shrouding forest, the still and glowing shrine, the sword lying where I had hidden it under the thatch of the shed, these held me there, serene and waiting. One never knows when the gods will call or come, but there are times when their servants feel them near, and this was such a time.

On the fifth night, as I carried in wood to build the fire, the hermit spoke to me from the bed. He was watching me from his pillows, and though he had not the strength to lift his head, his eyes were level and clear.

"Who are you?"

I set down the wood and went over to the bedside. "My name is Emrys. I was passing through the forest, and came on the shrine. I found you by the well, and brought you back to your bed."

"I . . . remember. I went to get water . . ." I could see the effort that the memory cost him, but intelligence was back in his eyes, and his speech, though blurred, was clear enough.

"You were taken ill," I told him. "Don't trouble yourself now. I'll get you something to drink, then you must rest again. I have a brew here which will strengthen you. I am a doctor; don't be afraid of it."

He drank, and after a while his colour seemed better, and his breathing easier. When I asked him if he was in pain, his lips said, "No," without sound, and he lay quietly for a while, watching the lamp beyond the doorway. I made the fire up and propped him higher on his pillows to ease his breathing, then sat down and waited with him. The night was still; from close outside came the hooting of the white owl. I thought: *You will not have long to wait, my friend.*

Towards midnight the old man turned his head easily on the pillows and asked me suddenly: "Are you a Christian?"

"I serve God."

"Will you keep the shrine for me when I am gone?"

"The shrine shall be kept. Trust me for it."

He nodded, as if satisfied, and lay quiet for a time. But I thought something still troubled him; I could see it working behind his eyes. I heated more wine and mixed the cordial and held it to his lips. He thanked me with courtesy, but as if he was thinking of something else, and his eyes went back to the lighted doorway of the shrine.

I said: "If you wish, I will ride down and bring you a Christian priest. But you will have to tell me the way."

He shook his head, and closed his eyes again. After a while he said, thinly: "Can you hear them?"

"I can hear nothing but the owl."

"Not that, no. The others."

"What others?"

"They crowd at the doors. Sometimes on a night of midsummer you can hear them crying like young birds, or like flocks on the far hills." He moved his head on the pillow. "Did I do wrong, I wonder, to shut them out?"

I understood him then. I thought of the bowl of sacrifice, the well outside, the unlit lamps in the sacred nine of an older religion than any. And I think some part of my mind was with the white shadow that floated through the forest boughs outside. The place, if my blood told me aright, had been holy time out of mind. I asked him gently: "Whose was the shrine, father?"

"It was called the place of the trees. After that the place of the stone. Then for a while it had another name . . . but now down in the village they call it the chapel in the green."

"What was the other name?"

He hesitated, then said: "The place of the sword."

I felt the nape of my neck prickle, as if the sword itself had touched me. "Why, father? Do you know?"

He was silent for a moment, and his eyes watched me,

considering. Then he gave the ghost of a nod, as if he had reached some conclusion that satisfied him. "Go into the shrine and draw the cloth from the altar."

I obeyed him, lifting the lamp down to the step in front of the altar, and taking off the cloth that had draped it to the ground. It had been possible to see even through the covering cloth that the altar was not a table such as the Christians commonly use, but as high as a man's waist, and of the Roman shape. Now I saw that this was indeed so. It was the twin of the one in Segontium, a Mithras altar with a squared front and the edge scrolled to frame the carving. And carving there had been, though it was there no longer. I could make out the words MITHRAE and INVICTO across the top, but on the panel below where other words had been, a sword had been cut clear through them, its hilt, like a cross, marking the center of the altar. The remains of the other letters had been gouged away, and the sword blade carved in high relief among them. It was rough carving, but clear, and as familiar to my eyes as that hilt was already familiar to my hand. I realized then, staring at it, that the sword in the stone was the only cross the chapel held. And above it, only the dedication to Mithras Unconquered remained. The rest of the altar was bare.

I went back to the old man's bedside. His eyes waited, with a question in them. I asked him: "What does Macsen's sword do here, carved like a cross in the altar?"

His eyes closed, then opened again, lightly. He fetched a long, light breath. "So. It is you. You have been sent. It was time. Sit down again, while I tell you." As I obeyed him, he said, strongly enough, but in a voice stretched thin as wire: "There is just time to tell you. Yes, it is Macsen's sword, him the Romans called Maximus, who was Emperor here in Britain before the Saxons ever came, and who married a British princess. The sword was forged south of here, they say, from iron found in Snow Hill within sight of the sea, and tempered with water that runs from that hill into the sea. It is a sword for the High King of Britain, and was made to defend Britain against her enemies."

"So when he took it to Rome, it availed him nothing?"

"It is a marvel it did not break in his hand. But after he was murdered they brought the sword home to Britain, and it is ready for the King's hand that can find it, and finding, raise."

"And you know where they hid it?"

"I never knew that, but when I was a boy and came here to serve the gods, the priest of the shrine told me that they had taken it back to the country where it was made, to Segontium. He told me the story, as it happened in this very place, years before his time. It was . . . it was after the Emperor Macsen had died at Aquileia by the Inland Sea, and those of the British who were left came home. They came through Brittany, and landed here on the west, and took the road home through the hills, and they came by here. Some of them were servants of Mithras, and when they saw this place was holy, they waited here for the summer midnight, and prayed. But most were Christians, and one was a priest, so when the others had done they asked him to say a mass. But there was neither cross nor cup, only the altar as you see it. So they talked together, and went to where their horses were standing, and took from the bundles tied there treasure beyond counting. And among the treasure was the sword, and a great krater, a grail of the Greek fashion, wide and deep. They stood the sword over against the altar for a cross, and they drank from the grail, and it was said afterwards that no man was there that day but found his spirit satisfied. They left gold for the shrine, but the sword and the grail they would not leave. One of them took a chisel and a hammer and made the altar as you see it. Then they rode away with the treasure, and did not come this way again."

"It's a strange story. I never heard it before."

"No man has heard it. The keeper of the shrine swore by the old gods and the new that he would say nothing save to the priest who came after. And I, in my turn, was told." He paused. "It is said that one day the sword itself will come back to the shrine, to stand here for a cross. So in my time I have struggled to keep the shrine clean of all but what you see. I took the lights away, and the offering bowls, and threw the crooked knife into the lake. The grass has grown now over the stone. I drove out the owl that nested in the roof, and I took the silver and copper coins from the well and gave them to the poor." Another long pause, so long that I thought he had gone. But then his eyes opened again. "Did I do right?"

"How can I tell? You did what you thought was right. No one can do more than that."

"What will you do?" he asked.

"The same."

"And you will tell no man what I have told you, save him who should know?"

"I promise."

He lay quietly, with trouble still in his face, and his eyes intent on something distant and long ago. Then, imperceptibly but as definitely as a man stepping into a cold stream to cross it, he made a decision. "Is the cloth still off the altar?"

"Yes."

"Then light the nine lamps and fill the bowl with wine and oil, and open the doors to the forest, and carry me where I can see the sword again."

I knew that if I lifted him, he would die in my hands. His breath laboured harshly in the thin chest, and the frail body shook with it. He turned his head on the pillows, feebly now.

"Make haste." When I hesitated, I saw fear touch his face. "I tell you I must see it. Do as I say."

I thought of the shrine scoured and swept of all its ancient sanctities; and then of the sword itself, hidden with the King's gold in the roof-beams of the stable outside. But it was too late even for that. "I cannot lift you, father," I said, "but lie still. I will bring the altar here to you."

"How can you—?" he began, then stopped with wonder growing in his face, and whispered: "Then bring it quickly, and let me go."

I knelt beside the bed, facing away from him, looking at the red heart of the fire. The logs had fallen from their blaze into a glowing cave, crystals glimmering in a globe of fire. Beside me the difficult breathing came and went like the painful beat of my own blood. The beat surged in my temples, hurting me. Deep in my belly the pain grew and burned. The sweat ran scalding down my face, and my bones shook in their sheath of flesh as, grain by grain and inch by shining inch, I built that altar-stone for him against the dark, blank wall. It rose slowly, solid, and blotted out the fire. The surface of the stone was lucent against the dark, and ripples of light touched it and wavered across it, as if it floated on sunlit water. Then, lamp by lamp, I lit the nine flames so that they floated with the stone like riding-lights. The wine brimmed in the bowl, and the censer smoked. INVICTO, I wrote, and groped, sweating, for the name of the god. But all that came was the single word INVICTO, and then the sword stood forward out of the stone like a blade from a splitting sheath, and the blade was white iron with runes running down it in the wavering water-light, below the flashing hilt and the word in the stone, TO HIM UNCONQUERED . . .

It was morning, and the first birds were stirring. Inside, the place was very quiet. He was dead, gone as lightly as the vision I had made for him out of shadows. It was I who, stiff and aching, moved like a ghost to cover the altar and tend the lamp.

BOOK III

THE SWORD

1

When I had promised the dying man to see that the chapel
was cared for, I had not thought of doing this myself. There
was a monastery in one of the little valleys not far from
Count Ector's castle, and it should not be hard to find someone from there who would live here and care for the place.
This did not mean I must hand over the sword's secret to
him; it was mine now, and the end of its story was in my
hands.

But as the days passed, I thought better of my decision to
approach the brothers. To begin with, I was forced to inaction, and given time to think.

I buried the old man's body, and just in time, as the next
day the snow came, falling thick, soft and silent, to shroud the
forest deep, and island the chapel and block the tracks. To tell
the truth I was glad to stay; there was enough food and
fuel, and both the mare and I needed the rest.

For two weeks or more the snow lay; I lost track of days,
but Christmas came and went, and the start of the year.
Arthur was nine years old.

So perforce I kept the shrine. I supposed that whoever
came as keeper would, like the old man, fight to keep the
place clear for his own God, but in the meantime I was
content to let what god would take the place. I would open
it again to any who would use it. So I put away the altar
cloth, and cleaned the three bronze lamps and set them about
the altar and lighted the nine flames. About the stone and the
spring I could do nothing until the snow melted. Nor could

I find the curving knife, and for this I was thankful; that Goddess is not one to whom I would willingly open a door. I kept the sweet holy-water in her bowl of sacrifice, and at morning and evening burned a pinch of incense. The white owl came and went at will. By night I shut the chapel door to keep out the cold and the wind, but it was never locked, and all day it stood open, with the lights shining out over the snow.

Some time after the turn of the year the snow melted, and the tracks through the forest showed black and deep in mire. Still I made no move. I had had time to think, and I saw that I must surely have been led up to the chapel by the same hand that had guided me to Segontium. Where better could I stay to be near Arthur without attracting attention? The chapel provided the perfect hiding-place. I knew well enough that the place would be held in awe, and its guardian with it. The "holy man of the forest" would be accepted without question. Word would go round that there was a new and younger holy man, but, country memories being long, folk would recall how each hermit as he died had been succeeded by his helper, and before long I would simply be "the hermit of the Wild Forest" in my turn and in my own right. And with the chapel as my home and my cure, I could visit the village for supplies, talk to the people, and in this way get news, at the same time ensuring that Count Ector would hear of my installation in the Wild Forest.

About a week after the thaw started, before I would risk taking Strawberry down through the knee-deep mud of the tracks, I had visitors. Two of the forest people; a small, thick-set dark man dressed in badly cured deerskins, which stank, and a girl, his daughter, wrapped in coarse woollen cloth. They had the same swarthy looks and black eyes as the hill men of Gwynedd, but under its weather-beaten brown the girl's face was pinched and grey. She was suffering, but dumbly like an animal; she neither moved nor made a sound when her father unwrapped the rags from her wrist and forearm swollen and black with poison.

"I have promised her that you will heal her," he said simply.

I made no comment then, but took her hand, speaking gently in the Old Tongue. She hung back, afraid, until I explained to the man—whose name was Mab—that I must heat water and cleanse my knife in the fire; then she let him lead her inside. I cut the swelling, and cleaned and bound the arm. It took a long time, and the girl made no sound throughout, but under the dirt her pallor grew, so when I had done and had wrapped clean bandages round the arm I heated wine for both of them, and brought out the last of my dried raisins, and meal cakes to go with them. These last I had made myself, trying my hand at them as I had so often watched my servant do at home. At first my cakes had been barely eatable, even when sopped in wine, but lately I had got the trick of it, and it gave me pleasure to see Mab and the girl eat eagerly, and then reach for more. So from magic and the voices of gods to the making of meal cakes: this, perhaps the lowest of my skills, was not the one in which I took least pride.

"Now," I said to Mab, "it seems that you knew I was here?"

"Word went through the forest. No, do not look like that, Myrddin Emrys. We tell no one. But we follow all who move in the forest, and we know all that passes."

"Yes. Your power. I was told so. I may need its help, while I stay here keeping the chapel."

"It's yours. You have lighted the lamps again."

"Then give me the news."

He drank, and wiped his mouth. "The winter has been quiet. The coasts are bound with storms. There was fighting in the south, but it is over and the borders are whole. Cissa has taken ship to Germany. Aelle stays, with his sons. In the north there is nothing. Gwarthegydd has quarrelled with his father Caw, but when did that breed ever rest quiet? He has fled to Ireland, but that is nothing. They say also that Riagath is with Niall in Ireland. Niall has feasted with Gilloman, and there is peace between them."

It was a bare recital of facts, told through with neither expression nor real understanding, as if learned by rote. But I could piece it together. The Saxons, Ireland, the Picts of the north; threats on all sides, but no more than threats: not yet.

"And the King?" I asked.

"Is himself, but not the man he was. Where he was brave, now he is angry. His followers fear him."

"And the King's son?" I waited for the answer. How much did these folk really see?

The black eyes were unreadable. "They say he is on the Isle of Glass, but then what do you do here in the Wild Forest, Myrddin Emrys?"

"I tend the shrine. You are welcome to it. All are welcome."

He was silent for a while. The girl crouched beside the fire, watching me, her fear apparently gone. She had finished eating, but I had seen her slip a couple of the meal cakes into the folds of her clothes, and smiled to myself.

I said to Mab: "If I should need to send a message, would your people take it?"

"Willingly."

"Even to the King?"

"We would contrive that it should reach him."

"As for the King's son," I said, "you say that you and your people see all that passes in the forest. If my magic should reach out to the King's son in his hiding-place, and call him to me through the forest, will he be safe?"

He made the strange sign that I had seen Llyd's men make, and nodded. "He will be safe. We will watch him for you. Did you not promise Llyd that he would be our King as well as the king of those in the cities of the south?"

"He is everyone's King," I said.

The girl's arm must have healed cleanly, for he did not bring her back. Two days later a freshly snared pheasant appeared at the back door, with a skin of the honey mead. In my turn I cleared the drifted snow from the stone, and put a cup in the place made for it above the spring. I never saw anyone near either, but there were signs I recognized, and when I left part of a new batch of meal cakes at the back door they would vanish overnight, and some offering appear in their place—a piece of venison, perhaps, or the leg of a hare.

As soon as the forest tracks were clear I saddled Strawberry and rode down towards Galava. The way led down the banks of the stream, and along the northern shore of a lake. This was a smaller lake than the great stretch of water at whose head Galava lay; it was little more than a mile long, and perhaps a third of a mile wide, with the forest crowding down on every hand right to the water. About midway along, but nearer the southern shore, was an island, not large, but thickly grown with trees, a piece of the surrounding forest broken off and thrown down into the quiet water. It was a rocky island, its trees crowding steeply up towards the high crags which reared at the center. These were of grey stone, outlined still with the last of the snow, and looking for all the world like the towers of a castle. On that day of leaden stillness there was about them a kind of burnished brightness. The island swam above its own reflection, the mirrored towers seeming to sink, fathoms deep, into the still center of the lake.

From the other end of this lake the stream flowed out again, this time as a young river, swollen with snow water, cutting its way deep and fast through beds of pallid rushes and black marshland seamed with willow and alder, towards Galava. In a mile or so the valley widened, and the marsh gave way to the cultivated land and the walls of small farms, and the cottages of the settlement crowding close under the protection of the castle walls. Beyond Ector's towers, jutting grey and uncompromising through the black winter trees, was the great lake which stretched as far as the eye could see, to merge with the sullen sky.

The first place I came to was a farm set a short way back from the river-side. It was not the kind of farm we have in the south and south-west, built on the Roman plan, but a place such as I had become used to seeing here in the north. There was a cluster of circular buildings, the farmhouse and the sheds for the beasts, all within a big irregular ring protected by a palisade of wood and stone. As I passed the gate a dog hurtled to the end of his chain, barking. A man, the owner by his dress, appeared in the doorway of a barn and stood staring. He had a billhook in his hand. I reined in and called a greeting. He came forward with a look of curiosity, but with the wariness that one saw everywhere in the country nowadays when a stranger approached.

"Where are you bound, stranger? For the Count's castle of Galava?"

"No. Only to the nearest place where I may buy food—meat and meal and perhaps some wine. I've come from the chapel up there in the forest. You know it?"

"Who doesn't? How does the old man up there, old Prosper? We've not seen him since before the snow."

"He died at Christmas."

He crossed himself. "You were with him?"

"Yes. I keep the chapel now." I gave no details. If he liked

308

to assume I had been there for some time, helping the chapel's keeper, that was all to the good. "My name is Myrddin," I told him. I had decided to use my own name, rather than the "Emrys." Myrddin was a common enough name in the west, and would not necessarily be connected with the vanished Merlin; on the other hand, if Arthur was still known as "Emrys," it might provoke questions if a stranger of that name suddenly appeared in the district, and began to spend time in the boy's company.

"Myrddin, eh? Where are you from?"

"I kept a hill shrine for a time in Dyfed."

"I see." His eyes summed me, found me harmless, and he nodded. "Well, each to his task. No doubt your prayers serve us in their way as much as the Count's sword when it's needed. Does he know of the change up yonder?"

"I've seen no one since I came. The snow fell just after Prosper died. What sort of man is this Count Ector?"

"A good lord and a good man. And his lady as good as he. You'll not lack while they hold the forest."

"Has he sons?"

"Two, and likely boys both. You'll see them, I dare say, when the weather loosens. They ride in the forest most days. No doubt the Count will send for you when he comes home; he's away now, and the elder son with him. They expect him back at the turn of spring." He turned his head and called, and a woman appeared in the doorway of the house. "Catra, here's the new man from the chapel. Old Prosper died at midwinter: you were right he wouldn't last the new year in. Have you bread to spare from the baking, and a skin of wine? Good sir, you'll take a bite with us till the fresh batch comes from the oven?"

I accepted, and they made me welcome, and found me all I needed, bread and meal and a skin of wine, sheeps' tallow to make candles, oil for the lamps and chopped feed for the mare. I paid for them, and Fedor—he told me his name—helped me pack my saddle-bags. I asked no more questions, but listened to all he told me of local news, and then, well content, rode back to the shrine. The news would get to Ector, and the name; he would be the one person who would immediately connect the new hermit of the Wild Forest with the Myrddin who had vanished with the winter from his cold hilltop in Wales.

I rode down again at the beginning of February, this time to the village itself, where I found that the folk knew all about my coming and, as I had guessed, accepted me already as part of the place. Had I tried to find a niche in village or castle I would still, I knew, have been "the foreigner" and "the stranger" and a subject of ceaseless gossip, but holy men were a class apart, and often wanderers, and the good folk took them as they came. I had been relieved to find that they never came up to the chapel; there was too much of its ancient awesomeness still hanging about the place. They were most of them Christians, and turned for their comfort to the community of brothers nearby, but old beliefs die hard, and I was regarded with more respect, I believe, than the abbot himself.

The same image of ancient holiness clung, I had found, about the island in the lake. I had asked one of the hill men about it. It was known, he told me, as Caer Bannog, which means the Castle in the Mountains, and was said to be haunted by Bilis the dwarf king of the Otherworld. It was reputed to appear and disappear at will, sometimes floating invisible, as if made of glass. No one would go near it, and though people fished on the lake in summer and animals were grazed on the flat grassland at the western end where the river flowed into the valley, no one ventured near the island. Once a fisherman, caught in a sudden storm, had had his boat driven onto the island, and had passed a night there.

When he came home next day he was mad, and talked of a year spent in a great castle made of gold and glass, where strange and terrible creatures guarded a hoard of treasure beyond man's counting. No one was tempted to go and look for the treasure, for the fisherman was dead, raving, within the week. So no man set foot now on the island, and though (they said) you could see the castle clearly sometimes of a fine sunset evening, when a boat rowed nearer it vanished clear away, and it was well known that if you set foot on the shore, the island would sink beneath you.

Such stories are not always to be dismissed as shepherds' tales. I had thought about it often, this other "isle of glass" that I found now almost on my doorstep, and wondered if its reputation would make it a safe hiding-place for Macsen's sword. It would be some years yet before the boy Arthur could take and lift the sword of Britain, and meanwhile it was neither safe nor fitting that it should be hidden in the roof of a beasts' shed out there in the forest. It was a marvel, I had sometimes thought, that it did not set light to the thatch. If it was indeed the King's sword of Britain, and Arthur was to be the King who would lift it, it must lie in a place as holy and as haunted as the shrine where I myself had found it. And when the day came the boy must be led to it himself, even as I had been led. I was the god's instrument, but I was not the god's hand.

So I had wondered about the island. And then, one day, I was sure.

I went down to the village again in March for my monthly supplies. When I rode back along the lake side the sun was setting, and a light mist wreathed along the water's surface. It made the island seem a long way off, and floating, so that one might well imagine it ghostly, and ready to sink under a random foot. The sun, sinking in splendour, caught the crags, and sent them flaming up from the dark hangers of trees behind. In this light the strange formations of the rock looked like high embattled towers, the crest of a sun-lit castle standing above the trees. I looked, thinking of the legends, then looked again, and reined Strawberry in sharply and sat staring. There, across the flat sheen of the lake, above the floating mist, was the tower of my dream again, Macsen's Tower, whole once more and built out of the sunset. The tower of the sword.

I took the sword across next day. The mist was thicker than ever, and hid me from anyone who might have been there to see.

The island lay less than two hundred paces from the south shore of the lake. I would have swum the mare across, but found that she could go through breast high. The lake was still as glass, and as silent. We forged across with no more splashing than the wild deer make, and saw no living thing but a pair of diver ducks, and a heron beating slowly past in the mist.

I left the mare grazing, and carried the sword up through the trees till I reached the foot of the towered crags. I think I knew what I would find. Bushes and young trees grew thickly along the scree at the foot of the cliffs, but the boughs were barely budding, and through them I could see an opening, giving on a narrow passageway which led steeply downwards into the cliffs. I had brought a torch with me. I lit it, then went quickly down the steep passage, and found myself in a deep inner cavern where no light came.

In front of my feet lay a sheet of water, black and still, flooring half the cavern. Beyond the pool, against the back of the cavern, stood a low block of stone; I could not tell if it was a natural ledge, or if men's hands had squared it, but it stood there like an altar, and to one side of it a bowl had been hollowed in the stone. This was full of water, which in the smoky torchlight looked red as blood. Here and there from the roof water welled slowly, dripping down. Where it struck the surface of the pool the water broke with the sound of a plucked harp-string, its echo rippling away with the widening rings of torchlight. But where it dripped dull on stone it had not, as you might expect, worn the rock into hollows, but had built pillars, and above these from the dripping rocks hung solid stone icicles that had grown to meet the pillars below. The place was a temple, pillared in pale marble and floored with glass. Even I, who was here by right, and hedged with power, felt my scalp tingle.

By land and water shall it go home, and lie hidden in the floating stone until by fire it shall be raised again. So had the Old Ones said, and they would have recognized this place as I did; as the dead fisherman did who came back from the Otherworld raving of the halls of the dark King. Here, in Bilis' antechamber, the sword would be safe till the youth came who had the right to lift it.

I waded forward through the pool. The floor sloped and the water deepened. Now I could see how the dark passageway ran on, back and down behind the stone table, until the roof met the water's surface and the passage vanished below the level of the lake. Ripples ringed and lapsed against the rock, and the echoes ran round the walls and broke between the pillars. The water was ice-cold. I laid the sword, still wrapped as I had found it, on the stone table. I went back across the pool. The place sang with echoes. I stood still, while they sank to a humming murmur and then died. My very breathing sounded all at once too loud, an intrusion. I left the sword to its silent waiting, and went quickly back up towards daylight. The shadows parted and let me through.

2

April came, when Ector was expected home. For the first week of the month it rained and blew, weather like winter, so that the forest roared like the sea and the draughts through the shrine kept the nine lights plunging sidelong and smoking. The white owl watched from the place where she sat her eggs in the roof.

Then I woke in the night to silence. The wind had dropped, the pines were still. I rose and threw my cloak about me and went out. Outside the moon was high, and there in the north the Bear wheeled so low and brilliant that one felt one could reach up and touch it, were it not that its touch would burn. My blood ran light and free; my body felt rinsed and new clean as the forest. For the rest of the night I slept no more than a lover does, and at first light rose and broke my fast and went to saddle Strawberry.

The sun rose brilliant in a clear sky, and its early light poured into the glade. Yesterday's rain lay thick and glittering on the grasses and the new young curls of fern; it dripped and steamed from the pines so that their scent pierced the air. Beyond their bloomed crests the encircling hills smoked white towards the sky.

I let the mare out of the shed, and was carrying the saddle over to her when suddenly she lifted her head from her grazing, and put her ears up. Seconds later I heard what she had heard, the beat of hoofs, coming at a fast gallop, far too fast for safety on a twisting path seamed with roots and overhung by branches. I set the saddle down, and waited.

A neat black horse, galloped hard on a tight rein, burst out of the forest, came to a sliding stop three paces from me, and the boy who had been lying along his back like a leech slid, all in the same movement, to the ground. The horse was sweating hard, and the bit dripped foam. Red showed inside the blown nostrils. That neat-footed gallop and the collected stop had been a matter of hard control, then. Nine years old? At his age I had been riding a fat pony which had to be kicked to a trot.

He gathered the reins competently in one hand and held the horse still when it tried to thrust past him to the water. He did it absently; his attention was all on me.

"Are you the new holy man?"

"Yes."

"Prosper was a friend of mine."

"I'm sorry."

"You don't much look like a hermit. Are you really keeping the chapel now?"

"Yes."

He chewed his lip thoughtfully, regarding me. It was a look of appraisal, a weighing-up. Under it, as under no other I had encountered, I could feel my muscles clench themselves to hold nerves and heart-beats steady. I waited. I knew that, as ever, my face gave nothing away. What he must be seeing was merely a harmless-looking man, unarmed, saddling an undistinguished horse for his routine ride down the valley for supplies.

He came apparently to a decision. "You won't tell anyone you saw me?"

"Why, who's looking for you?"

His lips parted, surprised. I got the impression that I had been supposed to say: "Very well, sir." Then he turned his head sharply, and I heard it, too. Hoofs coming, soft on the mossy ground. Fast, but not so fast as the hard-ridden black.

"You haven't seen me, remember?" I saw his hand start towards his pouch, then stop halfway. He grinned, and the sudden flash startled me: till that moment he had been so like Uther, but that sudden lighting of the face was Ambrosius', and the dark eyes were Ambrosius', too. Or mine.

"I'm sorry." He said it politely, but very fast. "I do assure you I'm not doing anything wrong. At least, not very. I'll let him catch me soon. But he won't let me ride the way I like to." He grabbed the saddle, ready to mount.

"If you ride like that on these tracks," I said, "I don't blame him. Do you need to go? Get inside there while I throw him off the scent, and I'll put your horse somewhere to cool off."

"I knew you weren't a holy man," he said, in the tone of someone conveying a compliment, and throwing me the reins, he vanished through the back doorway.

I led the black horse across to the shed, and shut the door on him. I stood there for a moment or two, breathing deeply as a man does when he comes out of rough water, steadying myself. Ten years, waiting for this. I had broken Tintagel's defenses for Uther, and killed Brithael its captain, with a steadier pulse than I had now. Well, he was here, and we should see. I went to the edge of the clearing to meet Ralf.

He was alone, and furious. His big chestnut came up the track at a slamming canter, with Ralf crouched low on its neck. There was a thin scarlet mark on one cheek where a branch had whipped his face.

The sun was full on the clearing, and he must have been dazzled. I thought for a moment he was going to ride right over me. Then he saw me, and reined his horse hard to its haunches.

"Hey, you! Did a boy ride through here a few minutes ago?"

"Yes." I spoke softly, and put my hand up to the rein. "But hold a moment—"

"Out of the way, fool!" The chestnut, feeling the spurs go home, reared violently, tearing the rein from my hand. On the same breath Ralf said, thunderstruck: "My lord!" and hauled the horse sideways. The striking hoofs missed me by inches. Ralf came out of the saddle as lightly as the boy Arthur, and reached for my hand to kiss it.

I drew it back quickly. "No. And get off your knee, man. He's here, so watch what you do."

"Sweet Christ, my lord, I nearly ran you down! The sun in my eyes—I couldn't see who it was!"

"So I imagined. A rather rough welcome, though, for the new hermit, Ralf? Are those the usual manners of the north?"

"My lord—my lord, I'm sorry. I was angry . . ." Then, honestly: "Only because he fooled me. And even when I sighted the young devil I couldn't come up with him. So I . . ." Then what I had said got through to him. His voice trailed off, and he stood back, taking me in from head to foot as if he could hardly believe his eyes. "The new hermit? *You?* You mean *you* are the 'Myrddin' of the shrine? . . . Of course! How stupid of me, I never connected him with you . . . And I'm sure no one else has—I haven't heard so much as a hint that it might be Merlin himself—"

"I hope you never will. All I am now is the keeper of the shrine, and so I shall remain, as long as it's necessary."

"Does Count Ector know?"

"Not yet. When is he due home?"

"Next week."

"Tell him then."

He nodded, and then laughed, the surprise giving way to excitement, and what looked like pleasure. "By the Rood, it's good to see you again, my lord! Are you well? How have you fared? How did you come here? And now—what will happen now?"

The questions came pouring out. I put up a hand, smiling. "Look," I said quickly, "we'll talk later. We'll arrange a time. But now, will you go and lose yourself for an hour or so, and let me make the boy's acquaintance on my own?"

"Of course. Will two hours do? You'll get a lot of credit for that—I'm not usually thrown off his track so easily." He glanced round the glade, but with his eyes only, not moving his head. The place was still in the morning sun, and silent but for the cock thrush singing. "Where is he? In the chapel? Then in case he's watching us, you'd better do some misdirecting."

"With pleasure." I turned and pointed up one of the tracks which led out of the glade. "Will that one do? I don't know where it goes, but it might suffice to lose you."

"If it doesn't kill me," he said resignedly. "Of course it had to be that one, didn't it? In the normal way I'd just call that a bad guess, but seeing it's you—"

"It was only a random choice, I assure you. I'm sorry. Is it so dangerous?"

"Well, if I'm supposed to be looking for Arthur there, it's guaranteed to keep me out of the way for quite some time." He gathered the reins, miming hasty agreement for the benefit of the unseen watcher. "No, seriously, my lord—"

" 'Myrddin.' No lord of yours now, nor of any man's."

"Myrddin, then. No, it's a rough track but it's rideable—just. What's more, it's just the way that devil's cub would have chosen to take . . . I told you, nothing you do can ever be quite random." He laughed. "Yes, it's good to have you back. I feel as if the world had been lifted off my shoulders. These last few years have been pretty full ones, believe me!"

"I believe you." He mounted, saluting, and I stepped back. He went across the glade at a canter, and then the sound of hoofs dwindled up the ferny track and was gone.

The boy was sitting on the table's edge, eating bread and honey. The honey was running off his chin. He slid to his feet when he saw me, wiped the honey off with the back of his hand, licked the hand and swallowed.

"Do you mind very much? There seemed to be plenty, and I was starving."

"Help yourself. There are dried figs in that bowl on the shelf."

"Not just now, thank you. I've had enough. I'd better water Star now, I think. I heard Ralf go."

As we led the horse across to the spring, he told me: "I call him Star for that white star on his forehead. Why did you smile then?"

"Only because when I was younger than you I had a pony called Aster; that means Star in Greek. And like you, I escaped from home one day and rode up into the hills and came across a hermit living alone—it was a cave he lived in, not a chapel, but it was just as lonely—and he gave me honey cakes and fruit."

"You mean you ran away?"

"Not really. Only for the day. I just wanted to get away alone. One has to, sometimes."

"Then you did understand? Is that why you sent Ralf away, and didn't tell him I was here? Most people would have told him straight away. They seem to think I need looking after," said Arthur in a tone of grievance. The horse lifted a streaming muzzle and blew the drops from its nostrils and turned from the water. We began to walk back across the clearing. He looked up. "I haven't thanked you yet. I'm much obliged to you. Ralf won't get into trouble, you know. I never tell when I give them the slip. My guardian would be angry, and it's not their fault. Ralf will come back this way, and I'll go with him then. And don't worry yourself, either; I won't let him harm you. It's always me he blames, anyway." That sudden grin again. "It's always my fault, as a matter of fact. Cei is older than me, but I get all the ideas."

We had reached the shed. He made as if to hand me the reins, then, as he had done before, stopped in mid-gesture, led the horse in himself and tied him up. I watched from the doorway.

"What's your name?" I asked.

"Emrys. What's yours?"

"Myrddin. And, oddly enough, Emrys. But then that's a common name where I come from. Who is your guardian?"

"Count Ector. He's Lord of Galava." He turned from his task, his cheeks flushed. I could see he was waiting for the next question, the inevitable question, but I did not ask it. I had spent twelve years myself having to tell every man who spoke to me that I was the bastard of an unknown father: I did not intend to force this boy through the same confession. Though there were differences. If I was any judge, he had better defenses already than I had had at twice his age. And as the well-guarded foster son of the Count of Galava, he did not have to live, as I had, with bastard shame. But then, I thought again, watching him, the differences between this child and myself went deeper: I had been content with very little, not guessing my power; this boy would never be content with less than all.

"And how old are you?" I asked him. "Ten?"

He looked pleased. "As a matter of fact I've just had my ninth birthday."

"And can ride already better than I do now."

"Well, you're only a—" He bit it off, and went scarlet.

"I only started work as a hermit at Christmas," I said mildly. "I've really ridden around the place quite a lot."

"What doing?"

"Travelling. Even fighting, when I had to."

"Fighting? Where?"

As we talked I had led him round to the front entrance of the chapel, and up the steps. These were mossed with age, and steep, and I was surprised at the child's lightness of foot as he trod up them beside me. He was a tall boy, sturdily built, with bones that gave promise of strength. There was another kind of promise, too, Uther's sort; he would be a handsome man. But the first impression one got of Arthur was of a controlled swiftness of movement almost like a dancer's or a skilled swordsman's. There was something in it of Uther's restlessness, but it was not the same; this sprang from some deep inner core of harmony. An athlete would have talked of co-ordination, an archer of a straight eye, a sculptor of a steady hand. Already in this boy, they came together in the impression of a blazing but controlled vitality.

"What battles were you in? You would be young, even when the Great Wars were being fought? My guardian says that I will have to wait until I am fourteen before I go to war. It's not fair, because Cei is three years older, and I can beat him three times out of four. Well, twice perhaps . . . Oh!"

As we went in through the chapel doorway the bright sunlight behind us had thrown our shadows forward, so that at first the altar had been hidden. Now, as we moved, the light reached it, the strong light of early morning, by some freak falling straight on the carved sword so that the blade seemed to lift clear and shining from its shadows on the stone.

Before I could say a word he had darted forward and

reached for the hilt. I saw his hand meet the stone, and the shock of it go through his flesh. He stood like that for seconds, as if tranced, then dropped the hand to his side and stepped back, still facing the altar.

He spoke without looking at me. "That was the queerest thing. I thought it was real. I thought, 'There is the most beautiful and deadly sword in the world, and it is for me.' And all the time it wasn't real."

"Oh, it's real," I said. Through the dazzling swirl of sun-motes I saw the boy, hazed with brightness, turn to stare at me. Behind him the altar shimmered white with the ice-cold fire. "It's real enough. Some day it will lie on this very altar, in the sight of all men. And he who then dares to touch and lift it from where it lies shall . . ."

"Shall what? What shall he do, Myrddin?"

I blinked, shook the sun from my eyes, and steadied myself. It is one thing to watch what is happening elsewhere on middle-earth; it is quite another to see what has not yet come out of the heavens. This last, which men call prophecy, and which they honour me for, is like being struck through the entrails by that whip of God that we call lightning. But even as my flesh winced from it I welcomed it as a woman welcomes the final pang of childbirth. In this flash of vision I had seen it as it would happen in this very place; the sword, the fire, the young King. So my own quest through the Middle Sea, the painful journey to Segontium, the shouldering of Prosper's tasks, the hiding of the sword in Caer Bannog—now I knew for certain that I had read the god's will aright. From now, it was only waiting.

"What shall I do?" the voice demanded, insistent.

I do not think the boy was conscious of the change in the question. He was fixed, serious, burning. The end of the lash had caught him, too. But it was not yet time. Slowly, fighting the other words away, I gave him all he could understand.

322

I said: "A man hands on his sword to his son. You will have to find your own. But when the time comes, it will be there for you to take, in the sight of all men."

The Otherworld drew back then, and let me through, back into the clear April morning. I wiped the sweat from my face and took a breath of sweet air. It felt like a first breath. I pushed back the damp hair and gave my head a shake. "They crowd me," I said irritably.

"Who do?"

"Oh," I said, "those who keep wake here." His eyes watched me, at stretch, ready for wonders. He came slowly down the altar steps. The stone table behind him was only a table, with a sword rudely carved. I smiled at him. "I have a gift, Emrys, which can be useful and very powerful, but which is at times inconvenient, and always damnably uncomfortable."

"You mean you can see things that aren't there?"

"Sometimes."

"Then you're a magician? Or a prophet?"

"A little of both, shall we say. But that is my secret, Emrys. I kept yours."

"I shan't tell anyone." That was all, no promises, no oaths, but I knew he would keep to it. "You were telling the future then? What did it mean?"

"One cannot always be sure. Even I am not always sure. But one thing for certain, some day, when you are ready, you will find your own sword, and it will be the most beautiful and deadly sword in the world. But now, just for the moment, would you find me a drink of water? There's a cup beside the spring."

He brought it, running. I thanked him and drank, then handed it back. "Now, what about those dried figs? Are you still hungry?"

"I'm always hungry."

"Then next time you come, bring your rations with you. You might pick a bad day."

"I'll bring you food if you want it. Are you very poor? You don't look it." He considered me again, head aslant. "At least, perhaps you do, but you don't speak as if you were. If there's anything you'd like, I'll try and get it for you."

"Don't trouble yourself. I have all I need, now," I said.

3

Ralf came back duly, with questions in his eyes, but none
on his lips except those he might ask a stranger.

He came too soon for me. There were nine years to get
through, and judgments to make. And too soon, I could
see, for the boy, though he received Ralf with courtesy, and
then stood silent under the lash of that eloquent young man's
tongue. I gathered from Arthur's expression that if it had
not been for my presence he might have been thrashed by
more than words. I understood that he lived under hard
discipline: that kings must be brought up harder than other
men he must have known, but not that the rule applied to
him. I wondered what rule applied to Cei, and what Arthur
thought the discrimination meant. He took it well, and when
it was finished and I offered Ralf the appeasement of wine,
went meekly enough to serve it.

When at length he was sent to lead the horses out, I said
quickly to Ralf: "Tell Count Ector I would rather not
come down to the castle. He'll understand that. The risks
are too great. He'll know where we can meet in safety, so
I'll leave it to him to suggest a place. Would he normally
come up here, or might that make people wonder?"

"He never came before, when Prosper was here."

"Then I'll come down whenever he sends a message. Now,
Ralf, there's not much time, but tell me this. You've no reason
to suppose that anyone has suspected who the boy is? There's
been no one watching about the place, nothing suspicious
at all?"

"Nothing."

I said slowly: "Something I saw, when you first brought him over from Brittany. On the journey across by the pass, your party was attacked. Who were they? Did you see?"

He stared. "You mean up there by the rocks between here and Mediobogdum? I remember it well. But how did you know that?"

"I saw it in the fire. I watched constantly then. What is it, Ralf? Why do you look so?"

"It was a queer thing," he said slowly. "I've never forgotten it. That night, when they attacked us, I thought I heard you call my name. A warning, clear as a trumpet, or a dog barking. And now you say you were watching." He shifted his shoulders as if at a sudden draught, then grinned. "I'd forgotten about you, my lord. I'll have to get used to it again, I suppose. Do you still watch us? It could be an awkward thought, at times."

I laughed. "Not really. If there was danger it would come through to me, I think. Otherwise it seems I can leave it to you. But come, tell me, did you ever find out who it was attacked you that night?"

"No. They wore no blazon. We killed two of them, and there was nothing on them to show whose men they were. Count Ector thought they must be outlaws or robbers. I think so, too. At any rate there's been nothing since then, nothing at all."

"I thought not. And now there must be nothing to connect Myrddin the hermit with Merlin the enchanter. What has been said about the new holy man of the chapel in the green?"

"Only that Prosper had died and that God had sent a new man at the appointed time, as he has always done. That the new man is young, and quiet-seeming, but not as quiet as he seems."

"And just what do they mean by that?"

"Just what they say. You don't always bear yourself just like a humble hermit, sir."

"Don't I? I can't think why not; it's what I normally am. I must guard myself."

"I believe you mean that." He was smiling, as if amused. "I shouldn't worry, they just think you must be holier than most. It's always been a haunted place, this, and more so now, it seems. There are stories of a spirit in the shape of a huge white bird that flies in men's faces if they venture too far up the track, and—oh, all the usual tales you always get about hauntings, silly country stories, things one can't believe. But two weeks back—did you know that a troop of men was riding this way from somewhere near Alauna, and a tree fell across the way, with no wind blowing, and no warning?"

"I hadn't heard that. Was anyone hurt?"

"No. There's another path; they used that."

"I see."

He was watching me curiously. "Your gods, my lord?"

"You might call them that. I hadn't realized I was to be so closely guarded."

"So you knew something like this might happen?"

"Not until you told me. But I know who did it, and why."

He frowned, thinking. "But if it was done deliberately . . . If I am to bring Emrys this way again—"

"Emrys will be safe. And he is your safe conduct, too, Ralf. Don't fear them."

I saw his brows twitch at the word "fear," then he nodded. I thought he seemed anxious, even tense. He asked me: "How long do you suppose you will be here?"

"It's hard to judge. You must know it depends on the High King's health. If Uther recovers fully, it may be that the boy will stay here until he is fourteen, and ready to go to his father. Why, Ralf? Can you not resign yourself to obscurity for a few more years? Or do you find it too taxing riding guard on that young gentleman?"

"No—that is, yes. But—it isn't that . . ." He stammered, flushing.

I said, amused: "Who is she?"

I did not quite understand his scowling look until, after a pause, he asked: "How much else did you see, when you watched Arthur in the fire?"

"My dear Ralf!" It was not just the moment to tell him that the stars tend only to mirror the fate of kings and the will of gods. I said mildly: "The Sight doesn't as a rule take me beyond bedchamber doors. I guessed. Your face is about as concealing as a gauze curtain. And you must remember to call him Emrys even when you are angry."

"I'm sorry. I didn't mean— Not that there was anything you couldn't have watched—I mean, I've never even been in her bedchamber . . . I mean, she's—oh, hell and damnation, I should have known you'd know all about it. I didn't mean to be insolent. I'd forgotten you never take anything the way other men do. I never know where I am with you. You've been away too long. . . . There are the horses now. He seems to have saddled yours as well. I thought you said you weren't coming down today after all?"

"I hadn't intended to. It must be Emrys' idea."

It was. As soon as he saw us in the doorway, Arthur called out: "I brought your horse, too, sir. Will you not ride down part of the way with us?"

"If we go at my pace, not yours."

"We'll walk the whole way if you like."

"Oh, I won't subject you to that. But we'll let Ralf lead the way, shall we?"

The first part of the descent was steep. Ralf went in front and Arthur behind him, and the black horse must have been very sure-footed indeed, for Arthur rode with his chin on his shoulder the whole way, talking to me. To anyone who did not know, it might have seemed that it was the boy who had nine years to make up; I hardly had to question him; all the detail, small and great, of his life came tumbling out, till I knew as much about Count Ector's household and the boy's place in it as he knew himself—and more besides.

We came at length down from the edge of the pines into a wood of oak and chestnut where the going was easier, and after half a mile or so struck into the easy track along the lake. Caer Bannog floated, sunlit, above its secret. The valley widened ahead of us, and presently, cloudy along its green curve, showed the line of willows that marked the river.

Where the river left the lake I checked my horse. As I took my leave of them the boy asked quickly: "May I come back soon?"

"Come whenever you like—whenever you can. But you must promise me one thing."

He looked wary, which meant that what he promised, he would keep. "What's that?"

"Don't come without Ralf, or whoever escorts you. Don't break away next time. This is not called the Wild Forest for nothing."

"Oh, I know it's supposed to be haunted, but I'm not afraid of what lives in the hills, not now that I've seen—" He checked, and changed direction without a tremor "—not with you there. And if it's wolves, I have my dagger, and wolves don't attack by day. Besides, there are no wolves that could catch Star."

"I was thinking of a different kind of wild beast."

"Bears? Boars?"

"No, men."

"Oh." The syllable was a shrug. It was bravery, of course; there were outlaws here as well as anywhere, and he must have heard stories, but it was innocence as well. Such had been Count Ector's care of him. The most vulnerable and sought-for head in the kingdoms, and danger was still only a story to him.

"All right," he said, "I promise." I was satisfied. The guardians from the hollow hills might watch him for me, but guarding him was another thing. That took Ector's kind of power, and mine.

"My greetings to Count Ector," I told Ralf, and saw that he had understood my thoughts. We parted then. I stood watching them ride off along the turf by the river, the black horse fighting to be away and snatching at the bit, Ralf's big chestnut simmering alongside, while the boy talked excitedly, gesturing. At length he must have got his way, for suddenly Ralf's heels moved, and the chestnut leaped forward into a gallop. The black, set alight a fraction later, tore after it. As the two flying figures vanished round a shaw of birch trees, the smaller turned in the saddle, and waved. It had begun.

He was back next day, trotting decorously into the clearing with Ralf half a length in the rear. Arthur carried a gift of eggs and honey cakes and the information that Count Ector was still away, but the Countess seemed to think contact with the holy man might do good where it was most needed, and was glad to let him come meanwhile. The Count would arrange to see me as soon as he got back.

Arthur gave me the message, not Ralf, and obviously saw nothing in it but the strict precautions of a guardian who he must have long ago decided was over-zealous to an uncomfortable degree.

Four of the eggs were broken. "Only Emrys," said Ralf, "could possibly have imagined he could carry eggs on that wild colt of his."

"You must admit he did very well only to break four."

"Oh, aye, only Emrys could have done it. I've never had a quieter ride since I last escorted you."

He went off then on some excuse. Arthur washed the eggs out of his horse's mane and then settled down to help me eat the honey cakes, and ply me with questions about the world that lay outside the Wild Forest.

A few days later Ector returned to Galava, and arranged through Ralf to meet me.

Word would have gone round by now that the boy Emrys had ridden up two or three times to the chapel in the green, and people might well expect Count Ector or his lady to send for the new incumbent to look him over. It was arranged that Ector and I were to meet as if by chance at Fedor's farm. Fedor himself and his wife could be trusted, I was told, with anything; the other folk there would only see the hermit calling for supplies as usual, and the Count riding by and taking the opportunity to speak with him.

We were shown into a smallish, smoke-filled room, and our host brought wine and then left us.

Ector had hardly altered, save to add a little grey to his hair and beard. When, after the first greetings were over, I told him so, he laughed. "That's hardly surprising. You tip a gilded cuckoo's egg into my quiet nest and think to find me carefree? No, no, man, I was only jesting. Neither Drusilla nor I would have been without the boy. Whatever comes of it in the end, these have been good years, and if we've done a good job, we had the finest stuff in the world to work on."

He plunged then into an account of his stewardship. Five years is a long time, and there was a great deal to say. I spoke hardly at all, but listened readily. Some of what he told me I knew already, from the fire, or from the boy's own talk. But if I was familiar enough with the tenor of

Arthur's life here in Galava, and could judge its results for myself, what came chiefly out of Ector's talk of him was the deep affection which he and his wife felt for their charge. Not only these two, but the rest of the household who had no idea who Arthur was held him, apparently, in the same affection. My impressions of him had been right; there was courage and quick wit and a burning desire to excel. Not enough cool sense and caution, perhaps—faults like his father's —"but who the devil wants a young boy to be cautious? That much he'll learn the first time he's hurt, or, worse, when he finds a man that can't be trusted," said Ector gruffly, obviously torn between pride in the boy and in his own successful guardianship.

When I began to talk of this, and to thank him for what he had done, he cut me off abruptly.

"Well, now, you've got yourself settled nicely in here, from all I hear about it. That was a fine chance, wasn't it, that led you up to the Green Chapel in time to take old Prosper's place?"

"Chance?" I said.

"Oh, aye, I'd forgotten who I was talking to. It's a long time since we had an enchanter in these parts. Well, to a jogging mortal like me it would have come as chance. Whatever it was, it's the best thing; you couldn't have taken a place in the castle, as it happens; we've got a man here who knows you well; Marcellus, him that married Valerius' sister. He's my master-at-arms. Maybe I shouldn't have taken him on, knowing you'd be likely to come back, but he's one of the best officers in the country, and God knows we're going to need all we have, here in the north. He's the best swordsman in the country, too. For the boy's sake, I couldn't miss the chance." He shot me a sharp look from under his brows. "What are you laughing at? Wasn't that chance, either?"

"No," I said, "it was Uther." I told him of the talk I had had with the King on the subject of Arthur's training. "How like Uther to send a man who knew me. But then he never did have room for more than one thought at a time. . . . Well, I'll keep away. Can you find a good reason for letting the boy ride up to see me?"

He nodded. "I've given it about that I know of you, and you're a learned man and have travelled widely, and there are things you can teach the boys that they'd not learn from Abbot Martin or the fathers. I'll let it be known that they may ride up your way whenever they wish."

" 'They?' Hasn't Cei outgrown a tutor, even an unorthodox one?"

"Oh, he wouldn't come for the learning." His father's voice held a kind of rueful pride. "He's like me, is Cei, not a thought in his head but what you might call the arts of the field. Not that even so he'll be the kind of swordsman Arthur's shaping for, but he's dogged and takes all the pains in the world. He'll not come twice if there's book learning to be discussed, but you know what boys are, what one has the other wants, and I couldn't keep him away if I tried, after all Arthur's been saying. He's talked of nothing else since I got home, even told Drusilla it was his holy duty to ride up there every day to see you got sufficient food. Yes, you may well laugh. Did you set a spell on him?"

"Not that I'm aware of. I'd like to see Cei again. He was a fine boy."

"It's not easy for him," said Ector, "knowing the younger one is near as good as he is already, for all the three years' difference, and is likely to surpass him when they both come to man. And when they were younger it was always 'Remember to let Emrys have as much as you—he's the foster-son, and a guest.' It might have been easier if there'd been others. Drusilla's had the hardest time of it, not liking to

333

favour one or the other, but having to let Cei see all the way that he was the real son, without letting Arthur feel he was on the outside. Cei's done well enough by the other boy, even if he does tend to jealousy, but there'll be nothing to fear in the future, I assure you. Show him where he can be loyal, and no one will shift him. Like his father; a slow dog, but where he grips, he holds." He talked on a little longer, and I listened, remembering my own very different upbringing as the bastard and outsider at another court. Where I had been quiet and showed no talents that could rouse jealousy in boy or man, Arthur by his very nature must shine out among the other boys in the castle like a young dragon hatching in a clutch of pond newts.

At last Ector sighed, drank, and set down his cup. "But there, those are nursery tales now, and long past. Cei stays by me now, among the men, and there's Bedwyr to keep Arthur company. When I said 'they' I wasn't thinking of Cei. We've another boy with us now. I brought him back with me from York. Bedwyr, his name is, son of Ban of Benoic. Know him?"

"I've met him."

"He asked me to take Bedwyr for a year or two. He'd heard Marcellus was here with me, and wanted Bedwyr to learn from him. He's about the same age as Arthur, so I wasn't sorry when Ban made the suggestion. You'll like Bedwyr. A quiet boy; not a great brain, so Abbot Martin tells me, but a good lad, and seems to like Emrys. Even Cei thinks twice before he tangles with the pair of them. Well, that's that, isn't it? It's just to be hoped Abbot Martin doesn't try to spoke the wheel."

"Is it likely?"

"Well, the boy was baptized a Christian. It's thought that Prosper served God in the later years, but it's well known that the Green Chapel has housed other gods than the true

334

Christ in its time. What do you do now, up there in the forest?"

"I believe in giving due honour to whatever god confronts you," I said. "That's common sense in these days, as well as courtesy. Sometimes I think the gods themselves have not yet got it clear. The chapel is open to the air and the forest, and they come in who will."

"And Arthur?"

"In a Christian household, Arthur will owe duty to Christ's God. What he does on the field of battle may be another matter. I don't know yet which god will give the boy his sword—though I doubt if Christ was much of a swordsman. But we shall see. May I pour you more wine?"

"What? Oh, thank you." Ector blinked, wetted his lips, and changed the subject. "Ralf was saying you'd asked about that ambush at Mediobogdum five years back. They were robbers, no more. Why do you ask? Have you reason to think that someone's interested now?"

"I had some small trouble on the way north," I said. "Ralf tells me there has been nothing here."

"Nothing. I've been twice myself to Winchester and once to London, and there's never a soul so much as questioned me, which they'd have been quick to do if anyone had thought the boy might be anywhere in the north."

"Lot has never approached you or shown interest?"

Another quick look. "Him, eh? Well, nothing would surprise me there. Some of the trouble we've been having in these parts might easily have been avoided if that same gentleman had minded his kingdom's business instead of paying court to a throne."

"So they say that, do they? It's the King's place he's after, not just a place at the King's side?"

"Whatever he's after, they're handfast now, he and Morgian: they'll be married as soon as the girl is twelve

335

years old. There's no way out of *that* union now, even if Uther wanted to end it."

"And you don't like it?"

"No one does, up in this part of the country. They say that Lot's stretching his borders all the time, and not always with the sword. There's talk of meetings. If he gets too much power by the time the High King fails, we might well find ourselves back in the time of the Wolf. The Saxons coming every spring and burning and raping as far as the Pennine Way, aye, and the Irish coming down to join them, and more of our men taking to the high hills and what cold comfort they can find there."

"How recently did you see the King?"

"Three weeks past. When he lay at York he sent for me, and asked privately about the boy."

"How did he look?"

"Well enough, but the cutting edge was gone. You understand me?"

"Very well. Was Cador of Cornwall with him?"

"No. He was still at Caerleon then. I have heard since—"

"At Caerleon?" I asked sharply. "Cador himself was there?"

"Yes," said Ector, surprised. "He'd be there just before you left home. Did you not know?"

"I should have known," I said. "He sent a party of armed men to search my home on Bryn Myrddin, and to watch my movements. I gave them the slip, I think, but what I didn't reckon on was being watched by two parties at the same time. Urien of Gore had men there in Maridunum, too, and they traced me north into Gwynedd." I told him about Crinas, and Urien's party, and he listened, frowning. I asked him: "You haven't heard reports of any such up here? They'd ask no questions openly, but wait and watch, and listen."

"No. If there were strangers, it would have been reported. You must have shaken them off. Be easy, Cador's men will never come this way. He's in Segontium now, did you know?"

"When I was there I heard he was expected. Do you know if he plans to make his headquarters at Segontium, now Uther's put him in charge of the Irish Shore defenses? Has there been talk of re-investing it?"

"There was talk, yes, but I doubt if it will ever come to anything. That's a task that'll take more time and money than Uther is likely to spare, or to have, just yet. If I can make a guess, Cador will garrison Segontium and the frontier fortresses, and base himself inland where he can keep his forces moving to the points of attack. Perhaps at Deva. Rheged himself is in Luguvallium. We do what we can."

"And Urien? I trust he's fixed on the east, where he belongs?"

"Well dug in on his rock," said Ector, with grim satisfaction. "And one thing's for sure. Until Lot marries Morgian with every bishop in the realm in attendance, and proof positive of consummation, he won't stir a hand to bring Uther down, or let Urien do so, either. Nor will he find Arthur. If they haven't had a sniff of the boy in nine years, they'll never pick the scent up now. So be easy. By the time Morgian is twelve, and ready for bedding, Arthur will be fourteen, and coming to the time when the King has promised to bring him before the kingdom. It will be time then to deal with Lot and Urien, and if the time comes before then, why, it is with God."

On that we parted, and I rode back alone to the shrine.

4

After this Arthur, sometimes with the other two boys, but usually just with Bedwyr, rode up to the chapel to see me two or three times a week. Cei was a big fair-haired boy, with a look of his father, and his manner to Arthur was a compound of patronage and hectoring affection which must have been galling at times to the younger boy. But Arthur seemed fond of his foster-brother, and eager to share with him the pleasure (for so he seemed to find it) of his visits to me. Cei enjoyed the tales I had to tell of foreign lands and the histories of fighting and conquests and battle, but he grew quickly tired of discussing the way the people lived and governed their countries, and the talk of their legends and beliefs, which Arthur loved. As time went by Cei stayed more often at home, going (the other two told me) on sport or business with his father; hunting sometimes, or on patrol, or accompanying Count Ector on his occasional visits to his neighbours. After the first year, I rarely saw Cei at all.

Bedwyr was quite different, a quiet boy of Arthur's own age, gentle and dreamy as a poet, and a natural follower. He and Arthur were like two sides of the same apple. Bedwyr trailed, doglike in devotion, after the other boy; he made no attempt to hide his love for Arthur, but there was nothing soft about him, for all his gentle ways and poet's eyes. He was a plain boy, with his nose flattened in some fight, and badly set, and the scar of some nursery burn on his cheek. But he had character and kindness, and Arthur loved him. As the son of Ban, a petty king, Bedwyr was the superior even of Cei, and as far as any of the boys knew, right out of Arthur's star. But this never occurred to either Bedwyr or Arthur; the one offered devotion, the other accepted it.

One day I said to them: "Do you know the story of Bisclavaret, the man who became a wolf?" Bedwyr, without troubling to answer, brought the harp out from under its shroud, and put it gently by me. Arthur, prone on the bed with chin on fist and eyes brilliant in the firelight—it was a chill afternoon of late spring—said impatiently: "Oh, let be. Never mind the music. The story." Then Bedwyr curled beside him on the blankets, and I tuned the strings and started.

It is an eerie tale, and Arthur took it with sparkling face, but Bedwyr grew quieter than ever, all eyes. It was growing dark when they went home, with a husky servant that day for escort. Arthur, alone with me next day, told me how Bedwyr had woken in the night with the nightmare. "But do you know, Myrddin, when we were on the way home yesterday, when he must have been full of the story, we saw something slink off beyond the trees and we thought it was a wolf, and Bedwyr made me ride between him and Leo. I know he was frightened, but he said it was his right to protect me, and I suppose it was, since he is a king's son, and I—"

He stopped. It was as near as he had ever got to the boggy ground. I said nothing, but waited.

"—and I was his friend."

I talked to him then about the nature of courage, and the moment passed. I remember what he said afterwards of Bedwyr. I was to remember it many times in later years, when, on even less certain ground, the trust between him and Bedwyr held true.

He said now, seriously, as if at nine years old he knew: "He is the bravest companion, and the truest friend in all the world."

Ector and Drusilla had, of course, taken care to see that Arthur knew all that was good to know about his father and the Queen. He knew, too, as much as everyone in the country knew about the young heir who waited—in Brittany, in the Isle of Glass, in Merlin's tower?—to succeed to the kingdom. He told me once, himself, the story that was current about the "rape at Tintagel." The legend had lost nothing in the telling. By now, it seemed, men believed that Merlin had spirited the King's party, horses and all, invisibly within the walls of the stronghold, and out again in the broad light of next morning.

"And they say," finished Arthur, "that a dragon curled on the turrets all night, and in the morning Merlin flew off on him, in a trail of fire."

"Do they? It's the first I heard of that."

"Don't you know the story?" asked Bedwyr.

"I know a song," I said, "which is closer to the truth than anything you've heard up here. I got it from a man who'd once been in Cornwall."

Ralf was there that day, listening silently, amused. I raised my brows at him and he shook his head slightly. I had not thought he would have let Arthur know he came from Tintagel, and indeed I doubt if anyone now would have guessed. He spoke as nearly as might be with the accent of the north.

So I told the boys the story, the truth as I knew it— and who knew better?—without the extra trimmings of fantasy that time and ignorance had added to it. And God knows it was magical enough without; God's will and human love driving forward together in the black night under the light of the great star, and the seed sown which would make a king.

"So God had his way, and the King through him, and

men—as men always do—made mistakes and died for them. And in the morning the enchanter rode away alone, to nurse his broken hand."

"No dragon?" This from Bedwyr.

"No dragon," I said.

"I prefer the dragon," said Bedwyr firmly. "I shall go on believing the dragon. Riding away alone, that's a let-down. A real enchanter wouldn't do that, would he, Ralf?"

"Of course not," said Ralf, getting to his feet. "But we must. Look, it's dusk already."

He was ignored. "I'll tell you what I don't understand," said Bedwyr, "and that's a King who would risk setting the whole kingdom at blaze for a woman. Keeping faith with your peers is surely more important than having any woman. I'd never risk losing anything that really mattered, just for that."

"Nor would I," said Arthur slowly. He had been thinking hard about it, I could see. "But I think I understand it, all the same. You have to reckon with love."

"But not to risk friendship for it," said Bedwyr quickly.

"Of course not," said Arthur. I could see that he was thinking in general terms, where Bedwyr meant one friendship, one love.

Ralf began to speak again, but at that moment something, a shadow, swept silently across the lamplight. The boys hardly glanced up; it was only the white owl, sailing silently in through the open window to its perch in the beams. But its shadow went across my skin like a hand of ice, and I shivered.

Arthur looked up quickly. "What is it, Myrddin? It's only the owl. You look as if you'd seen a ghost."

"It was nothing," I said. "I don't know."

I did not know, either, then, but I know now. We had

been speaking Latin, as we usually did, but the word he had used for the shadow across the light was the Celtic one, *guenhwyvar*.

Be sure I told them, too, about their own country, and about the times recently past, of Ambrosius and the war he had fought against Vortigern, and how he had knit the kingdoms together into one, and made himself High King, and brought to the length and breadth of the land justice, with a sword at its back, so that for a short span of years men could go peacefully about their affairs anywhere in the country, and not be molested; or if they were, could seek, and get, the King's justice equally for high or low. Others had given them the stories as history; but I had been there, and closer to affairs than most, being at the High King's side and, in some cases, the architect of what had happened. This, of course, they could not be allowed to guess: I told them merely that I had been with Ambrosius in Brittany, and thereafter at the battle of Kaerconan, and through the next years of the rebuilding. They never asked how or why I was there, and I think this was out of delicacy, in case I should be forced to confess how I had served in some humble capacity as assistant to the engineers, or even as a scribe. But I still remember the questions Arthur poured out about the way the Count of Britain—as Ambrosius then styled himself —had assembled, trained and equipped his army, how he had shipped it across the Narrow Sea to the land of the Dumnonii where he had set up his standard as High King before he swept northwards to burn Vortigern out of Doward, and finally to smash the vast army of the Saxons at Kaerconan. Every detail of organization, training, and strategy I had to recall for him as best I could, and every skirmish of which I could tell them anything was fought over and over again by the two boys, poring over maps drawn in the dust.

"They say there will be war again soon," said Arthur, "and I am too young to go." He mourned over it, openly, like a dog which is bidden to stay at home on a hunting morning. It was three months before his tenth birthday.

It was not all talk of war and high matters, of course. There were days when the boys played like young puppies, running and wrestling, racing their horses along the riverside, swimming naked in the lake and scaring every fish within miles, or taking bows with Ralf up to the hills to look for hares or pigeons. Sometimes I went with them, but hunting was not a sport I cared for. It was different when it occurred to me to rummage out the old hermit's fishing rod and take it to try the waters of the lake. We would pass the time happily there, Arthur fishing with more fury than success, myself watching him, and talking. Bedwyr did not care for fishing, and on these occasions went with Ralf, but Arthur, even on the days when wind or weather made fishing useless, seemed to prefer to stay with me rather than go with Ralf or even Bedwyr to look for sport in the forest.

Looking back, I do not remember now that I ever paused to question this. The boy was my whole life, my love for him so much a part of every day that I was content to take the time as it came, accepting straight from the gods the fact that the boy seemed to like above all else to be with me. I told myself merely that he needed to escape from the crowded household, from the patronage of an elder brother preparing now for a position which he himself could never hope for, and also a chance to be with Bedwyr in a world of imagination and brave deeds where he felt himself to belong. I would not allow myself to ascribe it to love, and if I had guessed the nature of the love, could have offered no comfort then.

Bedwyr stayed at Galava for more than a year, leaving

for home in the autumn before Arthur's eleventh birthday. He was to return the following summer. After he had gone Arthur moped visibly for a week, was unwontedly quiet for another, then recovered his spirits with a bound, and rode up to see me, in defiance of the weather, rather more often than before.

I have no idea what reasons Ector gave for letting him come so often. Probably he needed no reason: as a rule the boy rode out daily except in the foulest weather, and if nothing was volunteered as to where he went, nothing would be asked. It became known, as it was bound to, that he came often to the Green Chapel where the wise man lived, but if people thought about it at all, they commended the boy's sense in seeking out a man known for his learning, and let it be.

I never attempted to teach Arthur in the way that Galapas, my master, had taught me. He was not interested in reading or figuring, and I made no attempt to press them on him; as King, he would employ other men in these arts. What formal learning he needed, he received from Abbot Martin or others of the community. I detected in him something of my own ear for languages, and found that, besides the Celtic of the district where he lived, he had retained a smattering of Breton from his babyhood, and Ector, mindful of the future, had been at pains to correct his northern accent into something which the British of all parts would understand. I decided to teach him the Old Tongue, but was amazed to find that he already knew enough of it to follow a sentence spoken slowly. When I asked where he had learned it he looked surprised and said: "From the hill people, of course. They are the only ones who speak it now."

"And you have spoken with them?"

"Oh, yes. When I was little once I was out with one of the soldiers and he was thrown and hurt himself, and two of the hill people came to help me. They seemed to know who I was."

"Did they indeed?"

"Yes. After that I saw them quite often, here and there, and I learned to speak with them a little. But I'd like to learn more."

Of my other skills, music and medicine, and all the knowledge I had so gladly amassed about the beasts and birds and wild things, I taught him nothing. He would have no need of them. He cared only about beasts to hunt them, and there, already, he knew almost as much as I about the ways of wild deer and wolf and boar. Nor did I share with him much of my knowledge about engines; here again it would be other men who would make and assemble them; he needed only to learn their uses, and most of this he was taught along with the arts of war he learned from Ector's soldiers. But as Galapas had done with me, I taught him how to make maps and read them, and I showed him the map of the sky.

One day he said to me: "Why do you look at me sometimes as if I reminded you of someone else?"

"Do I?"

"You know you do. Who is it?"

"Myself, a little."

His head came up from the map we were studying. "What do you mean?"

"I told you, when I was your age I used to ride up into the hills to see my friend Galapas. I was remembering the first time he taught me to read a map. He made me work a great deal harder than ever I make you."

"I see." He said no more, but I thought he was downcast. I wondered why he should imagine I could tell him anything about his parentage; then it occurred to me that he might expect me to "see" such things at will. But he never asked me.

5

There was no war that year, or the next. In the spring after Arthur's twelfth birthday Octa and Eosa at last broke from prison, and fled south to take refuge behind the boundaries of the Federated Saxons. The whisper went that they had been helped by lords who professed themselves loyal to Uther. Lot could not be blamed directly, nor Cador; no one knew who were the traitors, but rumours were rife, and helped to swell the feeling of unease throughout the country. It seemed as if Ambrosius' forceful uniting of the kingdoms were to go for nothing: each petty king, taking Lot's example, carved and kept his own boundaries. And Uther, no longer the flashing warrior men had admired and feared, depended too much on the strength of his allies, and turned a blind eye to the power they were amassing.

The rest of that year passed quietly enough, but for the usual tale of forays from north and south of the wild debatable land to either side of Hadrian's Wall, and summer landings on the east coast which were not (it was said) wholeheartedly repelled by the defenders there. Storms in the Irish Sea kept the west peaceful, and Cador, I was told, had made a beginning on the fortifications at Segontium. King Uther, heedless of the advisers who told him that when trouble came it would come first from the north, stayed between London and Winchester, throwing his energies into keeping the Saxon Shore patrolled and Ambrosius' Wall fortified, with his main force ready to move and strike wherever the invaders broke the boundaries. Indeed there seemed little to turn him yet towards the north: the talk of a great alliance of invaders was still only talk, and the small raids continued along the southern coast throughout the year, keeping the King down there to combat them. The Queen left Cornwall at this time, and moved to Winchester with all her train. Whenever the King could, he joined her there. It was observed, of course, that he no longer frequented other women as he had been used to do, but no rumour of impotence had gone around: it seemed as if the girls who had known of it had seen it simply as a passing phase of his illness, and said nothing. When it was seen now that he spent all his time with the Queen, the story went round that he had taken vows of fidelity. So, though the girls might mourn their lover, those citizens rejoiced who had been wont to lock their daughters away when word went round that the King was coming, and praised him for adding goodness to his powers as a fighting man.

These latter he certainly seemed to have recovered, though there were stories of the uncertain temper he showed, and of sudden ferocities in the treatment of defeated enemies. But on the whole this was welcomed as a sign of strength at a time when strength was needed.

I myself seemed to have managed to drop safely out of sight. If people wondered from time to time where I had gone, some said that I had crossed the Narrow Sea again and resumed my travels, others, that I had retired once more into a new solitude to continue my studies. I heard from Ralf and Ector—and sometimes, innocently, from Arthur— that there were rumours of me from all parts of the country. It was said that when the King first fell sick, Merlin had appeared immediately in a golden ship with a scarlet sail and ridden to the palace to heal him, and afterwards vanished into the air. He had been seen next at Bryn Myrddin, though none had seen him ride there. (This in spite of the fact that I had changed horses at the usual places, and stayed every night in a public tavern.) And since then, the talk went, Merlin the enchanter had been wont to appear and vanish here and there all over the country. He had healed a sick woman near Aquae Sulis, and a week later had been seen in the Caledonian Forest, four hundred miles away. The host of tales grew, coined by idle folk anxious for the importance that such "news" would give them. Sometimes, as had happened before, wandering healers or would-be prophets would style themselves "another Merlin," or even use my very name: this inspired trust in the healers, and if the patient recovered, did no harm. If the patient died, folk tended to say simply, "It cannot have been Merlin after all; *his* magic would have succeeded." And since the false Merlin would by that time have completely vanished, my reputation would survive the imposture. So I kept my secret, and lost nothing. Certainly no wandering suspicion lighted on the quiet keeper of the Green Chapel.

I had contrived from time to time to send messages of reassurance to the King. My chief fear was that he would grow impatient, and either send for the boy too soon, or by some hasty inadvertence betray Ector or myself to the people who watched him. But he remained silent. Ector, speaking of it to me, wondered if the King still thought the danger of treachery too great to have the boy by him in London, or if he still hoped against bitter hope that some day he would get another son.

Myself I think it was neither. He was beset, was Uther, with treachery and trouble and the lack of the fine health that he was used to; and besides, the Queen started to ail that winter. He had neither time nor mind to give to the young stranger who was waiting to take what he himself found it harder and harder to hold.

As for the Queen, there had been many times during the

years when I had wondered at her silence. Ralf had, through means of his own, kept secretly in touch with his grandmother who served Ygraine, and through her had assured the Queen of her son's well-being. But from all accounts Ygraine, though she loved her daughter Morgian, and would have loved her son as dearly, was able to watch—indifferently enough, it seemed—her children used as tools of royal policy. Morgian and Arthur were, to her, pledges only of her love for the King, and having given them birth, she turned back to her husband's side. Arthur she had barely seen, and was content to know that one day he would emerge from his fastness safe and strong, in the King's time of need. Morgian, to whom she had given all the mother-love of which she was capable, was to be sent (without a backward glance, said Marcia in a letter to Ralf) to the marriage bed which would join the cold northern kingdom and its grim lord to Uther's side in the coming struggle. When I had tried to show Arthur something of the all-consuming sexual love which had obsessed Uther and Ygraine, I had spoken only half the truth. She was Uther's first, then she was Queen; and though she was the bearer of princes, she cared no more than the hawk does when its fledglings fly. As things stood, for her sake, it was better so; and, I thought, for Arthur too. All he needed now, he had from Ector and his gentle wife.

I kept no contact with Bryn Myrddin, but in some roundabout way Ector got news for me. Stilicho had married Mai, the miller's girl, and the child was a boy. I sent my felicitations and a gift of money, and a threat of various dire enchantments should he let either of his new family touch the books and the instruments that remained at the cave. Then I forgot about them.

Ralf married, too, during my second summer in the Wild Forest. His reason was not the same as Stilicho's; he had

349

wooed the girl long enough, and only found his happiness in her bed after a Christian wedding. Even if I had not known the girl was virtuous, and that Ralf had been fretting after her like a curbed colt for a year or more, I could have guessed it from his relaxed and glowing strength as the weeks went by. She was a beautiful girl, gay and good, and with her maidenhead gave him all her worship. As for Ralf, he was a normal young man and had looked here and there, as young men will, but after his marriage I never knew him to look aside again, though he was handsome, and in later years was not unnaturally high in the King's favour and found many who tried to use him as a stepping stone to power as much as to pleasure. But he was never to be used.

I believe that there were those in Galava who wondered why such an able young gentleman was kept riding guard on Ector's foster-son when even young Cei joined his father and the troops whenever there was an alarm, but Ralf had a high temper, and a fine self-assurance these days, and had, besides, the Count's orders to quote. It might have been hard if his wife had taunted him, but she was soon with child, and too thankful to have him tied at home near her ever to question it. Ralf himself fretted a little, I know, but he confessed to me once when we were alone that if he could only see Arthur acknowledged and set in his rightful place beside the High King, he would count it a good life's work.

"You told me the gods were driving us that night at Tintagel," he said. "I am no familiar of the gods, as you are, but I can think of no youth I have known who is worthier to take up the High King's sword when he has to lay it down."

All reports bore this out. When I went down to the village for supplies, or to the tavern for gossip, I heard plenty about Ector's foster-son "Emrys." Even then his was a personality that gathers legend as a drip-stone gathers lime.

I heard a man say once, in the crowded tavern room: "I tell you this, if you told me he was one of the Dragon's breed, a bastard of the High King that's gone, I'd believe you."

There were nods, and someone said: "Well, why not? He could be a bastard of Uther's, couldn't he? It's always surprised me that there aren't more of those around. He was one for the women, sure enough, before his sickness put the fear of hell on him."

Someone else said: "If there were more, you can be sure he'd have acknowledged them."

"Aye, indeed," said the fellow who had spoken first. "That's true. He never showed any more shame than the farm bull, and why should he? They say that the girl he got in Brittany—Morgause, was it?—is high in his favour at court, and goes everywhere with him. Those are all we know of, the two girls, and the prince that's being reared at some foreign court."

Then the talk passed, as it often did these days, to the succession, and the young Prince Arthur growing up somewhere in the foreign kingdom to which Merlin the enchanter had secretly spirited him away.

Though how long he might be kept hidden I could not guess. Watching him come riding up the forest track, or diving and wrestling with Bedwyr in the summer waters of the lake, or drinking in the wonders I showed him as the earth absorbs rain, it was a marvel to me that everyone did not see, as I could, the kingship shining from him as it had shone in that moment's flashing vision from the sword in the altar-stone.

6

Then came the year that, even now, is called the Black Year. It was the year after Arthur's thirteenth birthday. The Saxon leader Octa died at Rutupiae, of some infection caught in the long imprisonment; but his cousin Eosa went to Germany, and there met Octa's son Colgrim, and it was not hard to guess at their counsels. The King of Ireland crossed the sea, but not to the Irish Shore, where Cador waited for him at Deva, and Maelgon of Gwynedd behind the scrambled-up fortifications of Segontium; but his sails were watched from Rheged's shore as he made landfall in Strathclyde and was received kindly by the Pictish kings there. These latter had had a treaty with Britain since Macsen's time, renewed with Ambrosius; but what answer they would make now to Ireland's proposals no man could guess.

Other troubles hit nearer home and more immediately. It was a year of starvation. The spring was long and cold and wet, the fields everywhere flooded, long past the time when corn should have been sown and growing. Cattle disease was everywhere in the south, and in Galava even the hardy blue-fleeced hill sheep died, their feet rotted away so that they could not move on the fells to feed themselves. Late frost blasted the fruit buds, and even as the green corn grew, it turned brown and rotted in the stagnant fields. Strange tales came north. A druid had run mad and attacked Uther for leading the country away from the Old Religion; and a Christian bishop stood up in church and railed against him for being a pagan. There was a story of an attempt on the

King's life, and of the hideous way in which the King had punished the men responsible.

So spring and summer wore through, in disaster, and by the beginning of autumn the country lay like a waste land. People died of starvation. Folk talked of a curse laid on the country; but whether God was angry because the country shrines still claimed their sacrifices, or whether the old gods of hill and woodland exacted vengeance for neglect, no one was sure. All that was certain was that there was a blight on the land, and the King ailed. There was a meeting of nobles in London demanding that Uther should name his heir. But it seemed—Ector told me this—as if he still feared, not knowing friend from foe; all he would say was that his son lived and thrived, and would be presented to the nobles at the next Easter feast. Meanwhile his daughter Morgian passed her twelfth birthday, and would be taken north for her wedding at Christmas.

With the autumn the weather changed, and a mild, dry season set in. It was too late to help the crops or the dying cattle, but grateful to men starved of the sun, and the bright weather came in time to ripen some of the fruit that the spring storms and the summer rot had left on the trees. In the Wild Forest the mists curled through the pines in the early morning, and the September dews glittered everywhere on the cobwebs. Ector left Galava to meet with Rheged and his allies at Luguvallium. The King of Ireland had sailed for home and there was still peace in Strathclyde, but the defense line along the Ituna Estuary from Alauna to Luguvallium was to be manned, and there was talk of Ector as its commander. Cei went with his father. Arthur, scarce three months from his fourteenth birthday, tall enough for sixteen, and already (according to Ralf) a notable swordsman, fretted visibly, and grew daily more silent. He spent all his days now in the forest, often with me (though not so much as formerly), but most of the time, Ralf told me, hunting or taking breakneck rides through the rough country.

"If only the King would make some move," said Ralf to me. "The boy will kill himself else. It's as if he knew that there was something in the future for him, something un-guessed at, but that gives him no peace. I'm afraid he'll break his neck before it happens. That new horse of his— Canrith he calls it—I wouldn't care to get astride it myself, and that's the truth. I can't think what possessed Ector to give it to him; a guilt gift perhaps."

I thought he was right. The white stallion had been left for Arthur when Ector took Cei up to Luguvallium with him. Bedwyr had gone, too, though he was no older than Arthur. Ector was hard put to it to explain to Arthur why he could not go. But until Uther spoke, we could do nothing.

The full moon came, the September moon that they call the harvester. It shone out in a dry mild night over the rotting fields, doing no good that anyone could see except light the outlaws who crept out of their fastnesses to pillage the outlying farms, or the troops who were constantly on the move these days to one or the other point of threat.

I could not sleep. My head ached, and phantoms crowded close, as they do when they bring vision; but nothing came forward into light or shape; nothing spoke. It was like suffering the threat of thunder, as close as the blankets that wrapped me, but without the lightning to break it, or the cleansing rain to bring a clear sky. When day broke at last, grey and misty, I rose, took bread, and a handful of olives from the crock, and went down through the forest to the lake, to wash the aching of the night away.

It was a quiet morning, so still that you could not tell where the mist ended and the surface of the lake began. The water met the flattened shingle of the beach without movement and without sound. Behind me the forest stood wrapped in the mist, its scents still sleeping. It seemed a kind of desecration to break the hush and plunge into that virgin water, but the fresh chill of it washed away the clinging strands of the night, and when I came out and was dry again and dressed, I ate my breakfast with pleasure, then settled down with my fishing rod to wait for the morning rise, and hope for a breeze at sun-up to ruffle the glassy water.

The sun came up at last, pale through the mist, but brought no breeze with it. The tops of the trees swam up out of the greyness, and at the far side of the lake the dark forest lifted, cloudy, towards the smoking hilltops. The water was bloomed with mist, like a pearl.

No ring or ripple broke the glassy water, no sign of a breeze to come. I had just decided that I might as well go, when I heard something coming fast through the forest at my back. Not a horseman; too light for that, and coming too fast through the brake.

I stayed as I was, half-turned, waiting. A prickling ran up the skin of my back, and I remembered the night's sleepless pain. The tingling ran into my fingers; I found I was clutching the rod until it hurt the flesh. All night, then, this had been coming. All night this had been waiting to happen. All night? If I was not mistaken, I had been waiting for this for fourteen years.

Fifty paces along the lake-side from where I sat, a stag broke cover. He saw me immediately, and stopped short, head high, poised to break the other way. He was white. In contrast the wide branches on his brow looked like polished bronze, and his eyes showed red as garnet. But he was real; there were stains of sweat on the white hide, and the thick hair of belly and neck was tagged with damp. A trail of yellow loosestrife had caught round his neck, and hung there like a collar. He looked back over his shoulder, then, stiff-legged, leaped from the bank into the water, and in two more bounds was shoulder-deep and swimming straight out into the lake.

The polished water broke and arrowed back. The splash was echoed by a crashing deep in the forest. Another beast coming, headlong.

I had been wrong in thinking that nothing could come through the forest as fast as a fleeing deer. Arthur's white hound, Cabal, broke from the trees exactly where the stag had broken, and hurled himself into the water. Seconds later Arthur himself, on the stallion Canrith, burst out after it.

He checked his horse on the shore, bringing it up rearing, fetlock deep. He had his bow strung ready in his hand. He pulled the stallion sideways and raised the bow, sighting from the back of the plunging horse. But deer swim low; only the stag's head showed above water, a wedge spearing away fast, its antlers flat behind it on the surface like boughs trailing. The hound, swimming strongly, was in line with it. Arthur lowered the bow, and turned the stallion back to breast the bank. In the moment before his spurs struck he saw me. He shouted something, and came cantering along the shingle.

His face was blazing with excitement. "Did you see him? Snow-white, and a head like an emperor! I never saw the like in my life! I'm going round. Cabal was closing, he'll hold him till I get there. Sorry I spoiled your fishing."

"Emrys—"

He checked impatiently. "What?"

"Look. He's making for the island."

He swung to look where I pointed. The stag had vanished into the mist, and the hound with him. There was no sign of them but the fading ripples flattening towards the shore.

"The island, is it? Are you sure?"

"Certain."

"All the devils of hell," he said angrily. "What a cursed

piece of luck! I thought I had him when Cabal sprang him so close." He hung on the rein, hesitating, staring out over the clouded lake while the stallion fretted, sidling. I suppose he was as much in awe of the place as anyone brought up in that valley. Then he set his mouth, curbing Canrith sharply. "I'm going to the island. I can say goodbye to the stag, I suppose—that was too good to be true—but I'm damned if I lose Cabal. Bedwyr gave him to me, and I've no mind to lose him to Bilis or anyone else, either in this world or the other." He put two fingers to his mouth and whistled shrilly. "Cabal! Cabal! Here, sir, here!"

"It's no good, you'll hardly turn him now."

"No." He took a breath. "Well, there's nothing for it, it'll have to be the island. If your magic will reach that far, Myrddin, send it with me now."

"It's with you always, you know that. You're not going to swim him across, are you?"

"He'll go," said Arthur, a little breathlessly, as he forced the reluctant stallion towards the water. "It's too far to go round. If that beast takes to the crags, and Cabal follows it—"

"Why not take the boat? It's quicker, and that way you can bring Cabal back."

"Yes, but the wretched thing'll need bailing. It always does."

"I bailed it this morning. It's quite ready."

"Did you? That's the first bit of luck today! You were going out, then? Will you come with me?"

"No. I'll stay here. Come now, Emrys, go and find your hound."

For a moment boy and horse were quite still. Arthur stared down at me, something showing in his face that was half speculation, half awe, but which was quickly swallowed up in the larger impatience. He slid off the stallion's back and pushed the reins into my hand. Then he unstrung his bow

357

and slung it across his shoulder and ran to the boat. This was a primitive flat-bottomed affair which usually lay beached in a reedy inlet a short way along the shore. He launched it with one flying shove, and jumped in. I stood on the shingle, holding the horse, watching him. He poled it out through the shallows, then had the oars out, and began to row.

I pulled the rolled cloth from behind the horse's saddle, slung it over the animal's steaming back, then tethered him where he could graze, and went back to my seat at the edge of the lake.

The sun was well up now, and gaining power. A kingfisher flashed by. Gauze-winged flies danced over the water. There was a smell of wild mint, and a dabchick crept out from a tangle of water forget-me-not. A dragonfly, tiny, with a scarlet body, clung pulsing to a reed. Under the sun the mist moved gently, smoking off the glassy water, shifting and restless like the phantoms of the night, like the smoke of the enchanted fire. . . .

The shore, the scarlet dragonfly, the white horse grazing, the cloudy forest at my back, faded, became phantoms themselves. I watched, my eyes wide and fixed on that silent and sightless cloud of pearl.

He was rowing hard, chin on shoulder as he neared the island. It loomed first as a swimming shape of shadow, growing to a shoreline hung over with the low boughs of trees. Behind the trees, misty and unreal, the shapes of rocks soared like a great castle brooding on its crag. Where the strand met the water lay a line of gleaming silver, drawn sharp between the island and its image. The cloudy trees and the high towers of the crags floated weightless on the water, phantoms themselves in the phantom mist.

The boat forged ahead. Arthur glanced over his shoulder, calling the hound's name.

"Cabal! Cabal!"

The call echoed loudly across the water, swam up the high crags, and died. There was no sign of either hound or stag. He bent to his oars again, sending the light boat leaping through the water.

Its bottom grated on shingle. He jumped out. He pulled it up and trod up through the narrow verge of grass. The light was stronger now as the sun rose higher, reflecting from white mist and white water. Over the shore the boughs of birch and rowan reached low, still heavy with moisture. The rowan berries were red as flame, and glossy. The turf was powdered with daisies and speedwell and small yellow pimpernel. Late foxgloves crowded down the banks, their spires thrusting through the trails of blackberry. Meadowsweet, rusting over with autumn, filled the air with its thick honey-scent.

The boy thrust the hanging boughs aside, plunged through the bramble trails, and stood squarely on the flowery turf, narrowing his eyes at the crags above him. He called again, and again the sound echoed away emptily, and died. The mist was lifting faster now, rolling upwards towards the tops, showing the lower reaches of rock bathed in a clear but swimming light. Suddenly he stiffened, gazing upwards. Midway up the crags, along what looked no more than a seam in the rock, the white stag cantered easily, light as a drift of the mist that wreathed away to air below it.

Arthur ran forward up the slope. His footsteps on the thick turf made no sound. He brushed waist-high through brakes of yellowing fern, sending the bright drops scattering, and came out at the foot of the cliff.

He paused again, looking about him. He seemed held by the same awe that had touched him earlier. He looked, not afraid, but as a man looks who knows that by a movement he may start something of which he cannot see the end. He craned his neck, searching the towering crags above him. There was no sign of the white stag, but the rocks looked more than ever like a castle crowned with the sun.

He took a breath, shaking his head as if he came out of water, then he spoke again, but quietly. "Cabal? Cabal?"

From somewhere very near him, bursting the awed silence, came the baying of the hound. There was something in it of excitement, something of fear. It came from the cliff. The boy looked round him, sharply. Then, behind the green curtain of the trees, he saw the cave. As he started forward Cabal bayed again, not in fear or pain, but like a beast questing.

With no more hesitation, Arthur plunged into the darkness of the cave.

He could never say afterwards how he found his way. I think he must have picked up the torch and flint I had left there, and lit it, but he remembers nothing of that. Perhaps what he does remember is the truth: there seemed, he said, to be everywhere some faintly diffused and swimming light, as if reflected from the burnished surface of the pool deep in the pillared cave.

There, beyond the shining pool, the sword lay on its table. From the rock above a trickle of water had run and dripped, the lime on it hardening through the years until the oiled leather of the wrappings, though proof enough to keep the metal bright, had hardened under the dripping till it felt like stone. In this the thing had rested, the crust of lime forming to hide all but its shape, the long slenderness of the weapon and the hilt formed like a cross.

It still looked like a sword, but a stone one, some random accident of dripping limestone. Perhaps he remembered the other hilt he had grasped in the Green Chapel, or perhaps for a moment he, too, saw the future break open in front of him. With an action too quick for thought, and too instinctive to prevent, he laid his hand to the hilt.

He spoke to me, as if I stood beside him. Indeed, I suppose I was as near to him, and as real, as the white hound that crouched, whining at the pool's edge.

"I pulled at it, and it came clear of the stone. It is the most beautiful sword in the world. I shall call it Caliburn."

The mist had gone from the forest now, sucked up by the sun. But it still lay over the island; this was invisible, floating on its sea of pearl.

I did not know how much time had passed. The sun was hot, beating down on the lake cupped in its hills. My eyes ached from the glare of water. I blinked them, moved, and stretched my stiff limbs.

There was a movement behind me; a sudden trampling, as if the white stallion had got loose. I turned quickly.

Thirty paces away, softly as a cloud, Cador of Cornwall rode out of the wood on a grey horse, with a troop at his back.

7

I believe that the thought uppermost in my mind was anger that I had not been warned. I was not only thinking of Arthur's guardians among the hill people; but even for me, Merlin, there had been no hint of danger in the sky, and the vision which had blanketed the troop's approach from my eyes and hearing had held nothing but light and promise leaping at last towards fulfillment. The only mitigation of my anger was that Arthur had not been found with me, and the only faint hope of safety lay in maintaining my character as hermit and trusting that Cador would not recognize me, and would ride on before the boy returned from the island.

All this went through my mind in the space it took Cador to raise a hand to halt the men behind him, and for me to pick up the discarded fishing rod and get to my feet. With some lie already forming on my lips I turned humbly to face Cador as he rode forward, to halt his grey ten paces off. Then all hope of remaining unrecognized vanished as behind him among the troop I saw Ralf with a gag in his mouth, and a trooper on either side of him.

I straightened. Cador bent his head, saluting me as low as he would have done the King. "Well met, Prince Merlin."

"Is it well met?" I was savagely angry. "Why have you taken my servant? He's none of yours now. Loose him."

He made a sign, and the troopers released Ralf's arms. He tore the gag from his mouth.

"Are you hurt?" I asked him.

"No." He was angry too, and bitter. "I'm sorry, sir. They fell on me as I was riding up through the forest. When they recognized me, they thought you might be near. They gagged me so that I could not give warning. They wanted to take you unawares."

"Don't blame yourself. It was no fault of yours." I had myself under control now, groping all the while for the shreds of the vision which had fled. Where was Arthur now? Still on the island, with Cabal and the wonderful sword? Or already on his way back through the mist? But I could see nothing except what was here, in plain daylight, and I knew that the spell was broken and I could not reach him.

I turned on Cador. "You go about your business strangely, Duke! Why did you lay hands on Ralf? You could have found me here any time you cared to ride this way. The forest is free to everyone, and the Green Chapel is open day and night. I would not have run from you."

"So you are the hermit of the chapel in the green?"

"I am he."

"And Ralf serves you?"

"He serves me."

He signed to his men to stay where they were, and himself rode forward, nearer where I stood. The white stallion screamed and plunged as the grey horse passed it. Cador drew to a halt beside me, and looked down, his brows raised. "And that horse? Is it yours? A strange choice for a hermit?"

I said acidly: "You know it is not mine. If you caught Ralf in the forest, then no doubt you saw one of Count Ector's sons as well. They were riding together. The boy came here to fish. I don't know how long he'll be; he often stays away half the day." I turned decisively away from the water. "Ralf, wait here for him. And you, my lord Duke, since you were so urgent to see me that you mishandled my servant, will you come with me now to the chapel, and say what you have to say in privacy? And you can tell me, too, what—besides this private hunt of yours—brings you and the men of Cornwall so far north?"

"War brings me; war, and the King's command. I doubt if even here you have been too isolated to know of Colgrim's threats? But you might say it was a happy chance that made me ride this way." He smiled, and added, pleasantly: "And this was hardly a private hunt. Did you not know, Prince Merlin, that men have been searching the length and breadth of the land to find you?"

"I was aware of it. I did not choose to be found. Now, Duke, will you come with me? Leave Ralf to wait here for the boy—"

"Count Ector's son, eh?" He had made no move to follow me away from the water's edge. He sat his big horse easily, still smiling. His manner was confident and assured. "And you really expect me to ride with you and leave Ralf to wait for this—son of Count Ector? No doubt to spirit him away for another span of years? Believe me, Prince—"

From the water, sharply, came Cabal's bark, the warning of a hound alert to danger. Then a word from Arthur, silencing the hound. The sound of oars as the boat jumped forward, suddenly driven hard through the water.

Cador swung his horse to face the sound, and in spite of myself I moved with him. My look must have been grim, for two of his officers spurred forward.

"Keep them back," I said sharply, and he flashed me a look and then lifted a hand. The men stopped short, a spear-cast off. I spoke quietly, for Cador alone:

"If you don't want Ector at your throat, with all Rheged behind him—yes, and Colgrim sweeping in to pick the fragments apart—let Ralf and the boy go now. Anything you have to say can be said to me. I shall not try to escape you.

364

But for my life, Duke Cador, the King himself will answer."

He hesitated, glancing from the misty lake to where his troopers stood. They had pricked to the alert. I did not think they had recognized me, or realized what quarry their Duke was hunting today; but they had seen his interest in the sounds from behind the mist, and though they stayed where they were near the edge of the wood, the spears stirred and rattled like a reed-bed in the wind.

"As to that—" began Cador, but he was interrupted.

The boat ran out of the mist's edge and cut through the shallows. Seconds before it grounded Cabal, with a growl in his throat, flung himself over the thwart and made for the shore. One of the officers swung his horse round and drew his sword. Cador heard it, and shouted something. The man hesitated, and the hound, leaping up the bank, silent now, went in a rush for Cador himself. The grey horse reared back. The hound missed his grab, caught the edge of the saddle-cloth. It tore, and a piece came away in his jaws.

Behind me, Arthur yelled at the hound and ran the boat hard ashore. Ralf jumped forward, intending, I could see, to grab Cabal, but the troopers nearest him spurred forward and crossed their spears with a clash, holding him back. Cabal tossed the torn cloth·over his shoulder and turned snarling to attack the men who held Ralf. One of them hefted his spear ready, and swords flashed out. Cador barked an order. The swords went up. The Duke lifted, not his sword, but his whip, and spurred the big grey round as the hound gathered himself to spring.

I took a stride forward under the whip, gripped the hound's collar, and threw my weight against his. I could scarcely hold him. Arthur's voice came fiercely, *"Cabal! Back!"* and even as the hound's pull slackened the boy jumped from the boat and in two strides was between me and Cador with the new sword naked and shining in his hand.

"You," he panted, "sir—whoever you are . . ." The sword's point slanted up at the Duke's breastbone. "Keep back! If you touch him, I swear I'll kill you, even if you had a thousand men at your back."

Cador slowly lowered the whip. I let Cabal go, and he sank to the ground behind Arthur, growling. Arthur stood squarely in front of me, angry and undoubtedly dangerous. But the Duke did not even seem to notice the sword or its threat. His eyes were on the boy's face. They flicked to mine, momentarily, then back to the boy.

All this had passed in a few breathless seconds. The Duke's men were still moving forward, the officers ranging to his side. As someone shouted an order, I shot a hand out and caught Arthur's arm and swung him round to face me, with his back to the Cornishmen.

"Emrys! What folly is this? There is no danger here, except from your hound. You should control him better. Take him now, and get yourself straight back to Galava with Ralf."

I had never spoken to him so in all the years he had known me. He stood still, his mouth slackening with surprise, like someone who has been struck for nothing. While he still stared dumbly I added, curtly: "This gentleman and I are acquainted. Why should you think he means me harm?"

"I—I thought—" he stammered. "I thought—they had Ralf—and swords drawn on you—"

"You thought wrongly. I'm grateful to you, but as you see, I need no help. Put up your sword now, and go."

His eyes searched my face again, briefly, then he looked down at the sword he held. The sunlight blazed from it and the jewelled hilt sparkled. His hand looked young and tense on the hilt. I remembered the feel and fit of that hilt, and the life that ran back from the blade, clear into the sinews and the leaping blood. He had braved the very halls of the Otherworld for this, and had brought the bright thing back from darkness into the light that owned it, to find his first danger waiting, and himself—with the wonderful sword —its equal. And I had spoken to him like this.

I gave his arm a little shake, and released it. "Go. No one will stop you."

He rubbed it where I had gripped him, not stirring. His colour was just beginning to come back, and with it a smoulder of anger. He looked so like Uther that I said, brutal with apprehension: "Go now and leave us, do you hear? I shall have time for you tomorrow."

"Emrys?" It was Cador, smoothly. Before I could stop him the boy had turned, and I saw that it was too late for pretense. Cador was looking from Arthur's face to mine, and there was excitement in his eyes.

"That is my name," said Arthur. He sounded sullen, narrowing his eyes up at the Duke against the sun. Then he seemed to notice the badge on the other's shoulder. "Cornwall? What are you doing so far north of your command, and with what authority do you lead your troops across our land?"

"Across your land? Count Ector's?"

"I'm his foster-son. But perhaps," said Arthur, silky with cold courtesy, "you have already passed Galava and spoken with his lady?"

He knew, of course, that Cador had not; he had not long ridden out of Galava himself. But Cador had given him the chance to recover the pride that I had damaged. He stood very straight, his back firmly turned to me, his eyes level on the Duke's.

Cador said: "So you are a ward of Count Ector's? Who is your father, then, Emrys?"

Arthur did not jib at this question now. He said coolly: "That, sir, I am not at liberty to tell you. But my breeding is not something of which I need to be ashamed."

This set Cador at pause. There was a curious expression on his face. He knew, of course. How could he not have known, the moment the boy flew out of the mist to my defense? From before that moment, it had been beyond repair. But there was still a chance that the others might not guess; Cador's big grey stood between Arthur and the troop, and even while the thought crossed my mind he turned and made a sign, and the officers and men moved back, once again beyond earshot.

I was calm now, knowing what I must do. The first thing was to salvage Arthur's pride, and whatever love I had not already destroyed by destroying this hour for him. I touched him gently on the shoulder. "Emrys, will you give us leave now? The Duke of Cornwall will not harm me, and he and I must talk together. Will you ride up to the chapel now with Ralf, and wait for me there?"

I expected Cador to intervene, but he sat without stirring. He was not watching the boy's face now, but the sword, still bare and flashing in Arthur's hand. Then he seemed to come to himself with a start. He signed to his men again, and Ralf, released, brought Canrith forward for Arthur, and mounted his own horse. He looked worried and questioning, wondering, probably, whether to take what I said at face value, or whether he must try to escape with Arthur into the forest.

I nodded to him. "Up to the shrine, Ralf. Wait for me there, if you will. Have no fear for me; I shall come later."

Arthur still hesitated, his hand on Canrith's bridle. Cador said: "It's true, Emrys, I mean him no harm. Don't be afraid to leave him. I know better than to tangle with enchanters. He'll come to you safely, never fear."

The boy threw me a strange look. He still looked doubtful, almost dazed. I said gently, not caring now who heard me: "Emrys—"

"Yes?"

"I have to thank you. It is true that I thought there was danger. I was afraid."

The sullen look lifted. He did not smile, but the anger died from his face, and life came back into it, as vividly as the bright sword leaping from its dull sheath. I knew then that nothing I had done had even smudged the edges of his love for me. He said, with little to be heard in his tone except exasperation: "How long will it be before you realize that I would give my life itself to keep you from hurt?"

He glanced down again at the sword in his hand, almost as if he wondered how it had got there. Then he looked up, straight at Cador.

"If you harm him in any way, the kingdoms will not be wide enough to hold us both. I swear it."

"Sir," said Cador, speaking, warrior to warrior, with grave courtesy, "that I well believe. I swear to you that I shall not harm him or anyone, save only the King's enemies."

The boy held his eyes for a moment longer, then nodded. He swallowed, and the tension went out of him. Then he leaped astride his horse, saluted Cador formally, and, without another word, rode off along the lake-side track. Cabal ran with him, and Ralf followed. I saw the boy glance back as he reached the bend in the track that would carry him out of my sight. Then they were gone, and I was alone with Cador and the men of Cornwall.

8

"Well, Duke?" I said.

He did not answer immediately, but sat biting his lip, staring down at the saddle-bow. Then, without turning, he signalled one of his officers who came forward and took his bridle as he dismounted. "Take the men down the shore a hundred paces. Water the horses, and wait for me there."

The man went, and the troop wheeled and clattered out of sight beyond a jut of woodland. Cador gathered his cloak over his arm and looked about him.

"Shall we talk here?"

We sat down where a flat rock overhung the water. He drew his dagger, for no worse purpose than to draw patterns in the wild thyme. When he had done a circle, and fitted a triangle inside it, he spoke to the ground. "He's a fine boy."

"He is."

"And like his sire."

I said nothing.

The dagger drove into the ground and stayed there. His head came up. "Merlin, why should you think I am his enemy?"

"Are you not his enemy?"

"No, by all the gods! I shall tell no one where he is unless you give me leave. There, you see? You look amazed. You thought of me as his enemy, and yours. Why?"

"If any man has reason for enmity, Cador, you have. It

370

was through my action and Uther's that your father was killed."

"That is not quite true. You planned to betray my father's bed, but not my father himself. It was his own rashness, or bravery if you like, that caused his death. I believe that you did not foresee it. Besides, if I am to hate you because of that night, how much more should I hate Uther Pendragon?"

"And do you not?"

"God's death, man, have you not heard that I ride beside him and serve him as his chief captain?"

"I had heard it. And I wondered why. You must know how I have doubted you."

He laughed, a harsh laugh, like his father's rough bark. "You made it clear. I don't blame you. No, I don't hate Uther Pendragon; neither, I confess, do I love him. But when I was a boy I saw enough of divided kingdoms; Cornwall is mine, but she cannot stand alone. There is only one future for Cornwall now, and this is the same future as Britain's. I am linked to Uther, whether I like it or not. I will not bring division again, to see the people suffer. So I am Uther's man . . . or, which is nearer the truth, the High King's."

I watched the kingfisher, reassured now that the troop had gone, dive in a jewelled splash below us. He came up with a fish, shook his feathers, and flashed away. I said: "Did you send men to spy on me in Maridunum, years back, before I came north?"

His lips thinned. "Those. Yes, they were mine . . . and fine work they made of it! You guessed straight away, didn't you?"

"It was an obvious conclusion. They were Cornish, and your troops were at Caerleon. I learned later that you yourself had been there. Am I to be blamed if I thought you were trying to find Arthur?"

"Not at all. That is exactly what I was trying to do. But not to harm him." He frowned down again at the dagger. "Remember those years, Prince Merlin, and think how it was with me then. The King ailing, and for all one could see, pledging more and more power to Lot and his friends. He offered Morgause in marriage before ever Morgian was born, did you know that? And even now, I doubt if he really sees where Lot's ambition is leading him . . . I tried to tell him myself, but from me it came like an echo of the same ambition. I feared what would happen to the kingdoms should Uther die—or should Uther's son die. And though I didn't doubt your power to protect that son in your own way, there's a place for my way as well." The dagger thudded back into the turf. "So I wanted to find him, and watch him. As, for a different reason, I have been watching Lot."

"I see. You never thought of approaching me yourself and telling me this?"

He looked sideways at me, the corners of his mouth lifting. "If I had, would you have believed me?"

"It's probable. I am not easy to deceive."

"And told me where the boy was?"

I smiled. "That. No."

He hunched a shoulder. "Well, there's your answer. I sent my foolish spies, and found nothing. I even lost you. But I never meant you harm, I swear it. And though I may once have been your enemy, I was never Arthur's. Will you believe that now?"

I looked around me at the tranquil day, the sunlit trees, the light mist lifting from the lake. "I should have known it long ago. All day I have been wondering why I had had no warning of danger."

"If I were Arthur's enemy," he said, smiling, "I would know better than to try and snatch him from under Mer-

372

lin's arm and eye. So if there had been danger in the air today, you would have known it?"

I drew a breath. I felt light again as the summer air around me. "I am sure of it. It worried me, that I had let you come so close today, and never felt the cold on my skin. Nor do I feel it now. Duke Cador, I should ask your forgiveness, if you will give it me."

"Willingly." He began to clean the tip of his dagger in the grass. "But if I am not his enemy, Merlin, there are those who are. I don't have to tell you about the dangers of this Christmas marriage; not only for Arthur's claim to the throne, but the dangers for the kingdom itself."

I nodded. "Division, strife, the dark end to a dark year. Yes. Is there anything more you can tell me about King Lot, that all men do not already know?"

"Nothing definite, not more than before. I am hardly in Lot's private councils. But I can tell you this; if Uther delays much longer over proclaiming his son, the nobles may decide to choose his successor among themselves. And the choice is there, ready, in Lot who is a tried and known warrior, who has fought at the King's hand, and is—will be soon— the King's son-in-law."

"Successor?" I said. "Or supplanter?"

"Not openly, no. Morgian would not see Lot stepping across her father's body to the kingdom. But once he is married to her, and is the King's apparent heir until Arthur is produced, then Arthur himself, when he does appear, will have to show both a stronger claim and a stronger backing."

"He has both."

"The claim, yes. But the backing? Lot has more men at his back than I." I said nothing, but after a bit he nodded. "Yes. I see. If he is backed by you, yourself in person . . . You can enforce his claim?"

"I can try. I shall have help. Yours, too, I hope?"

"You have it."

"You shame me, Cador."

"Hardly that," he said. "You were right. It was true that I hated you. I was young then, but I have come to see things differently; perhaps more clearly. For my own sake, if for nothing else, I cannot stand by and see Uther so bound to Lot, and Lot succeeding in his ambition. Arthur's is the one strong claim which can't be denied, and his is the one hand which can hold the kingdoms together—if any hand can do it now. Oh, yes, I would support him."

I was reflecting that even at fifteen Cador had been a realist; now, his tough-minded common sense was like a gust of cold air through a musty council-chamber. "Does Lot know this?" I asked him.

"I have made it clear, I think. Lot knows I would oppose him, and so would the northern lords of Rheged, and the kings of Wales. But there are others I am not sure of, and many who will be swayed either way if their lands are threatened. The times are dangerous, Merlin. You knew Eosa went to Germany, and was consorting with Colgrim and Badulf? Yes? Well, news came a short while ago that longships had been massing across the German Sea from Segedunum and that the Picts have opened their harbours to them."

"I had not heard that. Then there'll be fighting before winter?"

He nodded. "Before the month is out. That's why I am here. Maelgon stays on the Irish Shore, but the danger is not on the west; not yet. The attack will come from east and north."

"Ah." I smiled. "Then certain things will be made clear very soon, I think."

He had been watching me intently. Now his mouth relaxed, and he nodded again. "You see it? Of course you do. Yes, one good thing may come out of this clash—Lot must declare himself. If, as rumour has it, he has been making advances to the Saxons, then he will have to declare for Colgrim. If he wants Morgian, and the High Kingdom along with her, he'll have to fight for Uther." He laughed with genuine amusement. "It's Octa's death that has brought Colgrim raging straight across the German Sea, and forced Lot's hand. If he'd waited for the spring, Lot would have had Morgian, and could have received Colgrim too, and used the Saxons to set himself up as High King, like Vortigern before him. As it is, we shall see."

"Where is the King?" I asked.

"On his way north. He should be at Luguvallium within the week."

"He'll lead the field himself?"

"He intends to, though as you know he's a sick man. It seems that Colgrim may have forced Uther's hand, too. I think he will send for Arthur now. I think he will have to."

"Whether he sends or not," I said, "Arthur will be there." I saw the excitement spring to Cador's face again, and asked him: "Will you give him escort, Duke?"

"Willingly, by God! You'll come with him?"

I said: "After this, where he is, I am."

"And you'll be needed," he said meaningly. "Pray God Uther has not left it too late. Even with proof of Arthur's parentage, and the King's own sword fast in his hand, it won't be easy to persuade the nobles to declare for an untried boy . . . And Lot's faction will fight back every foot of the way. Better to take them by surprise, like this. The boy will need all you can throw into the scale for him."

I smiled. "He can throw in quite a lot himself. He's to be reckoned with, Cador, make no mistake. He's no kingmaker's toy."

He grinned. "You don't need to tell me that. Did you know he was more like you than ever like the King?"

I spoke with my eyes on the glittering surface of the lake. "I think it is my sword, not Uther's, which will carry him to the kingship."

He sat up sharply. "Yes. That sword. Where in middle-earth did he find that sword?"

"On Caer Bannog."

His eyes widened. "He went *there?* Then, by God, he's welcome to it and all it brings him! I'd not have dared! What took him there?"

"He went to save the hound. It had been given him by his friend. You might call it chance that took him there."

"Oh, aye. The same kind of chance that brought me along the lake-side today, to find a poor hermit, and a boy called Ambrosius, who holds a sword which might well befit a king?"

"Or an emperor," I said. "It's the sword of Macsen Wledig."

"*So?*" He drew in his breath. I saw the same look in his eyes as there had been in the Cornish troopers' when I spoke of the enchanted island. "This was the claim you were speaking of? You found that sword for him? You cast your net wide, Merlin."

"I cast no net. I go with the time."

"Yes. I see." He drew another long breath, and looked about him as if he saw the day for the first time, with all its sunlight and moving breezes and the island floating on the water. "And now for you, and for him and all of us, the time is come?"

"I think so. He found the sword where I had laid it, and you came, hard on its finding. All the year the King has been urged to make proclamation and he has done nothing. So instead, we will do it. You lie tonight at Galava?"

"Yes." He sat up, pushing the dagger home in its sheath with a rap. "You'll join us there? We ride at sun-up."

"I shall be there tonight," I said, "and Arthur with me. Today he stays with me in the forest. We have things to say to one another."

He looked at me curiously. "He knows nothing yet?"

"Nothing," I said. "I promised the King."

"Then until the King speaks publicly, I'll see he learns nothing. Some of my men may suspect, but they are all loyal. You needn't fear them."

I got to my feet, and he followed suit. He raised a hand to his watching officer in the distance. I heard the words of command, and the sounds of the troop mounting. They rode towards us along the lake-side.

"You have a horse?" asked Cador. "Or shall I leave one with you now?"

"Thank you, no. I have one. I'll walk back to the chapel when I'm ready. There's something I have to do first."

He looked again at the sunlit forest, the still lake, the dreaming hills, as if power or magic must be ready to fall on me from their light. "Something still to do? Here?"

"Indeed." I picked up the fishing rod. "I still have to catch my dinner, and for two now, instead of one. And see, this day of days has even produced a breeze for me. If Arthur can lift the sword of Maximus from the lake, surely I shall be granted at least two decent fish?"

9

Ralf met me at the edge of the clearing, but we could not have much talk, because Arthur was nearby, sitting in the sun on the chapel steps, with Cabal at his feet.

I told Ralf quickly what he must do. He was to ride down now to the castle and tell Drusilla what had happened, that Arthur was safe with me, and that we would join Duke Cador on the ride north tomorrow. A message was to go ahead to Count Ector, and one to the King. Meanwhile Ralf was to ask the Countess to arrange with Abbot Martin to have the shrine tended during my absence.

"And are you going to tell him now?" asked Ralf.

"No. It's for Uther to tell him."

"Don't you think he may guess already, after what happened down yonder? He's been silent ever since, but with a look to him as if he'd been given more than a sword. What is that sword, Merlin?"

"It's said that Weland Smith himself made it, long ago. What is sure is that the Emperor Maximus used it, and that his men brought it home for the King of Britain."

"*That* one? And he tells me he found it on Caer Bannog . . . I begin to see . . . And now you take him to the King. Are you trying to force Uther's hand? Do you think the King will accept him?"

"I am sure of it. Uther must claim him now. I think we may find that he has sent for him already. You'd better go, Ralf. There'll be time to talk later. You'll ride with us, of course."

"You think I'd let you leave me behind?" He spoke gaily,

but I could see that he was torn between relief and regret; on the one hand the knowledge that the long watch was over, on the other, that Arthur would now be taken from his care and committed to mine and the King's. But there was happiness, too, that he would soon be back in the press of affairs in an open position of trust, and able to wield his sword against the kingdom's enemies. He saluted me, smiling, then turned and rode off down the tracks towards Galava.

The hoof-beats faded down through the forest. Sunlight poured into the clearing. The last of the water-drops had vanished from the pines, and the smell of resin filled the air. A thrush was singing somewhere. Late harebells were thick among the grass, and small blue butterflies moved over the white flowers of the blackberry. There was a hive of wild bees under the roof of the chapel; their humming filled the air, the sound of summer's end.

Through a man's life there are milestones, things he remembers even into the hour of his death. God knows that I have had more than a man's share of rich memories; the lives and deaths of kings, the coming and going of gods, the founding and destroying of kingdoms. But it is not always these great events that stick in the mind. here, now, in this final darkness, it is the small times that come back to me most vividly, the quiet human moments which I should like to live again, rather than the flaming times of power. I can still see, how clearly, the golden sunlight of that quiet afternoon. There is the sound of the spring, and the falling liquid of the thrush's song, the humming of the wild bees, the sudden flurry of the white hound scratching for fleas, and the sizzling sound of cooking where Arthur knelt over the wood fire, turning the trout on a spit of hazel, his face solemn, exalted, calm, lighted from within by whatever it is that sets such men alight. It was his beginning, and he knew it.

He did not ask me much, though a thousand questions

must have been knocking at his lips. I think he knew, without knowing how, that we were on the threshold of events too great for talk. There are some things that one hesitates to bring down into words. Words change an idea by definitions too precise, meanings too hung about with the references of every day.

We ate in silence. I was wondering how to tell him, without breaking my promise to Uther, that I proposed to take him with me to the King. I thought that Ralf was wrong; the boy did not begin to guess the truth; but he must be wondering about the events of the day, not only the sword, but what there was between myself and Cador, and why Ralf had been so handled. But he said nothing, not even asking why Ralf had gone away and left him here alone with me. He seemed content with the moment. The angry little skirmish down by the lake might never have been.

We ate in the open air, and when we had finished, Arthur, without a word, removed the dishes and brought water in a bowl for me to wash with. Then he settled beside me on the chapel steps, lacing the fingers of his hands round one knee. The thrush still sang. Blue and shadowed, and misty with presence, the hills brooded, chin on knees, round the valley. I felt myself crowded already by the forces that waited there.

"The sword," he said. "You knew it was there, of course."

"Yes, I knew."

"He said . . . He called you an enchanter?" There was the faintest of queries in his voice. He wasn't looking at me. He sat on the step below me, head bent, looking down at the fingers laced round his knee.

"You knew that. You have seen me use magic."

"Yes. The first time I came here, when you showed me the sword in the stone altar, and I thought it was real . . ." He stopped abruptly, and his head came up. His voice was sharp with discovery. "It *was* real! This is the one, isn't it? The one the stone sword was carved from? Isn't it? Isn't it?"

"Yes."

"What sword is it, Myrddin?"

"Do you remember my telling you—you and Bedwyr— the story of Macsen Wledig?"

"Yes, I remember it well. You said that was the sword carved in the altar here." Again that note of discovery. "This is the same? His very sword?"

"Yes."

"How did it come there, on the island?"

I said: "I put it there, years back. I brought it from the place where it had been hidden."

He turned fully then, and looked at me. A long look. "You mean you found it? It's your sword?"

"I didn't say that."

"You found it by magic? Where?"

"I can't tell you that, Emrys. Some day you may need to search for the place yourself."

"Why should I?"

"I don't know. But a man's first need is a sword, to use against life, and conquer it. Once it is conquered, and he is older, he needs other food, for the spirit . . ."

After a bit I heard him say, softly: "What are you seeing, Myrddin?"

"I was seeing a settled and shining land, with corn growing rich in the valleys, and farmers working their fields in peace as they did in the time of the Romans. I was seeing a sword growing idle and discontented, and the days of peace stretching into bickering and division, and the need of a quest for the idle swords and the unfed spirits. Perhaps it was for this that the god took the grail and the spear back from me and hid them in the ground, so that one day you might set out to find the rest of Macsen's treasure. No, not you, but

Bedwyr . . . It is his spirit, not yours, which will hunger and thirst, and slake itself in the wrong fountains."

As if from far away, I heard my own voice die, and silence come back. The thrush had flown, the bees seemed quiet. The boy was on his feet now, and staring.

He said, with all the force of simplicity: "Who are you?"

"My name is Myrddin Emrys, but I am known as Merlin the enchanter."

"*Merlin?* But then—but that means you are—you were—" He stopped, and swallowed.

"Merlinus Ambrosius, son of Ambrosius the High King? Yes."

He stood silent for a long time. I could see him thinking back, remembering, assessing. Not guessing about himself— he had been too deeply rooted, and for too long, in the person of Ector's bastard foster-son. And, like everyone else in the kingdom, he assumed that the prince was being royally reared in some court beyond the sea.

He spoke at length quietly, but with such a kind of inward force and joy that one wondered how he could contain it. What he said surprised me. "Then the sword was yours. You found it, not I. I was only sent to bring it to you. It is yours. I will get it for you now."

"No, wait, Emrys—"

But he had already gone. He brought the sword, running, and held it out to me.

"Here. It's yours." He sounded breathless. "I ought to have guessed who you were . . . Not away in Brittany with the prince, as some people have it, but here, in your own country, waiting till the time came to help the High King. You are the seed of Ambrosius. Only you could have found it, and I found it only because you sent me there. It is for you. Take it."

"No. Not for me. Not for a bastard seed."

"Does that make a difference? Does it?"

"Yes," I said gently.

He was silent. The sword sank to his side and was quenched in his shadow. I mistook his silence, and I remember that at the time I was relieved merely that he said no more.

I got to my feet. "Bring it now into the chapel. We'll leave it there, where it belongs, on the god's altar. Whichever god is sovereign in this place will watch it for us. It must wait here till the time comes for it to be claimed in the sight of men, by the legitimate heir to the kingdom."

"So. That's why you sent me for it? To bring it for him?"

"Yes. In due time it will be his."

A little to my surprise he smiled, apparently satisfied. He nodded calmly. We took the sword together into the chapel. He laid it on the altar, above its carved replica. They were the same. His hand left the hilt, lingeringly, and he stepped back to my side.

"And now," I said, "I have something to tell you. The Duke of Cornwall brought news—"

I got no further. The sound of hoofs, approaching rapidly through the forest, brought Cabal up, roach-backed and growling. Arthur whipped round. His voice was sharp.

"Listen! Is that Cornwall's troop back again? Something must be wrong . . . Are you sure they mean you well?"

I put a hand to his arm and he stopped, then, at the look on my face, asked: "What is it, then? Were you expecting this?"

"No. Yes. I hardly know. Wait, Emrys. Yes, this had to come. I thought it must. The day is not over yet."

"What do you mean?"

I shook my head. "Come with me and meet them."

It was not Cornwall's troops that came clattering into the clearing. The Dragon glittered, red on gold. King's men. The officer halted his troop and rode forward. I saw his eye take in the wild clearing, the overgrown shrine, my own plain robes; it touched the boy at my side, no more than a touch, then came back to my face, and he saluted, bowing low.

The greeting was formal, in the King's name. It was followed by the news I had already had from Cador; that the King was marching north with his army, and would lie at Luguvallium, there to face the threat from Colgrim's forces. The man went on to tell me, looking troubled, that of late the King's sickness seemed to have taken hold of him again, and there were days when he had not the strength to ride, but proposed, if need be, to take the field in a litter. "And this is the message I was charged to give you, my lord. The High King, remembering the strength and help you gave to the army of his brother Aurelius Ambrosius, asks that you will come now out of your fastness, and go to him where he waits to meet his enemies." The message came, obviously, by rote. He finished: "My lord, I am to tell you that this is the summons you have been waiting for."

I bent my head. "I was expecting it. I had already sent to tell the King I was coming, and Emrys of Galava with me. You are to escort us? Then no doubt you will have the goodness to wait a while until we are ready. Emrys"—I turned to Arthur, standing in a white trance of excitement at my side—"come with me."

He followed me back into the chapel. As soon as we were out of sight of the troop he caught at my arm. "You're taking me? You're really taking me? And if it comes to a battle—"

"Then you shall fight in it."

"But my father, Count Ector . . . He may forbid it."

"You will not fight beside Count Ector. These are King's troops and you go with me. You will fight with the King."

He said joyously: "I knew this was a day of marvels! I

thought at first that the white stag had led me to the sword, that it was for me. But now I see that it was just a sign that today I should ride to my first battle . . . What are you doing?"

"Watch now," I said. "I told you I would leave the sword in the god's protection. It has lain long enough in the darkness. Let us leave it now in the light."

I stretched out my hands. From the air the pale fire came, running down the blade, so that runes—quivering and illegible—shimmered there. Then the fire spread, engulfing it, till, like a brand too brightly flaring, the flames died, and when they had gone, there stood the altar, pale stone, with nothing against it but the stone sword.

Arthur had not seen me use this kind of power before, and he watched open-mouthed as the flames broke out of the air and caught at the stone. He drew back, awed and a little frightened, and the only colour in his face was the wanlight cast by the flames.

When it was done he stood very still, licking dry lips. I smiled at him.

"Come, be comfortable. You have seen me use magic before."

"Yes. But seeing this—this kind of thing . . . All this time, when Bedwyr and I were with you, you never let us know what sort of man you were . . . This power; I had no idea. You told us nothing of it."

"There was nothing to tell. There was no need for me to use it, and it wasn't something you could learn from me. You will have different skills, you and Bedwyr. You won't need this one. Besides, if you do, I shall be there to give it to you."

"Will you? Always? I wish I could believe that."

"It is true."

"How can you know?"

385

"I know," I said.

He stared at me for a moment longer, and in his face I could see a whole world of uncertainty and bewilderment and desire. It was a boy's look, immature and lost, and it was gone in a moment, replaced by his normal armour of bright courage. He smiled then, and the sparkle was back. "You may regret that, you know! Bedwyr's the only person who can stand me for long."

I laughed. "I'll do my best. Now, if you will, tell them to bring our horses out."

When I was ready I went out to join the waiting men. Arthur was not mounted and fretting to be off, as I had expected; he was holding my horse for me, like a groom. I saw his eyes widen a little when he saw me; I had put on my best clothes, and my black mantle was lined with scarlet and pinned on the shoulder by the Dragon brooch of the royal house. He saw that I was amused and had guessed his thought, and smiled a little in return as he swung himself up on his white stallion. I took care that he should not see what I was thinking then; that the youth with the plain mantle and the bright, proud look did not need a brooch to declare himself Pendragon, and royal. But he drew the stallion soberly in behind my mild roan mare, and the men were watching me.

So we left the chapel of the Wild Forest in the care of whichever god owned it, and rode down towards Galava.

BOOK IV

THE KING

1

The danger from the Saxons had been more immediate even than Cador had supposed. Colgrim had moved fast. By the time Arthur and I with our escort approached Luguvallium we found, just south-east of the town, the King's forces and Cador's moving into position with the men of Rheged, to face an enemy already massing in great numbers for the attack.

The British leaders were closeted with the King in his tent. This had been pitched on the summit of a small hill which lay behind the field of battle. There had in times past been some kind of a fortress there, and a few ruined walls still stood, with the remains of a tower, and lower down on the slopes were the tumbled stones and weedy garths of an abandoned village. The place was a riot of blackberry and nettle, with huge old apple trees still standing among the fallen stones, golden with ripening fruit. Here, below the hill, the baggage trains were rumbling into place; the trees and the half-ruined walls would provide shelter for the emergency dressing station. Soon the apparent chaos would resolve itself; the King's armies still fought with a pattern of the Roman discipline enforced by Ambrosius. Looking at the huge spreading host of the enemy, the field of spears and axes and the horse-hair tossing in the breeze like the foam of an advancing sea, I thought that we would need every last scruple of strength and courage that we could muster. And I wondered about the King.

Uther's tent had been pitched on a little level lawn, before the ruined tower. As our troop rode towards it through the noise and bustle of the battalions assembling into fighting order, I saw men turn to stare, and even above the shouts of command and the clash of arms could hear the word go round. "It's Merlin. Merlin. Merlin the prophet is here. Merlin is with us." Men turned, stared, shouted, and elation seemed to spread like a buzz through the field. A fellow with the device of Dyfed shouted as I passed, in my own tongue: "Are you with us then, Myrddin Emrys, *braud*, and have you seen the shooting star for us today?"

I called back, clearly, so that it could be heard: "Today it is a rising star. Watch for it, and the victory."

As I dismounted with Arthur and Ralf at the foot of the hill, and walked up to Uther's tent, I heard the word spread through the field with a rush like the wind racing over ripe corn.

It was a bright September day, full of sunlight. Outside the King's tent the Dragon blew, scarlet on yellow. I went straight in, with Arthur on my heels. The boy had armed himself at Galava, and looked at every point a young warrior. I had expected him to appear with Ector's blazon, but he carried no device, and his cloak and tunic were of plain white wool. "It's my colour," he had said, when he saw me looking. "The white horse, the white hound, and I shall carry a white shield. Since I have no name, I shall write on it myself. My device will be my own, when I get it." I had said nothing, but I thought now, as the boy trod forward beside me across the King's tent, that if he had deliberately courted all men's eyes on the field of battle, he could not have done better. The unmarked white, and his air of eager and shining youth, stood out among the tossing brilliance of colour on that bright morning, as surely as if the trumpets had already proclaimed him prince. And as Uther greeted us, I could see the same thought in the eager and hungry gaze he fixed on the boy's face.

Myself, I was shocked at Uther's appearance. It bore out the reports I had had of him, of a man visibly failing, "as if a canker gnawed at his guts, not with pain but with daily wasting." He was thin and his colour was bad, and I noticed that from time to time his hand went to his chest, as if he found it hard to draw breath. He was splendidly dressed, with gold and jewels glinting on his armour; the stuff of his great cloak was gold, too, with scarlet dragons entwined. He held himself upright, kingly in the great chair. There was grey now in the reddish hair and beard, but his eyes were vivid and alive as ever, burning in their deep sockets. The thinness of his face made it look more hawk-like, and if possible more kingly than before. The flashing gold and jewels and the great cloak hid the thinness of his body. Only the wrists and bony hands showed where the long wasting sickness had gnawed the flesh away.

Arthur waited behind me with Ralf as I went forward. Count Ector was there, near the King, along with Coel of Rheged, and Cador, and a dozen other of Uther's leaders whom I knew. I saw Ector eyeing Arthur with a kind of wonder. I did not see Lot anywhere.

Uther greeted me with a courtesy only thinly overlaying the eagerness below. It is possible that he had intended there and then to present his son to the commanders, but there was no time. Trumpets were sounding outside. Uther hesitated, looking indecisive, then he made a sign to Ector who stepped forward and formally presented Arthur to the King as his foster-son Emrys of Galava. Arthur, with this new quiet and self-contained maturity, knelt to kiss the King's hand. I saw Uther's hand close on his, and I thought he would speak then, but at that moment the trumpets shrilled again, nearer, and the door of the tent was pulled open. Arthur stood back. Uther—the effort was apparent—tore his eyes from the boy's face and gave the word. The commanders saluted hurriedly and dispersed to mount and gallop away to their stations. The ground shook to the trampling of horses, and the air to the shouting and the clash of metal. Four men ran in with poles, and I saw then that Uther's chair was a kind of litter, a big carrying-chair, in which he could be borne onto the battlefield. Someone ran to him with his sword and put it into his hand, whispering as he did so, and the four fellows bent to the poles, waiting for the King's word.

I stood back. If any memory came to me of the young, tough commander who had fought so ably at his brother's side through all the early years of war, it touched me now with no feeling of pity or regret, as the King turned his head and smiled, the same fierce, eager smile that I knew. The years had dropped away from him. If it had not been for the litter, I could have sworn that he was a whole man. There was even colour in his cheeks, and his whole person glittered.

"My servant here tells me you have foretold us victory already?" He laughed, a young man's laugh, full and ringing. "Then you have indeed brought us today all that we could desire. Boy!"

Arthur, at the tent door speaking to Ector, stopped and looked back. The King beckoned. "Here. Stay by me."

Arthur flashed an enquiring look at his foster-father, then at me. I nodded. As the boy moved to obey the King I saw Ector make a sign to Ralf, and the latter moved quietly with Arthur to the left of the King's litter. Ector hung on his heel a moment in the tent doorway, but Uther was saying something to his son, and Arthur was bent to listen. The Count hitched his cloak over his shoulder, nodded abruptly to me, and went out. The trumpets sounded again, and then the sunshine and the shouting were all about us as the King's chair was carried out towards the waiting troops.

I did not follow it down the hillside, but stayed where I

was, on the high ground beside the tent, while below me on the wide field the armies formed. I saw the King's chair set down, and the King himself stand to speak to the men. From this distance I could hear nothing of what was said, but when he turned and pointed to where I stood high in the sight of the whole army, I heard the shout of "Merlin!" again, and the cheers. There was an answering shout from the enemy, a yell of derision and defiance, and then the clamour of trumpets and the thunder of the horses drowned everything, and shook the day.

Beside the tower wall stood an ancient apple tree, its bark now gnarled and thick with lichen like verdigris, but its boughs heavy with yellow fruit. In front of it was a tumble of stone with a plinth where perhaps there had once been an altar or a statue. I stepped up onto this, with my back to the laden apple tree, and watched the course of the fighting.

There was still no sign of Lot's banner. I beckoned a fellow running past—he was a medical orderly on his way to the dressing station lower down the hill—and asked him: "Lot of Lothian? Are his troops not come?"

"There's no sign of them yet, sir. I don't know why. Maybe they're to be held back as reserves on the right?"

I glanced where he was pointing. To the right of the field was the winding glimmer of a stream, flanked for some fifty paces to either hand by broken and sedgy ground. Beyond this the field rose through alder and willow and scrubby oak to thicker woodland. Between the trees the slope was rough and broken, but not too steep for horses, and the woods could well hide half an army. I thought I could see the glint of spear-heads through the thick of the trees. Lot, coming from the north-east, would have had early news of the Saxon advance, and would hardly have come late for the battle. He must be there, waiting and watching. But not, I was sure, by order as a reserve placed there by the King. The dilemma that Cador and I had spoken of might well be resolved today for Lot: if Uther looked like winning the victory, then Lot could throw his army in and share the time of triumph and its aftermath of reward and power; but if Colgrim should bear away the day, then Lot would have the chance of fixing his interest with the Saxon conquerors—in time, moreover, to deny his marriage with Morgian and take whatever power the new Saxon rule would offer him. I might well, I thought sourly, be doing the man an injustice, but my bones told me I was not. I wished there had been time to learn before the battle what Uther's dispositions had been. If Lot was anywhere at hand he would not miss this battle, of all battles, with the chances it held for him. I wondered how soon he would see me, or hear that I had come. And once he knew, he would have no doubt at all of the identity of the white-cloaked youth on the white horse, who fought so close on the King's left hand.

It was evident that the High King's presence, even in a litter, had cheered and fortified the British. Though, borne as he was in his chair, he could not lead the charge, he was there with the Dragon above him, right in the center of the field, and, though the press of his followers round him would hardly let an enemy get within striking distance, the fighting was fiercest round the Dragon, and from time to time I saw the flutter of the golden cloak and the flash of the King's own sword. Out on the right rode the King of Rheged, flanked by Caw and at least three of his sons. Ector too was on the right, fighting with dogged ferocity, while Cador on the left showed all the dash and dazzle of the Celt on his day of luck. Arthur I knew to be endowed by nature with the qualities of both, but today he would doubtless be more than content with his position guarding the King's left side. Ralf, in his turn, held himself back to guard Arthur's. I watched the chestnut horse swerve and turn and rear, never more than a pace away from the white stallion's flank.

This way and that the battle went Here a banner would go down, swamped apparently under the savage tide of attack, then somehow there would be a recovery, and the British would press forward under the swinging axes, and push back the yelling waves of Saxons. From time to time a solitary horseman—a messenger, it could be assumed— spurred off eastwards across the boggy land by the stream, and up into the trees. And now it was certain that Lot's force was there, hidden and waiting in the wood. And, as surely as if I had read his mind, I knew that he was waiting there by no orders from the King. Whatever calls for help those messengers brought to him, he would delay his coming until he saw how the day went. So, for two fierce hours, lengthening through midday to three, the British forces fought, deprived of what should have been their fresh fighting right. The King of Rheged fell wounded, and was carried back: his forces held their position, but it could be seen that they were wavering. And still the men of Lothian held back. Soon, if they did not come in, it might be too late.

All at once, it seemed that it was. There was a shout from the center, a shout of anger and despair. There, in the thick of the press round the King's chair, I saw the Dragon standard waver, rock violently, then slope to its fall. Suddenly, for all the distance, it was as if I was there, close by the King's chair, seeing it all clearly. A body of Saxons, huge fair giants, some of them red with unfelt wounds, had rushed the group that surrounded the King, breaking it, it seemed, with sheer weight and ferocity. Some were cut down, some were forced back by desperate fighting, but two got through. They smashed their way forward, axes whirling, on the King's left. One axe struck the shaft of the standard, which splintered, rocked, and began to fall. The man who had carried it went down with the blood spouting from his severed wrist, and disappeared under the mashing hoofs. With scarcely a pause the axe wheeled through its bright arc towards the King. Uther was on his feet, his sword up to meet the axeman, but Ralf's sword whirled and bit, and the Saxon fell clear across the King's chair, his blood gushing out over the golden cloak. The King was pinned back under the fallen man's weight. The other Saxon rushed forward yelling. Ralf, cursing, fought to thrust his horse between the helpless King and the new attacker, but the Saxon, towering above the British, brushed their weapons aside as a mad bull brushes the long grass, and charged forward. It seemed nothing could stop him reaching the King. I saw Arthur drive his horse forward, just as the rocking standard fell, striking the white stallion across the chest. The stallion reared, screaming. Arthur, holding the horse with his knees, seized the falling standard, and shouting flung it clear across the King's chair into a soldier's ready grip, then swung the screaming, striking horse right into the path of the giant Saxon. The great axe whirled into its flashing circle, and came down. The stallion swerved and leaped, and the blow missed, but glancing spent from the boy's sword, knocked it spinning from his hand. The stallion climbed high again, striking out with those killing forefeet, and the axeman's face vanished in a pash of bright blood. The white horse plunged back to the side of the King's chair and Arthur's hand went down to his dagger. Then quiet, but clear as a shout, the King called, "Here!" and flung his own sword, hilt first, into the air. Arthur's hand shot out and caught it by the hilt. I saw it catch the light. The white horse reared again. The standard was up, and streaming in the wind, scarlet on gold. There was a great shout, spreading out from the center of the field where the white stallion, treading blood, leaped forward under the

Dragon banner. Shouting, the men surged with him. I saw the standard-bearer hesitate fractionally, looking back at the King, but the King waved him forward, then lay back, smiling, in his chair.

And now, too late for whatever spectacular intervention Lot had intended, the Lothian troops swept down out of the woodland and swelled the ranks of the attacking British. But the day was already won. There was no man there on the field who had not seen what happened. There, white on a white horse, the King's fighting spirit had leaped, it seemed, out of his failing body, and run ahead, like the spark on the tip of a fighting spear, straight to the heart of the Saxon forces.

Soon, as the Saxons, breaking from stand to fighting stand, were pressed gradually backwards towards the marshes that fringed the field, and the British followed them with steadily growing ferocity and triumph, men started to run in behind the fighting troops to bring out the hurt and the dying. Uther's chair, which should have been borne back at the same time, was forging forward steadily in Arthur's wake. But the main press of the fighting was no longer round it; that was well forward of the field where, under the Dragon, everyone could see the white stallion and the white cloak and the flashing blade of the King's sword.

My post as a visible presence on the hill was no longer either heeded or necessary. I went down to where the emergency dressing station had been set up below the fallen tangles of the apple orchard. Already the tents were filling, and the orderlies were hard at work. I sent a boy running for my box of instruments and, taking off my cloak, slung it over the low boughs of an apple tree to make a shelter from the sun's rays; and as the next stretcher went by me I called to the bearers to set the wounded man down in the improvised shade.

One of the bearers was a lean and greying veteran whom I recognized. He had worked as orderly for me at Kaerconan. I said: "A moment, Paulus, don't hurry away. There are plenty to do the carrying; I'd rather have your help here."

He looked pleased that I had recognized him. "I thought you might need me, sir. I've got my kit with me." He knelt on the other side of the unconscious man, and together we began to slit the leather tunic away where it was torn open by a bloody gash.

"How is it with the King?" I asked him.

"Hard to say, sir. I thought he'd gone, and a lot else gone with him, but he's there now with Gandar, and sitting peaceful as a babe, and smiling. As well he might."

"Indeed . . . That's far enough, I think. Let me look . . ." It was an axe wound, and the leather and metal of the man's tunic had been driven deep into the hacked flesh and splintered bone. I said: "I doubt if there's much we can do here, but we'll try. God's on our side today, and he may well be on this poor fellow's, too. Hold this, will you? . . . As you were saying, well he might. The luck won't change now."

"Luck, is it? Luck on a white horse, you might say. A fair treat it was to see that youngster, the way he pushed through just at the right moment. It needed something like that, with the King falling back as if he was dead, and the Dragon going down. We were looking for King Lot then, but no sign of him. Believe me, sir, another half-minute and we'd have been going the other way. Battle's like that; it makes you wonder sometimes, to think what hangs on a few seconds and a bit of luck. A piece of nice timing like that, and the right person to do it—that's all it takes, and you've won or lost a kingdom."

We worked for a while in silence then, quickly, because the man was beginning to stir under my hands, and I had to finish before he woke to cruel life. When I had done all I could, and we were bandaging, Paulus said, ruminatively: "Funny thing."

"What?"

"Remember Kaerconan, sir?"

"Will I ever forget it?"

"Well, that youngster had a look of *him*—Ambrosius, I mean, that was Count of Britain then. White horse and all, and the Dragon flying over it. Men were saying so . . . And the name's the same, sir, isn't it? Emrys? Connection of yours, perhaps?"

"Perhaps."

"Ah, well," said Paulus, and asked no more questions. He did not need to say more; I knew already that rumours must have been flying round the camp from the moment that Arthur and I had ridden in with the escort. Let them run. Uther had shown his hand. And between the boy's bravery, and the luck of the battle and his own misjudgment, Lot would have a hard struggle of it now to change the King's mind, or to persuade the other nobles that Uther's son was no fit leader.

The man between us woke then and began to scream, and there was no more time for talking.

2

By nightfall the field was cleared of the fallen. The King had withdrawn when it was seen that the tide of victory was sure, and not to be stemmed by any late action of the Saxons. The battle over, the main forces of the British fell back on the township two miles to the north-west, leaving Cador, with Caw of Strathclyde, to hold the field. Lot had not stayed to test his position with the other leaders, but had withdrawn into the town as soon as the fighting was done, and had gone like Ajax to his quarters, since when no man had seen him. Already stories were going round about his fury at the King's action in favouring the strange youth on the battlefield, and his black silence when he heard that Emrys was bidden with me to the victory feast, where no doubt he would be further honoured. There were rumours, too, about the reason for the belated entrance into battle of Lot's troops. No one went so far as to speak of treachery, but it was said openly that, had he delayed much longer, and had not Arthur performed his small miracle, Lothian's inaction might have cost Uther the victory. Men wondered too, aloud, whether Lot would emerge from his sullen silence to share in the feast which was decreed for the following night. But I knew that he could not keep away. He dared not. Though he had said nothing, he must certainly know who "Emrys" was, and if he was ever to discredit him and seize the power he had schemed for, he would have to do it now.

After the emergency cases had been dealt with at the

orchard dressing station, the medical units had also moved back to the town, where a hospital had been set up. I went with them, and dealt with a steady stream of cases all afternoon and evening. Our losses had not been heavy as such things commonly go, but still the burial parties would be hard at work all night, watched by the wolves and the gathering ravens. From the marshes came the distant flicker of flames, where the Saxon dead were burning.

I finished work in the hospital at about midnight, and was in an outer room, watching while Paulus packed my instruments away, when I heard someone coming quickly across the court outside, and was aware of a stir near the door behind me.

Call me an old fool if you like, remembering back through the years to what never happened, and you may be more than half right; but it was not only love which made me recognize his coming before I even turned my head. A current of fresh sweet air blew with him, cutting through the fumes of drugs and the stench of sickness and fear. The very lamps burned brighter.

"Merlin?" He spoke softly, as one does in a sickroom, but the excitement of the day was still in his voice. I looked at him smiling, then more sharply.

"Are you hurt? You young fool, why didn't you come to me sooner? Let me see."

He drew back the arm in its stiffened sleeve. "Can't you tell black Saxon blood when you see it? I never had a scratch. Oh, Merlin, what a day! And what a King! To go out in the field crippled and in a chair—that's real courage, far more than it takes to ride into a fight with a good horse and a good sword. I'll swear I never even had to think . . . it was so easy . . . Merlin, it was splendid! It's what I was born for—I know it now! And did you see what happened? What the King did? His sword? I'll swear it pulled me forward of its own will, not mine . . . And then the shouting and the way the soldiers moved forward, like the sea. I never even had to use a spur on Canrith . . . Everything moved so fast, and yet so slowly and clearly, every moment seemed to last for ever. I never knew one could be blazing hot and ice-cold all at the same moment, did you?"

He did not wait for answers, but talked on, fast and sparkling, his eyes alight still with the thrill of battle and the overwhelming experience of the day. I hardly listened, but I watched him, and watched the faces of the orderlies and servants, and of those men who were still awake and near enough to hear us. I saw it begin: even so, after battle, Ambrosius' very presence had given the wounded strength, and the dying comfort. Whatever it was he had had about him, Arthur had the same; I was to see it often in the future; it seemed that he shed brightness and strength round him where he went, and still had it ever renewed in himself. As he grew older, I knew it would be renewed more hardly and at a cost, but now he was very young, with the flower of manhood still to come. After this, I thought, who could maintain that youth itself made him unfit for kingship? Not Lot, stiffened in his ambition, grimly scheming for a dead king's throne. It was Arthur's very youth which had whistled up today the best that men had in them, as a huntsman calls up the following pack, or an enchanter whistles up the wind.

He recognized, in one of the beds, a man who had fought near him, and went softly down the hospital room to speak to him, and then to others. Two of them, at least, I heard him call by name.

Give him the sword, my dream had said, *and his own nature will do the rest. Kings are not created out of dreams and prophecies: before ever you began to work for him, he was what you see now. All you have done is to guard him while he grew. You, Merlin, are a smith like Weland of the black forge; you made the sword and gave it a cutting edge, but it carves its own way.*

"I saw you up there beside the apple tree," said Arthur gaily. He had followed me out of the hospital room, and I had stopped in the anteroom to give instructions to a night orderly. "The men were saying it was an omen. That when you were there, above us on the hill, the fight was as good as won. And it's true, because through it all, even when I wasn't thinking, I could feel you watching me. Quite close beside me, too. It was like a shield at one's back. I even thought I heard—"

He stopped in mid-sentence. I saw his eyes widen and fix on something beyond me. I looked to see what had gagged him.

Morgause would be two and twenty now, and she was even lovelier than when I had last seen her. She wore grey, a long plain gown of dove-colour which should have made her look like a nun, but somehow did not. She wore no jewels, and needed none. Her skin was pale as marble, and the long eyes that I remembered were gold-green under the tawny lashes. Her hair, as befitted a woman still unwed, fell loose and shining over her shoulders, and was bound back from her brow with a broad band of white.

"Morgause!" I said, startled. "You should not be here!" Then I remembered her skills, and saw behind her two women and a page carrying boxes and linen cloths. She must have been working, as I had, among the wounded; or possibly she still attended the King, and had been with him. I added, quickly: "No, I see; forgive me, and forgive my lack of greeting. Your skill is welcome here. Tell me, how is the King?"

"He has recovered, my lord, and is resting. He seems well enough, and his spirits are good. It seems it was a notable fight. I wish I might have seen it." She glanced past me then

403

at Arthur, an interested, summing look. It was obvious that she recognized him as the youth who had won everyone's praise that day, but it seemed that the King had not yet told her who he was. There was no hint of such a knowledge in her face or voice as she made him a reverence. "Sir."

The colour was up in Arthur's face, bright as a banner. He stammered some kind of greeting, suddenly sounding no more than an awkward boy; he whose boyhood had never been awkward.

She took it coolly, then turned her eyes back to me, dismissing him as a woman of twenty dismisses a child. I thought: No, she does not know yet.

She said, in that light, sweet voice: "My lord Merlin, I came with a message to you from the King. Later, when you have rested, he would like to speak with you."

I said doubtfully: "It's very late. Would he not be better to sleep?"

"I think he would sleep better if he spoke with you first. He was impatient to see you as soon as he came back from the field, but he needed to rest, so I gave him a draught, and he slept then. He's awake now. Can you come within the hour?"

"Very well."

She curtsied again with lowered eyes, and went, as quietly as she had come.

3

I supped alone with Arthur. I had been allotted a room whose window overlooked a strip of garden on the river bank; the garden was a terrace enclosed by gates and high walls. Arthur's room adjoined mine, and both were approached through an anteroom where guards stood armed. Uther was taking no chances.

My room was large and well appointed, and a servant waited there with food and wine. We spoke little while we ate. I was tired and hungry, and Arthur showed his usual appetite, but after his flow of exalted spirits he had fallen strangely quiet, probably, I thought, out of deference to me. For my part I could think of little else but the coming interview with Uther, and of what the morrow might bring; at that moment I could bring nothing to them myself but a sort of weariness of the spirit, which I told myself was no more than reaction from a long journey and a hard day. But I thought it was more than that, and felt like a man who comes out of a sunlit plain into boggy ground, where mist hangs heavy.

Ulfin, Uther's body-servant, came to take me to the King. From the way his look lingered on Arthur I could see he knew the truth, but he said nothing of it as he led me through the corridors to the King's chamber. Indeed he seemed to have little room in his mind for anything but anxiety about the King's health. When I was ushered into Uther's presence, I could see why. Even since the morning, the change was startling. He was in bed, propped in a furred bedgown against pillows, and, shorn of the kingly trappings of armour and scarlet and gold tissue, anyone could see how mortally wasted his body was. Now I could see his death clearly in his face. It would not be tonight, nor should it be tomorrow, but it must come soon; and this, I told myself, must be the cause of the formless dread that was weighing on me. But, though weak and weary, the King seemed pleased to see me, and eager to talk, so I pushed my foreboding aside. Even with tonight and tomorrow, Uther and I and whatever was working for us should have time to see our soaring star riding high and safe to his bright zenith.

He talked first of the battle, and of the day's events. It was evident that all his doubts were set aside, and that (though he would not admit it) he was regretting the lost years since Arthur had come near manhood. He plied me with questions, and, though afraid of taxing him too much, I could see that he would rest better when he knew all I had to tell him. So, as clearly and quickly as I could, I told him the story of the past years, all the details of the boy's life in the Wild Forest that could not be put into the reports I had sent him. I told him, too, what suspicions and certainties I had had about Arthur's enemies; when I spoke about Lot he made no sign, but he heard me out without interruption. Of the sword of Maximus I said nothing. The King had himself today publicly put his own sword into his son's hand; he could not have declared more openly that the boy was his favoured heir. Macsen's sword, when there was need for it, would be given by the god. Between the two gifts was still a dark gap of fate through which I could not see; there was no need to trouble the King with it.

When I had done he lay back on his pillows a while in silence, his eyes on a far corner of the room, deep in thought. Then he spoke.

"You were right, Merlin. Even where it was hard to understand, and where not understanding I condemned you, you were right. The god had us all in his hand. And doubtless it was the god himself who put it in my mind to deny my son and leave him in your care, to be brought in safety and secrecy to such manhood as this. At least it has been granted me to see what manner of man I begot on that wild night at Tintagel, and what kind of a king will come after me. I should have trusted you better, bastard, as my brother did. I don't need to tell you that I am dying, do I? Gandar hums and haws and begs the question, but you'll admit the truth, King's prophet?"

The question was peremptory, requiring an answer. When I said, "Yes," he smiled briefly, with a look almost of satisfaction. I found myself liking Uther better now than I ever had before, seeing him bring this kind of bleak courage to his coming death. This was what Arthur had recognized in him today, the kingly quality to which he had come late, but not too late. It could be that now, almost in the moment of fulfillment of the past years, he and I found ourselves united in the person of the boy.

He nodded. The strain of the day and night was beginning to show, but his look was friendly and his manner still crisp. "Well, we've cleared the past. The future is with him, and with you. But I'm not dead yet, and I'm still High King. The present is with me. I sent for you to tell you that I shall proclaim Arthur my heir tomorrow at the victory feast. There'll never be a better moment. After what happened today no one can argue his fitness; he has already proved himself in public, more, in the sight of the army. Even if I wished to, I doubt if I could keep his secret any longer; rumour has run through the camp like a fire through straw. He knows nothing yet?"

"It seems not. I would have thought he would begin to guess, but it seems not. You'll tell him yourself tomorrow?"

"Yes. I'll send for him in the morning. For the rest of the time, Merlin, stay by him and keep him close."

He spoke then about his plans for the morrow. He would talk with Arthur, and then in the evening, when everyone had recovered from the fighting, and erased the scars of battle, Arthur would be brought with glory and acclaim in front of the nobles at the victory feast. As for Lot—he came to it flatly and without excuse—there was doubt as to what Lot would do, but he had lost too much public credit over his delay in the battle, and even as the betrothed of the King's daughter he would hardly dare (Uther insisted) stand up in public against the High King's own choice. He said nothing about the darker possibility, that Lot might even have thrown his weight onto the Saxons' side of the balance; he saw the delay only as a bid for credit—that Lot's intervention should seem to carry the British to victory. I listened, and said nothing. Whatever the truth of that, the trouble would soon be other men's, and not the King's.

He spoke then of Morgian, his daughter. The marriage, firmly contracted as it was, must go through; it could hardly be broken now without offering a mortal and dangerous insult to Lot and the northern kings who hunted with him. And as things had fallen out, it would be safer so; Lot would by the same token not dare to refuse the marriage, and by accepting it would bind himself publicly to Arthur; an Arthur already (months before the marriage) proclaimed, accepted, and established. Uther had almost said "and crowned," but let the sentence drift. He was looking tired now, and I made a move to leave him, but one of the thin hands lifted, and I waited. He did not speak for a few moments, but lay back with closed eyes. Somewhere a draught crept through the room, and the candles guttered. The shadows wavered, throwing dark across his face. Then the light steadied, and I could see his eyes, still bright in their deep sockets, watching me.

I heard his voice, thin with effort now, asking me something. Not asking, no. Uther the High King was begging me to stay beside Arthur, to finish the work I had begun, to watch him, advise him, guard him . . .

His voice faded, but the eyes watched me, intent, and I knew what they were saying. "*Tell me the future, Merlin, prophet of kings. Prophesy for me.*"

"I shall be with him," I said, "and the rest of it I have said before. He will bear a king's sword, and with that sword he will do all and more than men hope for. Under him the countries will be one, and there shall be peace, and light before darkness. And when there is peace I myself will go back into my solitude, but I will be there, waiting, always, to be called up as quickly as a man might whistle for the wind."

I was not speaking with vision: this was something which has never come to me when asked for, and besides, visions did not live easily in the same room as Uther. But to comfort him I spoke from remembered prophecies, and from a knowledge of men and times, which sometimes comes to the same thing. It satisfied him, which was all that was needed.

"That is all I wanted to know," he said. "That you will stay near him, and serve him at all times . . . Perhaps, if I had listened to my brother, and kept you near me . . . You have promised, Merlin. There is no man who has more power, not even the High King."

He said it without rancour, in the tone of one making a plain statement. His voice was tired suddenly, the voice of a sick man.

I got to my feet. "I'll leave you now, Uther. You had better sleep. What is the draught Morgause gives you?"

"I don't know. Some poppy-smelling thing; she puts it in warm wine."

"Does she sleep here, near you?"

"No. Along the corridor, in the first of the women's rooms. But don't disturb her now. There's some of the drug still in that jar yonder."

I crossed the room, picked up the jar, and sniffed it. The

potion, whatever it was, was already mixed in wine; the smell was sweet and heavy; poppy there was and other things I recognized, but it was not quite familiar. I dipped a finger in and put it to my lips. "Has anyone touched it since she mixed it?"

"Eh?" He had been drifting away, not in sleep, but as sick men do. "Touched it? No one that I have seen, but there's no one will try to poison me. It's well known that all my food is tasted. Call the boy in, if you wish."

"No need," I said. "Let him sleep." I poured some into a cup, but when I lifted it to my mouth he said with sudden vigour: "Don't be a fool! Let be!"

"I thought you said it would not be poisoned."

"No matter of that, we'll not take the chance."

"Do you not trust Morgause?"

"Morgause?" He knitted his brows, as if at an irrelevancy. "Of course, why not? When she has cared for me all these years, refusing to wed, even when . . . But no matter of that. Her fate is 'in the smoke,' she says, and she is content to wait for it. She riddles like you, sometimes, and I've scant patience with riddles, as you may remember. No, how could I doubt my daughter? But tonight of all nights we must be wary, and of all men, except my son, I can least spare you." He smiled then, momentarily the Uther that I remembered, hard and gay, and slightly malicious. "At least, not until he is proclaimed, and then no doubt you and I will well spare one another."

I smiled. "Meantime I'll taste your wine. Calm yourself, I can smell nothing hurtful, and I assure you that my death is not yet."

I did not add, "So let me make sure that you live to proclaim your son tomorrow." This strange shadow that brooded still behind my shoulder, it could not be my own death, nor (I knew) was it Arthur's, but it might, against all probability, be the King's. I took a sip, letting the wine rest for a moment on my tongue, then swallowed. The King lay back on his pillows and watched me, tranquil once more. I sipped again, then crossed the room to sit down by the great bed, and, more idly now, we talked: of the past seamed with memories; of the future, shadows still across glory. We understood one another tolerably well at the last, Uther and I. When it was patent that the wine was harmless I poured a draught for him, watched him drink it, then called his servant Ulfin, and left him to sleep.

4

All was so far well. Even if Uther died tonight—and nothing in his look or in my bones told me that he would—all was surely still set fair. I, with Cador's backing and Ector's support, could proclaim Arthur to the nobles as well as the King could, and prestige with power behind it had every chance of forcing the thing through. The King's gesture in flinging his sword to the boy in battle would be, to many of the soldiers, proof enough of Arthur's right to succeed him, and the warriors who had followed him so gladly today would follow him still. It was surely only the dissidents of the north-east who would not rejoice to see the days of uncertainty finished, and the succession pass clear and undoubted into Arthur's hands.

Then why, I thought, as I trod quietly along the corridors towards my own chamber, was my heart so heavy in me; what was this foreboding black enough for a death? Why, if this was a heavy matter that my blood prophesied, could I not see it? What shadow hung, clawed and waiting, over the day's bright success?

A moment later, as I nodded to the guard outside my ante-chamber, and went quietly through into the room itself, I saw the edge of the shadow. Beyond the doorway connecting Arthur's room to my own I could see his bed. It was empty.

I went quickly back to the antechamber, and had stooped to shake the sleeping servant awake, when my nostrils caught a familiar smell, the drug that had been in the King's wine. I dropped the man's shoulder and left him snoring, and in three swift strides was back in the corridor. Before I had said a word, the guard flattened himself back against the wall, as if afraid of what he saw in my face.

But I spoke softly: "Where is he?"

"My lord, he's safe. There's no reason for alarm . . . We had our orders, there was no harm could come to him. The other guard saw him right to the door, and stayed there—"

"*Where is he?*"

"In the women's rooms, my lord. When the girl came to him—"

"Girl?" I asked sharply.

"Indeed, my lord. She came here. We stopped her, of course, wouldn't let her in, but then he came out to the door himself. . . ." Reassured now by my silence, the man was relaxing. "Indeed, my lord, all's well. It was one of the Lady Morgause's women, the black-haired one, you may have noticed her, plump as a robin, and the prettiest, as was proper for my young lord this night—"

I had noticed her; small and rounded, with a high colour and black eyes bright as a bird's. A pretty creature, very young, and healthy as a summer's day. But I bit my lip. "How long ago?"

"Two hours, as near as might be." A grin touched his mouth. "Time enough. My lord, where's the harm? Even if we'd tried, how could we have stopped him? We didn't let her in; we'd had our orders, and he knew it; but when he said he'd go with her, what could we do? After all, it's a fair end to a man's first battle day."

I said something to him, and went back into my room. The fellow was right enough, the guards had done their duty as they saw it, and this was one situation in which no guard would have interfered. And where indeed was the harm? The boy had seized one half of his manhood today out under the sun; it was inevitable that the rest should come to him tonight.

413

As his sword had quenched its lust for blood, so the boy would burn alive till he quenched his own excitement in a girl's body. Anybody, I thought bitterly, but a god-bound prophet would have foreseen this. Any normal guardian would let this night take its normal course. But I was Merlin, and the room was full of shadows, and I was afraid.

I stood there alone, with the shadows pressing round me, controlling myself to coldness, facing the fear. The blackness came from my mind; very well, was it human merely, was it black jealousy, that Arthur at fourteen should take so easily a pleasure that at twenty I had burned for even as he, and had fumbled, failing? Or was it a fear worse than jealousy, the fear of losing or even sharing a love so dear and lately found; or was I fearful only for him, knowing what a girl could do to rob a man of power? And as this thought struck me I knew I was acquitted; the shadows were not from this. I had known, that day at twenty, when I fled from the girl's angry and derisive laughter, that for me there had been a cold choice between manhood and power, and I had chosen power. But Arthur's power would be different, that of full and fierce manhood, that of a king. He had shown me often enough that however much he might love and learn from me, he was Uther's son in the flesh; he wanted all that manhood could give. It was right that he should lie with his first girl tonight. I ought to smile, like the sentry, and go to bed myself and sleep, leaving him to his pleasure.

But the cold in my entrails and the sweat on my face were not there for nothing. I stood still, while the lamp flared and dimmed and flared again, and thought.

Morgause, I thought, one of Morgause's girls. And she'd drugged my servant, who might have come to tell me that Arthur had gone two hours since to her chamber. . . . And Morgause is Morgian's half-sister, and might be in Lot's pay, with the promise of some rich future should Lot become

414

King. True, she had made no attempt on the King, but she knew he always used a taster, and it would have served no purpose to be rid of him until Lot was married to Morgian and able to declare himself legitimately heir to the High Kingdom. But now Uther was dying, and Arthur had appeared, with a claim which would eclipse Lot's. If Morgause was indeed an enemy, and wanted Arthur put out of the way before tomorrow's feast, then the boy might even now be drugged, captive in Lot's hands, or dying . . .

This was folly. It was not for death that the god had given him the sword and shown him to me as High King. There was no reason for Morgause to wish him ill. As his half-sister she might expect more from Arthur as King than from Lot, her sister's husband. Arthur's death, I thought coldly, would not profit her. But death was here, in a form and with a smell I did not know. A smell like treachery, something remembered dimly from my childhood, when my uncle planned to betray his father's kingdom, and to murder me. It was not a matter of reason, but of knowing. Danger was here, and I had to find it.

I could not walk through the house, asking where Arthur was. If he was happily bedded with a girl, this was something he would never forgive me. I would have to find him by other means, and since I was Merlin, the means were here. Standing rigid there in the dim chamber, with my hands held stiff-fisted at my sides, I stared at the lamp. . . .

I know that I never moved from the place or left my chamber, but in my memory now it seems as if I went out, silent and invisible as a ghost, across the antechamber, past the guard, and along the dim corridor towards Morgause's door. The other sentry was there; he was full awake, and watching, but he never saw me.

There was no sound from within. I went in.

In the outer room the air was heavy and warm, and

smelled of scents and lotions such as women use. There were two beds there, and sleepers in them. On the threshold of the inner chamber Morgause's page was curled on the floor, sleeping.

Two beds, each with its sleeper. One was an old woman, grey-haired, mouth open, snoring slightly. The other slept silently, and over her pillow the long black hair lay heavy, braided for the night. The little dark girl slept alone.

I knew it now, the horror that oppressed me; the one thing that, looking for larger issues of death and treachery and loss, I had never thought of. I have said men with god's sight are often human-blind: when I exchanged my manhood for power it seemed I had made myself blind to the ways of women. If I had been simple man instead of wizard I would have seen the way eye answered eye back there at the hospital, have recognized Arthur's silence later, and known the woman's long assessing look for what it was.

Some magic she must have had, to blind me so. It may be that now, knowing I could do nothing, she let the magic lapse and thin; or let it waver as she sank towards sleep. Or it may be only that my power outstripped hers, and she had no shield against me. God knows I did not want to look, but I was nailed there by my own power, and because there is no power without knowledge, and no knowledge without suffering, the walls and door of Morgause's sleeping chamber dissolved in front of me, and I could see.

Time enough, the guard had said. They had indeed had time enough. The woman lay, naked and wide-legged, across the covers of the bed. The boy, brown against her whiteness, lay sprawled over her in the heavy abandonment of pleasure. His head was between her breasts, half turned from me; he was not asleep, but the next thing to it, his face close and quiet, his blind mouth searching her flesh as a puppy nuzzles for its mother's nipple. Her face I saw clearly. She held his head cradled, and about her body was the same heavy languor, but her face showed none of the tenderness that the gesture seemed to express. And none of the pleasure. It held a secret exultation as fierce as I have ever seen on a warrior's face in battle; the gilt-green eyes were wide and fixed on something invisible beyond the dark; and the small mouth smiled, a smile somewhere between triumph and contempt.

5

He came back to his room just before daylight. The first bird had whistled, and a few moments later the sudden jargoning of the early chorus almost drowned the clink of arms at the outer door, and his soft word to the guard. He came in, his eyes full of sleep, and stopped short just inside the door when he saw me sitting in the high-backed chair beside the window.

"Merlin! Up at this hour? Couldn't you sleep?"

"I haven't yet been to bed."

He came suddenly wide awake, sharpened and alert. "What is it? What's wrong? Is it the King?"

At least, I thought, he doesn't jump to the conclusion that I stayed awake to question his night's doings. And one thing he must never know; that I followed him through that door.

I said: "No, not the King. But you and I must talk before the day comes."

"Oh, the gods, not now, if you love me," he said, half laughing, and yawned. "Merlin, I've got to sleep. Did you guess where I'd gone, or did the guard tell you?"

As he came forward into the room I could smell her scent on him. I felt sickened, and I suppose I was shaken. I said curtly: "Yes, now. Wash yourself, and wake up. I have to talk to you."

I had put out all the lamps but one, and this was burning low, only half competing with the leaden light of dawn.

I saw his face go rigid. "By what right—?" He checked himself, and I saw the quick control come down over his anger. "Very well. I suppose you do have the right to question me, but I don't like the time you choose."

It was something altogether different from the injured boyish anger he had shown before, how short a time ago, beside the lake. So far they had already taken him between them, the sword and the woman. I said: "I have no right to question you, and I've no intention of doing so. Calm yourself, and listen. It's true I want to talk to you—among other things—about what happened tonight, but not for the reasons you seem to impute to me. Who do you think I am, Abbot Martin? I don't dispute your right to take your pleasure as and where you wish." He was still hostile, between anger and pride. To relax him and pass the moment over, I added mildly: "Perhaps it wasn't wise to venture through this house at night where there are men who hate you for what you did yesterday. But how can I blame you for going? You showed yourself a man in battle, why not then in your bed?" I smiled. "Though I've never lain with a woman myself, I've known what it is to want one. For the pleasure you had, I'm glad."

I stopped. His face had been pale with anger; now even in that lack of light I could see the anger drain away, and with it the last vestiges of colour. It was as if blood and breath had stopped together. His eyes looked black. He narrowed them at me as if he could not see me properly, or as if he were seeing me for the first time, and could not get me in focus. It was a discomforting look, and I am not easily discomforted.

"You have never lain with a woman?"

Somehow, to the matters boiling in my mind, the question came as sheer irrelevancy. I said, surprised: "I said so. I believe it's a matter of common knowledge. I also believe it's a fact that some men hold in contempt. But those—"

"Are you a eunuch, then?"

The question was cruel; his manner, harsh and abrupt, made it seem meant so. I had to wait a moment before I answered.

"No. I was going to add, that those who hold chastity in contempt are not men whose contempt would disturb me. Have I yours, then?"

"What?" He had obviously not heard a word of what I had been saying. He jerked himself free of whatever strong emotion was riding him, and made for his room like a man who is choking, and in need of air. As he went he said, muffled: "I'll go and wash."

The door shut behind him. I stood up quickly and set my hands on the window sill, leaning out into the chill September dawn. A cock was crowing; from farther off others answered it. I found that I was shaking; I, Merlin, who had watched while kings and priests and princes plotted my death openly in front of my eyes; who had talked with the dead; who could make storm and fire and call the wind. Well, I had called this wind; I must face it. But I had counted on his love for me to get us both through what I had to tell him. I had not reckoned on losing his respect—and for such a reason—at this moment.

I told myself that he was young; that he was Uther's son, fresh from his first woman, and in the flush of his new sexual pride. I told myself that I had been a fool to see love given back where I gave it, when what the boy was rendering to me was no more than I had given my own tutor Galapas, affection tinged with awe. I told myself these and other things, and by the time he came back I was seated again, calm and waiting, with two goblets of wine poured ready on a table at my hand. He took one without a word, then sat across the room from me, on the edge of my bed. He had washed even his hair; it was still damp, and clung to his brow. He had changed his bedgown for day dress, and in the short tunic, without mantle or weapon, looked like a boy again, the Arthur of the summer and the Wild Forest.

I had been casting round carefully for what to say, but now could find nothing. It was Arthur who broke the silence, not looking at me, turning the goblet round and round in his hands, watching the swirl of wine as if his life depended on it.

He said, flatly, and as if it explained everything, as I suppose it did:

"I thought you were my father."

It was like facing an opponent's sword, only to find that the sword and the enemy are in fact illusions, but in the same moment to feel that the very ground on which one has made one's stand is a shaking bog. I fought to rearrange my thoughts.

Respect and love, yes, I had had these from him, but they could have been given to me for the man I was; in fact, only in such a way does a boy give them to his father. But other things became suddenly plain; above all the deference which he would have given to no other man but Ector, his obedience, his assumption of my ready welcome, and more than all—I saw it like the sudden rift of daffodil sky which opened in the grey beyond the window—the shining anticipation with which he had come with me to Luguvallium. I remembered my own ceaseless childhood search for my father, and how I had looked for and seen him everywhere, in every man who looked my mother's way. Arthur had had only his foster-parents' story of noble bastardy, and a vague promise of recognition "when you are grown enough to bear arms."

As children do—as I had done—he had said little, but waited and wondered, ceaselessly. Then into this perpetual search and expectation I had come, with some mystery about me, and I suppose the air that Ralf had spoken of, of a man used to deference and moved by some strong purpose. The boy may have seen his own likeness to me; more likely others, Bedwyr even, had commented on it. So he had waited, reaching his own conclusions, prepared to give love, accept authority and trust me for the future. Then came the sword, a gift, it seemed, from me; father to son. And the discovery that had followed hard on it, that I was Ambrosius' son, and the Merlin of the thousand legends told at every fireside. Bastard or no, suddenly he had found himself, and he was royal.

So he had followed me to the King at Luguvallium, seeing himself as Ambrosius' grandson and great-nephew to Uther Pendragon. From this knowledge had come that flashing confidence in battle. He must have thought this was why Uther had flung him the sword, because in default of the absent prince, he, bastard or not, was the next in blood. So he had led the charge, and afterwards accepted the duties and the favours due to a prince.

It also explained why he had never seemed to suspect that he might be the "lost" prince. The stares and whispers and the deference he received he had put down to recognition as my son. He accepted, as most men did, the fact that the High King's heir was abroad at a foreign court, and thought nothing more about it. And once he imagined he had found his place, why should he think again? He was mine, and he was royal, and through me he had a place at the center of the kingdom. Now all at once, cruelly enough, as he must see it, he found himself not only deprived of ambition and the place he had dreamed of, but even of a place as a man's

422

acknowledged son. I, who had lived my youth as a bastard and a no-man's-child, knew how that canker can eat: Ector had tried to spare Arthur this by telling him that he would one day be acknowledged nobly; it had never struck me that he would count in love and confidence on the acknowledgment coming from me.

"Even my name, you see." The dull apology of his tone was worse than the cruelty that shock had brought from him before.

At least, if I could heal nothing else, I could heal his pride. The cost would be counted presently, but he had to know now. I had many times thought how, if it were left to me, I would tell him. Now I spoke straight, the simple truth. "We bear the same name because we are in fact kin to one another. You are not my son, but we are cousins. You, like me, are a grandson of Constantius and a descendant of Maximus the Emperor. Your true name is Arthur, and you are the legitimate son of the High King and Ygraine his Queen."

I thought the silence this time would never break. At my first word his eyes had come up from watching the swirling wine, and fastened on me. His brows were knitted like those of a deaf man straining to hear. The red washed through his face like blood staining a white cloth, and his lips parted. Then he set the goblet down very carefully, and standing up, came to the window near me, and, just as I had done earlier, set his hands on the sill and leaned out into the air.

A bird flew into the bough beside him and began to sing. The sky faded to heron's-egg green, then slowly cooled to hyacinth where thin flakes of cloud floated. Still he stood there, and I waited, without movement or speech.

At length, without turning, he spoke to the bough with its singing bird. "Why this way? Fourteen years. Why not where I belonged?"

So at last I told him the whole story. I began with the vision Ambrosius had shared with me, of the kingdoms united under one king, Dumnonia to Lothian, Dyfed to Rutupiae; Romano-Briton and Celt and loyal *foederatus* fighting as one to keep Britain clear of the black flood that was drowning the rest of the Empire; a version, humbler and more workable, of Maximus' imperial dream, adapted and handed down by my grandfather to my father, and lodged in me by my master's teaching and by the god who had marked me for his service. I told him about Ambrosius' death without other issue, and the ravelled clue the god had thrust into my hand, bidding me follow it. About the sudden passion of the new King Uther for Ygraine, wife of Cornwall's Duke, and about my own connivance at their union, shown by the god that this was the union which would bring its next king to Britain. About Gorlois' death and Uther's remorse, mingled as it was with relief at a death he had more than half wished, but wanted publicly to disclaim and disown; then the consequent banishment of myself and Ralf, and Uther's own threats to disown the child so begotten. Then finally, how pride and common sense between them prevailed, and the child had been handed to me to look after through the dangerous first years of Uther's reign; and how since then the King's illness and the growing power of his enemies had forced him to leave his son in hiding. About some things I said nothing: I did not tell Arthur what I had seen waiting for him, of greatness or pain or glory; and I said no word about Uther's impotence. Nor did I speak of the King's desperate wish for another son to supplant the "bastard" of Tintagel; these were Uther's secrets, and he would not have long now to keep them.

Arthur listened in silence, without interruption. Indeed, at first without movement, so that one might have thought his whole attention was on the slowly brightening sky outside the window, and the song of the blackbird on the bough. But after a while he turned and—though I was not looking at him—I felt his eyes on me at last. When I came to the Coronation feast, and the King's demand for me to bring him to Ygraine's bed, he moved again, going softly across to his former place on the bed. My tale of that wild night when he was begotten was told plainly, exactly as it had happened. But he listened as if it had been the same half-enchanted tale I had told him in the Wild Forest with Bedwyr beside him, himself curled half-sitting, half-lying on my bed, chin on fist, his dark eyes, calm now and shining, on my face.

As I came towards an end it was to be seen that the tale fitted in with all that I had taught him in the past, so that now I was just handing him the last links in the golden lineage and saying, in effect: "All that I have ever taught or told you is summed up in you, yourself."

I stopped at length, and took a draught of wine. He uncurled swiftly from the bed and, bringing the jug, poured more into my goblet. When I thanked him, he stooped and kissed me.

"You," he said quietly, "you, from the very beginning. I wasn't so far wrong after all, was I? I'm as much yours as the King's—more; and Ector's too . . . Then Ralf, I'm glad to know about Ralf. I see . . . Oh, yes, now I begin to see a lot of things." He paced about the room, talking in snatches, half to himself, as restless as Uther. "So much—it's too much to take in, I'll have to have time . . . I'm glad it was you who told me. Did the King mean to tell me himself?"

"Yes. He would have talked to you earlier, if there had been time. I hope there will still be time."

"What do you mean?"

"He's dying, Arthur. Are you ready to be King?"

He stood there, the wine-jug still in his hand, hollow-eyed with lack of sleep, thoughts crowding in on him too fast for expression. "*Today?*"

"I think so. I don't know. Soon."

"Will you be with me?"

"Of course. I told you so."

It was only then, as he set down the jug, smiling, and turned to put out the lamp, that the other thing struck him. I saw the moment when his breath stopped, then was let out again cautiously, the way a man tries his breathing after a mortal stroke.

He had his back to me, reaching up to quench the lamp. I saw that his hand was quite steady. But the other hand, which he tried to hide from me, was making the sign against evil. Then, being Arthur, he did not stay turned away, but faced me.

"I have something to tell *you* now."

"Yes?"

The words came like something being dragged up from a depth. "The woman I was with tonight was Morgause." Then, as I did not speak, sharply: "You knew?"

"Only when it was too late to stop you. But I should have known. Before I ever went to see the King, I knew that something was wrong. Oh, no, nothing of what it was, only that the shadows pressed on me."

"If I had stayed in my room, as you told me . . ."

"Arthur. The thing has happened. It's no use saying 'if this' and 'if that'; can't you see that you're innocent? You obeyed your nature, it's something young men will do. But I, I am to blame. You could curse me, if you wished, for my promise to the King, and for all this secrecy. If I had told you sooner about your birth—"

"You told me to stay here. Even if you didn't know what

ill was in the wind, you knew that if I obeyed you I would be safe. If I had obeyed you, I'd be more than safe, I would still be—" He bit off some word I did not quite hear, then finished, "—clean of this thing. Blame *you?* The blame is mine, and God knows it and will judge between us."

"God will judge us all."

He took three restless strides across the room and back again. "Of all women, my sister, my father's daughter . . ." The words came hard, like a morsel one gags on. I could see the horror clinging to him, like a slug to a green plant. His left hand still made the sign against evil: it is a pagan sign; the sin has been a heavy one before the gods since time began. He halted suddenly, squarely in front of me, even at this moment able to think beyond himself. "And Morgause herself? When she knows what you have just told me, what will she think, knowing the sin we've committed between us? What will she do? If she falls into despair—"

"She will not fall into despair."

"How can you know? You said you didn't know women. I believe that for women these matters are heavier." Horror struck at him again as he thought why. "Merlin, if there should be a child?"

I think there has been no moment in my life when I have had to exert more self-command. He was staring wildly at me; if I had let my thoughts show in my face, God only knows what he might have done. As he spoke the last sentence it was as if the formless shadows which had clawed and brooded over me all night suddenly took form and weight. They were there, clinging round my shoulders, vultures, heavy-feathered and stinking of carrion. I, who had schemed for Arthur's conception, had waited blind and idle while his death also was conceived.

"I shall have to tell her." His voice was edged, desperate.

"Straight away. Even before the High King declares me. There may be those who guess, and she may hear . . ."

He talked on, a little wildly, but I was too busy with my own thoughts to listen. I thought: if I tell him that she knew already, that she is corrupt and that her power, such as it is, is corrupt; if I tell him that she used him deliberately to gather more power to herself; if I tell him these things now, while he is shaken out of his wits by all that has happened in this last day and night, he will take his sword and kill her. And when she dies the seed will die that is to grow corrupt as she is, and eat at his glory as this slug of horror eats at his youth. But if he kills them now he will never use a sword again in God's service, and their corruption will have claimed him before his work is even begun.

I said calmly: "Arthur. Be still now, and listen. I told you, what is done is done, and men must learn to stand by their deeds. Now hear me. One day soon you will be High King, and as you know, I am the King's Prophet. So listen to the first prophecy I shall make for you. What you did, you did in innocence. You alone of Uther's seed are clean. Has no one ever told you the gods are jealous? They insure against too much glory. Every man carries the seed of his own death, and you will not be more than a man. You will have everything; you cannot have more; and there must come a term to every life. All that has happened tonight is that you yourself have set that term. What more could a man want, that he determines his own death? Every life has a death, and every light a shadow. Be content to stand in the light, and let the shadow fall where it will."

He grew quieter as he listened, and at length asked me, calmly enough: "Merlin, what must I do?"

"Leave this to me. For yourself, put it behind you, forget about the night, and think of the morning. Listen, there are the trumpets. Go now, and get some sleep before the day begins."

So, imperceptibly, was the first link forged in the new chain that bound us. He slept, to be ready for the great doings of the morrow, and I sat watchful, thinking, while the light grew and the day came.

6

Ulfin, the King's chamberer, came at length to bid Arthur to the King's presence. I woke the boy, and later saw him go, silent and self-contained, showing a sort of impossible calm like smooth ice over a whirlpool. I think that, being young, he had already begun to put behind him the shadow of the night; the burden was mine now. This was a pattern which was common in the years to come.

As soon as he was gone, ushered out with a ceremony wherein I could see Ulfin remembering that night so long ago, of the boy's conception, and which Arthur himself accepted as if he had known it all his life, I called a servant and bade him bring the Lady Morgause to me.

The man looked surprised, then doubtful; it was to be surmised that the lady was used to do her own summoning. I had neither time nor patience this morning for such things. I said briefly: "Do as I say," and the fellow went, scuttling.

She kept me waiting, of course, but she came. This morning she wore red, the colour of cherries, and over the shoulders of the gown her hair looked rosy fair, larch buds in spring, the colour of apricots. Her scent was heavy and sweet, apricots and honeysuckle mixed, and I felt my stomach twist at the memory. But there was no other resemblance to the girl I had loved—had tried to love—so long ago: in Morgause's long-lidded green eyes there was not even the pretense of innocence. She came in smiling that close-lipped smile, with the prick of a charming dimple at the corner of her mouth, and, making me a reverence, crossed the room gracefully to seat herself in the high-backed chair. She disposed her robe prettily about her, dismissed her women with a nod, then lifted her chin and looked at me enquiringly. Her hands lay still and folded against the soft swell of her belly, and in her the gesture was not demure, but possessive.

Somewhere, coldly, a memory stirred. My mother, standing with her hands held so, facing a man who would have murdered me. "I have a bastard to protect." I believe that Morgause read my thoughts. The dimple deepened prettily, and the gold-fringed lids drooped.

I did not sit, but remained standing across the window from her. I said, more harshly than I had intended: "You must know why I sent for you."

"And you must know, Prince Merlin, that I am not used to being sent for."

"Let us not waste time. You came, and it's just as well. I wish to speak with you while Arthur is still with the King."

She opened her eyes wide at me. "Arthur?"

"Don't make those innocent eyes at me, girl. You knew his name when you took him to your bed last night."

"Can the poor boy not even keep his bed secrets from you?" The light pretty voice was contemptuous, meant to sting. "Did he come running to your whistle to tell you about it, along with everything else? I'm surprised you let him off the chain long enough to take his pleasure last night. I wish you joy of him, Merlin the kingmaker. What sort of king is a half-trained puppy going to make?"

"The sort who is not ruled from his bed," I said. "You have had your night, and that was too much. The reckoning comes now."

Her hands moved slightly in her lap. "You can do me no harm."

"No, I shall do you no harm." The flicker in her eyes showed that she had noticed the change of phrase. "But I am also here," I said, "to see that you do Arthur no harm. You will leave Luguvallium today, and you will not come back to the court."

"I leave court? What nonsense is this? You know that I look after the King; he depends on me for his medicines, I am his nurse. I and his chamberer look after him in all things. You cannot imagine that the King will ever agree to let me go."

"After today," I said, "the King will never want to see you again."

She stared. Her colour was high. This, I could see, mattered to her. "How can you say that? Even you, Merlin, cannot stop me from seeing my father, and I assure you he will not want to let me go. You surely don't mean to tell him what has happened? He's a sick man, a shock might kill him."

"I shall not tell him."

"Then what will you say to him? Why should he agree to having me sent away?"

"That is not what I said, Morgause."

"You said that after today the King would never want to see me again."

"I was not speaking of your father."

"I don't see—" She took a sharp breath, and the green-gilt eyes widened. "But you said . . . the King?" Her breath shortened. "You were speaking of that boy?"

"Of your brother, yes. Where is your skill? Uther is marked for death."

Her hands were working together in her lap. "I know. But . . . you say it comes today?"

I echoed my own question. "Where is your magic? It comes today. So you had better leave, had you not? Once Uther is gone, who will protect you here?"

She thought for a moment. The lovely green-gilt eyes were narrow and sly, not lovely at all. "Against what? Against Arthur? You're so sure you can make them accept him as King? Even if you do, are you trying to tell me that I will need protection against him?"

"You know as well as I do that he will be King. You have skill enough for that, and—in spite of what you said to anger me—skill enough to know what kind of a king. You may not need protection against him, Morgause, but it is certain that you will need it against me." Our eyes locked. I nodded. "Yes. Where he is, I am. Be warned, and go while you can. I can protect him from the kind of magic you wove last night."

She was calm again, seeming to draw into herself. The small mouth tightened in its secret smile. Yes, she had power of a kind. "Are you so sure you are proof against women's magic? It will snare you in the end, Prince Merlin."

"I know it," I said calmly. "Do not think I have not seen my end. And all our ends, Morgause. I have seen power for you, and for the thing you carry, but no joy. No joy, now or ever."

Outside the window, against the wall, was an apricot tree. The sun warmed the fruit, globe on golden globe, scented and heavy. Warmth reflected from the stone wall, and wasps hummed among the glossy leaves, sleepy with scent. So, once before, in a sweet-smelling orchard, I had met hatred and murder, eye to eye.

She sat very still, her hands locked against her belly. Her eyes held mine, seeming to drink at them. The scent of honeysuckle thickened, visibly, drifting in green-gold haze across the lighted window, mingling with the sunshine and the smell of apricots. . . .

"Stop it!" I said contemptuously. "Do you really think that your girl's magic can touch me? No more now than it could before. And what are you trying to do? This is hardly a matter of magic. Arthur knows now who he is, and he knows what he did last night with you. Do you think he will bear you near him? Do you think that he will watch daily, monthly, while a child grows in your belly? He is not a cold or a patient man. And he has a conscience. He believes that you sinned in innocence, as he did. If he thought otherwise, he might act."

"Kill me, you mean?"

"Do you not deserve killing?"

"He sinned, if you call it sin, as much as I."

"He did not know he was sinning, and you did. No, don't waste your breath on me. Why pretend? Even without your magic, you must know that half the court has whispered it since he and I rode in together yesterday. You knew he was Uther's son."

For the first time there was a shade of fear in her face. She said obstinately: "I did not know. You cannot prove I knew. Why should I do such a thing?"

I folded my arms and leaned a shoulder back against the wall. "I will tell you why. First, because you are Uther's daughter, and like him a seeker after casual lusts. Because you have the Pendragon blood in you that makes you desire power, so you take it as it mostly offers itself to women, in a man's bed. You knew your father the King was dying, and feared that there would be no place of power for you as half-sister of the young King whose Queen would later dispossess you. I think you would not have hesitated to kill Arthur, but that you would have less standing, even, at Lot's court, with your own sister as Queen. Whoever became High King would have no need of you, as Uther has. You would be married to some small king and taken to some corner of the land where you would pass your time bearing his children

434

and weaving his war cloaks, with nothing in your hands but the petty power of a family, and what women's magic you have learned and can practise in your little kingdom. That is why you did what you did, Morgause. Because, no matter what it was, you wanted a claim on the young King, even if it was to be a claim of horror and of hatred. What you did last night you did coldly, in a bid for power."

"Who are you to talk to me so? You took power where you could find it."

"Not where I could find it; where it was given. What you have got you took, against all laws of God and men. If you had acted unknowingly, in simple lust, there would be no more to say. I told you, so far he thinks you have no blame. This morning, when he knew what he had done, his first thought was for your distress." I saw the flash of triumph in her eyes, and finished, gently: "But you are not dealing with him, you are dealing with me. And I say that you shall go."

She got swiftly to her feet. "Why did you not tell him then, and let him kill me? Would you not have wanted that?"

"To add another and worse sin? You talk like a fool."

"I shall go to the King!"

"To what purpose? He will spare no thought for you today."

"I am always by him. He will need his drugs."

"I am here now, and Gandar. He will not need you."

"He'll see me if I say I've come to say farewell! I tell you, I will go to him!"

"Then go," I said. "I'll not stop you. If you were thinking of telling him the truth, think again. If the shock kills him, Arthur will be High King all the sooner."

"He would not be accepted! They wouldn't accept him! Do you think Lot will stand by and listen to you? What if I tell *them* what Arthur did last night?"

"Then Lot would become High King," I said equably. "And how long would he let you live, bearing Arthur's child? Yes, you'd better think about it, hadn't you? Either way, there is nothing you can do, except go while you can. Once your sister is married at Christmas, get Lot to find you a husband. That way, you may be safe."

Suddenly, at this, she was angry, the anger of a spitting cat in a corner. "You condemn me, you! You were a bastard, too . . . All my life I have watched Morgian get everything. Morgian! That child to be a Queen, while I . . . Why, she even learns magic, but she has no more idea how to use it for her own ends than a kitten has! She'd do better in a nunnery than on a Queen's throne, and I—I . . ." She stopped on a little gasp, and caught her underlip in her teeth. I thought she changed what she had been about to say. ". . . I, who have something of the power which has made you great, Merlin my cousin, do you think I will be content to be nothing?" Her voice went flat, the voice of a wise-woman speaking a curse which will stick. "And that is what you will be, who are no man's friend, and no woman's lover. You are nothing, Merlin, you are nothing, and in the end you will only be a shadow and a name."

I smiled at her. "Do you think you can frighten me? I see further than you, I believe. I am nothing, yes; I am air and darkness, a word, a promise. I watch in the crystal and I wait in the hollow hills. But out there in the light I have a young king and a bright sword to do my work for me, and build what will stand when my name is only a word for forgotten songs and outworn wisdom, and when your name, Morgause, is only a hissing in the dark." I turned my head then, and called the servant. "Now enough of this, there is no more to say between us. Go and make yourself ready, and get you from court."

The man had come in, and was waiting inside the door glancing, I thought apprehensively, from one to the other of us. From his look, he was a black Celt from the mountains of the west; it is a race that still worships the old gods, so it is possible he could feel, if only partly, some of the stinging presences still haunting the room.

But for me, now, the girl was only a girl, tilting a pretty, troubled face to mine, so that the rose-gold hair streamed from her pale forehead down the cherry gown. To the servant waiting beside the door, it should have seemed an ordinary leave-taking, but for those stinging shadows. She never glanced his way, or guessed what he might see.

When she spoke her voice was composed, calm and low. "I shall go to my sister. She lies at York till the wedding."

"I shall see to it that an escort is ready. No doubt the wedding will still be at Christmas, according to plan. King Lot should join you soon, and give you a place at your sister's court."

There was a brief flash at that, discreetly veiled. I might have tried a guess at what she planned there—that she hoped, even at this late date, to take her sister's place at Lot's side— but I was weary of her. I said: "I'll bid you farewell, then, and a safe journey."

She made a reverence, saying, very low: "We shall meet again, cousin."

I said formally, "I shall look forward to it." She went then, slight, erect, hands folded close again, and the servant shut the door behind her.

I stood by the window, collecting my thoughts. I felt weary, and my eyes were gritty from lack of sleep, but my mind was clear and light, already free of the girl's presence. The fresh air of morning blew in to disperse the evil lingering in the room, till, with the last fading scent of honeysuckle, it was gone. When the servant came back I rinsed face and hands in cold water, then, bidding him follow me, went back to the hospital dormitory. The air was cleaner there, and the eyes of dying men easier to bear than the presence of the woman who was with child of Mordred, Arthur's nephew and bastard son.

7

King Lot, brooding on the edge of affairs, had not been idle. Certain busy gentlemen, friends of his, were seen to be hurrying here and there, protesting to anyone who would listen that it would be more appropriate for Uther to declare his heir from one of his great palaces in London or Winchester. This haste, they said, was unseemly: the thing should be done by custom, with due notice and ceremony, and backed by the blessing of the Church. But they whispered in vain. The ordinary people of Luguvallium, and the soldiers who at present outnumbered them, thought otherwise. It was obvious now that Uther was near his end, and it seemed not only necessary, but right, that he should declare his successor straight away, near the field where Arthur had in a fashion declared himself. And if there was no bishop present, what of it? This was a victory feast and was held, so to speak, still in the field.

The house where the King held court in Luguvallium was packed to the doors, and well beyond them. Outside, in the town and around it, where the troops held their own celebration, the air was blue with the smoke of fires, and thick with the smell of roasting meat. Officers on their way to the King's feast had to work quite hard to turn a blind eye to the drunkenness in camp and street, and a deaf ear to the squeals and giggles coming from quarters where women were not commonly allowed to be.

I hardly saw Arthur all day. He was closeted with the King until afternoon, and in the end only left to allow father to rest before the feast. I spent most of the day in the hospital. It was peaceful there, compared with the crush near the royal apartments. All day, it seemed, the corridors outside my rooms and Arthur's were besieged; by men who wanted favours from the new prince, or just his notice; by men who wanted to talk with me, or to court my favour by gifts; or simply by the curious. I let it be known that Arthur was with the King, and would speak with no one before the time of the feast. To the guards I gave private orders that if Lot should seek me out, I was to be called. But he made no approach. Nor, according to the servants I questioned, was he to be seen in the town.

But I took no chances, and early that morning sent to Caius Valerius, a King's officer and an old acquaintance of mine, for extra guards for my rooms and Arthur's, to reinforce the duty sentries outside the main door, in the antechamber, and even at the windows. And before I went to the hospital I made my way to the King's rooms, to have a word with Ulfin.

It may perhaps seem strange that a prophet who had seen Arthur's crowning so plain and clear and ringed with light should take such pains to guard him from his enemies. But those who have had to do with the gods know that when those gods make promises they hide them in light, and a smile on a god's lips is not always a sign that you may take his favour for granted. Men have a duty to make sure. The gods like the taste of salt; the sweat of human effort is the savour of their sacrifices.

The guards on duty at the King's door lifted their spears without a challenge and let me straight through into the outer chamber. Here pages and servants waited, while in the second chamber sat the women who helped to nurse the King. Ulfin was, as ever, beside the door of the King's room. He rose when he saw me, and we talked for a little while,

of the King's health, of Arthur, of the events of yesterday
and the prospects for tonight; then—we were talking softly,
apart from the women—I asked him:

"You knew Morgause had left the court?"

"I heard so, yes. Nobody knows why."

"Her sister Morgian is waiting in York for the wedding,"
I said, "and anxious for her company."

"Oh, yes, we heard that." It was to be inferred from
the woodenness of his expression that nobody had believed it.

"Did she come to see the King?" I asked.

"Three times." Ulfin smiled. It was apparent that Morgause
was no favourite of his. "And each time she was turned away
because the prince was still with him."

A favoured daughter for twenty years, and forgotten in as
many hours for a true-born son. *"You were a bastard, too,"*
she had reminded me. Years ago, I remembered, I had wondered what would become of her. She had had position and
authority of a sort here with Uther, and might well have
been fond of him. She had (the King had hinted yesterday)
refused marriage to stay near him. Perhaps I had been too
harsh with her, driven by the horror of foreknowledge and
my own single-minded love for the boy. I hesitated, then
asked him: "Did she seem much distressed?"

"Distressed?" said Ulfin crisply. "No, she looked angry.
She's bad to cross, is that lady. Always been so, from a
child. One of her maids was crying, too; I think she'd been
whipped." He nodded towards one of the pages, a fair
boy, very young, kicking his heels at a window. "He was
the one sent to turn her away the last time, and she laid his
cheek open with her nails."

"Then tell him to take care it does not fester," I said, and
such was my tone that Ulfin looked sharply at me, cocking
a brow. I nodded. "Yes, it was I who sent her away. Nor did
she go willingly. You'll know why, one day. Meanwhile,

I take it that you look in now and again upon the King? The interview isn't tiring him overmuch?"

"On the contrary, he's better than I've seen him for some time. You'd think the boy was a well to drink at; the King never takes his eyes from him, and gains strength by the hour. They'll take their midday meal together."

"Ah. Then it will be tasted? That's what I came to ask."

"Of course. You can be easy, my lord. The prince will be safe."

"The King must take some rest before the feast."

He nodded. "I've persuaded him to sleep this afternoon after he has eaten."

"Then will you also—which will be more difficult—persuade the prince that he should do the same? Or, if not rest, then at least go straight to his rooms, and stay in them till the hour of feasting?"

Ulfin looked dubious. "Will he consent to that?"

"If you tell him that the order—but you'd better call it a request—came from me."

"I'll do that, my lord."

"I shall be in the hospital. You'll send for me, of course, if the King needs me. But in any case you must send to tell me the moment the prince leaves him."

It was about the middle of the afternoon when the fair-haired page brought the message. The King was resting, he told me, and the prince had gone to his rooms. When Ulfin had given the prince my message the latter had scowled, impatient, and had said sharply (this part of the message came demurely, verbatim) that he was damned if he'd skulk indoors for the rest of the day. But when Ulfin had said the message came from Prince Merlin the prince had stopped short, shrugged, and then gone to his rooms without further word.

"Then I shall go, too," I said. "But first, child, let me see that scratched cheek." When I had put salve on it, and sent him scampering back to Ulfin, I made my way through corridors more thronged than ever to my rooms.

Arthur was by the window. He turned when he heard me.

"Bedwyr is here, did you know? I saw him, but could not get near. I sent a message that we'd ride out this afternoon. Now you say I may not."

"I'm sorry. There will be other times to talk to Bedwyr, better than this."

"Heaven and earth, they couldn't be worse! This place stifles me. What do they want with me, that pack in the corridors outside?"

"What most men want of their prince and future King. You will have to get used to it."

"So it seems. There's even a guard here, outside the window."

"I know. I put him there." Then, answering his look: "You have enemies, Arthur. Have I not made it clear?"

"Shall I always have to be hemmed in like this, surrounded? One might as well be a prisoner."

"Once you are undoubted King you can make your own dispositions. But until then, you must be guarded. Remember that here we are only in an emergency camp; once in the King's capital, or in one of his strong castles, you'll have your own household, chosen by yourself. You'll be able to see all you want of Bedwyr, or Cei, or anyone else you may appoint. It will be freedom of a sort, as much as you can ever have now. Neither you nor I can go back to the Wild Forest again, Emrys. That's over."

"It was better there," he said, then gave me a gentle look, and smiled. "Merlin."

"What is it?"

443

He started to say something, changed his mind, shook his head instead and said abruptly: "At this feast tonight. You'll be near me?"

"Be sure of it."

"The King has told me how he will present me to the nobles. Do you know what will happen then? These enemies you speak of—"

"Will try to prevent the assembly from accepting you as Uther's heir."

He considered for a moment, briefly. "May they carry arms in the hall?"

"No. They'll try some other way."

"Do you know how?"

I said: "They can hardly deny your birth to the King's face, and with me there and Count Ector they can't quarrel with your identity. They can only try to discredit you; shake the faith of the waverers, and try to swing the army's vote. It's your enemies' misfortune that this has come on a battlefield where the army outnumbers the council of nobles three to one—and after yesterday the army will take some convincing that you are not fit to lead them. It's my guess that there will be something staged, something that will take men by surprise and shake their belief in you, even in Uther."

"And in you, Merlin?"

I smiled. "It's the same thing. I'm sorry, I can't see further yet than that. I can see death and darkness, but not for you."

"For the King?" he asked sharply.

I did not answer. He was silent for a moment, watching me, then, as if I had answered, he nodded, and asked:

"Who are these enemies?"

"They are led by the King of Lothian."

"Ah," he said, and I could see he had not let his senses be stifled through the brief hours of that crowded day. He had seen and heard, watched and listened. "And Urien who runs with him, and Tudwal of Dinpelydr, and—whose is the green badge with the wolverine?"

"Aguisel's. Did the King say anything to you about these men?"

He shook his head. "We talked mostly of the past. Of course he has heard all about me from you and Ector over these past years, and"—he laughed—"I doubt if any son ever knew more about his father and his father's father than I, with all you have told me; but telling is not the same. There was a lot of knowing to make up."

He talked on for a little about the interview with the King, speaking of the missed years without regret, and with the cool common sense that I had come to see was part of his character. That much, I thought, was not from Uther; I had seen it in Ambrosius, and in myself, in what men called coldness. Arthur had been able to stand back from the events of his youth; he had thought the thing through, and with the clear sight that would make him a king he had set feeling aside and come to the truth. Even when he went on to speak of his mother it was evident that he saw the matter much as Ygraine had done, and with the same hard expediency of outlook. "If I had known that my mother was still alive, and had been so willingly parted from me, it might have come hard to me, as a child. But you and Ector spared me that by telling me she was dead, and now I see it as you say she saw it; that to be a prince one must be ruled always by necessity. She did not give me up for nothing." He smiled, but his voice was still serious. "It was true as I told you. I was better in the Wild Forest thinking myself motherless, and your bastard, than waiting yearly in my father's castle for the Queen to bear another child to supplant me."

In all those years I had never seen it so. I had been blinded by my larger purposes, thinking all the time of his safety, of the kingdom's future, of the gods' will. Until the boy Emrys had burst into my life that morning in the Wild Forest, he had hardly been a person to me, only a symbol, another life (as it were) for my father, a tool for me. After I came to know and love him I had seen only the deprivations we had subjected him to, with his high temper and leaping ambition to be first and best, and his quick generosity and affection. It was no use telling myself that without me he might never have come near his heritage at all; I had lived with guilt for all that he had been robbed of.

No question but that he had felt the deprivation, the bite of dispossession. But even here, even now in the moment of finding himself, he could see clearly what that princely childhood would have meant. I knew he was right. Even apart from the daily dangers, he would have had a hard time of it beside Uther, and the high qualities, wasting with time and hope deferred, might have turned sour. But the admission, to absolve me, had to come from him. Now it lifted my guilt from me as cool air lifts a marsh mist.

He was still speaking of his father. "I like him," he said. "He has been a good king as far as it was in him. Standing apart from him as I have done, I have been able to listen to men talking, and to judge. But as a father—as to how we would have dealt together, that's another matter. There is time still to know my mother. She will need comfort soon, I think."

He referred only once, briefly, to Morgause.

"They say she has left the town?"

"She went this morning while you were with the King."

"You spoke with her? How did she take it?"

"Without distress," I said, with perfect truth. "You needn't fear for her."

"Did you send her away?"

"I advised her to go. As I advise you to put it out of your mind. For the moment, at any rate, there is nothing to be done. Except—I suggest—sleep . . . Today has been hard, and will be harder for both of us before it's done. So if you can forget the crowds outside and the guard beyond the window, I suggest we both sleep till sundown."

He yawned suddenly, widely, like a young cat, then laughed. "Have you put a spell on me to make sure of it? Suddenly I feel I could sleep for a week. . . . All right, I'll do as you say, but may I send a message to Bedwyr?"

He did not speak of Morgause again, and I think that soon, in the final preparations for the evening's feast, he forgot her. Certainly the haunted look of the morning had left him, and it seemed to me that no shadow touched him now; doubt and apprehension would have wisped off his charged and shining youth like water-drops from white-hot metal. Even if he had guessed, as I did, what the future held —that it was greater than he could have imagined, and in the end more terrible—I doubt if it would have dimmed his brightness. When one is fourteen, death at forty seems still to be several lifetimes away.

An hour after sundown, they came for us to lead us to the hall of feasting.

8

The hall was packed to the doors. If the place had seemed crowded before, by the time the trumpets sounded for the feast there was barely breathing-room in the corridors; it seemed as if even those sturdy Roman-built walls must bulge and crumble under the press of excited humanity. For rumour had run like a forest fire through the countryside that this was no ordinary victory feast, and even from parts of the province twenty or thirty miles off people were pouring into Luguvallium to be there for the great occasion.

It would have been impossible to sift and select the followers of those privileged nobles who were allowed into the main hall where the King would sit. At a feast of this kind men expected to leave their weapons outside, and this was enforced, till the antechamber, stacked as it was with thickets of spears and swords, looked like a grove of the Wild Forest. More than this the guards could not do, save run an eye over each man's person as he entered the hall, to see that he carried only the knife or dagger he needed for his food.

By the time the company was assembled the sky outside was paling to dusk, and torches were lit. Soon, with the smoky torchlight and the mild evening, the food and wine and talk and laughter, the place was uncomfortably warm, and I watched the King anxiously. He seemed in good enough spirits, but his colour was too high and his skin had a glazed, transparent look that I have seen before in men who are pushed to the limits of their strength. But he was perfectly in command of himself, talking cheerfully and courteously to Arthur on his right, and to the others about him, though at times he would fall into silence and seem to be drifting, forgetfully, into some place far away from which he would recall himself with a jerk. At one point he asked me—I was seated on his left—if I knew why Morgause had not come to see him that day. He asked without concern, without even much interest; it was obvious that he had not taken in the fact that she had left the court. I told him that she had wanted to go to her sister at York, and that since the King had been unable to see her I myself had given her permission, and sent her with an escort. I added quickly that the King need have no fears for his health, since I was here and would attend him personally. He nodded and thanked me, but as if my offer of help was something no longer needed: "I have had the best doctors I could have had this day; victory, and this boy beside me." He laid a hand on Arthur's arm, and laughed. "You heard what the Saxon dogs were calling me? The half-dead King. I heard them shouting it when I was carried forward in my chair . . . And so in truth I think I was, but now I have both victory and life."

He had spoken clearly, and men leaned forward to listen, and afterwards murmured approval, while the King went back to picking at his food. Ulfin and I had both warned him that he must eat and drink sparingly, but there had been no need for such advice; he had little appetite, and Ulfin saw to it that his wine was well watered. And Arthur's, too. He sat beside his father, his back straight as a spear, and the tension and excitement of the occasion had taken some of the colour from his cheeks. For once he hardly seemed to notice what he was eating. He spoke little, and then only when he was addressed, answering briefly and obviously only for courtesy. Most of the time he sat silent, his eyes on the throng in the hall below the royal dais. I, who knew him, could see what he was doing; he was telling over face by face, blazon by blazon, the toll of the men who were there, and noting where they sat. Noting also how they looked. This face was hostile, that friendly, this undecided and ready to be swayed by promises of power or gain, that foolish or merely curious. I could read them myself, as clearly as if they were red and white pieces ready on the board to play, but for a youth not yet turned fifteen, and on such a highly charged occasion, it was a marvel that he could collect himself to watch them so. Years afterwards he was still able to tally exactly the forces which assembled for and against him that first night of his power. Only twice did that cool look linger and soften; on Ector, not far from where we sat, solid, dependable Ector, beaming a little moist-eyed across his wine as he watched his foster-son jewelled and resplendent in white and silver at the High King's side. (I thought that Cei's glance beside him was less than enthusiastic, but Cei had, at best, low brows and a narrow face that gave even his enthusiasms a grudging look.) Down the hall, beside his father the King of Benoic, was Bedwyr, his plain face flushed and his soul, as they say, in his eyes. The two boys' eyes met and met again during the feasting. Here, already, the next strong thread was being woven of the new kingdom's pattern.

The feast wore on. I watched Uther carefully, wondering if he could last until the proclamation was made and the thing done, or if he would lack the strength to see it through. In which case I would have to choose the moment to intervene, or the work would have to be done with fighting. But his strength held. At last he looked round and raised a hand, and the trumpets rang out for silence. The clamour hushed, and all eyes turned to the high table. This had been deliberately raised, for it was beyond the King's strength to stand. Even so, upright in his great chair, with the blaze of lights and banners behind him, he looked alert and splendid, commanding silence.

He laid his hands along the carved arms of his chair, and began to speak. He was smiling.

"My lords, you all know why we are met here tonight. Colgrim has been put to flight, and his brother Badulf, and already reports have been coming back that the enemy is fled in disorder back towards the coast, beyond the wild lands to the north." He went on to speak of the previous day's victory, as decisive, he said, as his brother's victory at Kaerconan had been, and as potent an augury for the future. "The power of our enemies, which has been massing and threatening for so many years, is broken and driven back for a time. We have a breathing space. But more important than this, my lords, we have seen how this breathing space was won; we have seen what unity can do, and what we might suffer from the lack of it. Singly, what could we do, the kings of the north, the kings of the south and west? But together, held and fighting together, with one leader and one plan, we can thrust the sword of Macsen again into the heart of the enemy."

He had spoken, of course, figuratively, but I caught Arthur's half-start of recollection, and the flash of a glance across at me, before he went back to his steady scrutiny of the hall.

The King had paused. Ulfin, behind him, moved forward with a goblet of wine, but the King motioned it aside, and began to speak again. His voice was stronger, with the ring almost of his old vigour. "For this is a lesson which the last years have taught us. There must be one leader, one strong High King to whom all the kingdoms pay undoubted homage. Without this, we are back where we were before the Romans came. We are divided and lost as Gaul and Germany have been divided and lost; we splinter into small peoples, fighting each other as wolves do for food and space, and never turning against the common enemy; we become a submerged province of Rome, sliding with her to her downfall, instead of a new kingdom emerging as a unit with its own laws, its own people, its own gods. With the right king, faithfully followed, I believe that this will come. Who knows, the Dragon of Britain may be lifted, if not as high as the Eagles of Rome, then with a pride and a vision that will be even farther seen."

The silence was absolute. It could have been Ambrosius speaking. Or Maximus himself, I thought. So do the gods speak when they are waited for.

This time the pause was longer. The King had contrived that it should seem like an orator's, a pause to gather eyes, but I saw how his hands whitened on the chair-arms, how carefully he used the pause to gather strength. I thought I was the only one who noticed; hardly an eye was on Uther, they all watched the boy at his right. All, that is, except the King of Lothian; he was watching the High King, with a kind of eagerness in his face. Ulfin, as the King paused, was beside him again with the goblet; catching my eye, he touched it to his own lips, tasted, then gave it to the King, who drank. There was no way of disguising the tremor in the hand which raised the goblet to his mouth, but before he could betray his weakness further, Ulfin had gently taken the thing from his hand, and set it down. All this, I saw, Lot had followed, still with that same concentrated eagerness. He must recognize how sick Uther was, and minute by minute he must be hoping for the High King's strength to fail him. Either Morgause had told him, or he had guessed what I knew for certain, that Uther would not live long enough physically to establish Arthur on the throne, and that in the free-for-all which might develop round the person of so young a ruler, Arthur's enemies would find their chance.

When Uther began to speak again his voice had lost much of its vigour, but the silence was so complete that he hardly needed to raise it. Even those men who had drunk too much were solemnly intent as the King began to speak again about the battle, about those who had distinguished themselves, and the men who had fallen; finally, about the part Arthur had played in saving the day, and then about Arthur himself.

"You have all known, for these many years, that my son by Ygraine my Queen was being nurtured and trained for the kingship in lands away from these, and in hands stronger than, alas, my own have been since my malady overtook me. You have known that when the time came, and he was grown, he would be declared by name, Arthur, as my heir, and your new King. Now be it known to all men where their lawful prince has spent the years of his youth; first under the protection of my cousin Hoel of Brittany, then in the house of my faithful servant and fellow-soldier, Count Ector of Galava. And all the time he has been guarded and taught by my kinsman Merlin called Ambrosius, to whose hands he was committed at his birth, and whose fitness for the guardianship no man can question. Nor will you question the reasons which prompted me to send the prince away until such time as he might publicly be shown to you. It is a practice common enough among the great, to rear their children in other courts, where they may stay unspoiled by arrogance, uncorrupted by flattery, and safe from the contriving of treachery and ambition." He waited for a moment to regain his breath. He was looking down at the table as he spoke, and met no one's eyes, but here and there a man shifted in his seat or glanced at another; and Arthur's cool gaze took note of it.

The King went on: "And those of you who had wondered what sort of shifts might be used to train a prince, other than sending him as a boy into battle, and into council alongside his father, have seen yesterday how he received the King's sword easily from the King's hand, and led the troops to victory as surely as if he had been High King himself and a seasoned warrior."

Uther's breath was short now, and his colour bad. I saw Lot's eyes intent, and Ulfin's worried look. Cador was frowning. I thought briefly back, with thankfulness, to the talk I had had with him beside the lake. Cador and Lot: had Cador been less his father's son, how easy it would have been for the two of them to tear the land north and south, parcel it out between them like a pair of fighting dogs, while the landless pup whined starving.

"And so," said the High King, and in the silence his gasping breath was horribly apparent, "I present to you all my true born and only son, Arthur called Pendragon, who will be High King after my death, and who will carry my sword in battle from this time on."

He reached his hand to Arthur, and the boy stood up, straight and unsmiling, while the shouting and the cheering went roaring up into the smoky roof. The noise must have been heard clear through the town. When men paused to draw breath the echoes of the acclamation could be heard running out through the streets as a fire runs through stubble on a dry day. There was approval in the shouting, there was obvious relief that at last the issue was clear, and there was joy. I saw Arthur, cool as a cloud, assessing which lay where. But from where I sat I could also see the pulse leaping below the rigid jawline. He stood as a swordsman stands, at rest after one victory, but alert for the next challenge.

It came. Clear above the shouting and the thumping of drinking-vessels on the boards came Lot's voice, harsh and carrying.

"I challenge the choice, King Uther!"

It was like throwing a boulder down into the path of a fast-flowing stream. The noise checked; men stared, muttered, shifted and looked about them. Then all at once it could be seen that the stream divided. There was cheering still for Arthur and the King's choice, but here and there were shouts of "Lothian! Lothian!" and through it all Lot said strongly: "An untried boy? A boy who has seen one battle? I tell you, Colgrim will be back all too soon, and are we to have a boy to lead us? If you must hand on your sword, King Uther, hand it to a tried and seasoned leader, to be held in trust for this young boy when he is grown!" He finished the challenge with a crash of his fist on the table, and round him the clamour broke out again: "Lothian! Lothian!" and then farther off down the hall, confusedly, other challenges being shouted down by "Pendragon!" and "Cornwall!" and even "Arthur!" It was to be seen then, as the clamour mounted, that only the fact that men were unarmed prevented worse things than insults being hurled from side to side of the hall. The servants had backed to the walls, and chamberlains bustled here and there, white-faced and placatory. The King, ashen, threw up a hand, but the gesture went almost unnoticed. Arthur neither moved nor spoke, but he had gone rather pale.

"My lords! My lords!" Uther was shaking, but with rage; and rage, as I knew, was as dangerous to him as a spear thrust. I saw that Lot knew it, too. I laid a hand on Uther's arm. "All will be well," I told him softly. "Sit back now and let them shout it out. Look, Ector is speaking."

"My lord King!" Ector's voice was brisk, friendly, matter-of-fact, cooling the atmosphere in the hall. He spoke as if addressing the King alone. The effect was noticeable; the hall grew quiet as men strained to hear him. "My lord King, the King of Lothian has challenged your choice. He has a right to speak, as all your subjects have a right to speak before you, but not to challenge, not even to question, what you have said tonight." Raising his voice a little he turned to the listening hall. "My lords, this is not a matter of choice or election; a king's heir is begotten, not chosen by him, and where chance has provided such a begetting as this, what question is there? Look at him now, this prince who has been presented to you. He has been in my household for ten years, and I, my lords, knowing him as I do, tell you that here is a prince to be followed—not later, not 'when he is further grown,' but now. Even if I could not stand before you here to attest his birth, you have only to look at him and to think back to yesterday's field, to know that here, with all fortune and God's blessing, we have our true and rightful King. This is not open to challenge, even to question. Look at him, my lords, and remember yesterday! Who more fit to unite the kings from all the corners of Britain? Who more fit to wield his father's sword?"

There were shouts of "True! True!" and "What doubt can there be? He is Pendragon, and therefore our King!" and a hubbub of voices that was louder and more confused even than before. Briefly, I remembered my father's councils, their power and order; then I saw again how Uther shook, ashen in his great chair. The times were different; this was the way he had had to do it; he could not enforce it other than by public acclaim.

Before he could speak, Lot was smoothly on his feet again. He was no longer shouting; he spoke weightily, with an air of reason, and a courteous inclination towards Ector. "It was not the prince's begetting that I challenged, it was the fitness of a young and untried youth to lead us. We know that the battle yesterday was only the preliminary, the first move in a longer and more deadly fight even than Ambrosius faced, a struggle such as we have not seen since the days of Maximus. We need better leadership than is shown by a day's luck in

456

a skirmish. We need, not a sick king's deputy, but a man vested with all the authority and God-given blessing of an anointed ruler. If this young prince is indeed fit to carry his father's sword, would his father be content to yield it to him now, before us all?"

Silence again, for three heart-beats. Every man there knew what it meant for the King formally to hand over the royal sword; it was abdication. Only I, of all the men in the hall except perhaps Ulfin, knew that it mattered nothing whether or not Uther abdicated now; Arthur would be King before night. But Uther did not know, and whether, even knowing his weakness, Uther was great enough to renounce publicly the power which had been the breath of life to him was not known even to me. He was sitting quite straight, apparently impassive, and only one as near to him as I could see how the palsy from time to time shook his body, so that light shivered in the circlet of red gold that bound his brow, and shook in the jewels on his fingers. I rose quietly from my chair and went to stand close beside him, at his left hand. Arthur, frowning, glanced questioningly at me. I shook my head at him.

The King licked his lips, hesitating. Lot's change of tone had puzzled him, as, it could be seen, it had puzzled others in the hall. But it had also relieved the waverers, those who were scared by the idea of rebellion, but found relief from their fear of the future in his air of reason and his deference to the High King. There were murmurs of approval and agreement. Lot spread his hands wide, as if including with him everyone in the body of the hall, and said, with that air of speaking reasonably for all of them: "My lords, if we could but see the King give his chosen heir the royal sword with his own hands, what could we do but acknowledge him? Afterwards, it will be time enough to discuss how best to face the coming wars."

Arthur's head turned slightly, like a hound's that catches an unfamiliar scent. Ector too looked round at the other men, surprised perhaps and distrustful of the apparent capitulation. Cador, silent at the other side of the room, stared at Lot as though he would drag his soul out from his eyes. Uther bent his head slightly, a gesture of abnegation which became him like nothing I had seen in him before.

"I am willing."

A chamberlain went running. Uther leaned back in the great chair, shaking his head as Ulfin proffered wine again. I dropped a hand unobtrusively to the wrist beside me; his pulse was all anyhow, a grasshopper pulse in a wrist gone suddenly frail and stringy, which before had been narrow with nerve and sinew. His lips were dry, and his tongue came out to moisten them. He said softly: "There's some trick here, but I can't see it. Can you?"

"Not yet."

"He has no real following. Not even among the army, after yesterday. But now . . . you may have to deal with it. They don't want facts, or even promises. You know them, what they want is a sign. Can you not give them one?"

"I don't know. Not yet. The gods come when they come."

Arthur had caught the whisper. He was as tight as a strung bow. Then he looked across the hall, and I saw his mouth relax slightly. I followed his look. It was Bedwyr, scarlet with fury, held down forcibly in his seat by his father's heavy hand. Otherwise I think that he would have been at Lot's throat with his bare hands.

The chamberlain came running, with Uther's battle sword laid, scabbarded, across his palms. The rubies in the hilt glinted balefully. The scabbard was of silver gilded, crusted with fine gold-work and gems. There was no man there but had seen the sword a hundred times at Uther's side. The man laid it flat on the table in front of the King. Uther's thin hand went out to the hilt, the fingers curving round it without thinking, fitting to the guard, a caress rather than a grip, the hold of the good fighting man. Arthur watched him, and I could see the flicker of puzzlement between his brows. He was thinking of the sword in the stone up there in the Wild Forest, wondering no doubt where that came into this formal scene of abdication.

But I, as the fire from the great rubies burned against my eyes, knew at last what the gods were doing. It was clear from the beginning, fire and dragon-star and the sword in the stone. And the message did not come through the smoke from the doubly-smiling god, it was clear as the flame in the ruby. Uther's sword would fail, as Uther himself had failed. But the other would not. It had come by water and by land and lay waiting now for this, to bring Arthur his kingdom, and keep and hold it, and afterwards go from men's sight for ever. . . .

The King laid firm hold of the hilt, and drew his sword. "I, Uther Pendragon, do by this token give to Arthur my son—"

There was a great gasp, then a hubbub of noise. Men cried out fearfully, "A sign! A sign!" and someone shouted, "Death! It means death!" and the whispers that had been stilled by victory, waking again: "What hope for us, a wasted land, and a maimed king, and a boy without a sword?"

As the sword came clear of the scabbard Uther lurched to his feet. He held it crookedly, half-lifted, staring down at it with ashen face and his mouth half open, struck still like a man out of his wits. The sword was broken. A handspan from the point the metal had snapped jaggedly, and the break shone raw and bright in the torchlight.

The King made some sound; it was as if he tried to speak, but the words choked in his throat. The sword sank with a clatter to the board. As his legs failed under him, Ulfin and I took him gently by the arms and eased him back into his chair. Arthur moved, fast as a mountain cat, to bend over him. "Sir? Sir?"

Then he straightened slowly, his eyes on me. There was no need for me to tell him what every man in the hall could see. Uther was dead.

9

Uther dead did more than Uther dying could have done to control the panic that had swept the hall. Every man there was held, silent and still, on his feet, watching the High King as we lowered him gently against the back of the chair. In the stillness the flames in the torches rustled like silk, and the goblet Ulfin had dropped rolled ringing in a half circle and back again. I leaned forward over the dead King and closed his eyes.

Then Lot's voice, collected and forceful: "A sign indeed! A dead king and a broken sword! Do you still say, Ector, that God has appointed this boy to lead us against the Saxon invader? A maimed land indeed, with nothing between us and the Terror but a boy with a broken sword!"

Confusion again. Men shouting, turning to one another, staring about them in fear and amazement. Part of my mind noted, coldly, that Lot had not been surprised. Arthur, eyes blazing in a face paler than ever with shock, straightened from his father's body and whipped round to face the shouting in the hall, but I said swiftly, "No. Wait," and he obeyed me. But his hand had dropped to his dagger and gripped there, whitening. I doubt if he knew it, or, knowing, could have stopped himself. The turmoil of astonishment and fear jarred from wall to wall like waves in the wind.

Through the commotion came Ector's voice again, harsh and shaken, but sturdily matter-of-fact as before, brushing aside the strands of superstitious fear like a broom clearing cobwebs. "My lords! Is this seemly? Our High King is dead,

461

here before our eyes. Dare we oppose his plain will when his eyes are hardly closed? We all saw what caused his death, the sight of the royal sword, which yesterday was whole, broken in its sheath. Are we to let this—accident"—he dropped the word heavily into the hush—"frighten us like children from doing what it is plain that we should do? If you look for a sign, there it is." He pointed at Arthur, standing straight as a pine beside the dead King's chair. "As one king falls, another is ready in his place. God sent him today for this. We must acknowledge him."

A pause, full of murmuring, while men looked at one another. There were nods, and shouts of agreement, but here and there still looks of doubt, and voices calling out, "But the sword? The broken sword?"

Ector said sturdily: "King Lot here called it a sign, this broken sword. A sign of what? I say, my lords, of treachery! This sword did not break in the High King's hand, nor in his son's."

"That's true," said another voice forcibly. Bedwyr's father, the King of Benoic, was on his feet. "We all saw it, whole in the battle. And by God, we saw it used!"

"But since then?" The questions came from every quarter of the hall. "Afterwards? Would the King have sent for it had he known it to be broken?" Then from some speaker at the end of the hall, invisible in the press: "But would the High King have consented to hand it to the boy, if it had still been whole?" And another voice, which I thought was Urien's: "He knew he was dying. He gave up the maimed land with the broken sword. It is for the strongest now to take up the kingship."

Ector, darkly flushed, broke in again: "I spoke the truth when I talked of treachery! In good time did the High King present his heir to us, or Britain would indeed be maimed, torn apart by disloyal dogs such as you, Urien of Gore!"

Urien shouted with anger, and his hand went to his dagger. Lot spoke to him, sharply, under cover of the tumult, and he subsided. Lot was smiling, his eyes narrow and watchful. His voice came smoothly: "We all know what interest Count Ector has in proclaiming his ward High King."

There was a sudden, still pause. I saw Ector glance round him, as if he would have conjured a weapon out of the air. Arthur's hand clenched tighter on his dagger's hilt. Then suddenly there was a stir from the right of the hall, where Cador stood forward among his men. The white Boar of Cornwall stretched and hunched itself on his sleeve as he moved. He looked round for quiet, and got it. Lot turned his head quickly; it was evident that he did not know what to expect. Ector controlled himself and subsided, rumbling. All around I saw the frightened men, the waverers, the time-servers, looking to Cador as men look for a lead in danger.

Cador's voice was clear and totally lacking in emotion. "What Ector says is true. I myself saw the High King's sword after the battle, when his son handed it back to him. It was whole and unmarked, save with the blood of the enemy."

"Then how is it broken? Is it treachery? Who broke it?"

"Who indeed?" said Cador. "Not the gods, for sure, whatever King Lot may think. The gods do not break the swords of the kings they favour with victory. They give them, and give them whole."

"Then if Arthur is our king," cried someone, "what sword have they given him?"

Cador looked up the hall: it was to be seen that he was expecting me to speak. But I said nothing. I had drawn back to stand behind Arthur in the shadow of the King's great chair. It was my place, and it was time they saw me take it. There was a kind of waiting pause, as heads turned to where I stood, a black shadow behind the boy's white and

463

silver. Men shuffled and murmured. There were those here who had known my power, and there was no man present who doubted it. Not even Lot; the whites of his eyes showed as he looked askance. But when I still did not speak, there were smiles. I could see the tension in Arthur's shoulders, and I spoke to him in silence with my will. *"Not yet, Arthur, not yet. Wait."*

He was silent. He had picked up the broken sword, and was gently fitting it back into its scabbard. As it went, it gave one sharp flash and then was quenched.

"You see?" said Cador to the hall. "Uther's sword is gone, and so is he. But Arthur has a sword, his own, and greater than this royal one that men have broken. The gods gave it to him. I saw it in his hand myself."

"When?" they asked. "Where? What gods? What sword was this?"

Cador waited, smiling, for the buzz of questions to die. He stood easily, a big man with that air of his of relaxed but ready power. Lot was biting his lip, and frowning. There was sweat thick on his forehead, and his eyes shifted round the hall, reckoning the tally of those who still supported him. From his look, he had still hoped that Cador might range himself against Arthur.

Cador had not looked at him. "I saw him once with Merlin," he told the company, "up in the Wild Forest, and he carried a sword more splendid than any I have seen before, jewelled like an Emperor's, and with a blade of light so bright that it burned the eyes."

Lot cleared his throat. "An illusion. It was done by magic. You said Merlin was there. We all know what that means. If Merlin is Arthur's master—"

A man interrupted, smallish, with black hair and a high colour. I recognized Gwyl from the western coast, on whose hills the druids meet still. "And if it was magic, what then?

Look you, a king who has magic in his hand is a king to follow."

This brought a yell of approval. Fists hammered on the tables. Many of the men in the hall were mountain Celts, and this was talk they understood. "That is true, that is true! Strength is good, but of what use is it without luck? And our new King, though he is young, has both. It was true what Uther said, good training and good counsel. What better counsel could he have, than Merlin to stand beside him?"

"Good training indeed," shouted a boy's voice, "that doesn't hang back in battle till it's almost too late!" It was Bedwyr, forgetting himself. His father quenched him with a cuff to the side of the head, but the blow fell lightly, and the admonitory hand slid over to ruffle the boy's hair. There were smiles. The heat was cooling. The ferment brought about by the stroke of superstitious fear had passed, and men were calming, ready now to listen and to think. One or two who had seemed to favour Lot and his faction were seen to withdraw a little from him. Then someone called out: "Why doesn't Merlin speak? Merlin knows what we should do. Let him tell us!" Then the shouting began: "Merlin! Merlin! Let Merlin speak!"

I let them shout for a few minutes. Then when they were ready to tear the hall stone from stone to hear me, I spoke. I neither moved nor raised my voice, standing there between the dead King and the living one, but they hushed, listening.

"I have two things to tell you," I said. "First, that the King of Lothian was wrong. I am not Arthur's master. I am his servant. And the second is what the Duke of Cornwall has already told you; that between us and the Saxon Terror is a King, young and whole, with a sword given straight into his hand by God."

Lot could see the moment slipping from him. He looked

around him, shouting: "A fine sword indeed, that appears in his hand as an illusion, and vanishes from it in battle!"

"Don't be a fool," said Ector gruffly. "That was one I lent him that was cut from him in the fight. My second best, too, so I'm not repining."

Someone laughed. There were smiles, and when Lot spoke again there was defeat under the sick rage in his voice. "Then where did he get this sword of marvels, and where is it now?"

I said: "He went alone to Caer Bannog and lifted it from its place below the lake."

Silence. There was no one here who did not know what that meant. I saw hands moving to make the sign against enchantment.

Cador stirred. "It is true. I myself saw Arthur come back from Caer Bannog with the thing in his hand, wrapped in an old scabbard as if it had lain in hiding for a hundred years."

"Which it had," I said into the silence. "Listen, my lords, and I will tell you what sword this is. It is the sword which Macsen Wledig took to Rome, and which was brought back to Britain by his people and hidden until it should please the gods to lead a King's son to find it. Must I remind you of the prophecy? It was not my prophecy, it was made before I was born; that the sword should come by water and by land, treasured in darkness and locked in stone, until he should come who is rightwise king born of all Britain, and lift it from its hiding-place. And there it has lain, my lords, safe in Caer Bannog, in Bilis' castle, until by magic signs sent from the gods did Arthur find it, and lifted it easily into his hand."

"Show us!" they cried. "Show us!"

"I shall show you. The sword lies now on the altar in the chapel of the Wild Forest where I laid it. It shall lie there till Arthur lifts it in the sight of you all."

466

Lot was beginning to be afraid; they were against him now, and by his actions he had confirmed himself as Arthur's enemy. But so far I had spoken quietly, without power, and he still saw a chance. The obstinacy which had driven him, and the stupidity of his own hope of power, sustained him now. "I have seen that sword, the sword in the altar of the Green Chapel. Many of you have seen it! It is Macsen's sword, yes, but it is made of stone!"

I moved then. I lifted my arms high. From somewhere, a breeze ran in through the open windows and stirred the coloured hangings so that behind Arthur the scarlet Dragon clawed up the golden banner, and sent my shadow towering like the Dragon's shadow, with arms raised like wings. The power was here. I heard it in my voice.

"And from the stone has he lifted it, and will lift it again, in the sight of you all. And from this day on, the chapel shall be called the Chapel Perilous, for if any man who is not the rightful King shall so much as touch the sword, it shall burn like levin in his hand."

Someone in the crowd said strongly: "If he has indeed got the sword of Macsen, he got it by God's gift, and if he has Merlin beside him, then by any god he follows, I follow him!"

"And I," said Cador.

"And I! And I!" came the shouts from the hall. "Let us all see this magic sword and this perilous altar!"

Every man was on his feet. The shouting rose and echoed in the roof. "Arthur! Arthur!"

I dropped my arms. *"Now, Arthur, it is now."*

He had not once looked at me, but he heard my thought, and I felt the power going out of me towards him. I could see it growing round him as he stood there, and every man in the hall could see it too. He raised a hand, and they

467

waited for him. His voice came clear and firm: no boy's voice, but that of a man who has fought his first decisive battles, there in the field, and here in the hall.

"My lords. You saw how fate sent me to my father without a sword, as was fitting. Now treachery has broken the weapon he would have given me, and treachery has tried to take with it my birthright that is proven in front of you all, and was attested by my father the High King in open hall. But as Merlin has told you, God had already put another, greater weapon into my hand, and I shall indeed take it up in front of you all, as soon as I may come with all this company, to the Perilous Chapel."

He paused. It is not easy to speak after the gods have spoken. He finished simply, cool water after the flames. The torches had died to red and my shadow had dwindled from the wall. The Dragon banner hung still.

"My lords, we shall ride there in the morning. But now it is seemly that we should attend the High King, and see his body laid in kingly fashion, and guards set, before it can be taken to its resting-place. Then those who will may take up their swords and spears, and ride with me."

He finished. Cador came striding up the hall and with him Ector, and Gwyl, and Bedwyr's father King Ban, and a score of others. I stepped quietly back, leaving Arthur standing there alone, with the King's guard behind him. I made a sign, and servants stooped to lift and carry out the chair where, all this time, the dead King had sat stiffening, with no man looking his way save only Ulfin, who was weeping.

10

As soon as I left the hall I sent a servant running with a
message that a swift horse was to be made ready for me.
Another fetched my sword and cloak, and very soon, without attracting much notice, I was able to slip quietly through
the thronged corridors and out to the courtyard.

The horse was there, ready. I thought I recognized it, then
saw from its housings that it was Ralf's big chestnut. Ralf
himself waited at its head, his face strained and anxious.
Beyond the high walls of the courtyard the town hummed
like a tumbled skep of bees, and lights were everywhere.

"What's this?" I asked him. "Didn't they get my message
right? I go alone."

"So they said. The horse is for you. He's faster than your
own, and sure on his feet, and he knows the forest tracks.
And if you do meet trouble—" He left the sentence un-
finished, but I understood him. The horse was trained to
battle, and would fight for me like an extra arm.

"Thank you." I took the reins from him, and mounted.
"They're expecting me at the gate?"

"Yes. Merlin"—he still kept a hand on the reins—"let me
come with you. You shouldn't ride alone. You've a bad
enemy there who'll stop at nothing."

"I know that. You'll serve me better by staying here and
seeing that no one rides after me. Are the gates shut?"

"Yes, I saw to it. No rider but you leaves this place now
until Arthur and the others ride out. But they tell me that

there were two men slipped out before the company left the hall."

I frowned. "Lot's?"

"No one seems clear on that. They said they were messengers taking the news of the King's death south."

"No messenger was sent," I said curtly. I had ordered this myself. The news of the High King's death, with the fear and uncertainty it would engender, must not be carried beyond the walls until there could go with it news of a new King and a new crowning.

Ralf nodded. "I know. These two got through just before the order came. It could just be someone hoping for a purse —one of the chamberlains, perhaps, sending word south as soon as it happened. But it could just as soon be Lot's men, you know it could. What could he be planning? To break Macsen's sword, as he broke Uther's?"

"You think he could?"

"N—no. But if he can do nothing, then why are you riding up there now? Why not wait and ride up with the prince?"

"Because it's true that Lot will stop at nothing now to destroy Arthur's claim. He's worse than ambitious now, he's frightened. He'll do anything to discredit me, and shake men's faith in the sword as God's gift. So I must go. God does not defend himself. Why are we here, if not to fight for him?"

"You mean—? I see. They could desecrate the shrine, or destroy the altar . . . If they could even prevent your being there to receive the King . . . And they may kill the servant you left to tend the shrine. Is that it?"

"Yes."

He took the chestnut by the bit, so roughly that it jibbed, snorting. "Then do you think that Lot would hesitate to murder you?"

"No. But I don't think he'll succeed. Now let me go, Ralf. I shall be safe enough."

"Ah." There was relief in his voice. "You mean there are no more deaths in the stars tonight?"

"There is death for someone. It's not for me, but I'll take no one with me, to put more at risk. Which is why you are not coming, Ralf."

"Oh, God, if that's all—"

I laid the reins on the chestnut's neck and it gathered itself, sidling. "We had this fight once before, Ralf, and I gave way. But not tonight. I can't force you to obey me; you are not mine now. But you are Arthur's, and your duty is to stay with him and bring him safely to the chapel. Now let me go. Which gate?"

There was a stretched pause, then he stepped back. "The south. God go with you, my dear lord."

He turned his head and called an order to the guard. The courtyard gate swung open, and crashed shut again behind my galloping horse.

There was half a moon, shadow-edged, thin silver. It lit the familiar track along the valley. The willows along the river's edge stood humped above blue shadows. The river ran fast, full with rain. The sky sparkled with stars, and brighter than any of them burned the Bear. Then moon, stars and river were blotted from sight as the chestnut, feeling my heels, stretched his great stride and carried me at his sure gallop into the blackness of the Wild Forest.

For the first part of the way the track went straight and smooth, and here and there through breaks in the leafage the pale moon sifted down, throwing a faint grey light to the forest floor. Roots, ribbing the pathway, rapped under the horse's hoofs. I lay low on his neck to avoid the sweeping branches. Presently the track began to climb, gently at first, then steep and twisting as the forest ran up into the foot-hills. Here and there the way bent sharply to avoid crags which thrust up among the crowded trees. Somewhere deep down on the left was the noise of a mountain stream, fed like the river with the autumn rains. Save for the horse's thudding gallop there was no sound. The trees hung still. No breeze could penetrate so far into the thick darkness. Nothing else stirred. If deer, or wolf, or fox were abroad that night, I never saw them.

The way grew steeper. The chestnut, sure-footed, breasted the rough track with heaving ribs and stride at last slackening to a heavy canter. Not far now. A gap in the boughs above let starlight through, and I could see ahead where a twist of the path took it round like a tunnel into yet thicker black-ness. An owl cried, away to the left. From the right, another answered. The sounds burst in my brain like a war cry as the chestnut took the bend, and I hauled at his mouth, throwing my whole weight back on the rein. A better horseman could have stopped him in time. But not I, and I had left it just too late.

He pulled to a plunging, trampling stop, but travelling as he was his hoofs ploughed up the muddy track, and he hurtled half-sideways towards the tree which lay fallen full across the way. A pine, dry and long-dead, with its branches thrusting out pointed and rigid as the spikes of a cavalry trap. Too high and too dense to jump, even had it lain in the open moonlight and not just at the darkest bend in the track. The place was well chosen. To one side of the track there was a steep and rocky drop forty feet to the rush of the stream; to the other a thicket of thorn and holly, too dense for a horseman to thrust through. There was no space even to swerve. Had we gone round the corner at a gallop, the horse would have been speared on the boughs, and I myself flung headlong against their crippling spikes.

If the enemy lay hidden, expecting me to gallop hard onto the spikes, there might be a few seconds in which we could get back from the ambush and off the track into deep forest. I turned the chestnut sharply and lashed the reins down. He came round fast, rearing, scoring his side along the wall of thorns and driving the sharp end of some branch deep into my thigh. Then suddenly, as if spurred, he snorted and hurled himself forward. Under us the path broke open with a crashing of boughs. A black pit gaped. The horse lurched, pitched half down, then went over in a thrashing of hoofs. I was flung clear over his shoulder into the space between the pit and the fallen tree. I lay for a moment half-stunned, while the horse, with a heave and a scramble, floundered out of the shallow pit and stood trembling, while two men, daggers in hand, broke out of the forest and came running.

I had been flung into the deepest of the dark shadow, and I suppose I was lying so still that for the moment I was invisible. The noise the stream made drowned most other sounds, and they may have thought I had been flung straight down into the gully. One of them ran to the edge, peering downwards, while the other pushed past the horse and came warily forward to the edge of the pit.

They had not had time to dig this deep enough, only deep enough to lame the horse and to throw me. Now in the black darkness it acted as a kind of protection, preventing them both from jumping me at once. The one near me called out to his fellow, but the rush of water below us drowned the words. Then he took a cautious step forward past the pit towards me. I saw the faint glimmer of the weapon in his hand.

I rolled, got him by the ankle, and heaved. He yelled, pitching forward half into the hole, then twisted free, slashed sideways with his dagger, and rolled away quickly to his feet. The other threw a knife. It struck the tree behind me and fell somewhere. One weapon the less. But now they knew where I was. They drew back beyond the pit, one to each side of the track. In the hand of one man I saw the glint of a sword, but could see nothing of the other. There was no sound but the rush of water.

At least the narrowness of the path, while it made for a good ambush, had effectively stopped them bringing up their own horses. Mine was dead lame. Their beasts must be tethered somewhere behind them in the trees. It was impossible to scramble through the fallen pine behind me; they would have caught and speared me there in seconds. Nor could I get through the wall of thorn. All that was left was the gully; if I could get down there unseen, somehow get past them and back into the open forest, perhaps even find their horses . . .

I moved cautiously sideways, towards the rim of the gully. I had my free hand out, feeling my way. There were bushes, and here and there saplings or young trees, rooted in the rocks. My hand met smooth bark, gripped it, tested it. I moved warily crabwise, over the edge. My eyes were still on that glimmer of metal, the sword beyond the pit. The man was still there. My groping foot slid down a sharp and muddy step, the rim of the gully. A bramble snatched at it.

So did a man's hand. He had used my own trick. He had slid quietly down the bank, flattened himself there, and waited. Now he flung his whole weight, sharply, on my foot and, caught off balance, I fell. His knife just missed me, biting deep into the bank bare inches from my face as I pitched down past him.

He had meant to send me crashing down the rocky bank, to be broken and stunned on the rocks below, where they could follow and finish me together. If he had been content with this, he might have succeeded. But his lunge with the knife shook his own balance, and besides, as he grabbed at me, instead of resisting I went with him, stamping hard downwards at the grabbing hand. My boot went into something soft; he grunted with pain, then yelled something as my weight broke his grip, and, loosing whatever hold he had, he went hurtling with me down the steep side of the gully.

I had been falling the faster of the two, and I landed first, halfway down, hard up against the stem of a young pine. My attacker rolled after me in a crash of broken bushes and a shower of stones. As he hurtled against me in a flying tangle of limbs I braced myself to meet him. I flung myself over him, clamping my body hard over his, clasping his arms with both of mine and pinning him with my weight. I heard him cry out with pain. One leg was doubled under him. He lashed out with the other, and I felt a spur rake my leg through the soft leather of my boot. He fought furiously, thrashing and twisting under me like a landed fish. At any moment he would dislodge me from my purchase against the pine, and we would fall together to the gully. I struggled to hold him, and to get my dagger hand free.

The other murderer had heard us fall. He shouted something from the brink above, then I could hear him letting himself down the slope towards us. He came cautiously, but fast. Too fast. I shifted my grip on the man beneath me, forcing my full weight down to hold his arms pinned. I heard something crack; it sounded like a dead twig, but the fellow screamed. I managed to drag my right hand from under him. My fist was clamped round the dagger and the hilt had bitten into the flesh. I lifted it. Some stray glimmer of moonlight touched his eyes, a foot from mine; I could smell the fear and pain and hatred. He gave a wild heave that nearly unseated me, wrenching his head sideways from the coming

475

blow. I reversed the dagger and struck with all the strength of the shortened blow at the exposed neck, just behind the ear.

The blow did not reach him. Something—a rock, a heavy billet of wood, hurled down from above—struck me hard on the point of the shoulder. My arm jerked out, useless, paralyzed. The dagger spun away into the blackness. The other murderer crashed down the last few feet through the bushes and rocks above me. I heard his drawn sword scrape on stone. The moon marked it as it whipped upwards to strike. I tried to wrench myself clear of my opponent, but he clung close, teeth and all, grappling like a hound, holding me there for that hacking sword to finish me.

It finished him. His companion jumped, and slashed downwards at the place where, a second before, my exposed back had been, plain in the moonlight. But I was already half free, and falling, my clothes tearing from my opponent's grasp, and my fist bloody from his teeth. It was his back that met the sword. It drove in. I heard the metal grate on bone, then the screams covered the sound, and I was free of him and half-sliding, half-falling, towards the noise of the water.

A bush checked me, tore at me, let me through. A bough whipped me across the throat. A net of brambles ripped what was left of my clothing to ribbons. Then my hurtling body hit a boulder, checked, lay breathless and half-stunned against it for the two long moments it took to let me hear the second murderer coming after me. Then with no warning but a sudden gentle shift of earth the boulder went from under me and I fell down the last sheer drop straight to the slab of rock over which the icy water slid, racing, towards the edge of a deep pool.

If I had fallen into the pool itself I might not have been hurt. If I had struck one of the great boulders where the water dashed and wrangled, I would probably have been killed. But I fell into a shallow, a long flat stretch of rock across which the water slid no more than a span deep, before plunging on and down into the next of the forest pools. I landed on my side, half-stunned and winded. The icy rush filled my mouth, nose, eyes, weighing down my heavy clothes, dragging at my bruised limbs. I was sliding with it along the greasy rock. My hands clawed for a hold, slipped, missed, scraped with bending nails.

Beside me with a thud and splash that shook the very rock, the second murderer landed, slipped, regained his foothold in the rushing water, and for the second time swung the sword high. It caught the moonlight. There were stars behind it. A sword lying clear across the night sky, in a blaze of stars. I took my hands from the rock, and the stream rolled me over to face the sword. The water blinded me. The noise of the cascade shook my bones apart. There was a flash like a shooting star, and the sword came down.

It was like a dream that repeated itself. Once before I had sat near a fire in the forest, with the small dark hill men waiting round me in a half circle, their eyes gleaming at the edge of the firelight like the eyes of forest creatures.

But this fire they had lit themselves. In front of it my torn clothes steamed, drying. Myself they had wrapped in their own cloaks; sheepskins, smelling too reminiscently of their first owners, but warm and dry. My bruises ached, and here and there a sharper pain told me where some stroke, unfelt in the scrimmage, had gone home. But my bones were whole.

I had not been unconscious long. Beyond the circle of firelight lay the two dead men, and near them a sharpened stake and a heavy club from which the blood had not yet been wiped. One of the men was still cleaning his long knife in the ground.

Mab brought me a bowl of hot wine, with something pungent overlying the taste of the grapes. I drank, sneezed, and pushed myself up straight.

"Did you find their horses?"

He nodded. "Over yonder. Your own is lame."

"Yes. Tend him for me, will you? When I get up to the shrine I'll send the servant down this way. He can lead the lame one home. Bring me one of the others now, and get me my clothes."

"They're still wet. It's barely ten minutes since we got you out of the pool."

"No matter," I said, "I must go. Mab, above here on the track there's a fallen tree, and a pit beside it. Will you ask your people to clear the path before morning?"

"They are there already. Listen."

I heard it then, beyond the rush of the stream and the crackling of the fire. Axe and mattock thudding, above us in the forest. Mab met my eyes. "Will the new King ride this way, then?"

"He may." I smiled. "How soon did you hear?"

"One of our people came from the town to tell us." He showed a gap of broken teeth. "Not by the gates you locked, master . . . But we knew before that. Did you not see the shooting star? It went across the heavens from end to end, crested like a dragon and riding a trail of smoke. So we knew you would come. But we were up beyond the Wolves' Road when the firedrake ran, and we were almost too late. I am sorry."

"You came in time," I said. "I'm in your debt for my life. I shan't forget it."

"I was in yours," he said. "Why did you ride alone? You should have known there was danger."

"I knew there was death, but I wanted no more deaths on my hands. Pain is another thing, and is soon over." I got to my feet, stiffly. "If I'm ever to move again, Mab, I must move now. My clothes?"

The clothes were wet still, a mass of mud and rents. But apart from the sheepskins there was nothing else; the hill people are small, and nothing of theirs would have fitted me. I shrugged myself into what was left of my court clothing, and took the bridle of a stolid brown horse from one of the men. The wound in my thigh was bleeding again, and from the feel of it there were splinters there. I got them to sling one of the sheepskins over the saddle, and climbed gingerly on.

"Shall we come with you?" they asked me.

I shook my head. "No. Stay and see the road cleared. In the morning, if you wish, come to the shrine. There will be a place there for you all."

The moonlit space at the forest's center was as still as a painted picture, and as unreal as a midnight dream. Moonlight edged the chapel roof and silvered the furred tops of the surrounding pines. The doorway showed an oblong of gold, where the nine lamps shone steadily round the altar.

As I rode softly round to the back the door opened there, and the servant peered fearfully out. All was well, he told me; no one had been by. But his eyes stretched wide when he saw the state I was in, and he was obviously glad when I handed the bridle to him and told him to leave me. Then I went in thankfully to the firelight to tend my hurts and change my clothing.

Slowly the silence seeped back. A brush of soft wind over the tree-tops swept the last sound of retreating hoofs away; it crept in through the chapel, thinning the lamp flames and drawing thin lines of smoke which smelled like sweet gums burning. Outside in the clearing the moon and stars poured their rare light down. The god was here. I knelt before the altar, emptying myself of mind and will, till through me I felt the full tide of God's will flowing, and bearing me with it.

The night lay silver and quiet, waiting for the torches and the trumpets.

11

They came at last. Lights and clamour and the trampling of horses flowed nearer through the forest, till the clearing was filled with flaring torchlight and excited voices. I heard them through the waking sleep of vision, dim, echoing, remote, like bells heard from the bottom of the sea.

The leaders had come forward. They paused in the doorway. Voices hushed, feet shuffled. All they would see was the swept and empty chapel, deserted but for one man standing facing them across the stone altar. Round the altar the nine lamps still dealt their steady glow, showing the carved stone sword and the legend MITHRAE INVICTO, and lying across the top of the altar the sword itself, unsheathed, bare on the bare stone.

"Put out the torches," I told them. "There will be no need of them."

They obeyed me, then at my signal pressed forward into the chapel.

The place was small, the throng of men great. But the awe of the occasion prevailed; orders were given, but subdued; soft commands which might have come from priests in ritual rather than warriors recently in battle. There were no rites to follow, but somehow men kept their places; kings and nobles and kings' guards within the chapel, the press of lesser men outside in the silent clearing and overflowing into the gloom of the forest itself. There, they still had lights; the clearing was ringed with light and sound where the horses waited and men stood with torches ready; but forward under the open sky men came lightless and weaponless, as beseemed them in the presence of God and their King. And still, this one night of all the great nights, there was no priest present; the only intermediary was myself, who had been used by the driving god for thirty years, and brought at last to this place.

At length all were assembled, according to order and precedence. It was as if they had divided by arrangement, or more likely by instinct. Outside, crowding the steps, waited the little men from the hills; they do not willingly come under a roof. Inside the chapel, to my right, stood Lot, King of Lothian, with his group of friends and followers; to the left Cador, and those who went with him. There were a hundred others, perhaps more, crowded into that small and echoing space, but these two, the white Boar of Cornwall, and the red Leopard of Lothian, seemed to face one another balefully from either side of the altar, with Ector four-square and watchful at the door between them. Then Ector, with Cei behind him, brought Arthur forward, and after that I saw no one but the boy.

The chapel swam with colour and the glint of jewels and gold. The air smelled cold and fragrant, of pines and water and scented smoke. The rustle and murmuring of the throng filled the air and sounded like the rustle of flames licking through a pile of fuel, taking hold. . . .

Flames from the nine lamps, flaring and then dying; flames licking up the stone of the altar; flames running along the blade of the sword until it glowed white hot. I stretched my hands out over it, palms flat. The fire licked my robe, blazing white from sleeve and finger, but where it touched, it did not even singe. It was the ice-cold fire, the fire called by a word out of the dark, with the searing heat at its heart, where the sword lay. The sword lay in its flames as a jewel lies embedded in white wool. *Whoso taketh this sword* . . . The runes danced along the metal: the emeralds burned. The chapel was a dark globe with a center of fire. The blaze from the altar threw my shadow upwards, gigantic, into the vaulted roof. I heard my own voice, ringing hollow from the vault like a voice in a dream.

"Take up the sword, he who dares."

Movement, and men's voices, full of dread. Then Cador: "That is the sword. I would know it anywhere. I saw it in his hand, full of light. It is his, God witness it. I would not touch it if Merlin himself bade me."

There were cries of, "Nor I, nor I," and then, "Let the King take it up, let the High King show us Macsen's sword."

Then finally, alone, Lot's voice, gruffly: "Yes. Let him take it. I have seen, by God's death, I have seen. If it is his indeed, then God is with him, and it is not for me."

Arthur came slowly forward. Behind him the place was dim, the crowd shrunk back into darkness, the shuffle and murmur of their presence no more than the breeze in the forest trees outside. Here between us, the white light blazed and the blade shivered. The darkness flashed and sparkled, a crystal cave of vision, crowded and whirling with bright images. A white stag, collared with gold. A shooting star, dragon-shaped, and trailing fire. A king, restless and desirous, with a dragon of red gold shimmering on the wall behind him. A woman, white-robed and queenly, and behind her in the shadows a sword standing in an altar like a cross. A circle of vast linked stones standing on a windy plain with a king's grave at its center. A child, handed into my arms on a winter night. A grail, shrouded in mouldering cloth, hidden in a dark vault. A young king, crowned.

He looked at me through the pulse and flash of vision. For him, they were flames only, flames which might burn, or not; that was for me. He waited, not doubtful, nor blindly trusting; waiting only.

"Come," I said gently. "It is yours."

He put his hand through the white blaze of fire and the hilt slid cool into the grip for which, a hundred and a hundred years before, it had been made.

Lot was the first to kneel. I suppose he had most need. Arthur raised him, speaking without either rancour or cordiality; the words of a sovereign lord who is able to see past a present wrong to a coming good.

"I could not find it in me, Lot of Lothian, to quarrel with any man this day, least of all my sister's lord. You shall see that your doubts of me were groundless, and you and your sons after you will help me guard and hold Britain as she should be held."

To Cador he said simply: "Until I get myself another heir, Cador of Cornwall, you are he."

To Ector he spoke long and quietly, so that no man could hear save they two, and when he raised him, kissed him.

Thereafter for a long span of time he stood by the altar, as men knelt before him and swore loyalty on the hilt of the sword. To each one he spoke, directly as a boy, and grandly as a king. Between his hands, held like a cross, Caliburn shone with his own light only, but the altar with its nine dead lamps was dark.

As each man took his oath and pledged himself, he withdrew, and the chapel slowly emptied. As it grew quieter, the encircling forest filled with life and expectation and noise, where they crowded, clamorously excited now, waiting for their sworn King. They were bringing up the horses out of the wood, and the clearing filled with torchlight and trampling and the jingling of accoutrements.

Last of all Mab and the men of the hills withdrew, and save for the bodyguard ranged back against the shadowed wall, the King and I were alone.

Stiffly, for pain still locked my bones, I came round the

altar till I stood before him. He was almost as tall as I. The eyes that looked back at me might have been my own.

I knelt in front of him and put out my hands for his. But he cried out at that, and pulled me to my feet, and kissed me.

"You do not kneel to me. Not you."

"You are High King, and I am your servant."

"What of it? The sword was yours, and we two know it. It doesn't matter what you call yourself, my servant, cousin, father, what you will—you are Merlin, and I'm nothing without you beside me." He laughed then, naturally, the grandeur of the occasion fitting him as easily as the hilt had fitted his hand. "What became of your state robe? Only you could have worn that dreadful old thing on such an occasion. I shall give you a robe of gold tissue, embroidered with stars, as befits your position. Will you wear it for me?"

"Not even for you."

He smiled. "Then come as you are. You'll ride down with me now, won't you?"

"Later. When you have time to look round for me, you will find that I am beside you. Listen, they are ready to take you to your place. It's time to go."

I went with him to the door. The torches still tossed flaring, though the moon had set long since and the last of the stars had died into a morning sky. Golden and tranquil, the light grew.

They had brought the white stallion up to the steps. When Arthur made to mount they would not let him, but Cador and Lot and half a dozen petty kings lifted him between them to the saddle, and at last men's hopes and joy rang up into the pines in a great shout. So they raised to be king Arthur the young.

I carried the nine lamps out of the chapel. Come daylight, I would take them where they now belonged, up to the caves of the hollow hills, where their gods had gone. Of the nine, all had been overturned, the oil spilled unburned along the floor. With them lay the stone bowl, shattered, and a pile of dust and crumbled fragments where the cold fire had struck. When I swept these away, with the oil that had soaked into them, it could be seen that the carving had gone from the front of the altar. These were the fragments that I held, caked with oil. All that was left of the carving on the altar's face was the hilt of the sword, and a word.

I swept and cleaned the place and made it fair again. I moved slowly, like an old man. I still remember how my body ached, and how at length, when I knelt again, my sight blurred and darkened as if still blind with vision, or with tears.

The tears showed me the altar now, bare of the nine-fold light that had pleasured the old, small gods; bare of the soldier's sword and the name of the soldiers' god. All it held now was the hilt of the carved sword standing in the stone like a cross, and the letters still deep and distinct above it: TO HIM UNCONQUERED.

THE LEGEND

When Aurelius Ambrosius was High King of Britain, Merlin, also called Ambrosius, brought the Giants' Dance out of Ireland and set it up near Amesbury, at Stonehenge. Shortly after this a great star appeared in the likeness of a dragon, and Merlin, knowing that it betokened Ambrosius' death, wept bitterly, and prophesied that Uther would be King under the sign of the Dragon, and that a son would be born to him "of surpassing mighty dominion, whose power shall extend over all the realms that lie beneath the ray (of the star)."

The following Easter, at the Coronation feast, King Uther fell in love with Ygraine, wife of Gorlois, Duke of Cornwall. He lavished attention on her, to the scandal of the court; she made no response, but her husband, in fury, retired from the court without leave, taking his wife and men-at-arms back to Cornwall. Uther, in anger, commanded him to return, but Gorlois refused to obey. Then the King, enraged beyond measure, gathered an army and marched into Cornwall, burning the cities and castles. Gorlois had not enough troops to withstand him, so he placed his wife in the castle of Tintagel, the safest refuge, and himself prepared to defend the castle of Dimilioc. Uther immediately laid siege to Dimilioc, holding Gorlois and his troops trapped there, while he cast about for some way of breaking into the castle of Tintagel to ravish Ygraine. After some days he asked advice from one of his familiars called Ulfin, who suggested that he send for Merlin. Merlin, moved by the King's apparent suffering, promised to help. By his magic arts he changed Uther into the likeness of Gorlois, Ulfin into Jordan, Gorlois' friend, and himself into Brithael, one of Gorlois' captains. The three of them rode to Tintagel, and were admitted by the porter. Ygraine, taking Uther to be her husband the Duke, welcomed him, and took him to her bed. So Uther lay with Ygraine that night, "and she had no thought to deny him in aught he might desire."

But in the meantime fighting had broken out at Dimilioc, and in the battle Ygraine's husband, the Duke, was killed. Messengers came to Tintagel to tell Ygraine of her husband's death. When they found "Gorlois," apparently still alive, closeted with Ygraine, they were speechless, but the King then confessed the deception, and a few days later married Ygraine. Some say that Ygraine's sister Morgause was married on the same day to Lot of Lothian, and the other sister Morgan le Fay was put to school in a nunnery, where she learned necromancy, and thereafter was wedded to King Urien of Gore. But others aver that Morgan was Arthur's own sister, born after him of the marriage of King Uther and Ygraine his Queen, and that Morgause was also his sister, but not by the same mother.

Uther Pendragon was to reign for fifteen more years, and during those years he saw nothing of his son Arthur. Before the child was born Merlin sought out the King and spoke with him. "Sir, ye must purvey you for the nourishing of your child." "As thou wilt," said the King, "be it." So on the night of his birth the child Arthur was carried down to the postern gate of Tintagel and delivered into the hands of Merlin, who took him to the castle of Sir Ector, a faithful knight. There Merlin had the child christened, and named him Arthur, and Sir Ector's wife took him as her foster son.

All through Uther's reign the country was sorely troubled by the Saxons and the Scots from Ireland. The two Saxon leaders whom the King had imprisoned managed to escape from London and fled thence to Germany, where they gathered a great army which struck terror throughout the kingdom. Uther himself was stricken with a grievous malady, and appointed Lot of Lothian, who was betrothed to his daughter Morgause, as his chief captain. But as often as Lot put the enemy to flight, they came back in even greater strength, and the country was laid waste. Finally Uther, though sorely ill, gathered his barons together and told them that he himself must lead the armies, so a litter was made for him, and he was carried in it at the head of his army against the enemy. When the Saxon leaders learned that the British King had taken the field against them in a litter, they disdained him, saying that he was half-dead already, and it would not become them to fight him. But Uther, with a return of his old strength, laughed and called out: "They call me the half-dead king, and so indeed I was. But I would rather conquer them in this wise, than be conquered by them and live in shame." So the army of the Britons defeated the Saxons. But the King's malady increased, and the woes of the kingdom. Finally, when the King lay close to death, Merlin appeared and approached him in the sight of all the lords and bade him acknowledge his son Arthur as the new King. Which he did, and afterwards died, and was buried by the side of his brother Aurelius Ambrosius within the Giants' Dance.

After his death the lords of Britain came together to find their new King. No one knew where Arthur was kept, or where Merlin was to be found, but they thought the King would be recognized by a sign. So Merlin had a great sword fashioned, and fixed it by his magic art into a great stone shaped like an altar, with an anvil of steel in it, and floated the stone on water to a great church in London, and set it up there in the churchyard. There were gold letters on the sword which said: "Whoso pulleth out this sword of this stone and anvil, is rightwise king born of all England." So a great feast was made, and at the feast all the lords came to try who could pull the sword from the stone. Among them came Sir Ector, and Kay his son, with Arthur, who had neither sword nor blazon, following as a squire. When they came to the jousting Sir Kay, who had forgotten his sword, sent Arthur back to look for it. But when Arthur returned to the house where they were lodging, everyone was gone and the doors were locked, so in impatience he rode to the churchyard, and drew the sword from the stone, and took it to Sir Kay. Then of course the sword was recognized, but even when Arthur showed that he alone of all men could pull it from the stone, there were those who cried out against him, saying it was great shame to them and to the realm to accept as king a boy of no high blood born, and that fresh trial must be made at Candlemas. So at Candlemas all the greatest in the land came together, and then again at Pentecost, but none of them could pull the sword from the stone, save only Arthur. But still some of the lords were angry and would not accept him, until in the end the common people cried out: "We will have Arthur unto our king, we will put him no more in delay, for we all see that it is God's will that he shall be our king, and who that holdeth against it, we will slay him." So Arthur was accepted by the people, high and low, and all men rich and poor kneeled to him and begged his mercy because they had delayed him so long, and he forgave them. Then Merlin told them all who Arthur was, and that he was no bastard, but begotten truly by King Uther upon Ygraine, three hours after the death of her husband the Duke. So they raised to be king Arthur the young.

AUTHOR'S NOTE

Like its predecessor, *The Crystal Cave*, this novel is a work
of the imagination, though firmly based in both history and
legend. Not perhaps equally in both: so little is known
about Britain in the fifth century A.D. (the beginning of the
"Dark Ages") that one is almost as dependent on tradition
and conjecture as on fact. I for one like to think that where
tradition is so persistent—and as immortal and self-perpetu-
ating as the stories of the Arthurian Legend—there must be
a grain of fact behind even the strangest of the tales which
have gathered round the meager central facts of Arthur's
existence. It is exciting to interpret these sometimes weird
and often nonsensical legends into a story which has some
sort of coherence as human experience and imaginative truth.

I have tried with *The Hollow Hills* to write a story which
stands on its own, without reference to its forerunner, *The
Crystal Cave*, or even to whatever explanatory notes follow
here. Indeed, I only add these notes for the benefit of those
readers whose interest may go beyond the novel itself, but
who are not familiar enough with the ramifications of the
Arthurian Legend to follow the thinking behind some parts
of my story. It may give them pleasure to trace for themselves the seeds of certain ideas and the origins of certain
references.

In *The Crystal Cave* I based my story mainly on the "history" related by Geoffrey of Monmouth,* which is the basis

* *History of the Kings of Britain*, translated by Sebastian Evans and re-
vised by Charles W. Dunn (Everyman's Library, 1912).

of the later and mainly mediaeval tales of "Arthur and his Court," but I set the action against the fifth-century Romano-British background, which is the real setting for all that we know of the Arthurian Fact.* We have no fixed dates, but I have followed some authorities who postulate 470 A.D. or thereabouts as the date of Arthur's birth. The story of *The Hollow Hills* covers the hidden years between that date and the raising of the young Arthur to be war-leader (*dux bellorum*) or, as legend has had it for more than a thousand years, King of Britain. What I would like to trace here are the threads I have woven to make this story of a period of Arthur's life which tradition barely touches, and history touches not at all.

That Arthur existed seems certain. We cannot say even that much for certain about Merlin. "Merlin the magician," as we know him, is a composite figure built almost entirely out of song and legend; but here again one feels that for such a legend to persist through the centuries, some man of power must have existed, with gifts that seemed miraculous to his own times. He first appears in legend as a youth, even then possessed of strange powers. On this story as related by Geoffrey of Monmouth I have built an imaginary character who seemed to me to grow out of and epitomize the time of confusion and seeking that we call the Dark Ages. Geoffrey Ashe, in his brilliant book *From Caesar to Arthur*,† describes this "multiplicity of vision":

> When Christianity prevailed and Celtic paganism crumbled into mythology, a great deal of this sort of

---

* See *Roman Britain and the English Settlements*, R. G. Collingwood and J. N. L. Myres (Oxford, 1937); *Celtic Britain*, Nora K. Chadwick Vol. 34 in the series *Ancient Peoples and Places*, ed. Glyn Daniel (Thames and Hudson, 1963).

† Published by Collins, 1960. See also *The Quest for Arthur's Britain*, ed. Geoffrey Ashe (Pall Mall Press, 1968).

thing was carried over. Water and islands retained their magic. Lake-sprites flitted to and fro, heroes travelled in strange boats. The haunted hills became fairy-hills, belonging to vivid fairy folk hardly to be paralleled among other nations. Where barrows existed they often fitted this role. Unseen realms intersected the visible, and there were secret means of communication and access. The fairies and the heroes, the ex-gods and the demi-gods, jostled the spirits of the dead in kaleidoscopic con-fusion . . . Everything grew ambiguous. Thus, long after the triumph of Christianity, there continued to be fairy-hills; but even those which were not barrows might be regarded as havens for disembodied souls . . . There were saints of whom miracles were reported; but similar mir-acles, not long since, might have been the business of fully identifiable gods. There were glass castles where a hero might lie an age entranced; there were blissful fairylands to be reached by water or by cave-passage-ways . . . Journeys and enchantments, combats and im-prisonments—theme by theme—the Celtic imagination articulated itself in story. Yet any given episode might be taken as fact or imagination or religious allegory or all three at once.

Merlin, the narrator of *The Hollow Hills*, the "enchanter" and healer gifted with the Sight, is able to move in and out of the different worlds at will. And as Merlin's legend is linked with the caves of glass, the invisible towers, the hollow hills where he now sleeps for all time, so I have seen him as the link between the worlds; the instrument by which, as he says, "all the kings become one King, and all the gods one God." For this he abnegates his own will and his desire for normal manhood. The hollow hills are the physical point of entry between this world and the Otherworld, and Merlin is their human counterpart, the meeting point for the inter-locking worlds of men, gods, beasts and twilight spirits.

One meeting of the real and the fantasy worlds can be seen in the figure of Maximus. Magnus Maximus, the soldier with the dream of empire, was a fact; he commanded at Segontium until the time when he crossed to Gaul in his vain bid for power. "Macsen Wledig" is a legend, one of the Celtic "seeking" stories later to flower into the Quest of the Holy Grail. In this novel I have linked the facts of Arthur's great precursor and his imperial dream to the sword episodes of the Arthurian Legend, and lent them the shape of a Quest story.

The tale of the "Sword of Maximus" is my invention. It follows the archetypal "seeking and finding" pattern of which the Quest of the Grail, which later attached itself to the Arthurian Legend, is only one example. The stories of the Holy Grail, identifying it with the Cup from the Last Supper, are twelfth-century tales modelled in their main elements on some early Celtic "quest" stories; in fact they have elements even older. These Grail stories show certain points in common, changing in detail, but fairly constant in form and idea. There is usually an unknown youth, the *bel inconnu*, who is brought up in the wilds, ignorant of his name or parentage. He leaves his home and rides out in search of his identity. He comes across a Waste Land, ruled by a maimed (impotent) king; there is a castle, usually on an island, on which the youth comes by chance. He reaches it in a boat belonging to a royal fisherman, the Fisher King of the Grail Legends. The Fisher King is sometimes identified with the impotent king of the Waste Land. The castle on the island is owned by a king of the Otherworld, and there the youth finds the object of his quest, sometimes a cup or a lance, sometimes a sword, broken or whole. At the quest's end he wakes by the side of the water with his horse tethered near him, and the island once again invisible. On his return from the Otherworld, fertility and peace are restored to the Waste Land.

Some tales figure a white stag collared with gold, who leads the youth to his destination.

For further reference see *Arthurian Literature in the Middle Ages;* A Collaborative History edited by R. S. Loomis (Oxford University Press, 1959); and *The Evolution of the Grail Legend* by D. D. R. Owen (University of St. Andrews Publications, 1968).

SOME OTHER BRIEF NOTES

Segontium. Geoffrey of Monmouth in the *Vita Merlini* tells us of cups made by Weland the Smith in Caer Seint (Segontium), which were given to Merlin. There is also another story of a sword made by Weland which was given to Merlin by a Welsh king. There is a brief reference in *The Anglo-Saxon Chronicle* for the year 418 A.D. "In this year the Romans collected all the treasures which were in Britain and hid some in the earth so that no one afterwards could find them, and some they took with them into Gaul."

Galava. The main body of legend places King Arthur in the Celtic countries of the west, Cornwall, Wales, Brittany. In this I have followed the legends. But there is evidence which supports another strong tradition of Arthur in the north of England and in Scotland. So this story moves north. I have placed the traditional "Sir Ector of the Forest Sauvage" (who reared the young Arthur) at Galava, the modern Ambleside in the Lake District. I have often wondered if "the fountain of Galabes * where he (Merlin) wont to haunt" could be identified with the Roman Galava or Galaba. (In *The Crystal Cave* I gave it a different interpretation. The mediaeval romancers make "Galapas" a gaint—a version of the old

* *Fontes galabes.*

495

guardian of the spring or waterway.) The fostering of Arthur on Ector, and the lodging at Galava of Bedwyr, are feasible; we find in Procopius that, as in later times, boys of good family were sent away to be educated. As for the "chapel in the green," once I had invented a shrine in the Wild Forest I could not resist calling it the Green Chapel, after the mediaeval Arthurian poem of *Sir Gawaine and the Green Knight*, which has its setting somewhere in the Lake District.

Ambrosius' Wall. This is the Wansdyke, or Woden's Dyke, so called by the Saxons, who saw it as the work of the gods. It ran from Newbury to the Severn, and parts of it are still traceable. It was probably built some time between 450 and 475 A.D., so I have ascribed it to Ambrosius.

Caer Bannog. This name, old Celtic for "the castle of the peaks," is my own interpretation of the various names— Carbonek, Corbenic, Caer Benoic, etc.—given to the castle where the youth finds the Grail.

There is a Celtic legend in which Arthur carries off a cauldron (magic vessel or grail) and a wonderful sword from Nuadda or Llyd, King of the Otherworld.

Cei and Bedwyr. They are Arthur's companions in legend. Cei was Ector's son and became Arthur's seneschal. Bedwyr's name was later mediaevalized to Bedivere, but in his relationship with Arthur he seems to be the original of Lancelot. Hence the reference to the *guenhwyvar* (white shadow: Guinevere) which falls between the boys on page 342.

Cador of Cornwall. When Arthur died without issue, we are told that he left his kingdom to Cador's son.

Morgause. On the subject of Arthur's unwitting incest with his sister, there is a rich confusion of legend. The most usual story is that he lay with his half-sister Morgause, wife (or mistress) of Lot, and begot Mordred, who was eventually his downfall. His own sister Morgan, or Morgian, became "Morgan le Fay," the enchantress. Morgause is said to have borne four sons to Lot, who later were to become Arthur's devoted followers. This seemed unlikely if Arthur had lain with her when she was Lot's wife, so I have taken my own way through the confusion of the stories, with the suggestion that after leaving the court Morgause will lose no time in taking her sister's place as Lot's queen. I believe there was in the fifth century a nunnery near Caer Eidyn (Edinburgh) in Lothian to which Morgian could have retired. This could be the "house of witches" or "wise women" of legend, and it is tempting to suppose that Morgian and her nuns came from there to take Arthur away and nurse him after his last battle against Mordred at Camlann.

Coel, King of Rheged, is the original of the Old King Cole of the nursery rhymes. We are told that Hueil, one of the nineteen sons of Caw of Strathclyde, was much disliked by Arthur. Another of the sons, Gildas the monk, seems to have returned this dislike. It is he who, in 540 A.D., wrote *The Loss and Conquest of Britain*, without once mentioning Arthur by name, though he refers to the Battle of Badon Hill, the last of Arthur's twelve great battles, in which he broke the Saxon power. From the tone of Gildas' book it is to be inferred that, if Arthur was a Christian at all, his Christianity went no further than lip-service. At any rate he was no friend to the monks.

Caliburn is the most pronounceable of the names for Arthur's sword, which was later romanticized as Excalibur. White was Arthur's colour; his white hound, Cabal, has a place in legend. Canrith means "white phantom."

It will be seen from these necessarily sketchy notes that any given episode of my story may—to quote Geoffrey Ashe again—"be taken as fact or imagination or religious allegory or all three at once." In this, if in nothing else, it is wholly true to its time.

M.S.

November 1970–November 1972

ABOUT THE AUTHOR

MARY STEWART was born in Sunderland, County Durham, England. She graduated from Durham University and worked there as a lecturer in English language and literature until 1956, when she moved with her husband to Edinburgh.

Lady Stewart's career as a novelist began in 1956 with *Madam, Will You Talk?* Since then, she has published nineteen novels, all bestsellers, most recently *The Prince and the Pilgrim*, and preceding that her Merlin Novels about the legendary enchanter Merlin and the young Arthur (*The Crystal Cave*, *The Hollow Hills*, and *The Last Enchantment*) and their sequel, *The Wicked Day*, the novel of Arthur and his son Mordred. Her books for children include *The Little Broomstick*, *Ludo and the Star Horse*, and *A Walk in Wolf Wood*. She has also published a book of poetry entitled *Frost on the Window*.

MARY STEWART

The Arthurian Novels